Praise for *Counting Down with You*

"A witty, romantic, deeply insightful debut that steals your heart from start to finish."
—Emma Lord, author of *Tweet Cute* and *You Have a Match*

"I'm completely heart-eyed over this book."
—Rachel Lynn Solomon, author of *Today Tonight Tomorrow*

"I. Love. This. Book."
—Mark Oshiro, award-winning author of *Anger Is a Gift*
and *Each of Us a Desert*

"Tashie Bhuiyan has done an excellent job of portraying the conflicts faced by many South Asian diaspora kids in this debut."
—Sabina Khan, author of *Zara Hossain Is Here*
and *The Love and Lies of Rukhsana Ali*

"A brisk and buoyant YA romance anchored by well-drawn family dynamics and anxiety issues."
—Jenn Bennett, author of *Alex, Approximately*

"Hand to fans of [the] Netflix hit *Never Have I Ever.*"
—*Booklist*

"With sarcastic, witty humor and a heartfelt exploration of familial relationships, Bhuiyan masterfully sucks you into Karina's world."
—*BuzzFeed*, New Young Adult Books Out Spring 2021

**Books by Tashie Bhuiyan
available from Inkyard Press**

*Counting Down with You
A Show for Two*

TASHIE BHUIYAN

Counting Down with You

ISBN-13: 978-1-335-42628-4

Counting Down with You

First published in 2021. This edition published in 2022.

For questions and comments about the quality of this book, please contact us at CustomerService@Harlequin.com.

Inkyard Press
22 Adelaide St. West, 41st Floor
Toronto, Ontario M5H 4E3, Canada
www.InkyardPress.com

Printed in U.S.A.

To Dadu and H, for teaching me to stay strong.

AUTHOR'S NOTE

Dear reader,

We're about to enter some big emo hours, so hold on tight. *Counting Down with You* is the story of my heart, and it was written as a love letter to young brown girls. It wasn't that long ago that I was a brown teenager, not that I really feel like the spitting image of an adult at twenty-one years old. The older I am, though, the more I realize that there is no "right" way to represent all of us, since we are not a monolith. We all come from different backgrounds and have different experiences. However, when I set out to write this story, I chose to write it from a deeply personal place. The main character of this novel, Karina Ahmed, represents one experience—my experience—but she does not represent all. In this book, my goal was to always give her agency, and give her room to grow. This is undeniably a love story, but Karina is not waiting for a knight in shining armor to rescue her from the challenges of life. At the end of the day, this is *her* story, and these are *her* decisions. Just like her, we can't rely on other people to come save us—we must be lionhearted on our own.

When I was younger, I often felt helpless. We don't always have the freedom we seek, and it's hard to rise up against our circumstances when we are young and have limited means to protect ourselves. But this is me telling you right now that it gets better. I know it's hard to believe that, especially when the future seems so bleak, but it's true. Someone gave me this advice at sixteen years old, and I hope to now impart it on you: *stay as strong as you can.* That's all we can do. We might not be able to fight back or run away, but we can continue to believe in a better future. As you follow Karina on her journey, I hope you find a sense of belonging and understanding. Being seen is the most tender form of love, and I see you. I do.

Thank you for taking the time to read this. If there is only one thing you take away from this book, let it be hope.

All the love,

Tashie

PART I

spark

1

T-MINUS 28 DAYS

Airports are the true chaotic evil.

There are too many things happening around me. Too many people in a hurry, too many people lazing around, too many announcements on the overhead speakers, and way too many tearful goodbyes.

Anarchy reigns in my little corner. My mom is on the phone, saying goodbye to her ten million friends, and my dad looks like he already regrets agreeing to go on a month-long trip to Bangladesh with her. Even with my earphones in, JFK Airport is too *loud*.

I wish I were anywhere else.

My younger brother, Samir, stands next to me as I sip the drink I forced him to buy me at Starbucks. In my other hand, I have a book flipped open to pass the time.

Dadu, my grandma on my paternal side, is busy fretting over my dad's shirt. "Tuck it *in*," she says in Bengali.

I hide my smile behind my drink when he reluctantly tucks in his shirt. Dadu isn't someone to mess with.

"How much longer do we have to wait?" I ask Samir, taking out an earphone.

"Who knows," he says. "Whenever Ma finally gets off the phone."

That was decidedly unhelpful. "So…never."

I still think the beginning of March is too chilly to go on vacation, but knowing my parents, plane tickets were probably cheapest today.

Even though I love my parents, I'm happy to see them leave for a month to visit my mom's side of the family. A part of me wishes I could go, since I love visiting Bangladesh and soaking in the beautiful, bustling energy of Dhaka, but the idea of spending an entire month surrounded by only my relatives is horrifying. Thankfully, high school takes priority over seeing extended family. Being sixteen is a good thing sometimes.

Only sometimes.

My mom finally gets off the phone and gestures to their suitcases. "Come help me, Samir."

While my brother helps them check in their luggage, I sidle up beside Dadu and lean my shoulder against hers. She's been at our house for a few days now, helping Ma and Baba pack for their trip.

"Hi Myra," she says, calling me by my dak nam, my familial name. I prefer my legal name, Karina, the bhalo nam all my friends use, but I don't mind when Dadu calls me Myra.

"Hey Dadu. Ready for your second Uber ride?" I ask. "Baba said we're going to have to take another one home."

"Another one?" she asks, squeezing my wrist. Her skin is wrinkled from old age and hours of hard work, but it's warm and familiar. "Do you think they'll try to kidnap us this time?"

"Inshallah," I say jokingly. *God willing.*

Dadu laughs and swats me on the shoulder. "Don't make silly jokes, Myra."

I grin. "Sorry."

It's nice to have a light and easy conversation like this. We don't have them often, because my grandma lives year-round in New Jersey. Every summer, I beg my parents to let me stay with her. They usually refuse until Dadu steps in and says she misses me, which is as good as saying *Your daughter's coming to visit me whether you like it or not.*

My parents return carrying only their handbags. My mom is shaking her head at my dad as he shows her something on his phone.

"Samir, you can download things from Netflix on your phone right, right?" my dad asks, looking pointedly at my mom.

Samir nods, but Ma narrows her eyes. "I told you already, I don't have any space."

"That's because you have a million prayer apps on your phone," Baba says under his breath. "Even Allah would agree one is enough."

My mom smacks his arm. "Don't say that in front of the kids. You're going to set a bad example. You know it's because of Candy Crush and Facebook. Why don't you download some movies *for* me?"

Baba snorts. "You wish. I already downloaded every episode of *Breaking Bad*. No room for your dramas."

Ma pinches the bridge of her nose. "We're all checked in. We have to leave right now if we want to make the flight," she says to my grandma before she turns to me, her gaze expectant.

My stomach flips uncertainly. I count backward in my head, trying to push away the uncomfortable weight pressing against my heart. *Ten, nine, eight, seven, six, five, four, three, two, one.*

I know I'm supposed to be emotional. I'm saying goodbye to my parents for a whole month, after all. We're going to be nearly eight thousand miles apart with a time difference of ten hours.

It's a lot.

It's too little.

T-28 days.

But they're still my parents, and I can't let them go without saying goodbye.

I lean forward to hug my mom. She smells like roses and citrus shampoo. The material of her salwar kameez scratches my cheek. I'm torn between wanting to hug her closer and wanting to be far, far away. "Bye, Ma," I say, and then I hug my dad, who smells like some God-awful cologne, probably worn to impress my mother's relatives. I smile and brush some lint off his shoulders as I step back. "Bye, Baba."

"Myra, make sure to call us *every* day," my mom says. "Dadu might be staying with you, but that doesn't mean you're allowed to do whatever you want. Make sure to behave properly and try to spend more time studying than reading these silly little books."

My smile strains. I feel like a dog being told to roll over. I have to remind myself she's saying it with my best interests at heart. "Of course, Ma."

My mom turns to my brother and starts cooing, brushing back his hair. I bite the inside of my cheek and try not to scowl. Naturally she has nothing condescending to say to him. "Tell Dadu whenever you're hungry, okay? She'll make you whatever you want, Samir."

"Stop it, Ma," my brother says, batting her hands away. He's grinning a hundred-watt smile that's hard to look at for more than one reason. I don't think I've ever smiled at my parents like that.

My dad steps forward, gaining my attention. His expression is only slightly easier to look at. "Keep us updated on your grades, Myra," he says, squeezing my shoulder. "It's junior year. You know you need all As if you want to become a doctor."

And what if I don't want to? What then?

"Of course, Baba," I say, because there isn't any other answer. "I will."

Between one blink and the next, they're walking toward security, leaving the three of us alone. I can still hear them bickering about Netflix.

"Come on, Myra," Dadu says, nudging my shoulder. I look away from my parents' retreating backs. "Let's find an Uber."

"I've got it," Samir says, whipping out his phone and waving me off as we start to walk to the exit.

I roll my eyes, unsurprised he wants to take the lead. I can't help but cast another glance over my shoulder at my parents, but Dadu gently tugs my ear.

"So what's your book about?" she asks.

I turn to her in surprise. I closed the book after my mom's rebuke, but the story is still fresh in my mind. "You want to know?"

"Of course," Dadu says, smiling warmly at me. "You can tell me during the Uber ride."

Something dislodges in my chest as we approach the exit. "That sounds great."

When I look back this time, there's no sign of my parents anywhere.

Even though I know it's wrong, all I feel is relief.

2

T-MINUS 27 DAYS

High school isn't as bad as television makes it out to be. I've never seen anyone pushed into a locker or publicly embarrassed in front of the cafeteria. I wouldn't *want* to. That sounds like a literal nightmare.

Here, the worst things I have to look forward to are the purple-and-gold banners decorated with large cartoonish wolves hanging from poles in front of the building. It's an attempt at school spirit that I think even our principal despises.

Midland High School is known for its science and math classes, which is why my parents thought it would be the best school in Long Island for my brother and me. Samir is a freshman and I'm a junior now, but during the six months he's been here, he's excelled more in math and science than I ever could. Especially since I hate those subjects.

Despite that, I've grown to love the school. With its bright yellow lockers, pastel walls, and sleek purple linoleum floors, it looks more like something out of a Dr. Seuss book than an academic institution.

When I walk into the cafeteria, my best friends are occupying a lime green table near the vending machines, and I head for them with a smile on my face. My mood is exceptionally bright today, since my grandma woke up early to make me a paratha and omelet. I'm used to being handed a granola bar, so it was a warm surprise.

"Good morning," I say, wrapping my arms around my two favorite girls. "Isn't it a beautiful day outside?"

Nandini rolls her eyes, running a hand through her short curls, still wet from the gloomy weather. "It's raining, Karina."

"Exactly," I say, slipping my way between her and Cora, who laughs as she scoots aside to make room.

The three of us met freshman year during Italian and have been tied together since. Every year we choose classes in the hopes of landing similar schedules and, so far, it's worked out.

This year, we have first period free every day, and all of us show up early just to spend time together.

"How's day one without the parental figures?" Cora asks, brushing her platinum blond hair over her shoulder and handing me a warm cup of coffee. "I see you've broken out the crop tops and ripped jeans."

I smile faintly, looking down at my outfit. It's not too wild, but it's still more skin than usual. "I've been hiding these in the back of my dresser for *months*."

"At least they're finally seeing the light of day," Nandini says, poking my belly button.

I laugh and take a sip from my cup. I try not to grimace at the bitter taste. Cora has a tendency to forget how I prefer my coffee, but I never complain, because she still went out of her way to bring it for me. "Last night I went to bed at one in the morning after binging three movies, and Dadu didn't say a *word*. Can you believe that? We truly love to see it."

"Ugh, wish I could relate. Ever since my grandparents

moved in, they hog the television *all* the time, and it's just not the same watching on my laptop." Nandini sighs heavily. "I'm considering spending my next paycheck on a TV for my room."

"You should," Cora says, her hazel eyes bright. "Imagine the movie marathons we could have."

Nandini grins before looking back at me. "Seriously though, babe. I'm happy for you. You needed this."

I offer her a small smile. "Yeah, I really did."

The last few months have been difficult, and both Nandini and Cora know it. We've never had a reason to keep secrets from each other. When Nandini decided during sophomore year that she didn't want to grow out her hair anymore, Sikh or not, we were the first people she told. We took her to the hair salon ourselves and held her hand the entire time. When Cora realized last year that she's bisexual, our group chat blew up my phone the entire night. We all showed up the next morning with matching dark circles underneath our eyes and smiled tiredly at each other in solidarity.

At the beginning of the year, I realized I didn't want to be a doctor or an engineer or anything relating to STEM. It was the most terrifying realization of my life. It still is.

When I hypothetically brought up pursuing something other than medicine to my parents—I didn't even *mention* being an English major—I received the worst lecture of my life. It went on for weeks upon weeks and stopped only when they began preparing their travel plans.

Their reaction was a horror story brought to life. Until then, I'd never realized I had anxiety. It was undeniable, though, when I found myself sitting alone in my room, struggling to breathe through my tears with an unknown pressure building in my chest.

In retrospect, I think I've always had it. It's just never been as bad as it is now, with the future looming over my head, so impossibly far away and yet closer than ever.

Nandini and Cora still think I should push for an English degree. I think my parents might actually disown me if I try.

But this next month means I don't have to worry about it. I'm free from the constant weight of their disapproving glares.

T-27 days. I'm going to try to make every single one of them count.

"How were your weekends?" I ask, leaning my elbows on the table.

Cora grins. "Okay, so I found the *cutest* pair of shoes at the mall. I'll Snapchat you a picture when I get home, but they're literally gorgeous. Perfect for junior prom."

"Not the junior prom thing again," Nandini says, leaning her chin on my shoulder. "Cora, that's for losers."

"You guys are so boring," Cora whines. "Come on, it'll be fun! We don't need to go with anyone. It can just be the three of us. It'll be like practice for real prom."

"Good luck convincing my parents to let me go to any kind of prom," I say. It comes out light, but both Nandini and Cora sober at the words.

Nandini is fully Indian and Cora is half-Chinese, yet my parents tend to be more strict than both of theirs combined. I'm rarely allowed to do things without guaranteed parental supervision. When I *do* break the rules, the hellish screaming that comes afterward is hardly ever worth it. I know it's because they're protective of me, but it's still a hindrance on my social life. The situation is complex.

And as of right now, prom is out of the question.

"I'm going to start a petition," Cora says, already taking out her planner to make a note. "I'd like to see your mom argue against five hundred signatures."

I choke back a laugh. "Where the hell do you think you're

going to get five hundred signatures? I don't think five hundred people even know who I *am*."

"Listen, they don't need to know you. This is a matter of social justice. Your parents are taking away your right to go to prom, and that should be illegal!" She raises her voice even louder. "This is your *space*. This is your *area*. They can't do that to you."

"Are you serious?" I ask, giggling. "Do you know how you sound right now? Is this because your dad is white?"

Nandini snorts. "That's exactly why," she says. "Cora, you silly, silly girl. I love you."

"Don't be condescending," Cora says, pointing a lead pencil at Nandini in warning. She hesitates and adds, "but I love you, too."

I snort. "You're both such clowns."

"Shut up." Nandini bumps her shoulder into mine. "If we have to kidnap you ourselves for junior prom, we'll do it. I could probably fit you in a duffel bag. It would take a little squeezing but between the three of us, we can make it work."

"Oh my God, does that mean we're doing it?" Cora says, nearly screeching in my ear. Some of the people at the end of the table give us dark looks, and I smile apologetically. "It's official! NCK is going to junior prom!"

"Why don't I ever think before I speak?" Nandini whispers, casting a glance skyward.

I lean my head against Nandini's shoulder, still smiling. My best friends might be clowns, but they're mine and I wouldn't trade them for the world.

Nandini slumps to accommodate me and on my other side, Cora interlaces our fingers. "I really wish we could all go to prom together," I say. "But with my parents… I don't know."

Cora squeezes my hand. "Karina, you know what the poets

say. If you want something badly enough, nothing can stop you or whatever. Right, Nandini?"

Nandini nods, grinning at my exasperated expression. She takes my other hand in hers, looping our pinkies together. "You can't let the world decide your future for you. It's your life, babe. If you want to go to prom, we should go to prom. You should put your happiness first every once in a while."

"I'm just being realistic," I say under my breath, but when they both squeeze my hands again, I return the gesture.

Nandini snorts. "Sure, Karina. We'll go with that."

"I am," I say, my voice rising.

Cora hums, arching a perfect brow. "I'll believe it when I see it."

"Whatever." I roll my eyes. "Don't you both have homework to catch up on?"

"Oh shit," Cora says, suddenly flipping through her binder. "Did either of you understand the Italian homework? Because I am *so* lost. What does question three even mean?"

I look on as Nandini explains, but I can't help but reflect on our conversation. My parents aren't here now, so I have more freedom than before, but that doesn't mean I can do whatever I want. This will last for only so long.

Twenty-seven days until they return and my gilded cage slams shut again.

3

T-MINUS 27 DAYS

We part ways for our first class of the day. I sit in the back of
the room and tune out my teacher, doodling aimlessly in my
journal. I'm not an artist, but sometimes poetry runs ram-
pant in my thoughts, so whenever I have a free moment, I
write it down.

I'm drowning in a pool of moonlight
my lungs are full of stars

When the bell rings, I pack my stuff and make my way to
my locker through the overcrowded hallways.

My locker is a visual representation of my brain. Pictures of
Nandini, Cora, and me are littered across every surface. There
are pictures of TV characters and fanart of my favorite book
scenes. Random things I need to remember are scribbled on
a whiteboard attached to the inside of my locker door. Hung
at the back is a replica of Desdemona's strawberry handker-
chief from *Othello*, and pinned to the bottom of the material
are a few of my poems.

I put away my textbook and head to my next—and favorite—class, English. It's a dearly needed breather after AP Physics. God forbid my parents ever realize how much I'm struggling in that class.

I slip into my English classroom and sit in the back corner, next to the window. Cora, Nandini, and I claimed this corner in the beginning of the year, since it's easier to text discreetly here.

"The wildest thing happened during gym," Nandini says as she drops into the seat beside me. Our teacher, Miss Cannon, is scrawling the opening activity onto the whiteboard, hardly paying attention to us. "I'll tell you and Cora during lunch."

I raise my eyebrows. "Can't wait."

As the bell rings, Cora rushes into class and takes a seat on the other side of Nandini. "I really had to pee," she says, chest heaving.

I sympathetically offer her my water bottle.

Miss Cannon claps, drawing attention to the front of the room. "Let's begin our discussion of *The Great Gatsby*..."

I'm in a good enough mood today that I raise my hand as soon as the discussion begins. Usually, I'm too flustered unless I have a really good talking point. I don't like having people's eyes on me unless I have something smart to say. "I don't think it truly matters whether Gatsby is telling the truth about himself or his past—because does it even affect his future? He could spin any tale, and it wouldn't matter nearly as much as the way his love for Daisy is presented. I'd argue it's the biggest facet of his entire persona."

"Interesting point, Karina," Miss Cannon says, smiling. "Would anyone like to counter or contribute further to that?"

Someone else raises their hand. "I agree with Karina. On page 150, it says..."

I nod, flipping to the mentioned page in the book.

The conversation continues for another ten minutes before

we split up into groups. Naturally, Cora, Nandini, and I push our desks closer together.

"Okay, so I didn't read any of it yet," Nandini admits after checking to make sure Miss Cannon is attending to a different group. "I had a late shift at the movie theater yesterday and I still had to finish the physics lab, so...something had to give."

"I skimmed most of it but didn't really understand," Cora says, scratching her nose. "Karina, can you explain?"

I roll my eyes, unsurprised. We all have our strengths when it comes to school subjects. Nandini loves science, Cora loves history, and I love literature. "So you basically want *Gatsby for Dummies*?"

"That's *exactly* what I want," Nandini says.

I sigh, but nod. "All right. So Nick and Gatsby are basically driving together, and Gatsby is like blah, blah, blah, here's my whole life story, and only God knows why Nick cares. Then Gatsby's all like bro, I've done all kinds of wild shit you wouldn't believe. I collected all these jewels in Europe and hunted big game and had mad medals awarded to me during World War I from tons of European countries. And Nick is like...huh? And Gatsby is all like look here's my medal from Montenegro and me and my bros playing cricket in Oxford, yada, yada, yada."

"I love you," Cora says sincerely. "You are an angel and I would absolutely die for you. I am never going to read a book again."

"That is the exact opposite of what you should do," I say, kicking her underneath the desk. "*Please* read a book."

"We'll see," Cora says, waving a nonchalant hand.

I explain the rest of the chapter, and we decide on a talking point for our homework just before the bell rings. We stand up to head for lunch, which we have next, but as we head for the door, Miss Cannon says, "Karina, can you come here for a second?"

I falter and look at my friends.

"We'll wait outside," Nandini says, patting my arm. I smile gratefully and go over to Miss Cannon's desk, which is overflowing with books and papers.

Miss Cannon is my favorite teacher. She's only a few years older than us and always has the most interesting lessons. When I told her I love to read everything from classics to young adult fiction, she offered me some of the best recommendations and then asked me if I'd be her assistant during after-school tutoring, which runs for an hour every day after ninth period.

I hesitated at first, because I'm not good outside my social bubble of Nandini and Cora. But tutoring means helping someone one-on-one for a few minutes, and even for me, that's manageable.

Getting my parents' permission was another problem, but Miss Cannon talked to them. Unsurprisingly, they demanded an in-person meeting before agreeing to let me stay after school from 3:00 to 4:00 p.m. every day.

Of course, they have no qualms about me staying late for Pre-Med Society on Tuesdays, even though it means *another* hour at school, since clubs don't start until after tutoring. I wish they were as lenient with everything else, but that's asking too much. I rarely go to the meetings anyway. No one cares if you skip club activities unless you're on the e-board. And I most *certainly* am not on the e-board for Pre-Med Society.

As soon as I lean against one of the desks, Miss Cannon says, "Before you say no, hear me out."

"Yikes," I say. "That doesn't sound promising, Miss Cannon."

"I know, I know." Miss Cannon sighs quietly, toying with a red dreadlock. "As you know, the English Regents are coming up."

I nod. Regents Exams are state-mandated exams we have to take every year as per New York law. This year, I have them for English, Physics, Italian, and US History.

"A student in my class reached out for help," Miss Cannon says. "We've worked together a little, but I think he'd benefit more from one of his fellow classmates' perspectives. Would you consider privately tutoring him?"

I raise my eyebrows. "Me? I think you're talking to the wrong person."

"No, I definitely chose the right person," Miss Cannon says, smiling, before her expression shifts to serious again, her lips pursed. "I know it's a lot to ask, but instead of helping me during after-school tutoring sessions, you could spend that time with him."

My mouth dries. "For *five* days a week?"

Miss Cannon winces. "Yes, preferably, since it'll be substituting the time you spend helping me here. It's only for three months, and you're my best student, Karina. I know you can do this."

I shake my head, my pulse hammering. "Miss Cannon, I don't know if—"

"If you do, you'll be excused from having to do the poetry project," Miss Cannon says, cutting me off. "I'll count this as your grade instead."

I falter. The poetry project is worth twenty percent of our grade. She wants us to write ten original pieces following the specific parameters of different poetry formats—haikus, limericks, freestyle, and so on. We have to turn it in next month and choose one of the ten poems to present in front of the class.

Even though I *love* poetry, I hate public speaking. More

than that, I hate the thought of saying my deepest, most vulnerable thoughts aloud. Being free of that obligation just to tutor some random dude during the time I'd be helping Miss Cannon anyway? It might be worth it.

But still...

"Karina, your grades are consistently the highest in the class, and you've been a great help to the other students," Miss Cannon says, squeezing my shoulder. "No one is more capable than you."

I know she's trying to encourage me, but her words are making me more anxious. I don't want to let Miss Cannon down, not when she believes in me this much.

The idea of facing her disappointment twists my stomach.

With painstaking reluctance, I say, "Okay."

Miss Cannon's face lights up with a grin. "Thank you so much, Karina."

"So...who's the student?" I ask, shoving my hands in my pockets to hide the way my fingers are shaking.

"He's in this class," she says, waving a hand toward the left side of the room. "Alistair."

An uneasy feeling spreads through me, like a heavy weight settling on my shoulders. *Ten, nine, eight, seven, six, five, four, three, two, one.*

"Alistair?" I repeat. "*Alistair Clyde*? As in Ace Clyde?"

Miss Cannon pauses. "Yes. Will that be a problem?"

I almost laugh hysterically. The world is clearly plotting against me. "No. Of course not."

She eyes me, her brows rising as she scrutinizes my expression.

Her face starts to fall, and my heart feels like it's pushing against my rib cage, making it difficult to breathe. The smallest hint of disapproval always sets off my anxiety beyond words. It's hard to believe I never realized this until a few months ago, because it's so achingly obvious now.

"Should I still come to your classroom after ninth period?" I ask, pushing forward. I can do this. I *will* do this.

Miss Cannon is still staring at me, so I paste a smile on my face, swallowing past the uncomfortable lump in my throat.

Slowly, she smiles back. "If you could go directly to the library, that'd be perfect. I'll tell him to meet you there," Miss Cannon says, handing over a folder. "I've already outlined a tutoring schedule, but feel free to deviate if you find a better way that works for both of you."

My smile strains. "Okay. Thank you, Miss Cannon."

After putting the folder away in my bag, I leave the room and see Nandini and Cora standing across the hall, speaking quietly.

They both smile when they see me, but Cora's face falls almost immediately. "Are you good? Are you in trouble?"

"No," I say, clutching the straps of my bag tighter. "Everything's fine. Everything is…" I falter, unable to say more.

Cora starts to move toward me, her features clouded in concern, but Nandini wraps a hand around her wrist.

"Cora, give her some space," Nandini says. A silent understanding passes between us, and I feel so grateful I could cry. "What's up, babe?"

I shake my head and run for the closest bathroom. Inside, I enter a stall and slam the door shut, then force myself to take a deep breath, pushing the heels of my palms into my eyes. I just need a moment. A moment, and I'll be okay again.

I barely know Ace Clyde, but tutoring him sounds like my worst nightmare. He's notorious for slacking off.

The idea of letting Miss Cannon down causes my lungs to constrict painfully. *How* am I going to do this?

Ten, nine, eight, seven, six, five, four, three, two, one.

Ten, nine, eight, seven, six, five, four, three, two, one.

Okay. I'm okay. I can face the world again without fear of bursting into tears.

I lift my head and unlock the stall. Cora and Nandini are standing in the bathroom doorway, but they don't say anything as I walk to the sink and splash my face.

I look in the smudged mirror and have a vivid flashback to the night I asked my parents about hypothetically changing my major. My expression then was worse, tear-streaked and devastated. But the manic light in my eyes is still the same as then.

I grappled with the concept of having anxiety for a while. It took me a lot of Google searches and conversations with Nandini and Cora, but I've slowly come to accept it. It's part of me, and it always will be. I just have to remember my countdown, and everything will be fine.

It'd be nice to get professional help, but that would require telling my parents. Maybe one day, when I'm in college and have more freedom, I can attend counseling. Until then, I have to make do with what I have.

I force myself to take one final deep breath. I'm *okay*.

"So?" Cora asks, shifting forward to stand in front of me. She holds out a pack of tissues. "What did Miss Cannon want?"

I offer her a tight smile. *Ten, nine, eight, seven, six, five, four, three, two, one.* "She wants me to tutor Ace Clyde."

There's a beat of silence.

Another.

Another.

Another…

…And then Cora drops the tissues. *"What?"*

4

T-MINUS 27 DAYS

Nandini slides me a slice of pizza as soon as she comes off the lunch line, and I smile in thanks. "You're the best."

"Don't ignore me, Karina. Are you being serious right now?" Cora asks, poking at her salad far too violently. "Ace Clyde?"

I roll my eyes and toss a napkin at her. My heart has calmed down to a respectable pace, and even though I'm still on edge, being around my friends helps significantly. "You're such a gossip."

"And what about it?" Cora says, flipping her hair. "But seriously, Ace Clyde?"

"Yes," I say, sighing. "Ace Clyde. Now can you stop saying his name over and over? I feel like he's going to appear over my shoulder like Bloody Mary."

"Nandini, I think I'm going to faint," Cora says. "How is she so calm?"

"Honestly? I think she's in shock," Nandini says, shaking

her head. "Maybe she doesn't understand the gravity of the situation."

"Oh my God, yes, I *understand*," I say, shoving her half-heartedly.

Cora and Nandini are infinitely more in tune to Midland High's social life than I am. It doesn't help that we have over two thousand students. Everyone usually sticks to their own grades and their own social circles. Aside from the people who have been in my classes through the years, I know only a handful of freshmen because of my brother, and *know* is a stretch.

But even with my small social circle, it would be impossible not to know the big names of our junior class. Ace is one of them.

His older brother, Xander Clyde, is Midland High's student body president. He's a senior, and beautiful, rich, popular, and intelligent. Almost all of the girls—and some of the boys—want to date him. Everyone else wants to be him.

Ace is also beautiful and rich. Whether he's popular and intelligent are debatable.

He's definitely infamous among our classmates, though. He sits alone at his own table, tells everyone who looks at him wrong to fuck off, wears leather jackets over designer sweaters, and spends half his time pissing off the school faculty.

"I really don't feel like you get it." Cora shakes my arm. "Do you know who he is?"

"Yes, Cora. And I know this is going to be a *nightmare*," I say bitterly. Of all people, I had to get stuck with the school's resident preppy bad boy. "Why would Miss Cannon do this to me?"

"How are you complaining right now?" Cora says, throwing her hands up. "Ace is the *hottest* guy in our grade."

"I hate enabling Cora, but she's right," Nandini says, shrugging when I give her an incredulous look. "Have you seen him? Karina, he's literally gorgeous."

My friends are ridiculous. I love them, but they really are.

"Yeah, well, I'm tutoring him. Not dating him. I'm more concerned that this dude never pays attention in class. How am I supposed to teach him anything?"

"Karina, you're the worst," Cora says, pouting. "How can you think about studying at a time like this? We're talking about Alistair Clyde! Oh my God, you have to get him to fall in love with you so we can live vicariously through you. Karina, this is what your entire life has been leading up to."

"Stop clowning around," I say, shaking my head. "The last thing I have room for in my life right now is a guy, much less *Ace*. It'll be a miracle if I can even talk to the dude without making a fool of myself."

"Karina and Alistair sitting in a tree, K-I-S-S-I-N-G," Cora sings, swaying side to side. I give up, knowing it's a lost cause when she gets like this.

I turn to Nandini for support, but she's staring at me in contemplation. The look in her eyes makes my skin crawl, because she looks like that only when she's scheming.

"I'm tired of you both," I say, flipping them off before returning to my pizza. "I need new friends."

Cora laughs but Nandini taps her chin thoughtfully. "I wonder what we'll wear to the wedding. He's white, which is a tragedy, but maybe you can convince him to have a brown wedding."

"Putting aside how senseless all of that is, you think my parents would let me marry a *white boy*?" I ask incredulously. "Have you met them?"

Nandini considers that for a moment. "Maybe we just won't invite them. Samir could walk you down the aisle instead."

I sigh, shaking my head. "Say less. Say so much less."

"I'm just pointing out that there's a lot of potential here," Nandini says, holding her hands out in defense.

"What potential? You think that all the people in our school who throw themselves at Ace, he would decide to date the random brown girl tutoring him in English? You've lost the plot," I say, before pointing a finger at her. "Earlier you said something wild happened during gym. Let's talk about that instead."

"You're no fun." Cora wrinkles her nose, but she also turns her gaze toward Nandini, which means the conversation is effectively over. Alhamdulillah.

As Nandini talks about some dude from her gym period who flashed the whole class, my mind drifts.

I shouldn't be surprised Ace is struggling with English. I *am* surprised he reached out for help.

I just wish I wasn't the one stuck helping him.

Ace doesn't show up.

I sit in the library, waiting for a whole thirty minutes, and he doesn't show up. It's beyond frustrating and, if the thought didn't tie my stomach into painful knots, I'd head upstairs right now to tell Miss Cannon.

But I don't want her to think I gave up before I even tried.

I wait a few more minutes, then decide to check out a US History textbook so I can work on my homework in my newfound free time. If I have to be here, I can at least be productive.

At four, the bell rings, signaling an end to after-school tutoring. Students start to leave the library, heading for their respective clubs.

I try to tamp down my annoyance at the empty seat across from me.

My group chat with Nandini and Cora buzzes with notifications, distracting me from homework.

Cora Zhang-Agreste:
SO??? HOW DID IT GO??? IS #KARSTAIR
OFFICIALLY A THING?

Nandini Kaur:
I want it on record that I prefer #ACEKARINA!!!
but also YEAH UPDATE US WHAT IS GOING
ONNNN

Me:
I literally cannot stand EITHER of you!!! he hasn't
even showed up so... [pretends to be shocked]

Cora Zhang-Agreste:
ugh men are such flops

Cora Zhang-Agreste:
they really can't do a single thing right

Nandini Kaur:
I guess we should've known but damn. it was nice
to have hope for like 2 seconds lmao

Me:
not to say I told you so but I told you so!!! plus I'M
NOT TRYING TO DATE HIM SO CAN Y'ALL CHILL

Cora Zhang-Agreste:
chilling? never heard of that concept!

I go to my locker, pack my things, and grab an umbrella. It's raining outside, though it wasn't an hour ago. Another reason to be irritated.

If I had a confrontational bone in my body, I would hunt down Ace and demand to know why he's forcing me into this awkward and horribly anxiety-inducing situation.

As it is, all I can do is wait for tomorrow.

5

T-MINUS 26 DAYS

During my free period the next day, I finish the study guide I started working on last night. Admittedly, I did it more for Miss Cannon than Ace. I want her to know I gave this every effort, that I actively tried to help him. It's not much, but it's *something* to show initiative on my part.

Giving him a study guide also means I won't have to deal with this tutoring situation anymore. The problem will be out of my hands.

My annoyance might have slipped in while I was writing it, though. In place of formal descriptions are the crude recaps I usually give to my friends. I probably should've kept it more professional, but it's not *my* fault he didn't show up.

Nandini and Cora insist I go to the library again, saying maybe Ace had an emergency and I should give him a second chance. I have to remind them exasperatedly that I'm not trying to date him.

God forbid I ever do. My parents would *murder* me.

There are far too many rules in my household, and not dating is one of the big ones. Some of them, I can understand, but others are more difficult to get behind. I have to be careful with the way I spend my time, I have to be careful with who I decide to hang out with, and I have to be careful about what kind of goals I choose to pursue.

With all of that in mind, getting an English degree is more or less a pipe dream.

Abiding by all these rules day in and day out is exhausting, but my parents have sacrificed too much for me to throw it all away by being selfish. They left behind their lives in Bangladesh and moved here in the hopes of giving me a better life. They want me to grow up and be successful, to be financially stable, to be focused and diligent and hardworking.

I know they're thinking about my future, but I don't know how to be the daughter they can gloat about at our community parties, the daughter whose achievements they can praise to their coworkers, the daughter who never steps a toe out of line and does everything exactly as they wish. Still, a part of me wants that—to be enough for them, to have them be proud of me. The rest of me wishes I could crawl into a hole.

I try not to think about it too much.

When I get to English, I don't see Ace, so I leave the study guide on his usual desk with a scribbled note explaining what it is. Miss Cannon watches me curiously but only offers a smile when our eyes meet.

I exhale in relief. If she saw how *awful* my commentary was, I think I'd have to drop out of school.

I wait on the edge of my seat for Ace's arrival, but the clock keeps ticking, Miss Cannon keeps teaching, and the door to the classroom remains closed.

He's ditching? Seriously?

Right before class ends, someone knocks on the front door.

Xander Clyde pops his head into our classroom, and everyone falls silent.

His eyes are a stunning pale blue, and his dark brown hair is slicked back. He looks like every Ivy League college's wet dream, with his brown loafers, tan khakis, and tucked-in button-down shirt.

When he grins at Miss Cannon, I glance at Cora. As much as she jokingly encouraged me to pursue Ace, I think she'd have an aneurysm if any of us even *looked* at Xander romantically. Ever since he beat her out for student body president, she's been seething with contempt for him.

"Sorry, Miss Cannon, do you have a minute?" Xander asks, leaning against the doorway.

She furrows her brows but nods. "Class, continue to discuss. I'll be right back."

"I wonder what that's about," Nandini says, turning toward us as the door closes behind them. "Do you think it has to do with Ace?"

As if her words are a trigger, the front door slams open, and a different figure enters. It's obviously Ace, but there's a hood over his head, so I barely catch a glimpse of his expression as he stalks toward his desk, snags my study guide with ringed fingers, and walks back out.

The class immediately bursts into confused clamor.

"What the hell was that?" I ask, staring after him. "Did Miss Cannon mention I left something for him? Do you think she knows he ditched our study session yesterday?"

Nandini looks as bemused as I feel. "Maybe?"

Cora is stretching her neck, trying to catch a glimpse of them through the back door's window. "I bet his asshole brother has something to do with it."

"Not everything is Xander's fault," Nandini says, nudging her.

Cora harrumphs, her eyes narrowed at the door.

When it opens again, we all watch with bated breath, but only Miss Cannon steps through.

She gives the entire class a pointed look. "I trust you all had a productive discussion in my absence."

Everyone mutters an affirmative, but I doubt *anyone* discussed anything aside from Ace and Xander.

When class finally ends, Miss Cannon calls me over. I walk slowly to her desk, ignoring the too-fast beat of my heart as I try to anticipate how the conversation will play out.

"How did it go yesterday?" she asks with a bright grin, and my brain short-circuits.

She doesn't know.

For a moment, I consider telling the truth. Then I imagine her face wiped clean of joy and abandon that idea. My anxiety demands I refrain from disappointing Miss Cannon. She has enough on her plate, with over a hundred students to monitor each day.

"It's a work in progress," I say, which is the truth. He *did* take the study guide. "I haven't quite gotten a feel for the situation yet. I have high hopes, though."

"I'm so glad to hear that." Miss Cannon releases a low sigh. "You're an angel, Karina. Thank you so much for doing this."

"It's no big deal," I say, waving a hand. "I'll keep you updated."

On my way out, I falter at the sight of a packet of papers in the recycling bin outside the classroom.

No way.

I march into the hallway and fish it out of the otherwise-empty bin, staring at it incredulously. He *threw out* my study guide? I know it was a little unrefined, but this is ridiculous.

Nandini and Cora meet me in the hallway, looking between the study guide and my face.

"Jesus. I guess they're both assholes," Cora says, shaking her head. "At least they make good eye candy. Whatever. On the bright side, that means you're free after school today, right? I know we were going to work on our Italian project over FaceTime this weekend, but since we're already here…"

I blink at them, still grappling with the fact that Ace tossed my study guide away. "I—but my parents…"

"They're not around," Nandini says, bumping hips with me. She steals the study guide from me, unzips my bag, and unceremoniously shoves it inside. "Plus your Dadu thinks you're tutoring after school anyway, right?"

"I mean, I guess," I say, licking my lips uncertainly. "But I—"

"Come on," Cora says, pouting at me. "Shouldn't we make the most of your time? We could even grab food afterward. It's not like you ever go to Pre-Med Society anyway."

"It's not my fault it's so *boring*," I say, and realize they're both laughing at me. I sigh, a smile tugging at my mouth. "Yeah, okay. It's not like anyone will notice I'm gone."

"Hey, maybe we'll run into Ace," Cora says, pulling me down the hall, in the direction of the cafeteria. There's a sharp grin on her face. "Wouldn't that be fun?"

"No," I say and pray that Ace stays far, far away from the library today. "That would *not* be fun."

6

T-MINUS 26 DAYS

At the library, the three of us split up to find different books for the Italian project. I'm in charge of books on the Italian economy, and I find them quickly, too used to navigating these aisles.

I sit down at our table, opening a fresh page and writing out the project's requirements.

A shadow looms over me, taller than both Nandini and Cora. I turn around slowly, and my eyes almost bulge out of my head when I see Alistair "Ace" Clyde leaning against a bookshelf, watching me.

My first stupid thought is: Why is he so tall?

My second stupid thought is: Who wears a leather jacket with a designer sweater?

My third stupid thought is: Why is he *looking* at me like that?

Ace is as beautiful as everyone says he is. I've seen him in class and around the hallways, but I've never been the subject of his intense stare before.

His skin is incredibly pale, and the first metaphor that comes to mind is that he's moonlight woven into a human being. It sounds pretentious, but it's true. His dark hair—on the edge between brown and black—is messy and rumpled as if he spends hours running his hands through it. His eyes are some strange kaleidoscopic mix of green and blue, and they twinkle in the faint sunlight that comes through the dusty library windows.

He shares the same strong jaw as his older brother, and his eyebrows are thicker than mine, which is saying something. Unlike his brother, he's tall and lanky. He probably has nine inches on me, at the very least, since I'm five-two.

A lollipop stick hangs in the corner of his mouth, and I try not to fixate on it. The last thing I want is for him to think I'm staring at his lips.

As if he can read my thoughts, he reaches up to take the lollipop out, and I see his fingers are covered in rings of all shapes, sizes, and colors.

"Karina Ahmed?"

It's a miracle I don't jolt at the sound of my name.

"Alistair Clyde," I say. "What are you doing here?"

He raises his eyebrows. "Don't we have a study session?"

I blink at him. "You're here to study? After you *tossed* my study guide in the recycling bin?" Immediately, I bite my lip, the weight of dead butterflies heavy in my stomach. I shouldn't have said that. I don't have the energy to argue with Ace Clyde over a study guide. "Never mind. Forget it."

One corner of his mouth turns up, but I wouldn't call it a smile. "No one calls me Alistair."

"Miss Cannon does," I say mildly, still reeling from this turn of events.

He tilts his head in consideration. "So she does."

A moment passes before Ace saunters around the table and sits across from me, sprawling on the chair. "So, Ahmed. You didn't tell Miss Cannon I bailed yesterday. Why?"

I gape at him. Why does it matter? Why is he *here*?

"I have no interest in landing you in unnecessary trouble," I say after a few seconds.

Ace hums and pops his lollipop back into his mouth. I avert my gaze, looking down at the Italian project.

"Karina, I found the—" Nandini says and falters, staring at me and then Ace with wide eyes. "Oh. Hi."

Ace leans back in his seat and salutes her with two fingers.

Nandini gives me a wide-eyed look. "Are you two...studying?"

I shake my head, opening my mouth to express my own confusion, when Ace places his hand on top of my homework, his rings clacking against the table. "Yes, we are."

"We are?" I repeat.

If he's actually here to study, one would think he'd show a little more effort than manspreading in a chair while sucking on candy.

Cora comes around the corner then, carrying a stack of textbooks. "I think we can divide the work by—" Her mouth snaps shut. Nandini reaches out and steadies the tower of books before they can fall over. "What's going on?"

I grimace, knowing Cora is about to have a field day. I turn back to Ace, smoothing my expression out before he can read my irritation. "You actually want to study?"

Ace meets my gaze evenly. "Why else would I be here?"

"Right." I look at Cora and Nandini, hoping it's clear from my expression I am *begging* them not to leave me alone with this dude.

Cora grins brightly. "You know what? I just remembered my mom wants me home early for dinner. She's making sesame chicken today."

Nandini stifles a giggle. "You should definitely head out then." She takes a step back, wiggling her fingers in farewell.

"I also just remembered I have to work on my Comic-Con costume."

I gape at them. I know Nandini saved up to buy tickets to San Diego Comic-Con, but that's in *July*. It's March. And last I heard, Cora's mom is out of town for some kind of financial conference.

"Wait, but what about—"

"No, it's fine, Karina!" Cora says cheerfully, already moving to the table to start packing up her things. "We wouldn't want to distract you guys."

Nandini nods, shoving her notebook into her Captain America tote bag. "Yeah. We'll see you during first period tomorrow."

Before I can protest anymore, they both press a kiss to the top of my head and disappear behind the tall shelves, laughing among themselves.

Wow. My friends are the *worst*.

I painstakingly look back at Ace. He's watching me with arched brows, his lollipop spinning between his fingers. I sigh, pushing away my resentment for the time being.

He's still a dickhead for not showing up yesterday, and he's an even bigger dickhead for showing up today without an apology.

But fine.

If he wants to study, we'll study. I'm not going to hold a grudge over the study guide. He *is* here, after all. I don't have to let Miss Cannon down.

I take out the rumpled study guide and place it on the table between us. Something flashes across his face—regret, maybe?—but it passes too quickly for me to decipher.

I purse my lips. "I thought we could start with the texts we're learning in class, and closer to the Regents we could focus on individual parts of the exam. Is that okay with you?"

"Whatever you think works best," he says, reaching for the study guide. He flips through it idly, but as his eyes flicker over the text, his eyebrows rise. I wince, remembering my irritation when I was making it.

"Ignore that," I say, reaching over to take it back. He lets me without protest but as he reclines, he watches me with a different look in his eye. He bites his lollipop, and I hear the sharp crunch of candy.

I tuck the study guide into my binder. Ace keeps watching me as he sets the leftover stick on the table. Even though it's *so* unhygienic, I restrain my urge to throw the stick away. I don't know if Ace would still be here when I got back.

"Okay, do you want to start with *The Great Gatsby*, *The Merchant of Venice*, or *The Scarlet Letter*?"

"Never heard of any of those," he says, reaching forward to steal my pencil.

I stare at him, wondering if he's being serious. There's no way he doesn't know those titles. I have to believe he's joking for my own sanity.

"I'll choose then," I say, moving along. "Let's start with *The Scarlet Letter*."

Ace gestures for me to go ahead with a flick of his fingers. He hasn't stopped staring at me, and his intense gaze is making me increasingly restless.

"Okay," I murmur, taking *The Scarlet Letter* from my bag and flipping it open. "I thought we could begin with chapter analyses. Since we already read this book in the fall, we're familiar with the themes and underlying messages, which means we can be more analytical with foresight. Why don't you tell me your overall thoughts on the book so we can figure out which angle we want to tackle first?"

Ace furrows his thick eyebrows. "What angle do *you* want to tackle first? I've seriously never read it. I only know it by name."

I clench my hands but somehow withhold a sigh.

"Okay. Well, I prefer looking at Hester's character in a feminist light and how, despite feminism not existing within the time period this was written, Hawthorne wrote her as being resilient, rebellious, and free to think in ways that stood apart from the rest of society," I say, pointing to the book. My words are rushing into each other, as I actively try not to ramble. "I know some people think Hester's choice to continue wearing the *A* at the end of the book is her conforming to misogynistic ideals, but I think by *choosing* to wear it instead of being *forced* to wear it, she's claiming back her agency."

Ace leans forward, and his combat boots knock into my worn-in Converse. His eyes are too pretty and too disconcerting. "You like English."

I stare at him blankly, mostly because my expression is threatening to twist with incredulity. What is he *talking* about? Why would I be here if I didn't enjoy English? I sure as hell wouldn't be a math tutor. "Yes."

"How strange," he murmurs, flipping my pencil between his fingers. His mouth pulls up a little higher in the corner, but it's still not a smile. "Do you enjoy anything else, Ahmed?"

On the tip of my tongue is: *when people actually listen to me.* I'd sooner die than actually say it.

Instead I set my shoulders and say, "Listen, Ace. I don't want to waste your time or mine. If you don't want to study, tell Miss Cannon. I'm sure she can figure something else out."

And then it won't be my fault.

"I didn't say this was a waste of time," Ace says. "I'm simply curious about my illustrious tutor."

"I promise the book is much more interesting than me," I say. "Come on, just read the first few chapters. They're only ten pages each."

Ace taps my pencil against his bottom lip in consideration.

"Okay." He holds his hand out for the book, and I pass it over easily.

He starts to read, and I take the opportunity to write some discussion questions. After thinking of two, I look up to see how much progress he's made and find him staring at me again.

"What?" I look down at my outfit, another crop top paired with ripped jeans, and wonder if my mom was right to warn me off them. "Is something wrong?"

"This is boring, Ahmed," he says, drawing my attention back to him.

"English isn't boring," I say, exasperated. "*The Scarlet Letter* is one of the better books in our curriculum."

Ace shakes his head. "I think we need to liven it up."

I pause. What does that mean? "What are you thinking?"

"There's a sweet shop down the block," Ace says. The look on his face is challenging, which is unfortunate. I generally like to go with the flow, and Ace seems like the person who *determines* the flow. "Let's study there instead."

"I don't know," I say and my voice wavers. "I have Pre-Med Society at 4:00."

I'm not actually going to go, but that's none of his business.

"Just this one time," Ace says. His gaze is almost titillating. "It'll help me focus, and I'll pay for whatever you want."

In my head I hear Cora yell, *OH MY GOD, HE'S ASKING YOU OUT ON A DATE!* even though I'm almost positive this is just his attempt to get out of studying.

Speaking of Cora...

"I need to use the bathroom," I say. Without waiting for his response, I stand and head for the exit.

I stop in the hallway and take out my phone. There's an unanswered text from my mom, and I click on it first. She must be jet-lagged if she's sending messages at this ungodly hour.

Myra, call us when you get home.
Your Nanu and Nana want to say hi.

I grimace. That conversation is going to be…fun.

Okay, I text back and move on, shifting to the NCK group chat.

Me:
I CAN'T BELIEVE YOU LEFT ME ALONE?? now
ace wants to go study in some bakery and it's ALL
YOUR FAULT

Cora Zhang-Agreste:
HE ACTUALLY SHOWED UP BITCH WHAT WERE
WE GONNA DO??? STAY THERE??? in this house
we do NOT cockblock our friends

Nandini Kaur:
back up a sec did you say BAKERY… ARE YOU
JOKING WTF

Me:
NO I'M SERIOUS PLS HELP ME INSTEAD OF YELLING

Cora Zhang-Agreste:
oh my god oh my god oh mY GOD KARINA

Me:
H E L P

Nandini Kaur:
SAY YES GIRLIE WHAT ARE YOU WAITING FOR OMG

Cora Zhang-Agreste:
OK BUT THIS IS BASICALLY A DATE GO SAY YES
OMG GO GO GO

Nandini Kaur:
YEAH STOP TEXTING US AND GO GET UR
MANS???

Me:
he is NOT my mans!!!!!!!!!

I put my phone on Do Not Disturb and lean my head against the wall. That was absolutely no help at all.

With a sigh, I dial my home phone number. After two rings, my grandma picks up. "As-salaam alaikum!"

"Wa-alaikum salaam," I say. "Dadu, I might be a little later than usual today. Is that okay, or do you need me to come home?"

"Oh, Myra!" my grandma says happily. "I'm glad you called. What do you want to eat tonight? Vegetable pulao or khichuri?"

"Khichuri," I say before reining the conversation back in. "Dadu, did you hear what I said? Can I stay late, or do you need me to come home? Do you need help cooking?"

"No, no, Myra," my grandma says. "Focus on your education. You have your club today, yes? Don't worry about me. I'll make dinner and have it ready for you when you come home. Stay safe."

"Okay, Dadu. Love you."

"Love you," she says. "Khoda hafiz!" *Goodbye.*

"Khoda hafiz," I say, before slumping against the wall, staring down at my phone. Part of me was seriously hoping she'd say no. My parents definitely would've, and it'd be a good excuse to give Ace.

Now? I'm out of options. I've cornered myself.

With a sigh, I head back into the library to tell Ace we can go to the sweet shop.

7

T-MINUS 26 DAYS

Pietra's Sweet Tooth is a little shop across the street, tucked between two larger brand stores. When we walk in, I'm taken aback by how warm and inviting it is. The walls are painted a pretty shade of baby pink and cute little plush cupcakes hang from the ceilings. There's a corner with board games and books on display, and the booths are filled with fluffy pastel throw pillows.

The menu showcases a wide selection of desserts, from ice cream to cake to doughnuts. A wonderful aroma wafts through the air, making my mouth water.

The counter has seats hanging from the ceiling like swings, and all the employees wear adorable animal ears. The girl behind the register is wearing bunny ears, and she smiles brightly when we make eye contact.

I smile back even though I feel like I'm having some kind of strange out-of-body experience.

"Hi! Welcome to Pietra's Sweet Tooth," she says before noticing Ace behind me and grinning even brighter. "Hi Ace. Your usual?"

He's here often enough to have a usual? I've never even heard of this place.

"Yes, please," he says, before nudging me. I jump at the contact, and a hint of a smile flashes across his face. "The strawberry sorbet is amazing."

"I don't like strawberries," I say, although it's not true. Still, I feel weird taking Ace's suggestions. I barely know him, and this entire situation is ridiculous. To the girl, I say, "Can I have a slice of cheesecake?"

"Of course," she says. "That'll be eight dollars."

Before I can open my mouth to ask why the hell a slice of cheesecake costs eight dollars, Ace slips in front of me, gently pushing me behind him. "I've got it."

Right. Ace Clyde is paying for my food. I'm clearly living in some kind of alternate universe. "Thanks," I say out of obligation.

"Grab a seat, Ahmed. I'll bring the food," Ace says, waving at the booths.

"Aye, aye, Captain," I mutter. He shoots me an amused look, and my cheeks warm. I head for the booth near the book display, wondering why I said that. I glance at my phone and see thirty-five unopened texts from the NCK group chat, which comforts me a little. At least some things will always be the same.

Sitting down, I take out our study materials and spread them across the table. I'm going to make sure we get at least *some* work done.

When Ace comes back, he's holding a platter with a large slice of cheesecake, a bowl of mint chocolate chip ice cream, and two milkshakes. He sets it down and offers me a drink. "It's vanilla."

Do I even want to know how much this cost him? Probably not.

"Thanks," I say again. "Are you ready to start studying?"

"Give me a moment," he says, sipping his chocolate milkshake. "I have to acclimate."

"That's a big word for someone who needs to be tutored in English," I say before biting my tongue, eyes wide at myself. Ace isn't Nandini or Cora. I can't just say whatever I want to him. I'm losing my mind.

"I have my moments," Ace says. Thankfully, if his calm expression is anything to go by, he seems unbothered. It's so weird, because I've heard the most horrible things about him.

It all began last year. Rumors started spreading that Ace tried to sabotage Xander's presidential campaign—rumors that back Cora's insistence that Ace is the superior Clyde brother—although no one has ever provided proof.

Before those rumors, Ace could be found hanging around the same social circles as Xander. Everyone knows that with beauty and wealth comes popularity. But even back then, it was pretty obvious he preferred to be on his own.

Aside from that, he's been seen in detention on numerous occasions for reasons unknown. People have taken to creating ludicrous excuses—he fistfought a teacher, he blew up a chem lab, he broke into the principal's office, he graffitied the boys' locker room.

I don't buy into any of it and I don't really care, either. But I *do* know that he has a certain kind of intimidating aura that makes it hard to stare at him for too long, much less hold a conversation. On occasion, I've seen people stop by his lunch table and speak to him briefly—maybe his old friends? But they've never stayed long enough to still be considered that.

Most people can barely say *Hi!* to him in the hallways without being met with a glare. I, however, can insult him and receive nothing but apathy in return. I wish I understood anything about what was happening right now.

My confusion grows when Ace says, "So what's your deal, Karina Ahmed?"

"My deal?" I repeat. "What do you mean?"

"I mean who are you? Obviously, you're the best student in our English class, but that's all I know about you."

I don't know how, but Cora is responsible for this entire situation. I know in my heart I'm here because of her. "We're supposed to be studying."

"We have three months to study," he says, waving off my concern. His rings glint in the sunlight streaming through the shop's wide-paneled windows.

Without meaning to, I admire his hands; how long his fingers are, the slope of his knuckles, the rings on his middle and pinky finger—and a hint of something dark on his wrist that I can't quite see past the sleeve of his leather jacket.

I realize he's waiting for an answer and look back at my notes. "You also have three months to get to know me, so let's do that another day. We should spend as much time studying as possible. I want you to do well on the Regents."

Ace presses his lips together before nodding. He reaches for his ice cream and says, "I'm listening."

Surprisingly, he does.

I outline the first chapters of *The Scarlet Letter*, because it's clear he's not going to read it. Not today, at least. Maybe in a week or two, once I've shown him English doesn't have to be boring. I manage to keep my cool the entire time, which is nothing short of a miracle.

I lay out the themes and write down discussion questions for our study session tomorrow. Ace doesn't interrupt me, but he also never contributes, so I'm not sure who's winning our little tug-of-war. I would say it's me, because my grade doesn't hinge on this, but I also just lost an hour of my life, so…yeah.

As I explain, I pause to eat. The cheesecake is the best cheesecake I've ever had, and I kind of understand why it's eight dollars. I think Ace can tell, because there's a hint of mirth in his eyes—which now look more green than blue, but are still somehow a mix of the two—when he sees me take my last bite.

"Would you like another slice?" he asks, and I get the distinct feeling he's making fun of me.

"I'm fine," I say and glance at my phone for the time. I nearly have a heart attack when I see *5:30 p.m.* "Oh shit," I say and start shoving my things in my bag, not bothering to put my papers back into their assorted folders. "I have to go."

My parents are going to kill—oh.

I falter and stare at my own hands as if they're strangers. My parents are eight thousand miles away. They're not here.

"Ahmed?" Ace says, looking at me with a bemused expression. "Are you okay?"

"Sorry, I—" I don't know how to explain the irrational anxiety that rose up inside me at seeing the time. I don't know if he would understand. I'm not scared of my parents—but I am scared of disappointing them. "Sorry," I finish weakly.

"What's going on?" His eyebrows are furrowed now. "Do you need me to take you home?"

"No, it's not—" I stumble, trying to find the right words. Finally, it seems easier to tell the truth, if only the bare bones of it. "I have a curfew, and I thought I broke it. But my parents are out of the country right now, so it's fine. Just a force of habit, I guess."

Ace looks at his watch with a frown. "You have a curfew of 5:30 p.m.?"

I smile bitterly. "5:15, actually."

He blinks at me like he's unsure what to say, and I don't blame him. I've seen enough movies and read enough books to know that most sixteen-year-olds have a curfew of 8:00 p.m. at the earliest. But I'm not like them. My parents are the way they are, which means there are a million things other people can do that I'll never be able to.

"So are you...all right? Are you going to be in trouble?" he asks.

I shake my head. "They don't come back for a month," I say and bite the inside of my cheek. Ace doesn't need to know about my family life. In fact, this conversation doesn't need to happen at all. "I should head home anyway. We'll reconvene tomorrow in the library? You'll actually be there this time?"

Ace keeps staring at me, and my stomach twists. The look on his face makes me feel like he understands more than he's supposed to, and I've known him for all of a day.

"Well?" I ask, forcing myself to speak up despite the unease weaving through me.

He leans back in his seat and flicks his fingers in another salute. "Yeah. See you then."

I nod and gather my stuff in a calmer manner. I put everything away neatly before grabbing my paper plate and milkshake to throw out. "Thanks for the food."

Ace tilts his head, his stormy eyes meeting my dark brown ones. "Any time, Ahmed."

Right. I doubt he'll even remember who I am after the Regents. Still, I wave as I head for the door. I check my texts and snort at the ninety unread messages from Nandini and Cora.

As I walk home, I can't help but wonder who Ace really is beneath his intense stares. Even though I don't plan to act on it, I think I'm just as curious about him as he is about me.

Maybe in these next three months I'll come to know the real Ace Clyde. Based on our study session today, I don't think I'd mind all that much if that were the case.

8

T-MINUS 26 DAYS

"Myra, you look so tired," Dadu says, pressing her wrinkled hands against my cheeks as she observes the dark circles underneath my eyes. "Did you get enough sleep last night?"

"I'm fine, Dadu," I say, gently pulling her hands away. "I'll sleep a lot tonight, if that'll make you feel better."

We're sitting in the living room, Dadu and I on the couch and Samir on the floor in front of us.

My house isn't the largest on the block, but it's warm and comforting. My parents worked hard to buy it, so I never let myself appear ungrateful for it. They've done everything they can to ensure that Samir and I have a bright future ahead of us.

Our walls are painted sky blue, and our worn, mismatched furniture follows a similar color scheme. Surahs from the Quran hang as decoration from the walls, alongside paintings picked out by my mother. Flowerpots line the window sills, and I remind myself to water them in Baba's absence. If his favorite marigolds die, he might burn down the entire house.

Ma stole some books from my shelves to display on the coffee table, but right now they're hidden beneath Samir's over-flowing folders. Half the floor is wood paneled and the rest is covered by lilac carpet. There's a smattering of blue from when Cora, Nandini, and I dropped nail polish last time they were over, and it's a miracle my mother hasn't noticed the stain yet.

Right now, a spectrum of colors is reflected against the living room walls as Samir plays a video game on the large, flat-screen television. Dadu and I both wince when a particularly gruesome death shows up on the screen.

I have to be careful not to jump at the gunshots, especially since a plate of steaming khichuri and dimer korma sits in my lap. There's no way my mom won't notice—or *smell*—the stain if I somehow tip my plate over.

I try to help Dadu with cooking when I can, though I'm not the best at it. We don't talk about it a lot, but Dadu had a daughter who passed away when she was only seven. My dad barely got to know his younger sister—my would-be aunt—and no one ever brings it up for obvious reasons.

I think that's part of why Dadu goes easier on all the girls in our family than our actual parents do. I have a plethora of girl cousins, and she treats every single one of them with incredible tenderness, as if to make up for her loss. My paternal grandpa, Dada, used to do the same before he passed away a year ago. I can't begin to explain how much I cherish that.

I finish eating and set the plate down on the table before checking my phone. My feet are warm in my grandma's lap as she reads the Bengali newspaper, her glasses sliding down her nose. Samir must have gotten it for her after his shift at the deli nearby, owned by one of my mom's friends from the mosque.

I send Cora and Nandini a Snapchat of Samir and caption it: omg he's STILL hogging the TV I could be watching a rerun of rupaul's drag race rn!!! Almost immediately they send back matching Snapchats expressing sympathy for me.

I'm in the midst of replying when my ringtone blares, Dua Lipa's voice blasting loud enough that I drop my phone. I forgot I left the sound on so I wouldn't miss any of my parents' calls.

I huff but answer the phone, holding it in front of my face as my mother comes into view.

"Myra, why didn't you call us yet?" my mom demands.

We're off to a great start. "I've had a lot of homework. Sorry?"

"Samir called us yesterday," she says, her voice thick with accusation. I cast my brother a glare and see that he's grinning at me. He sticks out his tongue when I catch his eye. Sometimes I think he has no idea how much his achievements highlight my failures. Other times, I think there's no way he can be that oblivious.

"Sorry," I say again.

My mom passes the phone to Nanu and Nana, who eye my flimsy T-shirt skeptically. I cross my chest with one arm and give them a forced smile. "As-salaam alaikum."

After several agonizing minutes of them asking about my upcoming college applications, my mom takes back the phone. I can't help but be low-key bitter my grandparents are even awake this late, presumably to catch up with my parents on everything they've missed.

"Are my plants still alive?" my dad asks, smushing his face against my mother's. Neither of them know how to properly angle their phones for video chatting. I think that might just be a parent thing across the board.

"Yes," I say. "I'm taking good care of them."

"Thank God," he says, the lines of his face relaxing. But then he purses his lips, considering me. "How is your homework going?"

"I have a US History term paper due soon," I say. "I was

assigned President Jimmy Carter. He's actually pretty interesting. Did you know—"

"What about physics?" my dad asks, as my mom's gaze grows heavy.

I bite my lip to withhold a sigh. Why would my parents want to hear a cool fact about Jimmy Carter anyway? "Yes, I've been doing my physics homework, too. We had an interesting lab assignment today. We had to weigh our shoes for it, so I was walking around in only my socks."

"And precalculus?"

I don't even have an answer for that one. "It's fine."

My dad's eyes narrow, mirroring my mother's expression, but before he can say anything, I turn the phone toward my grandma. "Dadu, Baba is on the phone."

She looks up from her newspaper in surprise and reaches for my phone. I'm pretty sure she tunes me and Samir out half the time, unless we're talking directly to her, and I don't blame her.

Ever since Dada passed away, she has these days where she's incredibly low-spirited. I know she misses him horribly, even if she never talks about it.

There are so many burdens she carries that I wish I could help her with, but there's only so much I can do.

I busy myself with taking my plate to the kitchen and washing it. When I come back, Samir is on the couch with my grandma, leaning over my phone.

"Have you been eating enough?" my mom asks. When I take the seat next to Samir, I can see the worry etched into her expression. Again, I withhold a sigh. It'd be nice to receive some of that concern. I know my parents love and care about me, but they never show it the way they do for my brother.

"Yeah, Ma," Samir says, holding up his arms to flex. "Look at my muscles. They're growing!"

I pretend to gag, unimpressed, but he doesn't notice, too busy kissing his nonexistent muscles.

My mom starts cooing like she always does around Samir, and I roll my eyes, reaching for the remote to switch the channel now that he's not playing video games anymore.

"Hey," he complains, trying to knock the remote out of my hand.

"Hey what?" I say, smacking his arm. "You're not even using the TV now. You've been hogging it all day."

"I was in the middle of something!" he says, stretching his body across mine. I wriggle out from underneath him and clutch the remote behind my back. "Myra Apu, give it back!"

"No," I say, pushing him away. "You use the TV every day, I just want it for an hour to—"

"Myra, give Samir the remote."

I fall silent and stare at my phone, still held in my grandma's hand. My mom doesn't say anything else, but saying it once is enough. Almost robotically, I give my brother the remote and sit down beside my grandma.

Between my parents, my mom has always been more strict. I think it's because Dadu raised my dad. Yet he still follows my mom's lead, so it's not like it really helps.

My maternal side tends to be more conservative in nature, even if they're all really nice people. We clash on quite a few of our views, partly because I'm part of the Bangladeshi diaspora, and partly because my outlook on life tends to be more liberal. While I firmly believe there's nothing wrong with being a more conservative Muslim, it's hard to relate to my family when I feel so on the outside of what they expect from me. I try my best to always be open and understanding about how everyone interprets their faith, because I'd want the same courtesy for myself.

I've always believed that Islam on its own is beautiful. Islam in the hands of people who are determined to tear others down—not as beautiful. It's the same way with any culture, any religion. There will always be people who carry out beliefs without stopping to think of the meaning behind them, who follow without question, who don't think about who they might hurt in the process.

I partake in religious activities when I have the time—praying helps with my anxiety—whereas Dadu prays five times a day and constantly rereads the Quran. She's much more religious than I am, but that's never been a problem between us. She loves me, and I love her, and we're both devoted to Allah in different ways.

With my parents...things are more complicated.

Dadu presses her leg against mine, drawing my attention to her. She offers me a small smile before turning back to my phone.

I don't say anything else as she bids them goodbye. Before she hangs up, my mom says, "And Myra, make sure my Hindi serials are being recorded. I want to watch them when I get back, so don't fill up the DVR with those silly reality shows you like to watch. And be nice to your brother. We're not there to look after him, so you have to do it."

"Ma," my brother whines, dragging the word out. "Nobody needs to look out for me."

Ten, nine, eight, seven, six, five, four, three, two, one.

Ten, nine, eight, seven, six, five, four, three, two, one.

What were the other things Google said about coping with anxiety? Aromatherapy? Maybe I need to buy some candles.

"Myra?"

My grandma is holding out my phone, the screen dark. I take it and start to get off the couch, but before I can, my grandma wraps her fingers around my wrist. "What were you saying earlier?"

My brain feels like it's filled with white noise. "What?"

"About that president you like. What did he do?"

"Uh…" I shake my head, trying to clear my thoughts. President… Oh. I didn't realize she was paying attention. "Right. So President Jimmy Carter ran for governor of Georgia before he was president. He campaigned on a super Republican-esque platform while being a Democrat and basically said he would support racism against Black people, which is obviously whack. But then when he was elected, he was all like *just kidding!* and said Black people deserve the same opportunities as everyone else and should be treated equally. All the racist people who voted for him were *so* appalled because they thought he would support their views, but he really just scammed them into voting for him. Isn't that interesting?"

I'm not sure Dadu caught half of what I said, because I started interspersing English with Bengali halfway through, but she's beaming like she understands, so I'll take it. "Very interesting."

A smile finally graces my lips. "Thanks, Dadu."

She runs a hand over the back of my head affectionately. "Always, Myra."

I return to my room, hoping to find a distraction when I catch sight of the clock. I still have time to do the Isha prayer. I head for my closet, grabbing a headscarf and a janamaz prayer mat. Maybe this will help with the unease still coursing through me.

As I set my phone down, an Instagram notification appears at the top of my screen. Ace Clyde (@AlistairClyde) has requested to follow you.

I stare at it for several moments before accepting. His profile is on private, but I press the button to follow back anyway, and wait for him to accept my follow request in return.

In the meantime, I send a screenshot to Nandini and Cora

and ignore the twenty texts of screaming that follow, returning to my janamaz. Still, I'm tempted to join them. With the way things are playing out, I can only imagine what tomorrow will bring.

9

T-MINUS 25 DAYS

The school library is different. Nothing about it is out of place compared to yesterday, but it's definitely different. It feels like everyone is holding their breath, waiting for something.

Or maybe it's just me.

Xander Clyde, student body president and Ace's brother, appears in my peripheral vision. I watch surreptitiously as he peruses the aisle ahead of me, looking through *cookbooks*.

I blink.

He finally seems to find the one he's looking for and, when he turns the cover my way, I glimpse something about Italian recipes.

Huh.

Xander makes for the self-checkout and I look away, returning to my task of finding another copy of *The Scarlet Letter* so Ace and I don't have to share mine. I spot it on the upper shelves and grimace. The upper shelves are my enemies.

I stretch on my tiptoes. I'm almost there, my fingers brushing against the spine, when someone laughs behind me and I jump, my hand knocking into the book. It falls forward, nearly smacking me in the face on its way down.

I part my lips, too shocked to fully process it. What—?

A hand reaches for the book at my feet, and when I look up, Ace is standing there with mirth lining his eyes. He looks like the midnight sky, from the dark vastness of the night to the bright moon and shining stars, and it's slowly driving me up the wall.

"You could have just asked someone for help." He looks far too self-satisfied as he leans against a shelf, and I can't help the indignant noise I release.

"Thanks," I say, taking the book. I don't wait for a response, walking past him and back to my table. As I make my way through the aisles, I curse at myself for getting riled up over nothing.

His footsteps sound behind me, and I withhold the urge to roll my eyes. At least he showed up on time today.

As I sit down, he says, "You seem tired," while looking me over.

I am tired. But that's too much information. I don't want him to assume my exhaustion is because of his little Instagram spectacle.

In reality, I'm tired because I spent the better part of last night scouring the internet for better anxiety-coping mechanisms. I decided to try them out for a few days each, to see what sticks. The first one I picked was writing down my thoughts, but even if it does help, I know it won't be instantaneous.

But I'll always have my countdown for that. Nandini found the technique on TikTok and sent it to me a few months ago. I've adopted it as mine ever since.

When I look up, Ace is still watching me. I feel too hot and too small in my oversized sweater, the sleeves slipping over my wrists. After the phone call with my parents yesterday, I didn't have it in me to wear a crop top again today.

"Thanks," I say and point to our books. "Let's study."

"Hold on." Ace disappears between the shelves. I stare after him for a moment before sighing, burying my face in my hands.

Even though I can feel my exhaustion viscerally, I didn't realize I *looked* tired. I never wear makeup, mostly because I'm lazy, but I should've done the bare minimum and put some color corrector beneath my eyes. I'm sure Nandini would've let me borrow hers if I'd thought to ask. We have a similar light brown skin tone.

I shoot Nandini a text asking her to bring it tomorrow, and she immediately replies, did ace say something rude? I'll throw hands in ur honor!!!

I smile. nothing I wouldn't say myself!! dw ♥

Ace reappears holding a book. I squint, trying to make out the title.

It's a book about different types of monkeys…

Monkeys?

Maybe the Clydes made a pact to confuse me with their reading choices.

Unable to help myself, I write it down. *A boy who looks like moonlight and reads strange books about monkeys.* There's a poem hidden somewhere in that sentence.

"Did you know some monkeys don't have tails?" Ace asks as if he can feel my gaze on him. My own lips start to betray me and turn up in amusement. "How weird is that? It can't be a monkey without a tail, right?"

I bite the inside of my cheek, trying to stop whatever the hell it is my lips are trying to do. "Apparently it can."

Ace looks up and grins. I shift uncomfortably, because my

stomach feels like it's twisting into knots. He has dimples? Jesus Christ. Ya Allah. All of the above.

Either way, this is *bad*. I want no part of it. If I look at his face for another minute, I might give in to Nandini and Cora's delusions, and then where would we be?

"You get it, Ahmed," Ace says, clearly pleased. He closes the book about monkeys—I'm still confused—and gives me his full attention. I can still see a hint of a dimple in his left cheek, and it makes me want to scream.

And yet, even though this entire conversation is ridiculous, the longer it goes on, the better I feel. The cloud that's been hanging over my head all day begins to evaporate.

"I think you're distracting me to keep from studying," I say after a moment. "Let's get to work, Ace."

"Boring," Ace mutters, but not a second later, he sits down across from me. When he grins this time, I actually feel normal. Maybe I can build an immunity to his smile. There's hope for me yet.

I get through about twenty minutes of the session I outlined before he interrupts. "Let's go."

"What?" I look down at my notes, trying to figure out his train of thought. "Go where?"

"Pietra's Sweet Tooth," he says, reaching for the leather jacket he hung on the back of his chair. He gestures for me to stand.

I give him a dubious look. "Why would we go there again? We have to study, Ace."

"I'm more productive there," he says.

On one hand, it's kind of true. On another hand, it wastes precious time. On a third hand I don't even have, the library is my favorite place to be. Pietra's Sweet Tooth is lovely, but this place feels like a warm hug.

"We're studying for school. We should study *in* school."

"Don't be a bore, Ahmed," Ace says, but his voice is teasing. I'm thrown by the change. Has he been switched out for
a look-alike? He's so different from the person I keep expecting him to be. "A little ice cream never killed anybody."

"A lot of people die from high blood sugar, actually."

Ace shakes his head. "Do you have an answer for everything?"

I grin widely, unable to help myself. "It's because I read.
You should try it sometime."

Almost immediately, my muscles tense. I'm not supposed
to say things like that to him.

But...he doesn't look like he minds, so maybe it's okay.

Slowly, I relax.

"Come on, Ahmed. I'll pay again," Ace says, offering me
his hand.

I blink down at it once, twice, thrice.

Even with my mother across the world, I can almost physi-
cally see her standing over Ace's shoulder with a sharp look in
her eye. According to her, it's inappropriate to interact with
boys aside from neutral pleasantries.

I don't really understand it, but her warnings are still in-
grained in me like decaying roots.

I push his hand back, pressing his fingers down gently until
they curl into his palm. "We really have to study."

He sighs and leans back in his seat. "Fine."

Our lesson goes completely downhill after that. His gaze
keeps drifting away, as if he's searching the aisles for something.
His entire body is rigid for reasons I can't begin to fathom.

Ten minutes later, I give up. I'm a people pleaser, and this
situation clearly isn't working for either of us. "Okay. You're
not paying attention. Let's just go."

Ace shifts his gaze from a bookshelf past my shoulder with

a guilty expression on his face. Then my words seem to penetrate his thick skull. "Really?"

"Yes, really." I roll my eyes. "But from now on we have to spend thirty minutes in the library and thirty minutes there. You can't slack off during the library time. Okay?"

I'm hoping he'll agree to the compromise, because I don't think there's any other mutually beneficial solution. Thankfully, Ace nods.

Five minutes later, he opens the door to the shop for me and I slip inside, this time inspecting the different doughnut flavors.

The same girl is behind the register, and she looks surprised when she notices me. I didn't realize yesterday but her name tag says Pietra. She looks only a year or two older than me, though, which doesn't make sense.

Pietra gestures to her name tag when she sees me looking. "My dad owns the shop. He named it after me."

"That's sweet," I say honestly, trying not to wonder if my parents would do something like that for me. I hope so, but I have no idea. "Can I get a jelly-filled doughnut please?"

"And I'll have my usual," Ace says over my head.

"If you're going to get me a drink, do you mind getting me coffee?" I ask him before I can lose the nerve. "Milk with three spoons of sugar? I can pay you back if you want."

"Don't worry about it." Ace nods toward the booths. "I'll bring it when it's ready."

We sit at the same booth again and I take some time to admire it in more detail. It's bubblegum pink with soft cushioned seats. The table is polished rosewood with an arrangement of condiments in animal-themed bottles. I push the frilly sky-blue throw pillows to the side to make room for my backpack.

I'm admiring a painting hung beside me, of sunflowers on a rainy day, when Ace returns.

"Do you paint?" he asks, sliding me my doughnut and coffee.

"I don't have a single artistic bone in my body," I say, looking away from the painting. "That doesn't matter. Let's study."

"Ahmed, you are the most difficult person I've ever met," Ace says under his breath.

I gape at him. No one has ever described me as *difficult* before. Shy, maybe. Quiet, often. A know-it-all, sometimes. Difficult? No. "Excuse me?"

"All you care about is studying," he says, shaking his head. "I don't understand."

I want to flail my arms in disbelief, but I think that might be counterproductive. I settle for saying, "I'm your *tutor*, Ace. Of course I'm going to focus on studying."

Ace makes a face, but the expression disappears before I can scrutinize it. "Okay. Back to Hawthorne. I'm listening."

I frown. I don't want this experience to be miserable for him, but I also don't think us talking about other things is going to be conducive to his studying. "Right. So Hawthorne…"

Before I know it, it's half past five again. It's definitely way past the half hour we were supposed to spend in Pietra's Sweet Tooth, but it's easy to lose myself in literature. I have no idea what Ace's excuse is for not noticing, especially since he seems to pay only half attention to the books in front of us.

I don't have a heart attack upon noticing the time today, but my anxiety still sets in, more from habit than anything else. I start jiggling my leg up and down and clicking my pen incessantly. *Ten, nine, eight, seven, six, five, four, three, two, one.*

I stop when Ace's hand closes over mine. It doesn't really help, because it causes me to spasm and he jerks back, an apology written across his face. "Sorry. I called your name like five times, but you weren't responding. Are you okay?"

"Great!" I say and wince. I don't sound great. Ace can probably tell, too. "Sorry. I'm just antsy. Anyway, I think we're finished for today."

Ace looks me over, his lips pressed together and his eyes focused on my leg, still jiggling up and down. "Can I help?"

"No. No. Uh, I should probably head home. You probably should too, right? I saw your brother Xander earlier in the library, checking out an Italian cookbook. Maybe he's cooking dinner for your family tonight. Or maybe it's for school, I have no idea. Does he take AP Italian? I heard rumors during freshmen orientation that the AP class cooks Italian cuisine. That's why I took Italian over Spanish in the first place. We haven't cooked yet, but—" I abruptly cut myself off, blood rushing to my cheeks. "Sorry, I'm rambling."

Ace is watching me in bemusement. "You saw Xander doing what?"

"Nothing," I say, quickly packing up my things. My mouth is far too dry. "I'll see you tomorrow, right?"

Ace is still staring at me, lips parted on an unasked question.

"Right?" I ask again, almost insistently. I know I'm a nervous wreck, but hopefully he doesn't take that as a reason to end our tutoring arrangement.

After a moment, Ace leans an elbow on the table and sets his chin in his hand, looking up at me through dark lashes. "I'll see you tomorrow, Ahmed."

I slump in relief. "Yeah, see you then."

As I walk away, I can feel his gaze burning a hole in the back of my head. I turn and meet Ace's eyes one last time, and his lingering stare feels like a warning.

10

T-MINUS 24 DAYS

"I'm a horrible tutor," I say, slamming my locker with an air of finality and revealing Cora and Nandini on the other side. "Why did I agree to this when I'm a *mess* of a human being who can barely keep my head on straight? I doubt he's learned a single thing."

"Is that really your fault?" Nandini asks, scratching her neck. "It sounds like he's being difficult."

"Don't even use the word *difficult*," I hiss before pinching the bridge of my nose. "I'm clearly destined to make a fool of myself, and it doesn't help that he's *barely* trying to learn. I don't even know why he asked to be tutored." I drag my fingers down my face, trying not to groan. "As much as I hate my parents' rules, maybe they were onto something with the boy one."

Cora laughs into her elbow, attempting to disguise it into a cough. "Karina, sweetie…no. Boys are not the problem here."

My shoulders slump. "You would say that. At least you have girls to choose from, too! Nandini and I are stuck with these useless, uncommunicative, and unproductive *disasters*."

Nandini tuts sympathetically. "Have you tried marriage counseling?"

I reach out to smack her upside the head, but she ducks out of the way.

"It literally keeps me up at night," I continue. They're the only people I would ever feel comfortable confiding this in. "After I've finished all my homework, I'm like, 'How can I help Ace study?' and my brain keeps coming up blank. I just feel so *bad*. Miss Cannon asked me to do one thing, and I can't even do that."

The thought of letting my favorite teacher down is one of my worst nightmares. I feel like I'm constantly disappointing all the grownups in my life.

"Hey," Cora says, frowning. "Don't feel bad. You're doing your best."

"And if nothing else, at least it distracts you from worrying about college," Nandini says.

"Oh God, don't remind me." I can't even open the Common App without wanting to jump out my window.

"No, but seriously," Cora says, reaching forward and tugging one of my dark waves. "Maybe Nandini is right and this is good. You can focus on this instead of worrying about your parents. A win for everyone!"

"It's not that easy."

Nandini joins Cora in frowning. "Karina, you don't have to carry the weight of the world on your shoulders. You know that, right?"

"Yeah."

They both look skeptical at my reply. I don't blame them.

"Karina—"

"Let's just go to class," I say, ushering them toward the main staircase. "I'll see you guys in English."

"We're not finished with this conversation," Nandini says. "Right, Cora?"

Cora nods. "Right."

I sigh. "I hate when you two team up against me."

"We do it out of love," Cora says, reaching forward to flick my nose. "See you later, alligator."

My mouth quirks into half a smile. "In a while, crocodile."

We both expectantly look at Nandini and she shakes her head. "Screw you guys. I don't have a response that rhymes."

I laugh and reach forward to hug them both around the neck. Their arms wrap around me in return, and we stand like that until the bell rings, spurring us into action.

Maybe my friends are the worst, but they're also the best.

As usual, I'm the first to arrive to English. I take my seat in the back corner and pull out my notebook.

I'm writing down the date when someone drops into the seat beside me.

"Don't start with the marriage counselor thing again," I say without looking up.

"You wound me. Does our love mean so little to you?"

My head snaps up and I see Ace sitting next to me, spinning a wrapped lollipop between his fingers. I open and close my mouth, unsure what to say, and he raises an eyebrow at me. "Cat got your tongue, Ahmed?"

"Why are you sitting here?" I ask, glancing around for my friends. Nandini walks through the doorway and stops in her tracks, seeing Ace next to me.

She gives me an incredulous look and mouths, *What's going on?*

I hope my flustered expression lets her know I have absolutely no clue. There's no reason for Ace Clyde to be sitting next to me outside of our tutoring sessions. Not a *single* reason.

Cora walks in and falters at Nandini's side. Her eyes nearly pop out of her head and she shakes Nandini's arm. *"Nandini,"* she says, loud enough that I can hear it from where I am, which means Ace can, too.

I wince and look back at Ace, who's sucking on his lollipop now. When he notices me looking, he produces another lollipop from his leather jacket and holds it out in offering.

"No thanks," I say. "I prefer Sour Patch Kids."

"Your loss," Ace says before leaning back in his seat, slouching into his usual lazy posture. He doesn't even have a notebook on the desk. No wonder he's failing.

"Do you really not have even a *single* piece of loose-leaf paper?"

"Forgot my bag."

"As in…your book bag? You forgot your *book bag*?"

He shrugs and smirks in a way that's completely infuriating.

I sigh and face forward. Maybe my good work ethic can rub off on him through proximity. Osmosis and all that. Inshallah.

Miss Cannon finishes writing our opening activity on the board and turns around, but she falters at the sight of me and Ace in the back row together.

And then she *grins*. Like, beams. I've never seen her that happy in my life.

"Would you look at that?" Ace whispers.

Without thinking, I smack his arm. As soon as I realize what I did, I open my mouth in apology, horrified, but he's smiling, *too*. His dimples are on display, and he's never looked more annoying or beautiful.

mouths are strange and peculiar

they can be happy, they can be sad
a curve of a lip here, a downturn there

My classmates are staring at us in disbelief. Well, they're staring at him, and I'm more of an afterthought. I'm pretty sure Ace has never smiled in public before, so this is an anomaly for everyone.

It doesn't help that the person he's choosing to smile at is me.

I have no idea what's happening, but I do know I want to sink into the ground.

"Please stop looking at me," I whisper to him and untie my hair, trying to curtain my face from view. My heart is beating too fast, but at least I know I haven't done anything wrong, which helps significantly. Still, I don't like being looked at like I'm a spectacle.

"Juliet would never say that to Romeo," he says, quiet enough that I doubt anyone else can hear. "I'm appalled, Ahmed."

"Don't you *start*," I say, nearly hissing. "Focus on the lesson."

"Whatever makes you happy."

Ten, nine, eight, seven, six, five, four, three, two, one.

I take out a piece of paper and try implementing my latest anxiety coping strategy. Clear, coherent thoughts written out onto a page.

Everyone in class is looking at me. Everyone in class is looking at me. Everyone in class is looking at…

Ace.

People are looking at me, because Ace is sitting next to me. Is looking at me a bad thing? Are they judging me? It's not like I did anything, right…?

No. I definitely didn't. Ace is the one who sat next to me and smiled. They're probably curious about how I tie into this (and frankly, so am I), but they're not judging ★me★.

Ace is the focal point of this situation. I might be a part of the frame, but I'm just a blur. And yet everyone is. still. staring. at. me.

I sigh and stop writing. That didn't help as much as I hoped it would.

English class has never gone by so excruciatingly slowly.

When the bell rings, I'm ready to drag Ace into a corner and chew him out. However, before I can say a word, he stands up and walks over to Miss Cannon.

I can't hear what he's saying, but she looks so overjoyed that all my anger deflates. Fine. Whatever. Instead of bothering with Ace, I walk over to Nandini and Cora, who are sitting on the opposite side of the room, still packing their things.

"Boys are clowns," I say under my breath, eyes darting to the front of the classroom where Ace is taking his leave.

People are still staring at me, and I really wish they would stop. Ace isn't even in the *vicinity* anymore. But I know there's nothing I can do to dissuade my classmates, short of yelling, which would only draw more attention to me.

As soon as Cora finishes shoving her things in her bag, she grabs my hand. "Forget lunch. Let's find an empty hallway." She pulls me toward the door without a second thought. "I baked cookies last night for the student council meeting today. They're in my locker, and no one will notice if we eat some."

"And when we're done, we can try to figure out whether mercury is in retrograde, because Karina's life is devolving into chaos," Nandini suggests, following us. "Maybe some witches on TikTok hexed the moon again."

I groan and let Cora drag me toward her locker. As we enter the staircase, I see Ace in the corner of my eye, leaning against the wall. He's looking at me and, when he catches my eye, he winks.

Winks.

I contemplate flipping him off, but Cora drags me away before I have a chance.

11

T-MINUS 24 DAYS

I don't even bother waiting for Ace to show up in the library. I have ninth period free when I don't have gym, so I make my way to the chemistry wing, a scowl on my face. Cora had to ask a friend of a friend, but I eventually found out Ace's locker is right near my old AP Chem classroom on the second floor.

Nandini and Cora *screeched* in my ear all through lunch. It was mostly confused screeching, but still screeching. Rumors have spread through the junior class quickly, and everyone in my grade keeps looking at me as if I'm some kind of alien who randomly landed my UFO on top of Midland High.

No matter how much I want to, I don't say, *What are you looking at?*

Nandini does it for me a few times, though.

I was prepared to wait for Ace, but he's already sitting there, earphones plugged in and head leaning against the wall. His eyes are closed, which is good, because I just stand there for a moment and stare at him.

I've been trying to figure out all afternoon why he sat next to me in English, and I haven't come up with a single answer. Ace is supposed to be this broody bad-boy delinquent who doesn't give anyone the time of day. He's still kind of all of those things, but he's also so much more. He's ridiculous and mischievous and smiles more than I ever imagined he could. He's also a pain in the ass.

The longer I stare at him, the more fired up I get. I run with that metaphor, imagining my nonconfrontational exterior melting off like a second skin, heated by the fire inside me and pooling at my feet in a disgusting puddle. It doesn't make a lot of sense, but it works for me.

Finally, I walk over and wrench the earphones out of his ears with more gusto than I would with anyone else.

Ace immediately opens his eyes, his gaze flashing with irritation. "What the fuck—?" He cuts himself off when he sees me, and his eyes light up with recognition. "Ahmed."

That one moment of animosity is more in tune to what I've heard about him than anything I've personally seen. But now he's back to the Ace I know, his expression relaxed. It's strange and perplexing.

"What were you *doing* today?" I ask, voice hushed. The hallway is void except for the two of us, but classes are still ongoing down the hall, and someone could step out at any moment to use the bathroom or water fountain.

Ace raises an eyebrow. "What was I doing today? Hm. I got up this morning and had some oatmeal. I drove to school. I had AP Physics, Gym, Russian, English—you were there, of course—lunch, AP Calculus—"

"That is *not* what I meant."

"Clarify next time." Ace grins and his dimples press into his cheeks, little indents that brighten his entire face. "Can you rephrase your question?"

"Oh my God," I say, mostly to myself. I'm going to kill this boy. "Why did you sit next to me during English?"

Ace tilts his head. "I didn't know we had assigned seats."

"We don't, but you can't just—" I flail my hands, trying to make my point. Maybe I'm not cut out to be an English major after all, if I can't manage eloquence in a moment like this. "Why?"

Instead of answering, Ace stands up. "Do you always have ninth free?"

"You're avoiding the question."

"Answer mine and I'll answers yours."

I sigh. "I have ninth free on Mondays and Thursdays."

Ace tugs his earphones back from me, wrapping them around his phone before fitting it all in his back pocket. "I have it free every day. We should meet earlier on those days."

"Maybe I have things to do."

Ace shrugs. "Never mind then. If you want to, you know where to find me." He hitches a thumb toward where he was sitting.

Then he saunters toward the staircase, and I have no choice but to follow. "You didn't answer my question, Ace."

"I will, once we get to the library," he says over his shoulder.

As I trail after him, some of the juniors in the stairway give me incredulous looks, and my cheeks burn. I'm glad my skin is dark enough that it can be written off.

Soon, we're in the library and afforded a semblance of privacy. I take the lead once we're inside, heading for a table in the back, where people are least likely to stare at us.

"Explain," I say as I sit down.

Ace takes all the time in the world settling into his seat, even though he doesn't have a bag to situate. He slowly shrugs off his leather jacket, revealing yet another fancy designer sweater underneath it, and I give him an irate look.

Once he's finally done, he waves a hand toward my expression. "That's why."

"What?"

"How annoyed with me are you right now?"

I snort. "On a scale of one to ten? Fifty."

"Exactly."

"What are you *talking* about?"

Ace leans forward across the table, his gaze dark and hypnotic. "There's a spark in you, Karina Ahmed."

"A…spark?" I shake my head. Maybe Ace is high. Maybe he's been high all day. That would explain a lot, actually.

"A spark," he repeats. When he reaches for me this time, I don't shy away. He waits a beat, staring at me, but when I still don't move—I don't think I *can*—he slowly takes my hand, his fingers running down my palm lines. "I want to light a match and send you up in flames. You're a forest fire waiting to happen."

A fire. Is it possible Ace read my thoughts earlier?

"That was almost poetic," I say, even though my heart is beating irregularly now. I'm glad he doesn't have his fingers pressed against my wrist, where my pulse is jumping. The way he's looking at me through hooded lids is dangerous, his voice measured and careful like he's spent a lot of time thinking about this.

"I want to know what makes you come alive," he says, leaning even closer but he's grinning now. The brush of his skin against mine feels like a slow burn, lighting me up from the inside. "What are you passionate about?"

"You sound ridiculous," I say and attempt to turn the conversation back around, hoping it'll help me stop feeling like a stranger in my own skin. "What are *you* passionate about?"

Ace's gaze travels across the planes of my face before he leans back. "I'll show you."

He pulls his phone out from his pocket again and unwraps the earphones. I'm not sure what he's doing until he offers one to me.

"If it's a jump scare, I'm going to kill you," I say. I don't seem to have much restraint left in terms of speaking to him like I would Nandini and Cora. He's wormed his way under my skin faster than anyone I've ever met before.

He waits until I put it in my ear before he presses play on his phone. Lilting piano music begins to play, as hypnotic as Ace's gaze.

Unable to look at him any longer, I close my eyes and listen, waiting for the words to come.

But they never do. Instead, the music builds into something deeper and more intense. The sounds overlap, multiple melodies weaving together to create something beautiful and moving.

I blink my eyes open and find Ace staring at me, waiting for my response.

"You love music," I say breathlessly. "Classical music."

His lips are pulling up again, and this time his smile is warm. His eyes shift from the roaring sea into a calm and gentle river. "I like any kind of music, really. It doesn't have to be classical, but I do have a soft spot for instrumental music. The Cinematic Orchestra, Sleeping at Last, Lindsey Stirling, artists like that." He pauses. "I… I like to play the piano."

I blink. That's not something I would have ever predicted. "The piano?"

He nods, his gaze distant. "I've been playing since I was a kid. It feels like home for me, I guess."

"Wow." I blow out a breath. "I had no idea music meant so much to you."

"Maybe I would've told you, if you wanted to do anything besides study for more than two seconds," he points out, tugging the earphone away from me.

I bite my lip, chagrined. Perhaps I've been approaching this studying situation wrong. "I'm sorry."

"Don't be," he says, before lifting his chin at me. "What about you, Ahmed? What are you passionate about?"

"Literature," I say. He makes a face like he doesn't believe me, and I hurry to add, "Writing is what helped me gain confidence in myself. There's something really special about being able to express yourself with words. I love stories and I love poems and I love learning more and more with each word. I think it's amazing." My words run together in a nervous jumble, but it seems to be enough.

Ace's disbelieving expression melts off his face. "I'm sorry, too, then."

"Don't be," I say in return, giving him a half smile. The dead butterflies in my stomach are apparently practicing necromancy, because they're fluttering around now instead of weighing me down. "Maybe we can meet in the middle. I really do want to help you."

"Yeah," he says, considering the books in front of us. They're not ours, but a copy of *The Great Gatsby* is sitting at the top. "Maybe we can."

Our studying session that day is much more productive than I could ever have anticipated. I run through some analyses about *The Scarlet Letter*, and Ace listens attentively.

Every now and then, his gaze flickers across the room, but his eyes always eventually return to me.

Finally, I ask, "Are you looking for someone?"

He startles, as if he wasn't expecting me to bring attention to it. "Oh. Uh." He rubs the back of his neck, lowering his gaze. "Not really. I was looking for my brother. You said you saw him in here yesterday."

I furrow my brows. "Do you need to talk to him?"

"No." Ace's mouth curls with distaste. After a moment, he sighs. "I don't want him to know I'm being tutored. I'll never hear the end of it if he finds out."

I tilt my head, considering his expression. "Are you…embarrassed? It's okay to ask for help, you know."

"No, I'm not embarrassed," he says immediately. "My brother's just an asshole sometimes. It's better if he doesn't know."

It's clear from the tight set of his shoulders that there's more he isn't saying, but I decide to let it go. "Should we head to Pietra's then?"

Ace looks up and a breathtaking smile breaks across his face. "Really?"

I roll my eyes and tug his wrist. "Yeah. Let's go."

I pack up my things, and we head to the sweet shop. I get chocolate chip ice cream this time and when Ace says we should take a short break, I tentatively agree.

"So when do your parents get back?" Ace asks. "They're out of the country, right?"

The question feels personal, even though it's hardly revealing of anything. I think the best way to help Ace might be to be his friend, so I decide to answer instead of deflecting.

"Yeah," I say, toying with my spoon. "They're visiting family in Bangladesh. They come back April 1st."

"That's almost a whole month away," he says, raising his eyebrows. "What are you going to do with your newfound freedom? Attend parties every night? Go to a rave? Rob a library?"

He's teasing me. I know he's teasing me, but it hits home

that I would never even attempt any of those things, because even when they're gone, my parents are still with me.

I sigh more deeply than I intend. "Probably not."

"You should do *something* fun," Ace says, poking me with the end of his plastic spoon. "Who knows when you'll get another chance."

"Ace, let's not do this," I say, suddenly tired. There are certain things I will never be able to do, and I'm not in the mood to explain our cultural differences to him. The last thing I need is for a white boy to try to fix any of my problems. There's nothing he can do—and there's nothing I *want* him to do. "This isn't... Let's get back to studying."

Ace stares at me for a long beat of silence. "I didn't mean to overstep," he says quietly. "Teach away, Ahmed."

My lips curve upward, and the tension in him eases, a smile flitting past his own lips.

By the end of our session, I feel like we're genuinely making progress. Ace actually asks *me* a question about *The Scarlet Letter*, which is a huge victory.

I leave the shop with a hopeful light in my heart. Maybe this studying thing will go smoothly, after all.

12

T-MINUS 23 DAYS

As soon as I walk into the cafeteria Friday morning, my friends pounce. I yelp in alarm, trying to slip out from between them. "What is *wrong* with you?"

"Tell us everything," Cora says, clutching my arm. There's a wild look in her eye that is all-too-familiar and frightening. When Nandini had a boyfriend sophomore year, this was the same behavior Cora exhibited. It's extremely alarming that she's acting the same way right now.

"There's nothing to tell!" I look at Nandini pleadingly, but she shakes her head. "I told you everything last night."

"All you said was—" Cora pauses to pull out her phone. I glower at her for keeping receipts. "'Nvm, everything's fine. Ace is just being a weirdo.' What does that mean, Karina? Define *weirdo*."

"I mean he's a weirdo," I say, slipping out from underneath their arms. "He says he sees a spark in me or whatever."

"Karina Myra Ahmed, *what* did you just say?"

I wince. I shouldn't have dropped that casually into a sentence. "Nothing. I said nothing."

Cora looks at Nandini incredulously. "Do you hear her? I'm going to kill her. I really am. Will you bail me out?"

"Absolutely," Nandini says, holding her pinky up. Cora hooks their pinkies together and they shake on it.

I roll my eyes. "Good. Please do. At least then I won't have to become a doctor."

"You can't just say things like that and then pretend it never happened," Cora says, linking her arm with mine. Nandini does the same on my other side and we exit the cafeteria together, heading for Nandini's locker since it's the closest. "What do you mean he sees a spark in you? What did he actually say?"

I sigh and relay the conversation in a hushed tone as we settle in front of Nandini's locker. By the end, they're both staring at me wide-eyed.

"What?" I ask self-consciously.

"I'm not even going to say it," Cora says, turning away and pressing her face against the side of a locker. "You're not going to hear a peep from me."

I squint at her, trying to make sense of those words or catch a glimpse of her expression behind her blond hair, to no avail.

"What is she talking about?" I ask Nandini.

"You'll see, dude," Nandini says, patting my head. "You'll see."

It really doesn't get any more cryptic than that. I sigh again and resign myself to the fact that my friends are chaotic neutrals.

Ace sits next to me in English again. This time, I don't do anything aside from pointedly slide him a piece of paper and a pencil. "Bring your book bag next time."

"You're no fun." Ace takes the paper and pencil, but not before he pokes me in the side using the eraser. "Also I need to talk to you after class."

I give him a sidelong look. "About what?"

"I'll tell you later," he says, turning his gaze on the whiteboard. *Now* he wants to pay attention?

The urge to grumble is hard to resist, but I make it through class without a single muttered insult. I consider patting myself on the back for that. I deserve it.

When Nandini and Cora wait for me expectantly at the door, I wave them off. Nandini raises her eyebrows, her gaze flickering toward Ace before she nods.

Cora says, "What—" but doesn't get to finish her sentence before Nandini pulls her into the hallway.

I turn to Ace. "What did you want to talk about?"

"I can't make it to the study session today," he says, his voice quiet. "I have a family thing."

I blink. "A family thing."

"My dad insists on having family dinners every Friday," Ace says, shrugging. "He usually leaves for business trips afterward, so we eat pretty early." He looks uncomfortable again, like when we spoke about Xander. It piques my curiosity, but not enough to pry.

Then his words register.

"So you'll be skipping our lesson *every* Friday?" I ask in disbelief.

I've been following Miss Cannon's outline as a base for our sessions. If I turn five weekly meetings into four, every single lesson will have to be adjusted in order to accommodate the change.

Ace grimaces. "Listen, I know but… I can't *not* attend."

The reluctant look on his face is one that I understand all too well. Sometimes our parents don't give us a choice.

I frown. "I get it. I really do. But that's so many days un-accounted for..."

Before Ace can reply, Miss Cannon appears in front of our desks, beaming. "I assume your study sessions are going well?"

I hesitate and look at Ace. He looks back at me with his lips pressed together harshly, and I'm reminded that when he showed up at our first session together, he was shocked that I hadn't complained to Miss Cannon about him.

"Great," I say, turning my attention back to Miss Cannon. "Alistair has shown a lot of initiative."

"Do you feel you're learning a lot from Karina?" Miss Cannon asks Ace, still grinning. Her happiness is infectious and, despite my concerns, I smile in return.

"More than I expected," Ace says. He's staring at me instead of Miss Cannon. "I hope to continue learning more."

The weight overlaying his words makes me squirm, heat rushing to my cheeks. "I hope so, too."

Miss Cannon sighs happily, folding her hands together and clutching them to her chest. "I'm so glad this is working out."

Ace doesn't look away as he says, "Me too."

Without much left to contribute, I start packing up my things and head for the door. Miss Cannon lets me slip past her with a small smile. As soon as I pass through the doors and into the hallway, fingers wrap gently around my wrist and pull me back beside a row of yellow lockers.

I look up at Ace in surprise. His rings are cold against my skin. "What?"

"I thought you were going to tell her about me bailing today," he says. He doesn't phrase it as a question, but his gaze is imploring as he looks at me.

I shrug. "I thought we could figure it out between us first."

Ace is quiet as he reaches up, taking a lock of my hair between his fingers. I'm hyperaware of the fact that we're only inches apart, and I almost wish we were closer.

"Come to my house. We can study before dinner as long as my dad knows I'm at home and not skipping out."

I must be hallucinating. "You want me to go to your... house."

He nods, apparently unaware of the existential crisis I'm having. He wants me to come to the *Clyde* residence?

"You can leave before the dinner, but at least we'll have some time to study."

I shake my head, trying not to let the shock show on my face. There are a million reasons to say no, the first of which is: "My parents would kill me."

Ace furrows his brows. "Aren't they out of the country?"

"I mean, yes, but... I can't go to your *house*. They'd know somehow."

"How?" he asks, seeming genuinely confused. "Are you going to tell them?"

I'd sooner die than tell my parents that I'm going to a boy's house unsupervised. "Of course not."

"Then what's the harm?" He tugs on my lock of hair, causing me to take an uneven step forward. "Live a little, Ahmed."

"By going to your house to study," I say dubiously. Does Ace hear himself when he speaks? I can't imagine what it's like to glide through life like this.

He nods and, this time, I know I have to say something, before this goes further. "You know we're from two different worlds, right? I can't just *do* the things you do, and I'm not going to suddenly turn my life upside down to work around your schedule. My family..." I trail off, unsure how to finish that sentence.

Ace makes a face, the twist of his mouth rueful. "Sorry. I didn't mean—I did it again, didn't I? I overstepped." He sighs, shifting backward, running a hand over his face. "I only meant that I'd like to study with you today, especially since I missed Monday already. Will you be in trouble if you come to my house?"

I bite my lip. I guess it's not like I'd *really* be doing anything wrong by going to his house. "No, I suppose not."

He nods, eyes scanning my face. "So then…what do you have to lose?"

My *dignity*, probably. Definitely my eardrums when Cora and Nandini hear about it. My life, if my parents ever find out against all odds.

He must see the answer on my face, because he changes tactics. "You don't have to if you don't want to. But I'd really like you to come if you can."

I open my mouth, but I'm stumped. I don't have a response to that.

"If you're up for it, meet me by my car after ninth. It's parked in spot 28," he says, finally stepping away. "See you later, Ahmed."

He walks off, leaving me to stare after him and wonder how my school life turned upside down within the span of a week.

13

T-MINUS 23 DAYS

The main reason I end up in front of Ace's car after gym is because Cora and Nandini both threaten to brutally murder me if I don't go. I have a few regrets, the biggest one being telling them at all. But if I didn't, I'd probably start screaming incoherently into the void and never stop.

I call my grandma first, nervously pacing in the parking lot while waiting for her to pick up. My anxiety is returning in anticipation of the conversation, and I have to repeatedly wipe my hands on my jeans to get rid of excess sweat.

I think if I tried to write my thoughts down right now, I'd break my pencil.

"Myra?" Dadu says, after our customary greetings. "What's wrong?"

"Nothing," I say quickly. *Ten, nine, eight, seven, six, five, four, three, two, one.* "I might get home a little later than usual today. I have to finish up something for school. Is that okay?"

I brace myself for the blowback, expecting to be reprimanded. There's silence and then, "That's fine. Do you want me to leave your food in the fridge, sweetheart?"

For some reason, I keep waiting. Surely that can't be it.

There has to be more. There's always more.

"Myra, did you hear me?" Dadu asks. "Are you sure you're okay?"

I shake my head and lean against Ace's car, trying to gain a hold of myself. "Yeah, I'm fine, Dadu. I'd love if you left my food in the fridge. I'll call you when I'm on my way home, if that's okay?"

"Of course, Myra," Dadu says, her voice warm. "Thank you for letting me know. I'll see you later."

"See you later," I echo.

I stare at my phone after we disconnect, more shocked than I should be. My grandma has never reprimanded me, but I still thought there would be *some* resistance. Easy acceptance is the last thing I expected.

Then again, maybe I should have. It's Dadu, after all.

I inhale. *Ten, nine, eight, seven, six, five, four, three, two, one.* I exhale.

Better. Not perfect, but better.

I look down at the hand not holding my phone, then *immediately* jump away from Ace's car, realizing I'm leaving smudge marks on the exterior.

The car is far too ostentatious. It's some sort of Mercedes, black and sleek. It probably cost as much as my future student loans.

I try to wipe away the smudges but only make it worse, so I give up and resign myself to apologizing when he shows up.

As I'm waiting, Xander walks up to the car beside the Mercedes. It's fancy, too, but I don't look at the logo, mostly because I'm ducking my head and hoping not to make eye contact.

Does Ace's family even know I'm coming home with him? This is a disaster waiting to happen.

As fate would have it, Xander stops in front of Ace's car and stares at me as he toys with his keys. "Are you waiting for my brother?"

Oh shit. I open my mouth...and nothing comes out.

He looks me over in a way that sets my hair on end. As if he's dissecting me for weaknesses. "No... You're Cora Zhang-Agreste's friend, aren't you?"

My back straightens at his tone. "Yeah. So?"

Xander smiles. "Then you wouldn't associate with the likes of my brother. Sorry for bothering you."

He disappears into his car and drives away, and I watch with narrowed eyes. I'm still looking into the distance when Ace appears five minutes later, a girl with thick, beautiful hair and dark skin following him and speaking animatedly.

There's a gentle expression on his face as he answers her. I've never seen him look at anyone that way before. I wonder who she is, racking my brain for whether anyone has been mentioned in relation to Ace in the last few months.

"Ahmed." Ace cocks his head and offers me a small smile. "You made it."

I bite my lip, shrugging. "You only live once and all that, right?"

The girl next to him smiles at me but turns an accusing look on Ace. "She's really pretty, Ace. You didn't tell me she was pretty."

I tuck a curl of dark hair behind my ear, averting my gaze. Compliments given by girls always feel a hundred times more special. "You don't have to say that. Thank you."

"Don't thank her, Ahmed," Ace says, his smile slipping off his face as he narrows his eyes at the girl. "Stop looking at her."

"I was just saying!" the girl says, raising her hands in defeat, but she's laughing. "You're so annoying, Ace."

Well. She's not wrong.

"She's too old for you," Ace says back, unlocking the car. To me, he says, "Ignore Mia."

"Don't ignore me, I'm awesome," the girl—Mia—says. "*And* I have access to Ace's baby photos. I'm the better friend to have."

I blink, unsure what to make of this situation. "I'll take your word for it."

"Also I have a girlfriend, you asshole," she says to Ace, pulling a face. "I'm not hitting on your tutoring buddy. I just wanted to tell her she's pretty."

That clears up a lot but also so little. She's not romantically involved with Ace, but they must have some kind of personal relationship. I don't think I've seen her before, so she's probably not in our grade, but that leaves me at a loss as to how Ace knows her.

Ace opens the door to the passenger side, gesturing for me to get inside. I hesitate, glancing at Mia but she's already slipping into the back seat.

I slide into the seat slowly, my skin prickling. Did Ace invite someone *else* to his family dinner?

Once Ace is inside, he double-checks his mirrors and pulls the car out in one easy glide.

"He's a good driver, don't worry," Mia says from over my shoulder. I jump in my seat, not expecting her to be so close.

"Jeez, you came out of nowhere," I say, rubbing my chest as I try to calm down. "So, uh, how do you and Ace know each other?"

"Ace is my stepbrother," Mia says, which is news to me. I didn't realize there was another Clyde sibling at our school. As if she can read my mind, Mia adds, "I'm a freshman and my last name is Jackson instead of Clyde, so it makes sense you didn't know."

"It's nice to meet you," I say, offering my hand. "I would say I've heard so much about you, but Ace hasn't said anything. He *is* annoying."

Mia snickers and takes my hand. "I like her."

Ace shakes his head and fiddles with the console. Instrumental music starts playing through the speakers.

Mia leans back in her seat and hums along. Ace smiles, his gaze flickering to his rearview mirror to look at his stepsister before turning to me.

"Ready to rumble?" he asks.

"Ready to study."

He grins. "Same thing. My stepmom is going to love you."

"I'm not talking to your family," I say, rolling my eyes. "I'm leaving as soon as we're done studying."

Ace laughs and changes the gear from Reverse to Drive. "Whatever you say, Ahmed."

I wrinkle my nose as a sense of foreboding rushes through me. I watch him tap his fingers against the steering wheel and try to push the strange feeling away.

It's just a study session. What's the worst that could happen?

14

T-MINUS 23 DAYS

The Clyde estate is huge. I knew Ace's father was rich, but seeing it is an entirely different thing. There are actual gates in the front of the house and a keypad that Ace has to pull up to so he can type in a lengthy code.

We drive past a beautiful garden, a huge fountain, and a perfectly trimmed lawn, elegantly designed hedges scattered every few feet. There are even marble statues littered across the estate. I try not to gape.

His "house" is an honest-to-God mansion. It's designed in a Roman architectural fashion, with a large porch and grand arches and stone columns. I wouldn't be surprised to find the Obamas taking a casual stroll down the lawn.

Mia runs off almost immediately, after jumping up to kiss Ace's cheek and promising to catch up with us before she disappears into the house.

Ace is slower, listening to the last notes of the song playing on the stereo, before shutting down the car and following me out. "Mia can be a lot."

"She seems sweet," I say, slowly walking down the stone path until I reach the porch. "I didn't know you had steps-iblings."

"Just the one," he says, before nodding toward the front door. "Ladies first."

"What a gentleman." I step inside and I can't contain the way my jaw drops. The inside of the house is just as beautiful as the outside, with exquisite paintings in the foyer and lavish furniture extending into the hallway. There's a diamond chandelier in the entryway, and I pause to stare at it in disbelief.

"How much money do you have?" I ask, because I apparently don't have a shred of decency or any sense of tact. Ace doesn't seem to mind. He's watching me in amusement.

"Enough," he says. "I can't touch most of it, since it's in a trust fund, but my dad gives me and my siblings a monthly allowance."

I know Cora also gets an allowance, but I think my parents would sooner kick me out of the house than hand me a lump sum every month. Instead, I have to rely on birthday and Eidi money to last me through the year.

I want to ask Ace more, because all of this is a *lot*, but he starts walking down the hall. I immediately follow. The house is so big, I'm afraid I might get lost otherwise.

As we walk, my jaw nearly unhinges. *Who* has paintings on their walls? There's even an uncanny amount of vases. I've seen the Bollywood film *Kabhi Khushi Kabhie Gham* enough times to steer clear of those. If I broke one, I'd probably die on the spot.

Ace leads me up a spiraling marble staircase, and we're walking down the hallway when I hear a loud bark behind me and freeze. I turn slowly and see a large golden retriever bounding toward us.

"Down, boy!" Ace says, but the dog comes at us full speed anyway.

I squeak in terror and hide behind Ace, clutching his leather jacket.

Dogs are adorable. Objectively, I know this. However, my parents heavily warned me off them because they're basically haram, so I'm at an impasse. I *wish* my body didn't lock up the second that I see one, especially because they look so cuddly and fun to be around.

"Ahmed, he's not gonna hurt you," Ace says, his voice heavy with amusement as he pets his dog.

"Dogs scare me," I whisper, too embarrassed to say it any louder than that.

Ace turns to look at me, eyebrows furrowed. "Seriously?"

I nod, still clutching on to him. "It's a whole thing. My parents taught me to be afraid of them."

"They *what*?"

I sigh and explain how my parents projected their view of dogs onto me, going as far as telling me I was allergic when I was younger so I would stay away from them. When I'm done, he's frowning deeply. "Why did they do that?"

"Some conservative Muslims don't like dogs because they're seen as impure," I say, eyeing the golden retriever, who's wagging his tail happily. "Personally, I think dogs are cute, but my parents freaked me out about it really bad when I was younger, so I'm kind of...hesitant now."

"Spade won't hurt you," Ace says, before holding out a hand toward me. "I'll show you if you want."

I shake my head. It's not like I've never petted a dog before. I have. But it's always so intimidating, and I have to work up the nerve to do it.

Then I have a different thought. "Your name is Ace and you named your dog Spade?"

"I was ten," Ace says, shrugging. "Spade seemed fitting. Isn't that right, boy?"

Ace leans down and nuzzles Spade, running his hands through the dog's fur coat. "You like the name Spade, don't you?"

The dog barks happily, licking Ace's face.

Ace laughs, pushing Spade away with a light touch. "See, Ahmed? He's gentle." He offers me his hand again. "Are you sure you don't want to pet him? It's up to you, but I'll be with you the whole time."

I bite my lip, considering my options. Ace *and* the dog are giving me puppy dog eyes now, which should be illegal. Despite my nerves, I slowly put my hand forward and Ace takes it.

Spade is quiet and patient as he waits for me to near him. Ace places my hand between his ears, and his fur is soft and fluffy beneath my palm. "See?"

I waver before giving the dog a careful rub. Spade's mouth opens into a wide grin, his tail wagging again.

"He likes you," Ace says, smiling as he lets go of my hand and leans against the wall. "He's a good judge of character."

"Oh, shut up," I say. God, I'm getting way too comfortable being around him.

Ace raises his hands above his head. "I can't even give you a compliment?"

"No." I pet Spade once more, feeling warm inside, before pulling away. Ace was right. He is gentle. "Now let's get to work. That's why I'm here, isn't it?"

"If we can't take a break to pet dogs, Ahmed, then what do we have left?"

"Your dramatics, apparently."

Ace reaches out and flicks my nose. I allow it, more out of shock than anything else. I've initiated more physical contact between us than he has at this point, but it's strange that we've somehow gained this level of familiarity in such a short time. Ace clearly thinks nothing of it, because he turns around and starts walking again. I follow him, and Spade happily trots along at my side.

"Welcome to my humble abode," Ace says, pushing open the door at the end of the hall.

I step inside and stop in my tracks, gazing around in wide-eyed wonder. The room is large, with high ceilings and copious amounts of free space. Solar systems are painted all along the walls, with small planets hanging on thin wires from built-in ceiling spotlights. A telescope sits by his dresser, and near his window is a sleek black grand piano covered in sheet music.

"You really do play," I say, glancing at one of the pages, unintelligible scribbles written in the margins.

He nods, his fingers ghosting over the keys. "Yeah, my mom taught me when I was four," he says, his gaze far away. "I used to practice in the living room, but since I usually play for three hours a day, it kind of…disrupts the peace. After my stepmother and Mia moved in, it was just easier to keep the piano in my room."

"Wait. Three hours a *day*?" I repeat, looking at him in surprise. "Are you any good?"

"I hope so," he says, offering me a mild smile. "My instructor says I'm not his worst student, for whatever that counts. Don't think I'd fly out for international competitions otherwise."

I blink. "*International*? Where have you been?"

Ace plays a single note, eyes drifting up to meet mine. "London, Paris, Tokyo. The works. My last competition was in Vienna. After our sets, me and one of the other competitors—Ben—snuck out midway through the competition and went for ice cream instead. You should have seen the look on his girlfriend's face when she realized he didn't bring her any back. I seriously thought she was about to dump him and book the next train to Slovakia just to get away from him."

I snort at the mental image. "Sounds fun."

"It was," Ace says, his smile stretching wide across his face. "You would like Vienna."

My brows raise of their own accord. "Would I?"

He nods, fingers skating along the keys one last time before he moves away from the piano. I almost want to ask him to play me something, but it feels too intrusive. I wouldn't want him to ask about my poetry.

the moon falls from the sky
and a boy rises from the ruins
carved by celestial dust

My gaze catches on the telescope again and I gesture vaguely. "And…what about this? Are you into space, too?"

He shrugs a shoulder, sitting down on his bed. "Somewhat."

"What do you mean, 'somewhat'?" Then I realize something far more important. "Oh my God, you like space and your name is Ace. Space. Ace. This is incredible."

"Yeah, yeah, I've heard it all before from Mia," Ace says, rolling his eyes. "Rest assured, if there's a space pun with my name involved, I've been a victim of it."

"Can you blame her?" I ask, reaching up to touch one of the low hanging planets. I'm still in awe of how beautiful it is. My moonlight metaphor grows more powerful by the minute. "All of this is so cool. Are you actually into astronomy or do you just like the aesthetic?"

He raises an eyebrow. "You think I have a telescope for the aesthetic?"

"You're rich," I say. "I definitely think it's within the realm of possibility that you would buy a telescope for the aesthetic."

Ace contemplates that and concedes to my statement with

a shrug. "Fair enough. It's not, though. I genuinely enjoy astronomy."

I pause where I'm examining a scattering of stars on his wall and look back at him curiously. "Okay, no offense, but… are you actually smart? Have you been holding out on me? Everyone talks about you like you're failing *all* your classes."

Ace startles into a laugh. "Are you asking if I'm stupid, Ahmed?"

My cheeks warm. "I—that's not…sorry?"

He keeps laughing, his eyes crinkling. "Jesus Christ. You're bold."

"I didn't mean to insult you," I say, flustered. I'm starting to think *I* might be the stupid one. Who even asks something like that? I've lost my mind.

"You didn't," Ace says, his laughter settling into a wide grin. "I'm not stupid, contrary to popular belief. I have As in most of my classes. I just don't *care* about most of them."

I squint. "How can you not care about your classes?"

"They're just not interesting." He gestures to the room around us. "But space is cool."

I don't say it, but I can't help but think that's such a privileged way to approach academics. I can't imagine doing the same. Despite hating math and science, I still put in a *lot* of effort to retain the GPA my parents expect to see.

"You're lucky you don't have to care," I say quietly before gesturing to his desk. "Should we start studying?"

Ace's expression falls. "Did I say—"

Before he can finish his sentence, the door opens, and Xander Clyde sticks his head inside.

I bite my tongue in surprise. I should have expected to see him again sooner rather than later, but I also thought Ace's room would afford us privacy. Apparently not.

His hair is a little more rumpled now, and the top button

of his shirt is loose, but he still looks intimidating. I try not to cower when his gaze lands on me.

"Alistair, Mia said you had a guest," Xander says, his eyes lighting up in recognition. "I came over to introduce myself."

"Knock next time, Alexander," Ace says, his tone dark. "My guest knows who you are. There's no need for introductions."

"Ah, but I don't know your guest," Xander says, giving me a charming grin. He doesn't have dimples, so it's not quite as effective as his brother's. "I'm Xander. It's nice to see you again."

Ace's eyes narrow with the mention of *again*, but I ignore him.

Instead, I nod my head politely, even though I kind of want to disappear. I don't want to be on the student body president's radar. I should barely be on *Ace*'s radar. "I'm Karina. It's nice to meet you, too."

"How do you and Ace know each other?" Xander asks, leaning against Ace's doorway. "He's never mentioned you before."

I open my mouth to reply but suddenly Ace is standing up, blocking the view of his brother. "Get out."

His brother widens his eyes, but it looks too practiced. Xander Clyde is definitely a politician in the making. I guess Cora will have competition in the 2040 election, too. "What did I do, Alistair?"

"I said get *out*," Ace says, a muscle jumping in his jaw. "No one wants you here."

"Calm down, Alistair," Xander says dismissively. "I would hate to tell Dad you lost your temper."

Ace's expression grows infinitely darker. "Get the fuck out."

Without another word, Ace shuts his door and Xander jumps out of the way to avoid being hit in the face.

I blink, stunned. That was a little more Clyde family drama than I ever intended to witness. "Are you okay?"

Ace flinches and looks at me in surprise. I think he might have forgotten I was here.

"Yeah, sorry." He shakes his head, running his fingers through his messy hair. "My brother is just…a lot." He pauses, looking up at me. "You two have met?"

I shake my head. "Barely. He saw me waiting by your car earlier."

Ace takes a deep breath, pinching the bridge of his nose. "Of course he did. Wow."

A million questions rise to the tip of my tongue, but the look on Ace's face is enough to keep my lips closed. At least, in terms of invasive questions. I still say, "So…studying?"

Ace gives me an incredulous look before laughing breathlessly, the tension slipping out of him. "Yeah, Ahmed. Studying."

I lose track of time as we make our way through my notes.

It only hits me how late it is when someone knocks on the door. "Ace, may I come in?"

"Yeah," Ace says distractedly, his gaze focused on a list of study questions I slid his way. "Sure, Tina."

A beautiful dark-skinned woman who can only be Ace's stepmother pokes her head in the room.

"Hi," she greets, addressing me. I falter where I was writing something down. "I was just wondering, Ace, if your friend would—"

Ace immediately looks up, eyes wide, and shoves our notes underneath his comforter. I make a face, thinking of all the crinkles we're going to have to straighten out, but I don't say anything with his stepmother in the room.

I catch a glimpse of Ace's expression, which is a strange mixture of panic and warmth. His voice is strained when he says, "Sorry, Tina. What was that?"

Is he okay? Why does he look like he stubbed his toe and he's happy about it?

"Dinner is in five minutes. I was wondering if your friend would like to stay?" she asks. "We can set an extra plate."

I inhale sharply. I'm pretty sure my oxygen went down the wrong pipe. I look at Ace for help, but he has a passive expression on his face. "I—er—really should get going." I motion hopelessly toward the windows, but Ace's stepmother is too busy looking at Ace.

I have absolutely no idea what she reads on his face, but her expression lights up. "Nonsense. I'll call your parents if I need to. You're having dinner with us. I'm glad that's settled."

I don't even have a chance to refuse again before she walks out. I open and close my mouth twice before looking at Ace. "I really shouldn't—"

"She's not going to let you leave," he says. Instead of an apologetic smile, he's grinning cheerfully. There's something seriously wrong with him. "Might as well accept your fate. I'll do my best to get you out of here as quickly as possible."

I don't believe him. "I don't believe you."

"Consider it a practice in trust," Ace says, before holding out his hand. "Come on."

I ignore his hand but climb off his bed with a sigh. I had a pillow between us for separation but, when he stands, we're entirely too close. It makes our height difference extremely apparent, since the top of my head barely comes up to his chin.

His shoulder grazes mine, and I take a step back, hoping my blush isn't visible on my cheeks. "Let's go."

15

T-MINUS 23 DAYS

I don't know how it slipped my mind that dinner at the Clyde residence means dinner with *everyone*. That includes multi-millionaire businessman Albert Clyde, who's sitting at the end of a small table.

"Oh my God," I whisper and attempt to make a getaway. I have nothing against the man, but the same way that I don't want to be on Ace's or Xander's radar, I definitely don't want to be on Albert Clyde's radar. I don't make it far, because Ace's hand on my wrist immediately pulls me back.

"Relax," Ace says in a quiet voice. "He's not going to bite." A pause. "Or, well, he won't bite *you*, at least."

"Alistair, stop whispering in the doorway and join us at the table," Ace's father says. "And introduce your guest." His tone leaves no room for argument.

"This is Karina Ahmed," Ace says, gesturing to me with a wave of his hand. "Karina, this is my family."

I smile weakly. "Hello."

Ace hesitates, and I don't understand why until he points to the seat next to Mia. "You can sit there."

Which means Ace has to sit next to Xander, since there are only six seats at the table.

Usually, I would refuse because it doesn't take a rocket scientist to figure out Ace doesn't like his brother. However, I also don't want to sit next to Xander, and I definitely don't want to cause a scene, so I quietly take my seat across from Ace.

"Shall we say grace?"

Ya Allah, I'm in a sitcom. I'm the Muslim girl sitting at a table with a typical all-American family about to say grace. Well, Mia and her mother are Black so at least there's *some* solidarity, but this is still incredibly awkward.

"Dear God," Ace's father starts, and I bow my head in accordance, wanting to be respectful of their religion, even if this is one of the strangest situations I've ever been in. The few times I've been to Cora's house, her family has never done this even though they're Christian, too. My family doesn't even sit down together for meals.

We eat on a strange schedule, where lunch is whenever you come home and dinner is an hour before you sleep. Since the timing differs for all of us, we rarely have meals together unless we're hosting guests of some sort.

This family dinner laid out in front of me is very much uncharted territory.

"Thank you for your graciousness," Ace's father says. "Thank you for the roof over our head and the food on our table. Thank you for the meal we are about to enjoy, made by Tina's wonderful hands. Thank you for Alexander's acceptance into Yale University with a full scholarship. Thank you for allowing Cosmia to win first place in Midland High

School's talent show. Thank you for not landing Alistair in detention this week so he's able to attend our family dinner."

I wince. Not landing Alistair in detention this week? Who says that during grace?

Albert says some more things and finishes with, "Amen."

The rest of the family echoes, "Amen," and I stay silent, busy looking at Ace now that all our heads aren't bowed.

He looks unbothered by his father's statement, his posture as lazy as it usually is. His arms are splayed out on the arms of his gaudy chair, and his legs are spread wide enough that one of his knees is knocking into his brother's.

Xander roughly pulls away. "Alistair, move over."

"Am I bothering you?" Ace asks, raising his brows. "I thought nothing bothered you?"

Xander's grip tightens on his fork. "Aren't you tired of being so immature?"

"Immature?" Ace pretends to look shocked. "You know, Mom always says I'm too mature for my age—"

"Mom hasn't seen this side of you," Xander says, his tone biting. "Dad, do you see what I have to deal with?"

"Alistair, enough," his dad says.

Ace opens his mouth to argue but seems to think better of it after a glance in my direction.

My gaze flicks among the three of them with rapt awareness, and I look away only when my phone buzzes in my pocket.

I take it out briefly to see a text from my mom. My heart rate rises and I force myself to take a breath, clicking on the notification. Dadu says you're staying at school late, finishing up a project. What project?

There's another text from Samir earlier, which reads: bro I accidentally recorded over baba's basketball games on the DVR how mad do u think he's gonna be on a scale of 1-10??

I reply to my mom first, a lie already prepared. I make up some nonsense about a physics lab and send a selfie of me and Nandini in goggles, saved in my camera roll from last week.

Then I respond to Samir, saying: yikes... ask dadu if she'll take the blame bc he'd never be mad @ her. I don't think he'd be that mad at you anyway, but if you wanna avoid a lecture... that's ur best option lmao.

Samir's response is immediate. UR SO RIGHT thanks bro!!

I roll my eyes, looking back up as Ace's stepmother stands and starts uncovering the various dishes. I try not to sigh when I see a roasted ham as the main course. I don't eat pork because I'm Muslim, and I've never been so grateful Dadu offered to save my lunch in the fridge.

Bangladeshi food is one of my favorite parts of my culture. It's so rich and heady, yet so comforting at the same time. One of few things I dread about going to college is leaving behind my family's homecooked meals. I highly doubt aloo bhorta is on Columbia's lunch menu.

"I have snacks in my room," Mia whispers, drawing my attention as we start passing bowls around and scooping food onto our plates.

My eyebrows rise. "What?"

She gestures toward the ham. "You can't eat that, right? Come by my room afterward. I'll slip you some potato chips."

I blink in surprise, a smile pulling at my lips. "That's so sweet of you. Thank you."

"So Miss Ahmed," Ace's father says, and my neck nearly snaps as I turn to face him. He looks like he wants nothing more than to dissect me under a microscope. "How do you and Alistair know each other? He's never brought any of his friends to our home."

I open my mouth, but nothing comes out. Why is nothing coming out? I can't think of a *single* thing to say.

Ten, nine, eight, seven, six, five, four, three, two, one.

I lick my lips uncertainly. "Um…"

And then, the same way a meteor strikes a dying planet, Ace says the worst thing of all time: "Karina is my girlfriend."

16

T-MINUS 23 DAYS

Ten.

Nine.

Eight.

Seven.

Six.

Five.

Four.

Three.

Two.

One.

What? Did he really just say I'm his *girlfriend*?

I look at Ace in disbelief, but he's staring at his dad, a challenging expression on his face.

"Your girlfriend?" Ace's father repeats, his tone incredulous. "Since when?"

Ace shrugs. "I haven't been keeping track."

Neither have I, apparently.

"And you didn't think to inform any of us when this started?" his father asks, setting down his knife and fork.

"Mia knew," Ace says, waving a nonchalant hand.

His stepsister blinks slowly, clearly at as much of a loss as I am, but after a moment, she nods. "Yeah, Ace told me a while ago."

I try not to sigh. Of course Mia is going along with it.

Albert turns his gaze on me. "Is this true, Miss Ahmed?"

And now everyone is staring at me. Great.

Ace meets my eyes and offers me a hopeful smile. Is he being serious?

I have absolutely no clue why Ace is telling his dad I'm his *girlfriend* instead of his tutor, but I also can't bring myself to deny it. I'm not eager to be at the center of Clyde family drama—I'll yell at Ace in the privacy of his room and then he can figure out a way to explain to his family that he was lying.

But for now... I'll play along.

I laugh nervously. "I also haven't been keeping track. I'm sorry, Mr. Clyde."

Albert hums, his lips pressed together as he looks between me and his son. "It's a shame we haven't been introduced before then."

"Better late than never," Ace says. His foot nudges mine underneath the table, and I nearly jump out of my seat. "Isn't that right, sweetie?"

Sweetie. This boy wants to die by my hand.

"Yes, *honey.*"

Ace winks at me, and I resist the urge to throw my fork at him.

"We'd love to hear more about you, Karina," Ace's stepmother says, which is arguably the worst thing she's said to me so far. I hate being the center of attention, and I hate talking about myself. "How did you and Ace meet?"

"We're in the same English class," I say, because that at least is true. "He sat next to me and we just…clicked?"

Ace's smile widens into a blinding grin. I'm going to *kill* him. "I took her on a date to a local bakery. She ordered the cheesecake and said it wasn't nearly as sweet as me."

His foot is close enough that I step on it in retribution. He winces but quickly covers it up. It still brings me some satisfaction.

"Who can blame me?" I offer his stepmother a pretty smile. "He's just such a sweetheart."

"I've never seen you two together," Xander says, watching me like a hawk. If I thought he was assessing my weaknesses before, it's nothing compared to his sharp gaze now. "Have you even told Mom?"

"You didn't know who Karina was before today," Ace says, his grin obnoxious even as his gaze is dark. "Maybe that's why you failed to notice. Mom has known for a while now, just like Mia."

Xander's eyes narrow, but he doesn't make any further comment. I restrain the urge to step on Ace's foot again. There's no way his mother knows about this—he's mentioned her to me only *once* in the passing. Another tangled thread in this web of lies.

"What do your parents do, Miss Ahmed?" Albert asks after he shares a look with Xander that is far from reassuring.

"My mom works as a receptionist for a dermatologist," I say, ignoring the way the back of my neck is prickling. "And my dad is an accountant."

"And what about you? Do you have plans for college?"

I can't believe I'm being *screened* right now to see if I'm an acceptable girlfriend when I'm not even dating anyone. I can't believe this is a real situation that Ace has wrangled me into.

My smile is flimsy. "My parents are hoping I get into Columbia for their premed track, under a biology major." And I'm hoping I somehow whisk myself into an alternate universe before then.

"That's incredible," Ace's father says, and he sounds like he actually means it. His gaze is appraising, but then he looks at Ace and it becomes far less so. "So what are you doing with someone like my son? Do you know he has no intention of even attending college?"

Wait, *what*?

"Dad," Ace says, his voice cold.

Oh. Clearly it's an off-limit subject. It's not really my business anyway. I have other things to fuss at Ace about—namely, our newfound relationship.

"What? Shouldn't your girlfriend know about your aspirations?"

"If you think shaming me in front of her is going to make me change my mind and suddenly decide to apply to Yale, you're wrong," Ace says, his jaw clenched. "Karina, let's go."

"Uh." I look down at my still-full plate. It's barely been ten minutes. Then again, it's not like I'm going to sit here while Ace stomps away. I glance around the table apologetically. "I'm sorry. I hope you don't mind excusing us."

I push back my chair and mutter another apology under my breath as I chase after Ace, who's disappearing farther down the hallway. "Wait!"

Ace falters and looks at me. We're far enough away now that he appears more relaxed, but it reminds me of the calm before the storm. "See? I told you I'd get you out of there quickly."

I gape at him. "That's not—you didn't—what is the *matter* with you?"

Ace smiles bleakly. "Too much to list. Come on, I'll drive you home."

"I'm going to kill you," I say, reaching out to swat him on the arm. "What *was* that?"

"Shhh," Ace says, holding a finger to his lips. He points above us. "Cameras."

"What?" I'm definitely in a sitcom. Or maybe a drama. Normal people don't have surveillance cameras in their homes, even in sitcoms. "Why?"

"In case of intruders," Ace says, shrugging a shoulder. "Dad's a cutthroat businessman. Has a lot of enemies."

He seems like a cutthroat father figure too, but it isn't my place to comment. Maybe everyone's family is secretly messed up.

"We're going to talk about this later," I say, narrowing my eyes. "I have a lot of words I'd like to say to you."

A smile tugs at Ace's lips. "Save it for the bedroom, sweetie."

I call him a dick in Bengali so the cameras won't pick up on it. He raises an eyebrow but keeps smiling, so I don't really feel like I insulted him. I have a feeling he'd smile even if I said it in English.

"I told you there was a spark in you, Ahmed."

I groan and shove him, walking ahead to get to his room. "Just take me home."

Ace only laughs.

17

T-MINUS 23 DAYS

In the car, I don't have a chance to yell at Ace about the dating thing, because at the last minute Xander shows up and requests a ride to Walmart. There are approximately six cars in the Clyde estate's extensive driveway, and I know for a fact Xander has his license, because I saw him get into his own car earlier today.

There's obviously some ulterior motive here. Xander has a calculating look in his eye, and Ace looks one word away from punching his brother, so I quickly agree for the both of us.

When I put my address into Google Maps, Xander leans forward between the seats. "You don't know where your girlfriend lives?"

"No, he does," I say quickly. I have a feeling that if Ace replies, I'm never going to get home. "But he's never driven to my house before, and it's good to have Google Maps just in case, right? You can never be too safe."

Xander hums, clearly unconvinced. Ace's knuckles strain

as he tightens his grip on the steering wheel, but neither of them say anything as we turn onto the next street.

It's somehow the most awkward car ride of my life, and my family has had more than our fair share of awkward car rides.

Ace drops me at home first, and I mutter a goodbye before slipping inside my house, my mind whirring.

I'm home way later than usual, but all Dadu does is ruffle my hair and tell me to warm up my Mughlai paratha for a minute. I thank her with a hug, then wonder how my life came to this.

I take a moment to process the events of the night and blow out a harsh breath. God. What in the world?

I think about texting Nandini and Cora about this chaos but decide against it, because it'll blow over by the end of the weekend. If I haven't figured it out by Monday afternoon, I'll explain the situation to them. Otherwise, it isn't worth the headache.

As I'm going to bed, my phone starts ringing with a Face-Time call from my parents. After a moment of deliberation, I slide my thumb across the screen, answering it.

My dad's face greets me this time. "Myra, where is your brother?"

"Uh. I don't know?" I say, glancing in the direction of my bedroom door. "Is something wrong?"

"No," my dad says. "I wanted to ask him to send me a link for the last Knicks game. He said Dadu deleted it off the DVR, so I tried to find it online, but I can't."

Looks like Samir took my advice. "I can find it for you," I offer hesitantly. "If you want."

"Really?" Baba's eyebrows rise. "Can you show me how?"

"Yeah," I say and move to my laptop, opening up a You-Tube tab. I flip the camera so he can watch as I click the official NBA account and find a highlights reel of the game. "I'll text you the link so you can watch it."

"Thank you so much," my dad says and the gratitude in his eyes settles some of the rocks floating in my stomach. "So how was your physics lab? Did you finish it? Ma told me you were working on it late today."

"Yeah," I say, offering him a tight smile as I flip the camera back around. "Sorry I haven't called every day. There's been a lot of schoolwork recently. I think they're piling it on because spring break is in a week."

"Oh, right, I forgot about that," my dad says, scratching his beard. "Maybe you should use that time to work on those new SAT workbooks I bought for you."

"Yeah, definitely," I say, even though the idea of spending my break studying gives me a headache. "Do you think Cora and Nandini could come over to our house one of those days?"

"Ask your mom, not me," Baba says, shaking his head.

I sigh. "Can you ask her *for* me?"

He considers me for a moment. "Okay. No promises, though."

This time, my smile feels genuine. "Thanks. How is Bangladesh?"

Baba's face twists. "Your mother's family is…loud."

I snort, remembering the last time I visited, over five years ago. "I know."

He relays a little more about the last few days, and I listen until my eyes start to droop. My dad must notice, because he waves me off when I insist I'm still awake. "Get some rest, Myra. You worked hard on your lab tonight."

A flash of guilt runs through me. "Yeah."

"Good night," Baba says, waving at me through the camera.

"Good night," I say in return and set my phone aside after he hangs up.

I'm used to lying to my parents. I have no doubt Samir lies to them, too. It's the way it has to be. But sometimes, I can't help but feel bad about it. I remind myself that tutoring Ace is a white lie—nothing that has any bearing on my relationship with my parents. It's not something they have to know about.

I fall asleep to that thought.

T-MINUS 22 DAYS

When I wake up Saturday morning, I stare at the posters of poetry hung on my bright yellow ceiling and bask in the comfort of not being called lazy for getting up at 11:00 a.m.

My room is relatively sparse. My parents always say less is more, so I've kept the decor to a minimum. Instead, there are stacks and stacks of books piled against the walls. My shelves are overflowing, but my parents have yet to buy me new ones.

I'm idly eyeing the stack of books on my bedside, trying to pick one for my weekend read, when someone knocks on the door.

"Myra, are you awake?" Dadu asks.

"Yeah!"

The door opens and Dadu peeks her head in, smiling. It feels like a breath of fresh air. "Do you want to come grocery shopping with me after breakfast?"

I smile back. It's always nice to see Dadu in a good mood. "I'd love to."

Later, when I'm walking through the fruit aisle, my phone buzzes in my back pocket. I unlock it to see a text from Nandini: have you checked FB?

I frown. no, I barely go on fb unless it's for class!! why?

baaabe. april fools must've come early for ace lol

Cora sends a screenshot of her Facebook app to our group chat the next moment. Ace Clyde is in a relationship.

The first comment says Mia Jackson: lmao with whomst?

The second comment says Ace Clyde: karina ahmed, rmbr??

I curse in surprise, dropping my phone into the shopping cart.

Dadu comes up behind me, a concerned expression on her face. "What happened?"

"Nothing," I say, shoving my phone away and focusing on the bananas. Is Ace *insane*? I don't know what could possibly make him think that was a good decision but he's going to regret it dearly.

The most ridiculous part of this is that we're not even Facebook friends.

My phone buzzes in my pocket again, but I ignore it. I can't even think about this or I'll start screaming, and then I'll probably get carted out of the grocery store.

"Are you sure, Myra?" Dadu asks, cupping my face and turning it side to side as if she can diagnose me from a glance. "Are you ill? We have to go to Sana's birthday party on Friday. If you're feeling sick, we should get you medicine today, to make sure that you're healthy by then."

I laugh weakly. Going to my cousin Sana's party on Friday is the *least* of my concerns. *Ten, nine, eight, seven, six, five, four, three, two, one.* "I'm not sick, don't worry."

Dadu hums. "If you're sure. Let me know though, okay?" I nod, and she tugs my shirtsleeve. "Come on, let's pick the bananas together."

"Yeah, maybe some candles, too," I say, biting my bottom lip as I sift through the various bananas.

Dadu holds a bunch toward me, perfectly yellow with a few brown spots.

The strange block in my chest seems to come loose. "You know me so well," I say.

She smiles and pats my cheek. "Let's grab your candles, and then we can get your brother's cereal."

I roll my eyes at the mention of Samir's special cereal but follow my grandma anyway. "He should just eat the cereal the rest of us eat."

"Your brother should do a lot of things that he doesn't do," Dadu says, laughing.

"Yeah, but Ma and Baba let him do whatever he wants," I say under my breath, tossing a few oranges into our shopping cart as we turn from the fruit aisle.

Dadu pats my shoulder in understanding. "Boys have it so much easier, don't they?"

I snort, thinking of all the times Samir has gotten away with doing things I can't even contemplate. "That's an understatement."

Dadu would know. She grew up with *five* older brothers. The sheer thought is horrifying.

"Hey, how about this, Myra—when we're done here, we can go to that bookshop you like and I'll buy you a book for coming with me to the grocery store. They might even have nicer candles there. What do you think?"

"Really?" I ask, something like lightning zinging through me. "Dadu, you're the best."

She smiles and gives me a one-armed hug before getting distracted by an assortment of mixed vegetables.

I pull out my phone with the intention of Snapchatting Nandini and Cora about how awesome my grandma is, but then remember the predicament I'm in when I see all my missed notifications.

Ugh. Ace might not be excelling in his studies, but he's definitely excelling at giving me a headache.

T-MINUS 21 Days

Sunday morning brings a horde of Samir's friends to my house.

I leave my room at noon to grab breakfast but falter halfway down the stairs when I catch sight of several teenage boys in my living room, playing Wii Bowling.

I'm kind of hungry, but to pass through, I'd have to walk over their various belongings littered on the floor and make small talk.

I already dislike dealing with groups of strangers, and one consisting of excitable freshmen is arguably my worst nightmare. I don't even have a *bra* on. It's not worth it.

I try to catch Samir's eye as I hover on the staircase, hoping to tell him to hurry up and get his friends out of the living room, but he's too busy laughing as he shows one of them something on his phone.

Great. I discreetly go back upstairs and busy myself doing homework while I wait for them to leave. I force myself to ignore the sound of bowling pins falling over and over downstairs. I'm in the middle of attempting to finish my precalc assignment when I get a text from a number I don't recognize.

don't be mad @ me, I'll explain tmrw.

I frown at my phone. who's this???

In response, I receive a picture of a shirtless Ace and nearly break my phone when I throw it halfway across the room. I must be losing my mind.

There's absolutely no way Ace Clyde is texting me shirtless selfies right now. There's no way this is my life.

I inch toward my phone slowly. I can't help but feel like it's a bomb that's going to explode at any moment. When I pick it up, it's blessedly intact, but Ace's shirtless selfie is still looking back at me unanswered.

WHY are you shirtless? is the only response I can manage.

i was working out, Ace texts back.

I sigh. Ace might be a delinquent who separates himself from the rest of the high school crowd, but he's as clueless as any other teenage boy. I save his contact in my phone and say, pls don't text me shirtless pics of yourself dude!!! it's weird!!!

Alistair Clyde:
u asked who i was

Me:
and I regret it dearly

Alistair Clyde:
haha ur a comedian

Alistair Clyde:
anyway don't be mad. i'll explain everything tmrw morning ok?

Me:
you mean if I don't kill you first

Alistair Clyde:
I look forward to u trying ;)

I put down my phone and dig the heels of my palms into my eyes. My life is a mess.

"Myra, come down for food!" Dadu calls. "Samir's friends are gone!"

"Coming!" I say and toss my phone aside in favor of a book. After breakfast, I always read to Dadu for a while. She says it helps improve her English, but I think she just likes hearing me read. Either way, I don't mind—rather, I'm *happy* to do anything that puts her mind at momentary ease—but today, it has the extra benefit of giving me a chance to get out of my own head.

It's something I need desperately if Ace is determined to keep up this charade.

18

T-MINUS 20 DAYS

For the first time in my life, I walk into school with my hood over my head, not wanting to attract the attention of my classmates. I don't think anyone will stare if Ace isn't by my side, but I don't want to risk it. He still hasn't changed his relationship status, and upward of a dozen strangers have requested to follow me on Instagram and friend me on Facebook this morning alone.

"Good morning," I say to my friends, finally pulling down my hood. As I predicted, no one casts me a second glance aside from Nandini and Cora, who stare at me like I found the cure to cancer. "How were your weekends?"

"If you don't explain what the hell is happening *right now*, I'm going to pour my orange juice down your shirt," Cora threatens pleasantly. "I should not have to find out from Facebook that you got your first boyfriend."

"He's not my boyfriend," I say, exasperated. "He's just being stubborn."

Nandini shakes her head. "I'm with Cora on this. What is going *on*, dude?"

"I wish I could tell you, but I don't even know myself." I scratch the back of my head. "He didn't tell me he was going to do that. I honestly don't have a single clue what he's up to."

As if I've summoned him, Ace suddenly appears behind Nandini. Never have I more fully believed in the phrase *speak of the devil*.

"Morning," Ace says, setting down a paper bag and coffee cup in front of me. "Have a good day, sweetie. I'll see you later."

Then he kisses the top of my head, his lips warm against my hair, and casually walks away like I'm not having a heart attack.

What. The. Hell.

Nandini and Cora are staring at me with wide eyes, and I open my mouth, but I don't know what to say.

"I—" I shake my head, at a loss. My heart is beating too fast. "I'll be back."

I grab the breakfast he got me and hurry after him, ignoring my friends' loud protests and all the eyes burning holes into the back of my head. The head that Ace just kissed. What the *hell*.

I don't see him in the hallway, so I aim for the chemistry wing, hurrying up the steps. People are giving me odd looks, but I don't care. What was Ace thinking? In what world is it normal to come up to your tutor and her friends, bring her breakfast, and then kiss her on the head before disappearing?

I find him standing at his locker, sifting through his things. "What is *wrong* with you?"

Ace looks at me, frowning. "Did I get your coffee order wrong?"

I splutter. "My *coffee* order?"

He grabs the drink from my hand and takes a sip. "Milk with three spoons of sugar, right?"

"I mean. Yes. But no! Forget the coffee! What are you *doing*?" I try not to think about how Cora still gets my coffee wrong but Ace remembered after I told him my order once.

Ace gives me a curious look. "Talking to you."

"Okay, smartass," I say. "You owe me an explanation, remember?"

A look of understanding settles over Ace's expression. "Ah, that."

"Yes, that!" I move to close his locker but catch sight of a notebook still encased in plastic and fall short. "Did you buy a notebook?"

"You said to," Ace says and reaches behind his ear. I didn't notice but there's a pencil tucked there. "I even brought something to write with. Are you proud of me?"

I stare at him blankly. I am, oddly, kind of proud of him, but I can't make myself say that when I'm still righteously indignant.

He smiles. "I'll take that as a yes."

When he grabs my hand, I don't refuse and let him lead me to the stairway.

As we're walking, we run into Xander, and all three of us stop to look at each other. My skin starts itching nervously as Xander's gaze drops to our hands, still interlocked.

"Good morning, Karina," Xander says, his gaze rising to meet mine. He's calmer than he was Friday night.

I offer him a small smile. It feels stretched too thin on my face. "Good morning, Xander."

"I see you're still…dating my brother."

I laugh nervously and look at Ace, who looks completely tuned out. But his grip on my hand is tighter than ever, making it clear he's not as relaxed as he looks. "It seems so."

Xander tilts his head. "Have you met our mom yet?"

"Mom's in Italy," Ace says darkly, his first words to his brother. "How would Karina have met her?"

Xander's smile stretches wide. "Surely, you've introduced them through FaceTime or Skype. I can't imagine Mom wouldn't want to meet your first girlfriend."

Ace's grip tightens on my hand. "Worry less about my relationship and more about yourself."

"I'm always going to worry about you, Alistair," Xander says, reaching forward to pat Ace's shoulder. "Isn't that what big brothers do?"

"And big sisters," I add, pulling the attention away from Ace before the two of them can engage in an all-out brawl in the middle of the stairway. "Speaking of which, I actually need to find my little brother. You don't mind, do you?"

Xander considers me for a moment before he nods. "Of course. I was heading to class anyway. Unlike my brother, I prefer to arrive in a timely manner. I'll see you around, Karina." He inclines his head toward Ace. "Alistair."

He disappears through the door, and I can't help but mutter, "I sincerely hope not."

Ace laughs under his breath, his grip loosening. "Come on."

We continue up and up the stairs until we reach a locked dead end. There are no other students here, giving us a semblance of privacy.

"Before you kick me in the balls, I'd like to make a case for myself," Ace says, sitting on one of the steps. "I swear I have a good explanation."

I sigh and sit next to him. "Let's hear it."

Ace fiddles with the rings on his fingers, refusing to meet my gaze. It's my first giveaway that this conversation is going to be more serious than I anticipated. "My family is…complicated.

What you saw on Friday is only a small glimpse into what it's like at our house. Do you want the SparkNotes version?"

"Please don't tell me you use SparkNotes," I say, mostly because I don't know how else to respond.

Ace laughs lowly. "Of course that's what you got out of that, Ahmed."

I elbow Ace. "Just tell me."

Ace still doesn't look at me, but one of his cheeks dimples. "Yeah. Okay." He exhales. "Basically, my dad only gives a shit about me when I'm getting into trouble. My brother's kind of perfect, so I have to stand out in my own way. If my grades start slipping, he sits me down and lectures me. If I skip a piano lesson, he monitors my next one himself. I know how stupid this sounds, but it's almost like he only cares about me when I'm letting him down."

I reach out toward Ace unthinkingly, placing my hand over his. "I'm sorry." His words resonate in a painful way.

"It's not your fault," Ace says, running his free hand through his hair, further messing up his dark waves. "My point is that if my dad knew I had a tutor...my grades would be one less thing for him to care about. I can't let him find out."

Puzzle pieces slot together in my mind. "Is that why you didn't want Xander to see us in the library?" I pause. "Wait, your solution was to tell your family we're *dating*?"

"It wasn't the most well-thought-out plan." Ace offers me a sheepish glance. "I would've left it alone after the dinner, but Xander goes to school with us and he watches me *all* the time. He loves any excuse to make me look bad in front of our dad."

My mouth falls open. If he's implying what I think he's implying, I'm going to stab him with his own pencil. "So we have to pretend to date so your brother doesn't...what? *Tattle* on you? Is that what you're telling me?"

"Don't look at me like that, Ahmed," Ace says, his lips pursed in a pout. "It's not like I'm doing it for fun."

I shake my head incredulously. "No, you're doing it so your dad doesn't find out you're actually *trying* to get good grades. That's ridiculous! You have to hear how that sounds. Why don't you just tell your dad what's going on?"

Ace's pout shifts into something more serious; a deeper frown that looks wrong on his face. "It's not that simple."

"It sounds pretty simple to me. You want me to pretend to be your girlfriend to keep Xander from getting suspicious." I feel like I'm losing brain cells. "Ace, you can't be serious."

"It'll only be for a couple months," Ace says, his gaze dropping to the ground. "Or even just a few weeks. Enough time that it seems believable. We could fake our breakup at prom or something."

"I don't even know what to say to you right now," I say, throwing my hands up. "My parents would *kill* me if I ever dated anyone, even if it's just pretend."

"What? Why?"

Before I can answer, the bell rings, signaling the end of first period. I look around, flabbergasted at how quickly the time went, then turn back to Ace. "I don't have the time to explain the intricacies of my family politics to you, but we're *not* doing this."

I grab my stuff and hurry down the steps without waiting for Ace. I glance back only once to see him staring at me, a contemplative expression on his face.

19

T-MINUS 20 DAYS

Later, I'm walking into AP Physics when a hand reaches out and pulls me away from the doorway. At this point, I'm not even surprised to see Ace standing there.

"Don't you have class?"

He shrugs. "It's gym. Not a big deal."

I roll my eyes. "Well, I *definitely* have class, so if you don't mind moving?"

"Just hear me out for two seconds, Ahmed," Ace says, holding out his hands. His eyes are oddly serious. "I'll do anything for you to agree."

I snort. "Okay. Buy me a dozen books a week."

"Okay."

I pause, giving him an incredulous look. "I was joking."

Ace's expression doesn't shift. "I wasn't."

"Go to class," I say, shoving his shoulder lightly.

"Just—Karina, please," Ace says, his tone so earnest that I hesitate. "I'm serious. I'll do anything."

I stare at him hard, trying to discern how honest he's being.

I don't know what to say, because I obviously can't agree. My parents would have a conniption. *I* might have a conniption.

But there's something in his expression that's making it increasingly difficult to say no.

Strange feelings swim in my chest, pushing on my rib cage, tugging at my heartstrings. Maybe I have a weakness for beautiful boys with gentle hearts.

Ya Allah. How did I get here?

The bell rings and I sigh, pushing his shoulder again. "We'll talk later."

All through class, I wonder why I'm stupid enough to even consider his request. Pretending to date Ace Clyde means a tsunami of problems I'm not equipped to deal with, the first of which means being *stared* at. Already, at least four of my classmates are shooting me disbelieving looks when they think I can't see them.

I take out a piece of paper and start writing, trying to put my thoughts onto the page as coherently as I can. Today's my last day of trying this method.

Ace isn't popular. He might be infamous, but he's not popular. My classmates might be looking at me now, but I doubt it'll last longer than a week. I'm pretty sure he's never dated anyone in this school, so he doesn't have any exes out to make my life miserable. The only person who might cause issues is Xander, but what can Xander really do to *me*? He graduates within three months, and then I never have to see him again.

Which means the real problem is my family. Samir's head is stuck up his robotics club's ass, so I doubt he'd even realize I'm "dating" Ace. Plus, he's a freshman and I'm a junior... would this wave of gossip even reach him? Why would any of the freshman care who Ace Clyde dates? With 2,000 kids in our school, I think the freshmen have more to worry about than Ace's dating life.

But still, I should be careful and keep an eye out for Samir when I'm with Ace. Though, I *could* say I'm his tutor. I am his tutor. It's not technically a lie.

Maybe I should tell Samir right now...my brother's a dumbass, but he's not *evil*, and he wouldn't rat me out on purpose.

But accidents happen. If I bring this situation to Samir's attention, is it more likely he'll slip up and tell Ma and Baba without realizing? Is it better to leave him in the dark? We don't talk about our social lives with each other, so bringing it up unnecessarily might raise a red flag...

Maybe I should keep that disgusting can of worms closed. I'll just briefly mention I'm tutoring Ace, so if he sees us around it's not a big deal. If I keep my head down, I'm sure I can make this work somehow—

It takes me a second to realize the direction of my thoughts and my pencil halts. I groan, dropping my head into my hands. I might as well have agreed already if I'm planning out contingencies.

Writing out my thoughts didn't help my anxiety either, so I guess it's time to move on to the next technique on my list. Maybe I'm destined to ping-pong between coping methods until one lands.

By the time I sit down in English class, I've resigned myself to helping Ace. At least until my parents come back. When he drops into the seat next to me, I'm contemplating whether I can submit myself as a Nobel Peace Prize applicant.

Ace looks at me. "I've been thinking about it, and I—"

"Yes."

His mouth snaps shut. "Really?"

I sigh, avoiding his gaze. My heart is pounding unevenly with the knowledge of what this will bring. "Yes. But you only get three weeks. And I want my books. If you're going to use me, I get to use you, too."

Ace slumps into his seat, his eyes fluttering shut. "Thank God."

"Don't thank God, thank me," I say, nudging him with my shoe. "And take notes."

He sits up straighter and grins at me, dimples as sweet as ever. Allah, *why*? "As you wish."

"Don't quote *The Princess Bride* at me," I say under my breath.

My friends are staring from a few desks away, and I give them a look, which I hope they understand as *I'll explain later*. We're not in the business of keeping secrets, and I sure as hell am not going to break that rule.

"Is our entire relationship going to be you bossing me around?" Ace asks, reaching over to play with a strand of my hair.

I bat his hand away, heat rushing into my cheeks. If he's going to keep touching me, I'm going to spontaneously combust. "You signed up for this."

His expression is annoyingly smug when he says, "Yes, I did."

"You're *pretending* to date Ace Clyde?" Cora says in disbelief, her fork halfway to her mouth. "In exchange for *books*?"

Nandini looks between us. "Is this all a dream? Maybe we're in *Inception*?"

"I can't believe this is happening," Cora says, shaking her head. "Who *are* you? Are you Karina's wilder identical twin?"

"Shut up," I say, dropping my head to the table. Telling them about it is making this situation far too real. *Ten, nine, eight, seven, six, five, four, three, two, one.* "I don't know why I said yes. Why do I ever agree to anything?"

"Because you're too nice," Nandini says, patting my cheek. "You should've just told him to go fuck himself. I don't care if it means his dad knows he's being tutored. Babe, you're an anxious mess right now."

I don't bother asking how she knows that. I keep bouncing my leg and biting my nails, which is as sure a sign as any that there's an uncomfortable weight pressing against my lungs, making me want to roll over and die.

"Don't say that!" Cora says. "Ace is *hot* and he's offering to buy her books. That's like...perfect for Karina."

"Yeah, but in case *you* happened to forget, Karina's parents are batshit," Nandini says, "and if they find out about this, it doesn't matter how hot Ace is, because they're going to kill her."

"Kill me first," I beg hopelessly. "At least it'll be quick."

"See? This is why she should've told Ace to go fuck himself," Nandini says, running a soothing hand down my back.

They've both been around my parents enough to know how strict they are. Every time Nandini and Cora are over, my parents grill them about their future prospects and their grades and just anything and everything that no high schooler *ever* wants to talk about.

I've been to my friends' houses only a handful of times. Nandini's parents are chill and mostly leave us alone when we're over—though, that might be because she has older sisters who have already taken the brunt of their expectations. Cora's parents are a dream come true, always accepting us with open and welcoming arms, constantly checking in and offering anything we need.

Being around their parents explains their personalities. Cora is loud and bright with unconditional love. Nandini is calm and no-nonsense with everlasting support. Both of them are the best friends I could ask for, but even when they get it, they still don't *get* it. I don't expect them to.

"Her parents aren't going to find out," Cora says, rolling her eyes as she stabs another piece of lettuce. "Who's going to tell them? You? Me? Karina? Ace himself?"

"I wouldn't put it past him," I mutter.

When someone takes the seat beside me, I don't have to turn my head to know it's Ace, because both Nandini and Cora fall silent.

"What now?" I ask, sitting up straight to look at him. My heart is flipping uncertainly, but I manage to keep my expression mild.

Ace's countenance is cooler than I'm used to, but it's not entirely standoffish. "Nothing. I just wanted to sit with you."

"You...wanted to sit with me." This nightmare never ends. I'm going to die. Death by Ace being... *Ace.*

He turns to my friends. "Nandini Kaur and Cora Zhang-Agreste, right?"

They nod, eyes wide.

Ace hums and unwraps a lollipop, offering it to me. "Want one?"

"No," I say, shaking my head. "I—you know what. Sit wherever you want."

I turn my attention back to the girls, ignoring Ace's presence at my side. If I stare at him for another minute, I'm going to keel over. He seems more than content with that, plugging in his earphones and leaning his head against his hand so he can stare at me quietly.

"Let's move on," I say, wiping my sweaty palms against my jeans.

Nandini squints at me. "Are we all mass hallucinating?"

"I ask myself that every day," I say. "We should've known

the world was coming to an end when a Cheeto was elected president. No offense to Cheetos."

Cora's eyebrows furrow as she watches Ace watch me. It's incredibly convoluted. I'm trying not to think about it. "Can he *hear* us?"

"Probably," I say, offering Ace a glance. He doesn't show any visible reaction, but his foot hooks around mine underneath the table, making me pinch his leg in surprise.

Nandini ignores Ace's obnoxious grin, her eyes steady on mine. "Anyway, I was thinking we could all go see the new Marvel movie since your parents are out of the country. Maybe during spring break next week?"

I smile, gratitude blooming in my chest. "Sure. Should we catch the first show so it's half off?"

Nandini nods. "That's what I was thinking, too. And we'll have my employee discount, so it'll be even cheaper."

"Sounds great to me," I say, pushing Ace's hand away when he starts poking my rib cage. My entire body feels on edge, prickling with awareness of his warm gaze.

Going to the movies. Right. Usually, I ask Samir to cover for me when I sneak out with my friends, but since my parents are out of town, it's a nonissue. "What do you think, Cora? Are you down?"

"I'm sorry, I can't get over the fact that your…*boyfriend* is sitting with us," Cora says, still staring at Ace. "This is so weird."

I wave a hand in front of Cora's face. "He's just like anyone else. Pretend he's a stranger." I wish I could take my own advice.

Cora mutters something unintelligible under her breath. Then, "Maybe you should invite your boyfriend to come with us, Karina."

"Cora," Nandini hisses, slapping her arm. "It's a girl's trip."

"You're no fun."

Ace is smirking now. It's barely there, just a wry twist to his lips, but I see it all the same. "Stop being an asshole," I say to both Cora and Ace.

Cora snorts and squeezes my hand. "I love you, K."

I sigh, lacing our fingers together. The motion is grounding enough to calm my heart. "And I love you."

When I glance to the side, Ace is still watching me. As soon as our eyes meet, he playfully mouths, *I love you, too.*

God, he's a dumbass.

A dumbass I'm growing impossibly fond of.

When he continues to stare at me with mirth lining his features, I reach forward to flick his forehead. "Please do me a favor and take a long walk off a short pier."

"With you by my side? Without hesitation. I'd happily sink to the bottom of a lake with you."

Ugh. This entire situation was so much easier when he wasn't talking.

"Stop flirting," Cora says, her eyes bright with amusement.

I gape at them. "I just told him to die."

Nandini looks exasperated. "We're Gen Z, Karina. That's how we flirt."

"She's not wrong, Ahmed," Ace says, surprising all of us. He grins, and both Cora and Nandini look at him like he just grew a second head. "It sounds like you have a crush on me."

"If by crush, you mean a growing urge to choke you, then yes."

"Choke me, huh?" Ace smirks, reaching forward to wrap a lock of my hair around his finger.

Blood rushes to my cheeks. "Shut up."

Ace chuckles and lets go of my hair, letting it spring back to hit me in the face. "We'll talk more about this later."

I open my mouth to protest, but he leans forward, his lips brushing my forehead, soft and unexpected. I fall silent.

Ace stands up and leaves before I can scramble together a coherent thought that isn't just *WHAT ARE YOU DOING?*

"Oh my God," Nandini says.

I turn toward her, my cheeks heated. I forgot my friends were there.

Cora isn't even saying anything, her eyes so wide they look like they're about to pop out of her head as she stares after Ace's retreating back.

"Karina… Karina, what the *fuck*?" Nandini asks.

I shake my head. "I." I can't think of anything else to say. "Uh."

Cora finally turns back to me. "Karina. He has a crush on you."

"No," I say immediately. "He's being a clown. He needs to keep up his act."

"Dude," Nandini says, her voice high-pitched. "He definitely likes you. Stop acting clueless. I've had five different classes with him over the last three years, and he's never even *looked* in someone else's direction like that."

I shake my head, but my heart is pounding ridiculously hard in my chest. I know it's not real, that he's faking a relationship because of Xander, but my traitorous body apparently didn't get the memo. "I'm telling you. It's to keep up the act."

"Karina, I have read enough fan fiction to know exactly how this goes," Nandini says and Cora nods in agreement. "If he doesn't already have a crush on you, he *will*. It's only a matter of time."

I groan. "Real life isn't fan fiction."

Nandini gives me a pitying look and turns toward Cora. "When they inevitably end up together, do we get to say 'I told you so'?"

"Hell yes," Cora says, offering Nandini her pinky.

Nandini hooks their pinkies together without hesitating.

Apparently my body isn't the only traitor at this table. "It's a pinky swear."

I hook my own pinkies together pointedly. "And I swear I'll tell you *both* 'I told you so' when Ace moves on after we're done with our study sessions."

Cora offers me a wicked grin. "Those are going to be your famous last words, Karina Ahmed."

PART 2

blaze

20

T-MINUS 20 DAYS

"You know, you'll lose your little bad-boy reputation if you keep badgering me," I say as I sit down. "No one is going to think you're cool and aloof anymore."

In the last few periods, I've managed to calm down. As lunch came to an end, I saw Xander sitting only a few tables away from us. No wonder Ace was acting so boldly.

"I didn't ask for that reputation," Ace says, putting his feet on the table and crossing them at the ankle. He's wearing heavy combat boots that are at odds with his designer skinny jeans. "Though I am pretty cool and aloof."

I raise an eyebrow. "You like mint chocolate ice cream, playing the piano, and space."

"But only you know that," Ace says, taking out a black marker from his jacket and uncapping it. I nearly smack it out of his hands when he starts doodling on the table.

"Isn't that destruction of public property?" I say, hoping it will dissuade him, but he only snorts. "Ace, please stop?"

He looks up at me, his eyes more blue than green today, and his marker falters. "Yeah, okay."

I blink. "Really?" That was easier than I thought it would be.

"Yeah, Ahmed. What are we looking at today?"

It takes a moment for that to sink in before a smile pulls at my lips. "I was thinking we could take a break—"

"I've *been* saying that."

"—from reading comprehension and focus on poetry."

He sighs. "I suppose."

I roll my eyes. "Hear me out. Just pretend they're song lyrics. You love music, right? That's why I thought poetry might work better for you. We have that poetry project coming up next month, anyway."

He hums, looking at me with an inscrutable expression. "You're something else, Ahmed."

I frown. "What? Did I say something wrong?"

"It's not a bad thing," Ace says. "You're thoughtful. I like it."

"Oh." My clothes suddenly feel too hot. Is it possible to blush with your full body? I grab my bag and take out the collections I snagged from my bookshelf so I have something to do with my hands. "I brought some poetry books from home. Is that okay?"

"Of course," Ace says, reaching for one. "Can you show me your favorite poem?"

"Yeah, sure," I say and grab a translated Bengali poetry collection. I'm flipping through the pages when I realize Ace isn't holding a poetry book at all. *Oh shit.* "Hey, wait, Ace—"

"Did you write these?" Ace asks, gaze straying from the frayed brown journal in his hands to look at me.

My nose wrinkles and I wring my hands helplessly. I should've been more careful when taking my books out, but being around Ace makes me lose my head. "Yeah, but it's just for school. It's not anything serious."

"Karina, these are…breathtaking," Ace says, his gaze is filled with some kind of strange awe that feels heavy on my skin. "This poem, 'Unshakeable'? Is it finished?"

I know exactly which poem he's talking about, and it causes my heart to race uncomfortably, until I can hear the staccato beat in my ears. No one was ever supposed to see that. Usually, I write poetry as a response to the world around me. Rarely do I ever put myself on the pages.

The poem "Unshakable" is the one time I dared to try, and I couldn't find it in myself to finish.

somewhere there are birds that fly free
here, I am caged and can barely breathe
there is so much to say
these thoughts never fall from my lips
I am scared of so goddamn much
afraid these flames will burn
my fingers, they hurt from clinging so hard

I'm lost, I'm bruised, I don't know what to do
I never thought I'd give up
but I'm starting to think I'm going to lose

it's dark, it's light, a hand reaches out
………

"Ace, that's personal," I say, voice cracking. *Ten, nine, eight, seven, six, five, four, three, two, one.* My heart feels exposed, lying on the pages for Ace to poke and prod at as he pleases. "Can you please give it back?"

"Hey," Ace says, his voice quiet. "I'm sorry. I didn't mean to… I didn't realize. I'm sorry."

He slides my journal across the table, and I catch it with shaking hands. The irony of the moment isn't lost on me.

"I'm sorry," Ace repeats, reaching across the table and slowly taking one of my hands in his. His rings are cold against my skin, jarring me out of a strange sense of dissonance.

"No, it's not your fault," I say, shaking my head in abrupt, agitated movements. "*I'm* sorry, I didn't mean to freak out on you like that."

His fingers slowly slide against mine, interlacing them and bringing our hands to the center of the table. The longer we touch, the less I hear my heartbeat in my ears. The less I feel out of breath.

"Don't apologize to me," he says, his voice fierce. I look up and find his strange and beautiful eyes blazing in the sunlight coming from the windows behind me. The fire he keeps insisting I have inside of me is alive in his gaze.

I exhale deeply and sit back in my seat. "Sorry."

"No apologizing," Ace insists, squeezing my hand. "If you're feeling up to it, we can keep studying. I still want to see your favorite poem."

You're something else, I think to myself. The thought makes me feel both hot and cold.

"Okay," I say. "Okay."

"Okay," Ace says and lets go of my hand. I almost wish he hadn't.

There's change shifting in the air, and I don't know how I feel about it.

That night, my fingers itch as I sit next to Dadu in the dining room. She's peeling and cutting vegetables for tomorrow's meal, and I'm doing my homework while music plays in the background.

"Dadu?" I tap my pencil anxiously against my textbook. I've felt off all day, and even counting backward in my head hasn't helped. "When you met Dada, what was it like?"

My grandma fumbles with the potato she's peeling and stares up at me from beneath her glasses. "When I met Dada?"

A part of me feels bad for bringing it up. Talking about Dada is a sore topic. I see how deeply she misses him every day, because all of her sarees are white in mourning. One day, when I was visiting her in New Jersey, I came across an entire closet full of colored sarees with a thin layer of dust coating them. I never asked Dadu about them, but it made me horribly sad to know she'd locked away the color in her life.

"Yeah," I say, spinning my pencil between my fingers. "What was it like when you first met him?"

"Myra." Dadu's eyebrows pull together. "Your Dada and I had an arranged marriage."

It's probably stupid to compare an arranged marriage to an arranged tutoring situation. No, it's definitely stupid. But it's the closest way I can think of to relate to my grandma right now, so I press forward.

"I know. That's why I'm asking. You were just thrown into the situation together, right? What was your first impression of him?"

Dadu hums, setting her potato back down on the cutting board. "He was handsome," she says, smiling faintly. "I remember I was glad about that. He was very spas.t.abhaˉs.ıˉ, though. I didn't expect that."

I repeat that word, *spas.t.abhaˉs.ıˉ*. It's not a word I'm familiar with. "What does that mean?"

My grandma pauses for a long moment, clearly searching for the right way to explain it. "He spoke his mind," she says finally. "He said what he wanted and didn't care what other people thought of him. He was a city boy, born and raised, and I was a country girl. It was strange for me to see how bold he was. I admired that in him sometimes, and thought he was a rascal the rest of the time."

I laugh in surprise. Near the end of his life, Dada was always serious. It's strange to hear he wasn't always like that. "A rascal?"

Dadu grins, reaching over to run a hand over my hair. "A rascal. He would get us into all sorts of trouble. I thought I would handle it fine because of all of my older brothers, but he was just...different. He treated *me* differently. I never realized until I met your grandpa, but my brothers were always so careful around me. They treated me like a precious jewel that could break at any moment. Only once I met him did I realize how sheltered I had been to the absurdity of the world around me. It changed me to see the manner in which your grandfather approached things. It made me realize that maybe I wasn't the person I thought I was. My family believed me to be one way, but I was quickly learning that I was someone else altogether."

I'm not the way my family believes me to be, either is on the tip of my tongue. But that's not a conversation for right now.

Dadu swallows roughly, her eyes glimmering in the candlelight. "Your grandpa never treated me that way. He always saw me for who I was, even before I saw it myself. His equal. He was free with his thoughts and actions around me. Wild in a lovely and terrifying sort of way. It was so unfamiliar. I didn't know what to do with him at first."

That sounds increasingly familiar. "What *did* you do?"

"I calmed him down," Dadu says, her voice quieter. The words send a chill through me. "And I think he needed that on occasion, the same way I needed his boldness. I was able to ground him in reality."

"How did you do that?" I ask, equally hushed.

Dadu looks away, her gaze somewhere distant. "By loving him."

I inhale sharply, not having expected that answer. Dadu looks back at me, her eyes alert again. "Is there a reason you're asking, Myra?"

"No," I say, scratching my nose. "I was just curious."

Dadu considers my expression. I have no idea what I must look like to her, but I doubt it's the perfect picture of innocence.

"Myra Apu has a *cruuuush*," Samir's voice says behind me, and I turn to see him leaning against the dining room's entryway, holding a tray of Oreos, likely stolen from the pantry as a snack. There's an infuriating grin on his face.

My neck burns. "Shut up. I do not."

Samir wiggles his eyebrows at me suggestively. I reach for a napkin on the dining table, then toss it at his head. He ducks out of the way, sticking his tongue out at me. "Don't forget to call Ma," he says, laughing when I throw another napkin. "I was just on FaceTime with her, and she said you're ignoring her calls."

"I am not *ignoring* her," I say. *Ten, nine, eight, seven, six, five, four, three, two, one.* Samir's words about having a crush keep looping through my head, and I stand suddenly, making for him. He never *thinks* before speaking.

His eyes widen and he skitters away, toward the stairs. I move to follow him when Dadu says, "Myra."

I pause, looking back at her. "Yes?"

She's watching me with a small smile. "Can you grab me a sweater? I'm feeling cold."

I slump in sudden relief, which probably paints me as even guiltier. "Of course," I say and hurry to get it for her.

On my way, I knock on Samir's door. He opens it a crack, peering at me through the small gap. "What?"

"Don't do that," I say, my skin crawling as I meet his eyes. Samir often forgets that we have different consequences for our actions. It's insufferable and anxiety inducing. "You're going to get me in trouble. I don't have a crush on anyone."

He raises his brows. "I was just joking," he says, opening the door wider. There are faint noises in the background, his laptop open to some video game streaming app. "It's not a big deal. Dadu doesn't care."

I swallow past the lump in my throat. "I know, but just— don't, okay? I don't have a crush on anyone. Don't bring up that kind of stuff at home. Promise me you won't."

Samir holds up his hands in a placating gesture. "All right, all right. Relax. I promise I won't bring it up."

The stiffness in my frame eases. "Thanks."

He shrugs but falters. Another awful grin spreads across his face. He pokes my side, asking, "You're being pretty defensive. *Do* you have a crush on someone? You said you were tutoring that dude, right? What was his name again?"

I smack his hand away, even as my heart skips a beat. At least this proves Samir didn't even care enough to remember Ace's name. "No. He's just a classmate. And didn't I *just* say not to bring that up at home? Don't you have homework to do?"

"Sorry, sorry, I'll stop now," my brother says and snorts at the irritated expression on my face. "I'm already done, by the way. Maybe you should go do yours."

He shuts the door in my face before I can flip him off. I grumble under my breath, but my heart feels a little more at ease knowing he won't say anything like that again. I grab a sweater from Dadu's room and head back downstairs to the dining room.

On my way, I pause in the living room at the sight of my phone, which is playing a Top 40 playlist from Spotify on the speakers. I pick it up unthinkingly and search for a classical music playlist.

I click into the first one and press play. The sound of piano notes fills the room, and it's different from what I'm used to, but it isn't bad. Just unfamiliar. Hopeful.

"Is that new, Myra?" Dadu asks from the other room.

"Yes," I say, staring at my phone in consideration. "It is."

"I like it," Dadu says. I can almost see the smile on her face.

"Yeah, Dadu," I say, closing my eyes and letting the music wash over me. My vehement protest of having a crush feels even flimsier now. "I think I do, too."

21

T-MINUS 19 DAYS

"I'm telling you, my new manager is the devil incarnate," Nandini says, scowling. "I told her I can't work multiple shifts during the week because of school, but she keeps scheduling me in anyway."

"Murder is always an option," Cora says, filing her nails. "Say the word and I'm on it."

"I'll drive the getaway car," I add, squeezing Nandini's arm. "Are you sure you can't get a job somewhere else?"

"I *could*, but I love my coworkers too much to quit," she says, laying her head on the table. "This is the worst."

"I bet I can get her fired," Cora muses, turning her full attention toward us. "I'm not above throwing a tantrum in the movie theater."

Nandini snorts, and I'm glad to see the shift in her mood. "At this rate, I might take you up on that offer."

I smile faintly, running my hand through her short curls.

Ace shows up a minute later, dropping off coffee and a doughnut. I roll my eyes and pinch his arm with my free hand.

He grins down at me. "I need to ask you something later. I'll walk you from AP Physics to English so we can talk about it."

"What are you going to ask for now? My homework?" I ask, raising an eyebrow.

"Very funny, Ahmed," Ace says and leans down to kiss the crown of my head again before making his way out of the cafeteria.

I'm used to Nandini and Cora's incredulous stares by now, so I wave it off. It's a lot harder to wave off the rising warmth inside my chest, the sudden fluttering of my pulse. "It's part of the facade."

"This is ridiculous," Cora says, shaking her head. "At least tell him to stop bringing you coffee. I already do that."

Before I can stop her, she grabs the coffee Ace brought and takes a sip.

"He even got your order wrong," Cora says, gesturing at the cup. "This is too sweet."

I wince. This isn't a conversation I ever intended to have. "It's actually right."

Cora stares in disbelief. "This is right," she repeats.

I nod, grimacing. "I didn't want to say anything! It's so nice of you to even think of me in the mornings. I didn't want to complain."

"I keep telling you, you're too nice," Nandini says, flicking me on the forehead.

"Yeah!" Cora says, flicking me on the forehead right afterward. "I would've written it down so I didn't mess it up. Why didn't you say something?"

I shrug helplessly.

Nandini sighs. "Karina, you've got to stop letting life just *happen* to you."

"I don't let life just happen to me," I say, jutting out my bottom lip. "I just don't like making other people feel bad."

They both look at me and I turn away, unable to hold their gazes. Even though I know I often let life pass me by, hearing it still stings.

Cora sighs, shaking her head. She shifts her gaze to my coffee cup. "He remembered, huh?"

"Yeah," I say, scrutinizing the expression on her face. "Is that a bad thing?"

"No, Karina," Cora says softly. "Not at all."

As promised, Ace is waiting when I step out of AP Physics. "You're like an annoying stray cat that won't stop following me," I say before wiggling my fingers at him. "Want a scratch on the head?"

Instead of shying away like I hoped he would, Ace just smirks. "If you're offering, why not?"

"I was joking," I say, brushing past him. My skin feels like it's overheating, and I take a deep breath when he isn't looking. "You take the fun out of things."

"*Me?*" Ace asks, catching up to me. I nearly jump ten feet in the air when he throws a casual arm around my shoulders. "You're the one that likes studying for fun."

I give him an unimpressed look. "No one likes studying for fun. I like staying on topic during our designated *study* time so you can gain the most out of our sessions."

I try not to be hyperaware of the fact that other juniors in our class are staring at us as we walk together. It's hard, because I'm also trying not to pay attention to Ace's fingers toying with the end of my braid. I don't see Samir anywhere, so at least there's that. It'd be just my luck to have him pass us in the hallway the day after I said I don't have a crush on anyone.

If he sees us now, he'll *never* stop badgering me. And then it's only a matter of time before he slips up to our parents.

Even still, I don't like how my classmates are staring at me. I resist the urge to burrow into Ace's side to hide but can't help leaning closer to him. As if he can read my thoughts, he pulls us into a less populated staircase.

Ten, nine, eight, seven, six, five, four, three, two, one.

Some of the tension leaves my frame and I turn to look at him. "Sorry."

"What have I told you about apologizing?" Ace says, squeezing my shoulder. "Anyway, I said I wanted to talk to you before. I was thinking...will you go to prom with me?"

I stop breathing.

Prom? It was only days ago that Cora, Nandini, and I were joking about it. I never expected anyone to ask me. I didn't expect *Ace* to ask me.

"Ahmed?" Ace says, gently nudging my shoulder.

I inhale sharply, trying to gain a hold of my bearings. "Are you serious?"

Ace nods. "I would've done a promposal, but I figured you'd be against that. I didn't want to put you on the spot or anything. You can say no, obviously, but I thought it'd be nice to go together since we're pretending to date. What do you think?"

I blink at him several times. "You want to go to prom with *me*? As part of our fake dating facade? Isn't that past our three-week mark?"

He shrugs. "Just in case." Then a strange look passes over his face. "Unless...someone asked you already?"

"No," I say quickly. "No, no one's asked me. I just—I don't know if I can go. I don't know if my parents will let me."

Ace frowns. "You're not allowed to go to junior prom?"

"I'm not allowed to do a lot of things," I say with a thin

smile, but my pulse is still raging like an incessant drumbeat. "But, uh…"

A hopeful light enters his eyes. "Yeah?"

I swallow past the dryness of my mouth. "If I can go, I'd love to go with you. But right now, three weeks is all I can promise."

"Okay. Let me know then." A flush spreads across his cheeks and he laughs in chagrin. "That actually isn't what I wanted to ask you."

"There's something *else*?"

He shrugs, his eyes still dancing. "Mia wants us to join her and her girlfriend for a double date after school. I thought it'd be fun. What do you think?"

I raise both eyebrows at him. "A double date? But we're not…dating, Ace."

"*Technically*, we are," he says, nudging his hip against mine. "Come on. Remember the books I promised to buy you? I'll do it today, if you come with us."

I pause to consider that. Goodreads recently informed me that several books from my TBR list released this week, and I've been meaning to go to the bookstore anyway. "Which bookstore?"

He must realize that means yes, because he grins widely. I reach up to poke one of his dimples without thinking. If anything, that only widens his smile. "There's an independent bookstore across from the ice rink Mia wants to go to. I figured we'd support a local business, but if you want to go to Barnes & Noble, we can do that, too."

I stare at him in wonder. How strange that his thoughts align with mine. "No, that's perfect. I love indie bookstores."

"Great," Ace says as we exit the staircase, only a few steps away from our English classroom. "It's a date."

A date. Why does that make it sound so real? As if asking me to prom wasn't enough.

"I guess so," I say, ignoring the way my heartstrings are pulling taut. "We're studying in your car on the way there. And we have to study tomorrow morning during first period to make up for lost time."

He laughs. "I'd expect nothing less."

I smile at him, even as my nerves begin to devour me in preparation for the evening ahead.

22

T-MINUS 19 DAYS

The bookstore is a small two-storied building called Two Stories, which already makes me love it.

Ace opens the door and I step inside, eyes wide as I take in the store. It's warm and cozy, earth themed. There are tables on the right side designed to look like tree stumps and seats that resemble shrubbery. Rows of bookshelves are lined up in front of me, and a warm yellow light filters in from above, where stars hang from thin metal threads. It reminds me of Ace's room, and I glance at him surreptitiously.

"My mom loves reading," he says, seeing the look on my face. "She designed my room before my parents got divorced. This used to be her favorite bookstore before she moved away."

"It's pretty," I say and glance at him. "Do you miss her? Since she's so far away?"

"I do," he says, quieter. "But we talk every day if we can. I told her about you."

"You *did*?" I blink at him. "What'd you say?"

Ace smiles at me innocuously. "Who knows?"

"*You* know," I say, pinching his arm. He laughs, but when it becomes clear he isn't going to say any more, I sigh. "So how long has this place been around?"

"Since I was a kid," he says, lightly tugging me around a shelf of books. "The owner's daughter manages it now. Actually, there she is. Genesis! Hey."

A beautiful dark-haired woman a few years older than us stops sorting books to look in our direction. When she sees Ace, her expression brightens, and her eyes are curious when they land on me. "Hi, Ace. Who's your friend?"

"This is my girlfriend, Karina," Ace says, taking my hand in his. Hearing those words come out of his mouth is still jarring, but I manage to keep my smile in place through sheer effort.

"Hi," I say. "It's nice to meet you."

"She loves books," Ace says slyly, ignoring me when I elbow him. "I think you'll get along great."

Genesis beams. "Do you want some recommendations? What do you like to read?"

I name some genres, and Genesis leads me away to an assortment of books on the second floor. Ace trails after us idly, and when he catches me looking at him, he winks. "Go wild, sweetie."

"Is he paying?" Genesis asks. I nod, and she laughs. "Definitely rob him blind, Karina. He can afford it."

I snort. "That's excellent advice."

"Actually, you know what? We're in the process of adding a section on astronomy." Genesis gestures for both of us to follow her. "Ace, you'll want to see this."

I tag along, my heart warm and content from being around books. The astronomy section turns out to be through a door, and when we come out on the other side, I stop in my tracks to stare. The entire room is set in darkness with lowlight fixtures in the shape of stars on the ceiling. Two displays make up most of the room, and half the book jackets glow in the dark.

I gasp when Genesis dials up the brightness. There are beautiful constellations painted on the walls and drawings of children hidden between them, chasing after the stars. But I'm focused on the book display. All the covers look untouched, with beautiful jackets illustrated in vivid detail. Depictions of moons, stars, planets, and the endless wonder of space are detailed across several of them.

"Gorgeous, right?" Genesis asks.

"Absolutely stunning," I say, my voice full of hushed reverence.

Ace isn't saying anything, so I glance to the side to see his reaction. Instead of looking at the room, he's staring at me. He doesn't look away when our gazes meet. "I've never seen anything more beautiful," he says softly.

I blink at him, my mouth suddenly dry. My heart starts racing, and I don't know what to say, how to break this sudden silence. He's looking at me in a way that no one ever has before.

"Teenage love," Genesis says wistfully, her voice cutting through the tension like warm butter. I look away from Ace, my cheeks burning with such intense heat I'm surprised I'm not going up in flames.

"I'm going to go look at the books you mentioned before," I say, my voice high-pitched, and I leave before either of them can reply.

I disappear into the shelves and take my phone out to text Nandini and Cora. guysssssss I think I'm on a real date with ace clyde !?????

Cora Zhang-Agreste:
W H A T

Nandini Kaur:
I wish this was surprising tbh I'm more curious what
made you get your head out of your ass

Me:
well...he asked me to prom kind of??? but that's not
rlly relevant rn

Nandini Kaur:
!? WHAT

Cora Zhang-Agreste:
oh. my. GOD.

Me:
IT'S NOT LIKE I CAN GO ANYWAY IT'S WHATEVER

Cora Zhang-Agreste:
BITCH I'M FILING THE PROM PETITION RN

Nandini Kaur:
omw to sign it cora expect me in 5

Me:
omg STOP I doubt I can go

Me:
but anyway listen. so. idk ace took me to a bookstore today right

Cora Zhang-Agreste:
..............nandini. nandini I can't do this with her

Cora Zhang-Agreste:
I know karina is oblivious but this is TOO MUCH

Me:
LISTEN TO ME

Me:
we were in this fancy room thing or whatever and it was beautiful and it was that stupid meme where it's like the stars are beautiful outside u know the one

Nandini Kaur:
AND HE SAID YOU WERE MORE BEAUTIFUL? BROOOO

Me:
not exactly but yes kind of IDK IM PANICKING WHAT DO I DO I THOUGHT THIS WAS ALL A PART OF HIS FAKE DATING THING BUT WHAT IF IT'S NOT

Nandini Kaur:
you're definitely on a date. pls take pics and post them on IG

Me:
I'm NOT posting pictures of ace on instagram are you OUT OF IT????

Nandini Kaur:
your instagram is on priv it's not a big deal!!

Cora Zhang-Agreste:
if u don't post them I'll post *this* conversation to my story... :)

Me:
you wouldn't…

Nandini Kaur:
have you MET cora? yes tf she will

Me:
oh my god I hate this you're both so chaotic

Me:
I have to go he's gonna see me on my phone bye
DON'T POST ANYTHING

I tuck my phone away and lean my head against a bookshelf, wondering if I've truly lost the plot of my own life.

Eventually, I decide I need to do something to occupy myself, otherwise I'm going to start screaming. There are children meandering around, so that's probably not the best option.

I wander through the aisles, scanning for specific titles. Once I have five, I sit down at one of the tables and crack open a retelling of *Much Ado About Nothing*.

This should be distracting enough.

I'm two chapters in when a shadow looms over me. I look up, trying to ignore the way my palms suddenly feel sweaty. Instead of meeting the reproachful gaze I expect, Ace is smiling down at me.

"Did you get the books you wanted?" he asks.

I nod, gesturing to my stack. Words feel hard right now. I still don't know what to say to him, but I'm grateful he's not making it weird between us.

He takes heed of the one I'm reading and chuckles. "A Shakespeare retelling, huh? I guess I shouldn't be surprised."

It's too easy to say "Shut up," and everything seems to fall back into place after that. "He's a literary genius. It's not my fault you can't appreciate that."

"Hey, I respect old Willy here as much as anyone else," Ace says, sitting on the edge of the table.

I groan. "Don't call William Shakespeare 'old Willy.' He's not your friend."

"How would you know?" Ace asks, his teeth flashing in a grin. "Maybe I can talk to ghosts and me and Willy are best friends. Have you ever thought of that?"

I close my book to level him with a flat look, even though my stomach is somersaulting. "You're such a nuisance."

Ace doesn't seem bothered by my reaction, reaching for my books and carrying them in one hand, fingers are splayed out against the spines. "Come on, let's go buy these."

I exhale quietly, my shoulders slumping. "Okay."

When Genesis rings up our books, she slides me a coupon despite Ace saying, "Hey, I paid for it. Shouldn't I get the coupon?"

"No," she says, winking at me. "I'm all about supporting women. Equity and all that. Your mom would approve, Ace."

I can't help my laughter.

Ace sighs, but his expression is warm as he glances between us. "I guess I'll just have to bring Karina here all the time then."

When I reach for the bag of books, he grabs it first. "I've got it," he says, nudging me lightly. "I'll put it in the car, and we can head to the ice rink."

"Have fun, lovebirds!" Genesis says, grinning. Something twists uncomfortably in my chest, but I still manage to smile back at the bookstore manager.

I'm overthinking it. I just have to remember that this is all part of Ace's act. Nothing more, nothing less.

23

T-MINUS 19 DAYS

"No, Ahmed, just hold on to my hand," Ace says, only for me to fall again, hitting the cold ice with a painful thud.

Mia and her girlfriend, Daniela, laugh at me from a few feet away, and I groan. "Just leave me here to die."

From above me, Ace looks like every parent's nightmare. Tall, dark, and handsome with a giggling problem. Or maybe that's just my nightmare.

Or a dream come true, whispers a traitorous voice in my head.

"We're all in this together," Ace says firmly, reaching down to grab one of my hands, even though I resist.

"You just quoted *High School Musical* at me. What kind of bad boy *are* you?"

Ace gives up and crouches down beside me instead. "I'm not a bad boy just because I wear a leather jacket," he says, shaking his head. "And maybe I cut classes a few times. But that's it. You know, half the time that I'm not at school, it's for a piano competition, so the school faculty knows about it.

I've even won quite a few trophies for Midland High. I think that disqualifies me from being a 'bad boy,' Ahmed."

His hand is still holding mine. It's nice and warm, comforting in a way it shouldn't be.

"Ace, there's no point in denying it." I finally sit up. "Everyone knows the truth."

Ace laughs, throwing his head back. A warmth blooms in my chest, almost as if my heart is swelling from how ridiculously content I feel in this moment.

It's weird. It's really, really weird. I don't want it to go away.

I hold my other hand toward Ace. "Come on, show me how to ice skate. Otherwise I'll have to ask Mia."

Ace laughs again but takes my other hand, pulling me to my feet. I knock into his chest once I'm standing, but he wraps his arms around me to keep me from slipping again.

"You have to be more careful," he says, tapping my nose. "But you know what? I think we can work through this. Or maybe work, work, work it out. Something like that."

I gape at him. "Was that another *High School Musical* reference?"

"Don't let him fool you, he knows all the words by heart," Mia says as she skates closer to us. Daniela is holding her hand but neither of them are in danger of falling like I am. "Every time I have a marathon, he joins me. He even knows how to play some of the songs on piano."

I give Ace an incredulous look. "Who *are* you?"

Ace shrugs, a smirk tugging at his lips as he runs his fingers through his hair. "The man of your dreams, obviously."

"Does that work for you?" Mia asks, raising an eyebrow before looking at me. "Karina, you've got to raise your standards. You can't let my brother get away with saying shit like that."

"Oh, trust me, I don't," I say, shoving gently at Ace's chest.

All that accomplishes is me having to flail until I reach the metal bar at the edge of the rink.

Mia and Daniela are laughing again, but there's fondness infused in their expressions that stops me from feeling embarrassed. It helps that Ace is watching me with his own fond look.

"You're a safety hazard to yourself," Ace says, skating over effortlessly. "Come on, take my hand."

Before I do, I remember the threatening texts Nandini and Cora sent me earlier and I sigh, taking out my phone. "Before we continue, can you guys take a picture of Ace and me? For Instagram?" I look hopefully at Mia and Daniela.

"Of course," Mia says, expression lighting up as she accepts my phone. "We can do a little photo shoot! Daniela loves photography. Here you go, babe."

Daniela grabs the phone from Mia, eyes bright with delight. "We'll have to skate to the other side. There's better lighting there."

She and Mia take off before I can protest that I don't care about the lighting. "I'm not going to make it over there for another ten minutes," I complain, judging the distance between us and them.

"I've got you," Ace says, squeezing my hand. A jolt goes down my spine, strange and unfamiliar. "Just don't let go of me."

I nod my agreement, and he pulls us toward the other side of the rink. Halfway there, Ace gives me a contemplative look. "I didn't peg you as the type to post stuff like this on Instagram."

"I'm not," I say, biting my bottom lip as I search for a lie that isn't *I panicked about whether this was a date and got manipulated by my best friends into treating it like one.* "Cora and Nandini threatened to…murder me, if I didn't post a picture of me ice skating on there."

Ace raises an eyebrow. "They care that much about ice skating?"

"I guess so," I say under my breath. Wait. Is Ace asking because he doesn't *want* to be in a photo with me?

After he let me follow his Instagram, I looked through his profile. It's all but barren, except for one picture of the night sky. The location is Istanbul, Turkey, and the only person tagged is someone named Ben Wang. Probably the same Ben that Ace mentioned the other day.

Mine at least has pictures of Nandini, Cora, and me doing stupid things and the occasional selfie when they coerce me into posting one. "Do you not want to be in the photo?" I ask. "You don't have to be."

"No, I don't mind," Ace says, his gaze still thoughtful. "Will you send me the pictures when you're done?"

I squint. "For what?"

He takes one of my hands and raises it above my head. I don't understand what he's trying to do until he spins me around in a slow circle. Not far from us, I hear the sound of a camera shutter go off.

"To remember," he says as he turns me back toward him. "There's something magical about this moment I don't ever want to forget."

I think Ace is trying to kill me. That's the only explanation for why he keeps saying things like *that* and expecting me to have an appropriate response aside from slipping and breaking a bone.

I swallow roughly, my heart stuttering in my throat. "Okay. I'll send them."

Another clicking sound draws my attention to Daniela, who's on one knee, my phone tilted up toward us. She smiles when she catches my eye. "Ready for a mini photo shoot?"

Ace looks at me expectantly. I bite the inside of my cheek and nod. "As ready as I'll ever be."

Later, I lie on my couch, staring at my phone with wide eyes. My homework sits in front of me untouched. I'm too busy looking at my last Instagram post, which has nearly two hundred likes. That's basically *all* of the people who follow me.

"This is unbelievable," I say under my breath.

I let only people I know and trust follow my account, and I've never been more grateful for that than right now.

If this picture somehow got back to my parents, I would be done for. I don't even let *Samir* follow me for that reason alone.

I scroll through my feed, trying to discern why all of these people are suddenly showing an interest in my life and why they're commenting on my picture saying:

ugh cuties :(((absolutely outsold

#RelationshipGoals

INVENTED LOVE AND PHOTOGRAPHY??? (That one is Mia. Of course it is. She requested to follow me immediately after the ice skating date.)

so happy for you both ♥

WE HAVE TO STAN!!!

#karstair DID invent love, you're so right. (And that one is Cora. I shouldn't have expected anything else.)

waiting for my wedding invitation! (Just for that, Nandini isn't getting an invitation to my actual wedding, whoever it's with.)

you look beautiful (A comment from @AlistairClyde. The comment itself has thirty likes. I don't know what to make of it, but it's causing strange feelings to blossom inside me and flutter in my stomach.)

As I'm liking comments, my phone lights up with a call from my mother. All the butterflies in my stomach plummet as I debate whether to pick up.

Eventually, I give in, sliding my thumb across the screen. My mother looks back at me, her eyes squinted. "Myra!"

"As-salaam alaikum, Ma," I say, clearing my throat. "How are you?"

"Wa-alaikum salaam. I'd be better if you picked up the phone more often," she says pointedly and I wince, lowering my gaze. "What has you so busy?"

"Just school," I say, wondering how to shift the topic when I notice her henna. "Oh, your mehndi looks so good! Who did it?"

"Your cousin Zahra," Ma says, holding her hand out so I can see the design better. I'm always so impressed by the talent Bangladeshi artists have. Every year, I await Eid eagerly, for many reasons, but especially for the clothes, jewelry, and henna designs. "She's trying to teach me, but..." She holds out her other hand where the design looks as if it was drawn by a three-year-old.

I try not to laugh.

Ma sighs. "It's awful, isn't it?"

"No, it's great," I say through muffled giggles. She levels me with a flat look, and I grin. "Practice makes perfect?"

"I suppose," she says, considering her hands before looking up, scrutinizing me. "There's something different about you."

All my amusement dies. "Is there?"

She tilts her head, her eyebrows knitting together. "Did you change your skin routine?"

I roll with it immediately. "Yes," I say, nodding. Ever since my mom started working in a dermatology office as a receptionist, she's been hyperaware of skin products. "Cora's mom brought some face wash from her last business trip. My skin feels so rejuvenated."

"Which brand is it?" Ma asks curiously.

"Uh. Good question." I scratch my head. "I can't remember. I'll text you a picture later tonight, when I'm applying it." *Translation: I will text Cora begging for help.*

Ma nods, as if satisfied. "How is everything else? Baba told me you wanted to invite Cora and Nandini over?"

I nod slowly, trying not to look too overeager. "Can I? It's been so long since they last came over."

She hums. "Only if you clean the *entire* house. Promise?"

"Promise," I say, flashing her a shaky thumbs-up. "I'll start after I finish my precalc homework."

"Mashallah," my mother says, a smile spreading across her face. "I'm glad to see you're working hard."

Another nagging stab of guilt. "I try my best."

Our conversation ends soon after that, and I exhale deeply, trying to get rid of the lingering unease.

A text from Ace flashes across my screen.

Alistair Clyde:
i showed my mom ur insta post and she says we make a cute couple. i'm inclined to agree...

I grin despite myself. I'm obvs bringing the cute to the table... what's your contribution???

"Myra?"

I look up. Dadu stands over me holding a small bowl of rosogolla, spongy white sweets in sugary syrup. It's one of my favorite desserts, and it lightens the load on my shoulders.

I sit up and reach for it. She offers me a spoon before sitting beside me on the couch. "Thank you," I say.

"You look happy today," Dadu says as I take a bite.

I smile faintly, gesturing toward the bowl. "Well, you made rosogolla."

She shakes her head, eyes trailing over my expression. "No, not because of that. When you came in today, there was something different about you. Your steps seem lighter."

I shake my head, laughing. "What are you talking about?"

Dadu reaches for the bowl instead of answering. I let her take it without complaint and smile when she tries to feed me. I part my lips, and she gives me a large serving, causing my cheeks to puff out.

"I don't know why, but you're happy, Myra. I'm glad to see it. You deserve it."

I try to speak through my food but don't quite manage it.

Dadu smiles and wipes the side of my mouth with her saree. "I'm happy for you."

She leaves the bowl on the table and stands before I can finish chewing, making her way back to the kitchen. I stare after her retreating figure in bemusement.

After I finish my dessert, I open up Snapchat and look at myself in the front camera, trying to discern whether there's something noticeably different about my face.

I don't see anything, so I put it off to familial love. I'm the same girl I've always been.

As I'm closing the app, I get another text from Ace.

Alistair Clyde:
pls send me the pics?

Me:
hold onnnn

Me:
[14 attachments]

There's no response, which is unexpected, given that Ace usually replies within minutes.

Except then I get the strangest notification of my life.

@AlistairClyde tagged you in a photo.

Oh no.

I open Instagram incredulously. Staring back at me is one of the pictures Daniella took earlier today. It's the one where Ace is spinning me and I'm staring up at him, entirely overwhelmed.

There's a reddish tint to my face, as close to a blush as I can get with my brown skin. Ace is staring down at me, his expression cool, but there's an intensity in his gaze that causes my breath to stutter even now.

The caption of the photo is: *magic…*

I remember his words from earlier; *There's something magical about this moment I don't ever want to forget.*

The longer I look at the photo, the more I focus on myself rather than Ace. I think I might know what Dadu was talking about. I think I might know what my *mother* was talking about.

There's something different about me here, visible in the lines of my expression. I don't know how to put it into words, but maybe my grandma already did. I look happier.

Am I happier?

Is this what happiness feels like?

I don't have the answer, but that doesn't mean I can't find it. T-19 days until my parents come home and all of this ends. That's not nearly enough time, but it has to be.

24

T-MINUS 18 DAYS

After ten minutes of Cora and Nandini giving me pointed looks and giggling whenever Ace so much as glances my way, I drag him to the library to study instead. I thought that since it was first period, we could have a more leisure-based study session with my friends, but I underestimated how chaotic they can be.

Ace completely ruins the five seconds of peace I've acquired when he opens his mouth. "Wasn't yesterday fun?"

Yes, I want to say. *I wish we could have lived in that moment forever.*

Instead I sigh, sliding *The Great Gatsby* across the table. "I *guess*, but we have to study, Ace."

"Oh, so you're back to being boring," he says with a pout, but there's a teasing light in his eye.

"Shut up," I say, tapping the book pointedly. I can't think about the fact that, every time I look at him, my heart skips a beat. "You have to pass the English Regents."

"After all the hard work you've put in, I don't see how I could fail," he says but obligingly takes the book.

"I've tutored you for a week and a half," I say, shaking my head. Saying the time frame puts a lot of our interactions into perspective. I've clearly been spending too much time with him. "You're not ready to pass the Regents if you still can't focus on a book for more than ten minutes."

"I can focus on a book for more than ten minutes," he says. He even has the audacity to look fake offended as he unwraps a lollipop.

"Yeah?" I raise my eyebrows at him. "Prove it."

"I will," Ace says, a determined set to his lips. He cracks open the book and flips to the first page while sucking on his lollipop. The *first* page. Oh my God.

I leave him to his own devices, taking out the study guide I prepared for this week's sessions.

Ten minutes later, I look up, expecting him to be doodling on the table or staring at me. Instead, there's a furrow to his brows and his eyes are focused on the page. His lips are moving faintly around the lollipop, as if he's mouthing along to the words.

I've never seen this serious look on his face before. He flips to the next page without glancing up and continues reading.

I look away. If Ace is reading, if Ace is actually *studying*, this might be the best development yet. I don't want to ruin it by distracting him.

Another ten minutes pass as I work on some of my own stuff. When I look up again, one of his legs is pressed against his chest, bent at the knee, book resting atop it. He's reading with a thoughtful expression on his face, stormy eyes narrowed with focus.

I start smiling. I can't help it. This is the longest I've seen Ace pay attention during our tutoring sessions and the most earnest I've seen his efforts.

As if he can feel me watching him, he looks up, and our

eyes lock across the table. There's a moment of strange silence where we're just gazing at each other, but then he smiles back at me. His eyes are warm and familiar, and his grin is wide and sweet.

He's beautiful.

Oh. *Oh.*

Oh no.

My cheeks burn, and I look back down at my work, trying to temper my expression, but it's not going well. I glance up surreptitiously for half a second and find that his attention has turned back to the book. It's almost worse than if he was looking at me.

We're fake dating. I know that. It's all a pretense.

And yet, despite knowing that, I think I might have feelings for Ace Clyde. *Real* feelings.

This is really, really bad.

At the start of English, Ace passes me a brown paper bag. I look inside curiously, only to find a slice of cheesecake.

My lips part, my heart caught in my throat. "When did you get this?"

He shrugs, which almost certainly means he skipped part of his last class to get me dessert. There's something seriously wrong with him.

Yet my skin is warming all the same.

"Consider it my late promposal," he says, grinning. "Have to convince you to go past three weeks, right?"

There isn't enough air in my lungs.

"Right," I echo.

Nandini and Cora sit in front of us now that they're aware of the whole situation, but when Cora catches sight of me blushing, I wish they were anywhere else.

"Group chat, *now*," Cora says, and I sigh as I slip out my phone, hiding it behind my binder.

Ace doesn't seem to notice, his eyes focused on the white-board for once. Ugh, of course he is. Why is he doing this to me? For some reason beyond my understanding, him paying attention to school makes me feel *strange*.

Cora Zhang-Agreste:
KARINA IS BLUSHING WHAT IS HAPPENING

Nandini Kaur:
WHAT

Nandini glances back at me, and my cheeks burn even more, blood rushing up so fast that I have to suck in a deep breath to keep calm. Ace looks me over, his expression twisting with concern, and he rests a hand on my elbow.

I don't want to admit it, but his concern kind of helps. I offer him a small, grateful smile, and feel both Cora and Nandini's gazes sharpen on the side of my head.

Welp.

Me:
STOP STARING AT ME OMG WHAT IS WRONG
WITH YOU BOTH PAY ATTENTION TO THE
LESSON

Cora Zhang-Agreste:
wHY ARE YOU BLUSHING? WHAT'S IN THE BAG?
DID HE BRING CONDOMS?

Me:
WHAT? oh my god no he did not bring CONDOMS
what is wrong with you we're FAKE dating

Nandini Kaur:
so What's In The Bag

Cora Zhang-Agreste:
I've legit never seen u blush this is wild UR LITER-
ALLY TURNING RED???

Me:
omg stop please tell me ur joking

Nandini Kaur:
well...

Me:
he literally just brought me cheesecake!! it's not
that deep

Cora Zhang-Agreste:
and yet you're getting flustered...

Cora Zhang-Agreste:
why??????

Me:
STOP it's not that serious omg

Me:
he just said it was a late promposal

Nandini Kaur:
AND UR BLUSHING BC...? TRY AND TELL ME U
DON'T LIKE HIM

Me:
DOES IT MATTER? HE'S WHITE!!!!!!!

Cora Zhang-Agreste:
WHAT DO YOU *MEAN*

Nandini Kaur:
YEAH. HE'S WHITE. BUT LIKE??? PERHAPS THIS
ONE (1) SINGULAR WHITE BOY IS WORTH YOUR
TIME

Me:
that's not what I meant

Me:
my parents would MURDER me if I even THOUGHT
about a white boy

Me:
I told you guys before

Me:
no dating allowed. highkey wouldn't be surprised
if their plan is to find me a "perfect" husband after
college

Cora Zhang-Agreste:
that's a dumbass plan...

Cora Zhang-Agreste:
anyway! they don't need to know!!!!!!!!

Me:
you know it's not that easy

Me:
I just can't

Me:
even if I liked ace it would never work out

Me:
we don't have a future together

Nandini Kaur:
it's high school you don't NEED to have a future together

Cora Zhang-Agreste:
in all seriousness forget about ace for a minute

Cora Zhang-Agreste:
this isn't about some random white boy

Cora Zhang-Agreste:
this is about you!!!

Cora Zhang-Agreste:
I know there's obvs a lot I don't understand bc of
our cultural differences and stuff. but you know
what I do know?

Cora Zhang-Agreste:
you deserve to be happy

Me:
I don't want to talk about this anymore. can we
please pay attention to the lesson?

I flip my phone over and look at the whiteboard. My skin
is crawling and the room feels like it's shrinking around me.
Ten, nine, eight, seven, six, five, four, three, two, one.
Ten, nine, eight, seven, six, five, four, three, two, one.

Ten, nine, eight, seven, six, five, four, three, two, one.

The bell rings, jarring me out of my slow counting. I'm thrown for a moment. How did the class go by that fast?

"Hey, Karina," Nandini says, coming to stand in front of me. She's biting her lip. "Sorry about earlier. I know it's not our business. It's just—we want what's best for you. You're our best friend."

I shake my head. "It's fine." My voice is weaker than I want it to be, and Nandini's expression falls further. "I think I'm going to have lunch on my own today. I need some fresh air."

Cora comes up behind Nandini, frowning. "We're really sorry, Karina. Are you sure you don't want us to come with you?"

"It's fine," I say again, lowering my gaze. "Next time, okay?"

"Okay," Nandini says, reaching forward to squeeze my hand. Cora's hand comes on top of hers. The weight is heavy. Usually, it would be comforting, and I *am* grateful to my friends for being so understanding about my anxiety, but right now it just feels like too much. Just having someone touch me is causing nausea to bubble up inside my stomach.

"Love you," Cora says, retracting her hand after seeing my face.

"Love you," I say and pull my hand back into the safety of my lap.

Nandini sighs but nods at Cora, gesturing toward the door. They leave after one last glance at me.

I completely forget Ace is sitting next to me until he raps his knuckles against my seat. "What's going on?"

"I'm just not feeling well," I say quietly, willing him to understand.

Ace observes my expression. "Is there anything I can do?"

I shake my head. "I—" My voice falters. "I'll see you later for our studying session, okay?"

I pack my things, carefully tucking away the brown paper bag. Ace doesn't protest as I leave. I'm glad. How can I speak to him right now, knowing that if I ever act on the feelings sprouting in my chest, we're doomed to a relationship full of lies and secrets?

we'll pretend it's a game of lost and found
or maybe even hide-and-seek
and perhaps for a while
in the darkness of the night
it will be enough
until the sun comes bursting from the east
and we fall to the flames

25

T-MINUS 18 DAYS

I wander through the halls after gym class, my mind a haze of colors. I'm supposed to head toward the library for my tutoring session with Ace, but my feet seem to have a different plan.

Somehow, I end up in a staircase, my back against a radiator and my gaze somewhere far above me.

I can't stop thinking about what Cora and Nandini said. *You deserve to be happy.* Just yesterday, Dadu said I look happy.

But does this brand of happiness fit in my life? Can I *have* it? Am I allowed to?

Since childhood, I've always tried so hard to make my parents proud. If that meant behaving the way they wanted, then I did. If that meant cutting television time to study math and science, then I did. If that meant staying home while all my other friends went to each other's houses, then I did.

Everything they've asked of me, I've given. I've given and I've given and I've *given*, and I continue to give. But it's never enough. There's never a limit to what they ask of me.

There's never a limit to what I'm willing to give.

All the years flash through my mind rapidly, and a horrible feeling rises in my chest, pushing up and up, battering against my rib cage and spreading through my lungs. It creeps up my throat, past the God-awful lump that I can't get rid of, and through my veins.

Tears pool in my eyes and I suck in a deep breath, trying to hold them back, but they spill anyway, wet and hot, sliding down my cheeks.

I know everything that my parents have done for me. I know how much they sacrificed for me to be able to live in New York, to live in a house, to go to a good school. They uprooted their whole life so I could have these opportunities. I know all of that. I know they want me to do well in life.

But sometimes I wonder if they want me to do well for me, or if they want me to do well for them. If all my accomplishments are for their pleasure, rather than mine.

How can they justify everything I've had to go through? All the times they stripped my freedom from me? How could that have been for me?

It's small things that become bigger and bigger. It's the fact I'm terrified to wear shorts, because even flashing an ankle is dangerous in my household. It's the fact Samir can be as loud and bold as he wants, and I'm expected to be quiet and compliant. It's the fact that I can't go anywhere without some kind of parental supervision and, if I do, I face being berated for hours and then locked away in my room to wither in silence.

It's the fact that I'm expected to be this perfect daughter that I don't know how to be.

It's the fact that, for the first time in my life, I have freedom because they're not here to watch over me, and it's the best I've ever felt. It's the fact that Ace smiles at me when he thinks I can't see him, and pokes and prods at me, but is always thoughtful when I need him to be. It's the fact that my

friends want to go to junior prom, and a boy I like *asked* me
to go with him, but I don't know if I can. It's the fact that I
love English more than anything, but I can't pursue it in college because I'm expected to become a doctor.

And for what? So they can gloat about it to their coworkers? To their friends? To the people at our mosque? To the
rest of my extended family? Why do those people have more
of a stake in what I do with my future than I do?

Why am I selfish if I want to do what I love? It's my life and
my future. Not my parents'. Mine. They gave me the tools to
be here, but that shouldn't mean that they get to make every
choice for me.

I'm not a bad person for wanting a life different than what's
expected of me. I'm not a bad person for wanting to pursue
something I love.

I'm not a bad person for *wanting*. But I feel like I am.

Because I don't want to let them down. I want them to look
at me with love and pride. Not disappointment. I want to be
as perfect in their eyes as Samir.

I've known for a while that I can't have both. I can't live
my life the way I want and still expect my parents to love me.

There's this suffocating pressure on my shoulders, this suffocating weight of my parents' expectations, and I don't have
the strength to lift it up.

I am not Atlas, born to carry the weight of the world
I am Icarus, wanting and wanting and wanting
at the risk of exploding when I fly too close to the sun

Happiness. Such a simple word, and yet the most difficult
word I've ever had to hold in my hands. If happiness were a
bird, it would be fluttering weakly, its heartbeat so faint that
it disappears when you look away.

For the first time, I'm looking and I can hear it. *Thump, thump, thump.* But I don't know if it's mine to have. It's so close, yet so immeasurably far away.

I stare at my empty palms through blurry eyes, wondering what would happen if I choose to nurture this bird. This small seed of happiness.

You deserve to be happy.

But what if what would make me happy is to live my life the way I want without disappointing my parents? What if I want to get an English degree *and* I want my dad to pat me on the back with a smile on his face, and my mom to cry happy tears when I accomplish my dreams?

Why can't I have both? Why do I have to choose one or the other?

"Karina."

Through a thick wave of tears, I blink up at the person standing in front of me. Warm hands cup my face, thumbs wiping the tears away.

"Karina."

Ace's stormy eyes are looking back at me. "Hey," he says quietly. "You need to breathe, okay?"

Am I holding my breath? I inhale sharply and then exhale. Some of the tension in my chest releases.

I take rapid breaths, trying to fill my lungs, but what little control I have slips away fast. Before I know it, I'm heaving.

Ace shakes me lightly. "Karina, follow me. In and out. Watch me."

I look at him, half-hysterical. He starts taking exaggerated breaths, puffing out his chest before exhaling.

"In and out. Come on."

I try to follow along, watching the rise and fall of his chest, and my breathing slowly evens out. Tears still fall down my cheeks, but I blink past them to focus on Ace.

"Sorry," I choke out.

"No," Ace says, his thumbs swiping underneath my eyes again. "Don't ever apologize to me for this."

Ace finally lets go and sits down beside me. When he leads my head to rest on his shoulder, I'm too tired to refuse.

"You're okay, Karina," he says against my hair.

I nod, trying to believe that. I'm okay. My life isn't over. If I have to pursue medicine, then I'll pursue medicine. I'm not *dying*. My parents aren't asking for something unforgivable.

I close my eyes and turn my face into Ace's shoulder, focusing on my breathing.

His hand runs through my hair, careful and soothing. "Hey," Ace says. "I have something for you."

I blink my eyes open. In his free hand, he's holding a packet of Sour Patch Kids.

A choked laugh slips past my lips. "You remembered."

"I'd never forget anything about you," he murmurs. "Here."

He rips open the top and hands it to me. I sniffle gratefully and take the packet.

"Thank you," I say. A part of me is embarrassed at losing it like this in front of Ace. The bigger part of me is glad it's him and not some random stranger. His presence has somehow become comforting. Only Nandini and Cora feel this familiar to me.

Ace doesn't respond, but he hums against the top of my head. We sit in silence, and it doesn't feel uncomfortable or forced. It feels as natural as anything else.

I don't know how much time passes, but once I finish the packet of Sour Patch Kids, I sit up properly, scrubbing at my face. I can't imagine how disastrous I look. I don't want to know, frankly.

"I'll walk you home," Ace says.

I look at him in surprise. "You don't have to do that."

He shrugs. "I want to. Come on." He offers me a hand up and I take it, rubbing my nose with my sleeve.

"What about your car?"

Ace looks away, his lips pressed together. "I don't have it right now. My dad took away my keys."

I falter, searching his expression. "What happened?"

"Just Xander," Ace says quietly before shaking his head. "Don't worry about it."

"But how will you get home?" I ask. "You don't have to walk me—"

"I want to," he says again, squeezing my shoulder. "I'll call my dad's chauffeur to pick me up. It's not a big deal, I swear."

I open my mouth to protest, not wanting him to brave the cold any more than he has to, especially not for me. It's mid-March, but it's still chilly outside.

Before I can say anything, he gently claps a hand over my mouth. "No, Ahmed."

I sigh, conceding defeat. I don't have the energy to hold an argument anyway. "Okay. If you're sure."

Ace slings my bag over his shoulder before I can and gestures for me to go ahead.

We walk out of school together, and I can't help but notice the curious looks slanted our way by some familiar juniors. I wipe at my face again self-consciously, but Ace tugs my hand down, interlacing it with his.

I inhale quietly in surprise, staring down at our joined fingers. My entire arm feels like it's buzzing, electricity running up and down my veins.

"Fuck off," Ace says darkly to the people still watching us. Everyone quickly averts their gaze.

I push past my shock to squeeze his hand in thanks, and he squeezes back.

As I expected, it's cold outside. I glance sideways at Ace,

my cheeks warming. "You don't have to walk me home. It's really windy."

"Are you cold?" he asks, furrowing his brows. "God, I didn't even realize. You're only wearing a sweater. Here."

"That's not what I—"

Ace shrugs off his leather jacket and holds it out to me. I stare at it, uncomprehending. There's no way Ace is offering me his leather jacket right now.

"Take it," he says, waving it in my direction.

"Now *you're* only wearing a sweater," I say, still staring at the jacket.

"I run warm," he says, shrugging. "And you just had an anxiety attack. I think you need it more than I do."

Oh. He's caught on to the fact I have anxiety. I guess I wasn't really going out of my way to hide it, but even my parents have failed to pick up on it. Hell, *I* didn't even realize until a few months ago.

I'm not ashamed of it. I *refuse* to be, but I'm still shocked at how easily he's accepting it. I know the type of person Ace is, and I don't think he'd ever call me crazy or dismiss me, but I still expect *something* to go wrong. If my own parents would look down on me for having anxiety, there's every possibility Ace might, too.

Another spur of nerves runs through me, a creeping terror that this will affect his outlook of me even if he doesn't say anything, but Ace keeps looking at me with the same steady expression he always has.

The longer I look at him, the easier I can breathe.

"Thank you," I finally say, slipping my arms into the sleeves of the jacket. It's large on my frame, hanging to midthigh. There's also a familiar scent to it that I never fully picked up on from Ace. Now that I'm basking in it, I recognize it.

He smells like cinnamon. It's faint, but it's there.

Neither of us says anything as we walk, but our hands brush against each other until Ace finally reaches out and intertwines our fingers again.

I stare at our hands, unable to tear my gaze away. There's no one here except the two of us. No one to pretend for.

By the time we find our way to my house, it's later than I expected. The sun is slowly setting, the sky a mix of pinks, oranges, and blues.

We stop on my porch, and a sense of disappointment washes over me. I wish I could spend the entire night walking around aimlessly with Ace, comforted by our mutual silence.

But...maybe another day. Maybe there's a balance here. Maybe I can't pursue English, but I can have this in secret for the little time I have left.

"Well, this is it, I guess," I say, shrugging off the leather jacket and passing it back to him. I miss its weight and smell as soon as I take it off. "Thank you for walking me home."

Ace nods and cards his fingers through my hair one last time. I hold my breath when he leans forward and brushes his lips against my forehead. "Good night, Karina."

"Good night, Ace," I say, my pulse fluttering in my neck, an offbeat rhythm spurred by his touch.

I wait for him to leave and watch until he turns the corner before I slump against my door, suddenly exhausted. That wasn't how I expected my day to go.

But maybe in the dust of lingering defeat, there's room for some victory.

26

T-MINUS 17 DAYS

I completely give up on attending school the next morning.

After my alarm goes off, I stare at the ceiling for approximately ten seconds before I call it quits. My emotions are too overwrought to deal with people today. "Dadu!"

Not even a moment later, my grandma opens the door, her expression tinged with concern. "What's wrong, Myra?"

"I'm not feeling well," I say. It helps that I still look like a disaster.

Dadu makes a worried noise and comes into my room, pressing the back of her hand against my forehead. "Ya Allah, you're burning up," she says. Before I can say anything, she leaves, presumably to grab a thermometer.

Samir appears in my doorway, raising an eyebrow. He's holding some kind of strange robotic contraption in his arms and has his backpack slung across his shoulder. "Ditching? Imagine what Ma and Baba will say."

"Shut up," I say halfheartedly. "You've ditched school for *video games* before. I don't wanna hear it."

"Touché." He considers me, and the amusement falls from his expression. "Do you have a math test or something? You should've texted me. I would've come home from work earlier last night if you needed help."

Despite everything, I smile. "No, but thanks. I'm good."

Dadu reappears, waving the thermometer haphazardly. "Myra, sit up. Let me see."

"That would be my cue to leave," Samir says, grinning as he waves a hand. "See you later, Dadu. Later, slacker."

I roll my eyes as he leaves and Dadu comes to take my temperature. It's only slightly above average, but she still asks, "Do you need to go to the doctor?"

I shake my head. "Just one day of rest, I think."

This would *never* work with my parents, but Dadu likes to give everyone the benefit of the doubt. The stories of my father's childhood in Bangladesh sound like heaven—tales of him and his brothers playing hooky and skipping school to go to the beach, where they'd spend hours lying in the sun and fooling around. He usually leaves his late sister out of those stories. I don't blame him, but it makes me sad.

Maybe the loss of his sister made him more restrictive, the same way that it made Dadu more lenient. People react to grief differently.

I think being around my mom has furthered that restrictive behavior, since my maternal grandparents are a lot more strict than Dadu. Nanu and Nana have never been anything but kind to me, sending me gifts and the like, but I know they're the reason Ma expects so much from me. They raised her a certain way, and now she's trying to raise me the same way, even though our generations are vastly different. It's hard sometimes to separate my parents' beliefs from my culture and my religion, but at the end of the day, I know it has nothing to do with being Bangladeshi or being Muslim. Blaming it on either of those would be turning to a scapegoat. They both make me who I am.

I love Bangladeshi culture—from the lyrical poetry to the hearty food to the breathtaking fashion. And I find comfort in being Muslim, in praying, in believing. In my heart, I know that Allah loves me, no matter what. If only I could say the same for my parents.

Dadu pats my cheek. "Go back to sleep. I'll make chai and we can have a movie marathon later."

"Thank you, Dadu. I'd love that," I say and burrow into my blankets. Before I fall back asleep, I shoot Nandini and Cora a quick text saying: I'll be absent today :(I'm not feeling well, sorry guys!!!

At least next week is spring break. I just have to survive tomorrow, and then I'll have a whole week to myself.

I wake up around 10:00 a.m. and stumble into the dining room, a blanket around my shoulders. Dadu frets over me for a few minutes but then leaves me to eat.

After I finish breakfast, I take my chai and sit down next to Dadu in the living room. I take a moment to light a cinnamon-scented candle before I open Netflix to find a Bollywood film.

Dadu lets me choose without complaint. I click on *Kal Ho Naa Ho*, in the mood to cry over someone else's life. As the main character, Naina, starts her monologue about New York, I lean my head against my grandma's bony shoulder and toss a second blanket over our laps.

"I'm not as crazy as Naina's Dadi, right?" Dadu asks, glancing down at me as the grandmother character starts singing, horribly off-key.

"Not even," I say, patting her hand. "You're the coolest Dadu in the world." I pause. "But maybe don't start a singing career."

Dadu laughs. "I see. Should I refrain from setting you up with strange men, too?"

"*Please* never do that," I say, only half-joking. "There are enough strange men in my life."

Dadu raises an eyebrow but thankfully doesn't push the subject. If she did, I would've just mentioned Samir and my father, but she seems to know better than to ask.

Halfway through the movie, the doorbell rings.

I sit up, confused. It's barely noon, and our mail doesn't get delivered until three. It's probably a solicitor.

I'm about to sink back into the couch when the doorbell rings again, followed by someone knocking.

"Do you want me to see?" Dadu asks.

I shake my head. I don't want her to strain herself to understand English if I can help it. I stand up, keeping my blanket wrapped around my shoulders. "I'll be right back."

When I open the door, my grip on the blanket goes slack, and it falls to the floor. I must be hallucinating. The cinnamon-scented candle has to be playing tricks on my brain. "What are you doing here?"

Ace smiles at me from the other side of the door, holding a large brown paper bag. "I brought soup."

"*What?*"

"Your friends told me you were sick," he explains. "I thought I'd drop by."

I shake my head, aghast. "What about school? You can't skip class!"

Ace gestures to his side, and I realize he's carrying a book bag. For the first time *ever*. "I brought my notes. We can study."

My expression twists in disbelief. "You skipped school to study for school."

Ace snaps his fingers, nodding. "Now you get it."

Before I can comment, a warm hand situates my blanket on my shoulders again and I look back to see Dadu standing there, examining Ace.

"Myra, who's this?"

"As-salaam alaikum!" Ace says which is enough to give me a head rush. Did he just say *salaam* to my grandma? "You must be Karina's grandmother. It's so nice to meet you. I'm Alistair Clyde."

"Oh my God," I say under my breath. I can't believe he showed up here. My one relief is that my parents are far, *far* away, otherwise my head would already be on a pike on the lawn.

Dadu raises her eyebrows. "Wa-alaikum salaam." Even though she's far from fluent, she definitely knows enough English to understand Ace's introduction. Still, she continues in Bengali, "Myra, is he your friend?"

"Kind of?" I say, offering her an uncertain look. "I can tell him to go."

"No," Dadu says, and she *smiles*. The relief I feel at the up-turn of her lips is enough to unlock my muscles. "He can come inside. I'll start preparing lunch."

"But...our movie marathon," I say, glancing back at the television from the doorway.

She pats my cheek fondly. "There will be other movie marathons," she says before disappearing in the direction of the kitchen.

"What's the verdict? Does she like me?" Ace asks. "Can I come in?"

I shake my head, incredulous, but open the door wider. "I guess so. Did you really say as-salaam alaikum to her, or did I hallucinate that?"

"I Googled proper etiquette for addressing Muslim elders

on my way here," he admits, running a hand through his dark, unruly hair. "Did I butcher the pronunciation?"

"Surprisingly, no." I lead the way into my living room after Ace takes off his boots. "Welcome to my humble abode. Except mine is actually humble compared to your mansion."

He snorts. "It's not a mansion."

"You're not allowed to have an opinion." I take my seat on the couch again. I wiggle my foot toward the other couch, but Ace sits down next to me. I don't know why I even bothered.

"Watch yourself," I warn him lightly. He raises his eyebrows and I add, "My grandma could come back any second."

His response is to smirk, which is far from reassuring, but he makes a point of scooting over a few inches.

I sigh, shaking my head at him. I'd be more worried if Dadu hadn't invited Ace into our home, but as it stands, he's already here. So long as he keeps his hands to himself, it'll be fine.

I hope.

"Where'd she go anyway?" he asks, glancing toward the dining room. "Did I scare her away?"

"You give yourself too much credit," I say, leaning back in my seat. "She went to make lunch."

"But I brought soup," Ace says, bemused.

"That's a liquid," I say, laughing quietly at the thrown expression on his face. "She's making *real* food."

After a moment, it seems Ace decides not to question it. "So what have you been doing all day?" he asks instead, taking off his leather jacket and draping it across his lap. Underneath is a preppy designer sweater that's sure to heighten my grandma's impression of him.

I gesture to the television. "I've been watching Bollywood films."

"I thought you weren't Indian."

"I'm not. I can still watch Indian movies, asshole," I say,

rolling my eyes. It feels good to settle back into our usual routine.

"Feisty," Ace says, grinning at me. "Are there subtitles?"

"Well, I can't speak Hindi," I say, raising my brows. "So, yes, there are subtitles."

"That was a stupid question," he concedes. "Can you give me a rundown of what's happened so far?"

"Are...are you going to watch with me?" I ask.

He nods. "Yeah. I'm not going to make you change movies because I'm here. What's happened so far?"

"Uh." I rack my brain for a way to summarize the plot, but I'm having difficulty even processing the fact he's willing to sit here and watch a Bollywood film with me. "The main character, Naina, has a dysfunctional family, and she doesn't believe in love or happiness and all that. Then this dude Aman suddenly shows up and brings all this wonderful energy and brightens every aspect of her life by helping her family and friends and her. He encourages her to live life to the fullest and she...falls in love with him because of it."

Ace tilts his head, his eyes searching my expression. I purposefully keep it as blank as possible, because it's hitting me how similar this movie is to my current state of affairs. "Is that it so far?"

"No," I say and clear my throat. The rest of the movie isn't as relatable, thankfully. "Aman is also in love with Naina, but he has a terminal illness. Still, Aman wants her to be happy even when he's gone, so he hatches this plan to make Naina fall in love with her best friend, Rohit, who's also in love with her."

Ace blinks. "That's...rough. Does Aman die?"

I shrug and gesture to the screen. "I guess you'll have to watch and find out."

"What are we waiting for then? Press play."

I hide my smile behind my blanket and hit play.

I start crying not even five minutes later, when Aman reads a speech about loving Naina from Rohit's diary.

Ace looks at me in alarm. "Why are you crying?"

"He—" I sniffle, wiping my nose. "There's nothing in the diary. Those are Aman's real words."

Dadu comes in a moment later, holding out a box of tissues. I immediately gauge how much distance is between me and Ace—thankfully, still a safe amount.

"Be careful with her, she's an ocean," Dadu tells Ace in Bengali, handing him the entire box, before walking off.

He gives me a confused look. "What did she say?"

I laugh, the sound wet and choked off. "She said to be careful. I'm an ocean."

"More tears?" Ace says.

"More tears," I agree.

Ace sighs, leaning farther back into the couch. "He's definitely going to die."

I laugh again and shove his arm after making sure Dadu isn't looking. "Just watch the movie."

As we're watching, Ace's phone keeps buzzing. He glances at it a few times and irritation flickers across his face before he puts it away without replying. I'm tempted to ask, but it's not my business.

One of my favorite dance numbers comes on, and Ace nudges my foot. "How come you never dress up like that?"

I roll my eyes, though I've also been imagining myself in Naina's shimmery lehenga. "She hasn't been dressed up for the *entire* movie, Ace."

"Yeah, but she's dressed up now."

"This is her engagement party!"

"Why didn't you just say that?"

"Say *what*?"

"That someone needs to propose to you in order for you to dress up. You know, technically, I *did* prompose, so maybe you could wear one to prom—"

"Oh my God, be quiet."

Ace makes an *mhmm* sound but mimes zipping his lips shut when I shoot him a glare.

A scene with Aman's doctor comes up, and my skin crawls. It must show on my face, because Ace reaches forward to pause the film. "What's wrong?"

"Nothing," I say.

He frowns. "You're shaking."

I glance at my hand and realize my fingers are trembling. Ugh. I should've been more careful when choosing a film. I'm always extra sensitive the day after an anxiety attack, and things trigger me more easily. Right now, apparently *seeing* a doctor on the screen is enough to make my body protest.

I take a deep breath, trying to inhale the scent of cinnamon in the room. It helps a little. "Um…it's just. Doctors."

"Are you scared of them?" he asks, sounding baffled. His gaze darts to the candle on the table in front of us, and his eyes narrow before he looks back at me. "I thought you were in Pre-Med Society."

I smile faintly. "You would remember that."

"Don't change the subject, Ahmed."

Damn. I wasn't even *trying* to change the subject. I guess we're having this conversation then. "It's just…my parents want me to be a doctor. I don't really want to be one, but I don't think I have much of a choice at this point. It is what it is, I guess."

Ace turns his entire body toward me, his expression uncertain. "What do you mean you don't have a choice?"

I play with a loose thread of my blanket. "It's complicated. I don't want to let my parents down."

"What do *you* want to do?" Ace asks.

"It doesn't matter," I say.

"If it matters to you, it matters," he says softly. "What is it?"

I lean my head against the back of the couch and loll it to the side to look at him. "English. But my parents don't think that's a real degree."

Ace's gaze is heavy. "Why not? What do you want to be when you grow up?"

I laugh hoarsely. "I'm sixteen. I don't have the answer to that. Do you know what you want to be?"

Ace hesitates oddly. "No," he says, and it sounds like a lie. Before I can press, he follows with, "But you're so hardworking and focused. You must have *some* idea what you want to be. A teacher? A journalist? A lawyer?"

I bite my bottom lip, the tiny seedling of a dream eagerly sprouting to life between my ribs. "I think being a teacher would be cool. But I don't know. There are so many options."

"That's a real career, Ahmed. What about that isn't a real career?" Ace asks, his thick brows furrowed in genuine confusion.

I sigh, wishing there was an easy way to explain. Even Nandini and Cora often grow frustrated with me when it comes to this. They insist my dreams of pursuing English are just as valid as any other. I don't know how to say *I know, but who's going to tell my parents that?*

Even now with Ace, I'm empty of words. He's asking because he cares, just like my friends, but at the end of the day, none of it matters.

"It's just not in the cards for me," I say quietly. "Can we continue the movie?"

Ace observes my countenance for a moment before he presses play.

Ten minutes later, I'm bawling as Shah Rukh Khan's character, Aman, runs for his life.

Ace silently passes me three tissues, and I nod gratefully. His phone buzzes and, this time, he flicks the side of the screen, switching it to silent.

Five minutes from the end of the movie, I look over to see that Ace is crying, too. He's not bawling like me, but there's definitely a tear sliding down his cheek.

I want to poke fun at him for it, but it's sweet. He notices me watching him and hastily wipes at his face.

"What?" he asks defensively. "That was sad, Ahmed."

I offer him a watery smile. "Ready to watch another one?"

Ace glances hesitantly at the tissue box. "Will it be *as* sad?"

"Maybe not *as* sad. This one kind of takes the cake."

He nods slowly. "Put it on."

We switch movies and he reaches forward to grab the paper bag he brought, pulling out a container of soup and plastic bowls. "Here, you should try to have some of this before it gets cold."

"You're such a mother hen," I say, the realization causing fondness to spring up inside me.

Ace sticks out his tongue in reply and ladles soup into a bowl for me. He glances at his phone again, and his expression grows darker. When he notices me looking, his features soften and he hands me a spoon. "I hope you like shrimp."

Ten minutes into the movie, I reach forward to pause it.

"What?" Ace asks, looking me over. "Is everything okay?"

I worry my bottom lip between my teeth, trying to figure out how to express my gratitude. Finally, nothing seems to encompass it as wholly as, "Thank you."

His expression shifts with surprise and he tilts his head. "For what?"

I flush, feeling small under his inquisitive gaze. "I don't know. For bringing me soup and watching Bollywood films with me, I guess. Just being you."

Ace looks even more surprised at that. "You're thanking me for being me?"

For the first time in days, I feel shy in front of Ace. I duck my head and offer him a bashful smile. "Yeah, I am. For being you and not who others expect you to be." I shrug, my heart fluttering uncomfortably in my chest.

He's smiling now, his dimples digging craters into his cheeks. I can't help but think I've never seen someone so alarmingly beautiful in my entire life.

"You're kind of wonderful, you know that?" I add unthinkingly. Before I can fumble over my misstep, his grin becomes impossibly wider.

"You're not so bad yourself, Ahmed," Ace says before he checks over my shoulder—for Dadu, probably—then reaches over, taking my hand in his, and squeezing.

Dadu's words about Dada linger in the back of my head, about him turning out to be different from what she expected.

Ace isn't exactly what I had in mind, either.

27

T-MINUS 17 DAYS

We're figuring out a third movie when Dadu calls us for lunch. Ace looks a little wary. I understand why a second later when he whispers, "Is it going to be really spicy?"

I struggle not to laugh. "You're so white," I say, without considering whether I should watch my tongue.

Before I can regret it, Ace sighs and nods. "Mia tells me all the time. So is my tongue going to fall off?"

I snort. "You don't have to eat it if it's too spicy."

Ace gives me a sharp look. "Your grandmother made it. Of course I have to eat it."

"You're ridiculous," I say, grinning. He wants to impress my grandma. I don't know why that makes me so stupidly happy. "I don't eat things that are super spicy."

"So it's...*not* spicy?"

"No, Ace, it's not." Probably. Today would be the day that Dadu decides to throw all caution to the wind in order to spite the random white boy in our house.

It turns out Dadu made pulao with chicken korma on the

side, which is the *best*. Definitely not spicy. Still, I almost wish
I could have seen the look on Ace's face if my grandma had
made shutki.

I move to help Dadu in the kitchen, but Ace waves me
away. "I've got this."

I raise my eyebrows but stay silent as he goes to help my
grandma carry the food to the dining table. I can already hear
her praising him for his manners. Being polite always wins
points with Dadu.

As I sit down, my phone starts ringing with a FaceTime
call from Nandini. I glance at the top of my screen and realize it's almost 4:00 p.m., which means they're out of school.

I hesitate but ultimately pick up. Nandini and Cora's faces
come into view on the screen and they're grinning at me.
"Hey babe, how are you feeling?"

"Better," I say honestly. Being at home and watching feel-
good movies is always helpful and relieving for my anxiety.

"Mrs. Ahmed, this smells incredible," Ace says to my
grandma as they come into the dining room together, her
holding a plate of tuna kebabs and him holding the entire
pot of pulao.

"Thank you, Alistair," Dadu says, using her limited English.

"What did your Dadu just say?" Cora asks, her voice raising several octaves. "Did she just say thank you to someone
named *Alistair*?"

I sigh and turn the camera around, giving them a perfect
view of Dadu and Ace maneuvering around each other as they
set out table mats.

Ace notices the camera and raises his eyebrows at me. Before I can protest, he comes around the other side to lean his
chin on my chair, right behind my shoulder. He flips the camera and waves at Nandini and Cora. "I brought Karina soup."

"I could have made you soup," my grandma says under her breath, making me giggle.

She shoots me a fond look and disappears into the kitchen.

Ace nudges me. "What's so funny?"

"Nothing," I say, trying to keep my expression straight. I don't think I manage, because Ace shakes his head at me, and he's so close his nose brushes my cheek. I hold my breath, my gaze darting to Dadu, but she's too busy washing dishes to pay attention to us. Still, I shift minutely away, tucking my hair behind my ear.

Ace blinks at me, before his eyes lighten with understanding. "Sorry."

"It's okay," I say quietly, offering him a small smile. "She didn't notice."

"If you two are quite finished," Nandini says, drawing my attention back to my phone. "Ace, why didn't you say something? We would've come with you."

I roll my eyes. "He cut class to be here. Please don't follow his example."

Cora whispers something unintelligible to Nandini and then looks dead at the camera. "Ace, can we speak to you privately?"

Ace shrugs. "Sure."

"Wait, what—?"

He grabs the phone out of my hand and walks away. I blink after him in bemusement, but don't protest. I think if I did, they'd just call Ace instead and repeat this all over again.

"I'll see you in five minutes!" Ace says and disappears into the foyer. I hear the sound of the front door opening and shake my head in exasperation.

I start carefully piling food on my plate when something lights up in the corner of my vision. I realize it's Ace's phone, left unattended. I glance at it and freeze, staring at the screen.

He has ten unread texts and three missed calls from his father, twenty unread texts and one missed call from Xander, and one unread text from Mia.

I flip the phone over out of respect for his privacy, but I'm flabbergasted. Why doesn't he call back his family? Has he been ignoring them the whole time he's been here?

Ace returns a few minutes later, a sparkle in his eye as he sits next to me. I frown uncertainly, sliding him his phone. "I think your family is trying to get in touch with you."

He shakes his head, waving dismissively. "Don't worry about it. Here's your phone." He hands it to me. "Damn, Ahmed. Your friends can be terrifying when they want to be."

I stiffen, glancing between my phone and him. No. I have to believe they wouldn't embarrass me like that. "Did they *threaten* you?"

"Just a little," he says, scooping food onto his plate. Dadu comes in halfway and takes over, piling on immense servings from each dish while Ace watches with wide eyes.

"He's a growing boy, he needs to eat," Dadu says to me, pouring us both water.

I laugh, reaching over to squeeze her wrist. "You can let him starve, Dadu. I don't mind."

"*Myra*, stop," Dadu admonishes in English, whacking the top of my head with a dish towel, making me laugh harder. She switches back to Bengali. "He brought you soup."

"You just said you could have made me soup!" I say in protest.

She harrumphs and leaves the dining room after flicking me gently on the ear. I grin after her as she heads upstairs to pray Asr. When I turn back to Ace, he's still staring at the mountain of food on his plate.

"Am I supposed to eat all of this?"

"Hey, you're the one that wanted to impress my grandma,"

I say, shrugging a shoulder. "Back to my friends threatening you. What exactly was said?"

"I was told if I revealed anything about our conversation, my balls would be stapled to a tree," he says, poking his tuna kebab. "Ahmed, this is *so* much food. What am I going to do with all of this?"

I sigh. "As Dadu said, you're a growing boy, you need to eat."

"Did she actually say that?" There's a pained expression on his face. "I guess I have to eat it all, then."

"That's the spirit," I say, clapping him on the back. "If it helps, it tastes delicious."

He sighs but takes a spoonful of food.

Unsurprisingly, after he takes the first bite, the rest go by much faster. I wasn't exaggerating. Dadu is a great cook, and pulao is her specialty.

Halfway done, he turns to me, his head tilted. "Why did your grandma call you Myra?"

"In Bengali, we have two names," I say, forking a piece of chicken. "One is our official name that's on legal documents. Mine is Karina, obviously. But we have another nickname of sorts that we call each other within the community, and mine is Myra. I don't know if you've ever heard of my younger brother, but he's in the same year as Mia. His name is Rafiq Ahmed, but I call him Samir, because that's his community nickname."

"That's cool," Ace says. "So only other Bengali people can call you Myra?"

"No, I guess anyone can, but most people don't know it's an option."

"It's a pretty name," he says and reaches forward to tuck a strand of hair behind my ear. His fingers brush my skin, and a wave of heat descends over me, but I manage to retain eye contact. "But I like Karina better."

"And yet you only ever refer to me as Ahmed," I say, teasing. "Perhaps I should start calling you Clyde."

Ace makes a face, his spoon halfway to his mouth, and I burst into giggles.

"Let's stick with Ace," he says, but there's laughter hidden in the twist of his mouth. "And I'll call you by your name, too. What do you think, Karina?"

My smile nearly splits my face in half. "I think I'd like that, Ace."

I'm heading to bed when Dadu calls me back from her own doorway. "Myra, can I talk to you for a second?"

I pause halfway to my room and look back at her. "Of course. What's going on?"

Dadu grimaces. "That Alistair boy…is he your friend?"

My chest collapses. Why don't I ever *think*? I shouldn't have humored Ace. Of course Dadu wouldn't embarrass me in front of him, but that doesn't mean she *approves*, no matter how careful we were to keep our distance. *Ten, nine, eight, seven, six, five, four, three, two, one.* "He's—no, no. I have to tutor him. We're just classmates."

My grandma's frown deepens. "You two seemed very close. I'm unsure if you should…continue in this manner. I don't know if your parents would approve."

Oh God. There's never been a situation where Dadu hasn't supported me. This is the first one and of course, *of course*, it's because of Ace.

In the back of my head, I knew I was pushing it. I'm not dating Ace, but whatever it is that's between us is forbidden, and I know that. My parents would have a conniption if they knew I was spending this much time with *any* kind of boy, regardless of race or religion.

This friendship—this fake romance—all of it breaks unspoken rules. Spending time with him alone, flirting when no one is looking, accepting his invitation to prom; none of it is allowed. Even three weeks is too many.

I thought if I kept it secret, it would all be okay. But in doing that, I'm asking the universe of my grandma, when she's already given me the world.

Dadu is a saint, but even she has to have limits. In this case, I don't even think they're *her* limits, so much as the limits of my parents she feels obligated to uphold.

I have a feeling if it were up to Dadu, she'd let me do whatever makes me happy. That's the kind of person her experiences have shaped her into—from Dada, to the expectations put in place by her older brothers and parents, to the young girl she never had a chance to raise.

But my parents are still a part of this, even when they're not here. No matter what, they always will be.

My mouth is so dry it almost hurts to speak. "It's just for school. He's just a study buddy. It's nothing serious."

Dadu sighs and takes my hand. "Just be careful, Myra. I don't want to see this end poorly for you."

I nod. *Ten, nine, eight, seven, six, five, four, three, two, one.* "Don't worry about it, Dadu. I doubt you'll ever see him again."

This thing with Ace and me is so fragile that I'm afraid it'll shatter in the face of its first obstacle. I have to find a way to make this work. I don't know *how*, but I have to.

I don't know if I'm ready to lose this.

28

T-MINUS 16 DAYS

Friday rolls around, and Ace and I find ourselves at Pietra's Sweet Tooth, studying. He suddenly closes *The Scarlet Letter* with a loud thud that makes me jump in my seat. "Can we talk? Seriously?"

"Uh. Yes?" My tongue feels like it's glued to the roof of my mouth.

Maybe my study guides aren't working for him. I have a few different methods that we can try if that's the problem. I can't work on any of them tonight, because I have to go to my cousin Sana's birthday party, but I can start this weekend.

"Karina..." Ace sighs, running a hand through his dark hair. "There's—we're so different."

My heart falls. I should've been expecting that. This is when he's going to tell me all of this is a mistake. Everything we've done these last two weeks was for nothing. I knew it was coming. I knew he wouldn't want anything to do with me after our study sessions, but I didn't think he'd get tired of me *this* quickly.

Maybe Dadu's concern yesterday was the universe warning me.

"I know," I whisper. I don't think I can speak any louder.

"I don't know how to say this," Ace says, his expression troubled. "I don't know if I'm allowed to. But I can't sit here and just…not say anything anymore."

"Just say it," I say, bracing myself for the blow, tightly gripping the edge of the table.

"I didn't realize until yesterday," Ace says, toying with the rings on his fingers instead of looking at me. "I mean, I had an inkling but I didn't realize the full extent of it."

"Ace, just say it." I grit my teeth together and try to focus on the sunflower painting on the wall instead of Ace. "You don't want to study together anymore."

"What?" Ace looks up in surprise. "No. No, Jesus Christ. I'd love to study with you *forever*."

The words feel like a balm against my skin but they leave behind a deeper itching. "So what's the problem?"

"You," he says, a muscle jumping in his jaw. "Your willingness to put everyone and everything above your own needs."

I nearly stop breathing. "What?"

"Everything you do, you do because of other people. What do you do for yourself? *Is* there anything you do for yourself?"

"I don't know what you're talking about."

"Don't do this, Karina," he says, almost pleading. "You know exactly what I'm talking about. You let your parents rule your life. You're afraid to do anything that goes against their wishes."

I bite my tongue so hard I taste blood in my mouth. "They're my parents, Ace."

"Yeah, and you're their *child*. Not their prisoner. You don't have to do everything they say. You're allowed to do things for yourself."

"You don't know what you're talking about. It's not that easy," I say. I can't believe how many times I've been forced to have this conversation this week. "They're the reason I'm here. They've done so much for me. I can't—I can't just throw that back in their faces."

"You don't owe them your life in payment, though," Ace says, leaning forward in his seat. "You shouldn't live your life for other people. You deserve to live for yourself."

His expression is so earnest, yet I can't help but think how naive his outlook is.

"That's an *extremely* privileged way to look at things," I say slowly, willing him to listen to me. "Our worlds are different, Ace. In mine, I can't just *do* things because I want to. I can't let my parents down."

He sighs, holding his head in his hands. "Karina, I don't understand. What about what you want? Doesn't it matter?"

I swallow past the bitterness coating my throat. I believe that he doesn't understand. I believe that he genuinely wants to help. I think the only way to explain this to him is to turn it around. "Why were you ignoring your family yesterday?"

"What does that have to do with anything?" he asks, gazing at me through his fingers.

"Just answer the question."

"After I cut class yesterday, the school called my dad to see if I had a piano competition I forgot to mention. My family was just asking where I went. It's not a big deal."

"But it bothers you," I say. The answer is written clearly across his face, from the deep frown and the small indent between his thick brows. "So it is a big deal. It bothers you, because you care what they think of you. They're your family."

"But I would never let them rule my life, Karina. That's the difference."

"Is it?" I ask. "You said we're different. We are. But we're also the same. You know why? Because you *do* let your parents rule your life. Why aren't you going to college, Ace? Why won't you apply to Yale?"

Ace blinks at me, taken aback. "That has nothing to do with—"

"Yes, it does," I interrupt. "Because you're doing it to make a point to your dad and brother. Tell me I'm wrong. Look me in the eye and tell me."

Ace doesn't say anything.

"I'm right," I deduce, although I hate that I am. I hate the thought that Ace is throwing away his future. "What's the difference then, Ace? I'm pursuing medicine because of my family. You're refusing to apply to college because of yours. Both of our actions are because of our parents."

"It's not the same, Karina."

"How is it different?"

The tension between us is so thick even a knife couldn't cut through it. Ace is staring at me, his eyes a turbulent sea, but he doesn't say anything. I don't think he has an answer. I don't think anyone has ever said this to his face before.

"I'm sorry," I say, conceding defeat first. My shoulders slump and I avert my gaze.

"What did I say about saying sorry?" Ace asks. His voice isn't cold; it's as familiar as it's always been.

I chance a glance up, and he's watching me tiredly, as if he doesn't know what else to say.

"I need you to understand this isn't something you can fix for me, Ace," I say softly. It's the most honest I've ever been with anyone about this. "I'm not a princess waiting for a knight in shining armor to save me."

"I understand," he says, his shoulders slumping. "But I wish there was something I could do."

A wry smile breaks across my face. "I don't think there *is* anything you can do. We have different ways of approaching our issues. I can't begin to imagine living a life where I'm purposely pissing off my parents. I don't know how you do it."

Ace shakes his head. "And I can't imagine living by my parents' rules."

"I don't know where that leaves us," I say after a moment, the words quiet.

He runs his hands through his hair again before he stands up. My face falls. He's leaving.

But then, strangely enough, Ace holds out a hand to me. "Do you trust me?"

I stare at the offered hand, a mix of exhilarated and nervous. "This isn't *Aladdin*."

"It's not," he says. "But do you trust me?"

There's only one answer. I take his hand. "Yes."

"Then come on. I'm going to show you the world."

He takes us back to school. It's only a quarter past four, so it's still open for students to enter. We just have to swipe our ID cards before we're allowed inside.

"I have to leave in half an hour," I remind him as he leads us up the staircase. I have to get ready for Sana's birthday party soon, but we have a cushion of time before then.

"It's this way," he says, squeezing my hand.

When we reach the top floor, he crosses a hallway and stops in front of a locked door. When he takes out a lock pick set, I gape at him. "Why do you have that?"

"I forget my keys sometimes," he says, but he's smirking. "And my dad doesn't believe in spares."

"You forget your keys but not your lock pick set?"

"Hey, you're the one who kept insisting I was a bad boy."

I splutter. "There are cameras, Ace."

"Then you'd better hide me from view," he says, his smirk widening into a full-blown grin.

I reluctantly move forward, shielding his hands from the camera in the upper left corner of the hallway.

The lock clicks, and Ace pushes the door open. "Come on."

"Where are we even going?" I ask, squinting into the darkness. "Won't we get caught?"

"We'll just say someone left the door unlocked," Ace says, and I hear the laughter in his voice. "Give me a second and I'll show you why we're here."

He hits a switch, and small lights flicker into existence. He looks at me with bright eyes. "Welcome to the planetarium."

I gaze around in wonder, reaching out to brush a hand along the walls. I've never taken an astronomy class, so I haven't seen this room in all its glory. Constellations cover the dark walls, interspersed with planets and burning suns. "Why are we here?"

"It's my favorite place," Ace says. "It helps me when I feel like I'm going out of my head. I'll sit here for a while and remember we're just a small speck in the universe. My failures and worries are infinitesimal in the grand scheme of things."

"Infinitesimal," I repeat. "Big word."

Ace smiles at me, only faintly visible in the low lighting. "Maybe your tutoring is working."

"Maybe," I say, still looking around. "You really love space, huh?"

"Yeah." He sits down on the ground and pats the spot next to him. "C'mere."

I take a seat and continue staring up at the constellations. I've never spent much time looking at the stars, but there's something comforting about them.

"I love my father," Ace says quietly, surprising me. I glance to the side and notice he's still staring at the ceiling, so I follow suit. Maybe this is a conversation best said without prying eyes. "But he doesn't love me the way he loves Xander. Not since my mom left, anyway. I tried so hard at first, but nothing I do ever lives up to what my brother has already done. I'm tired of trying."

Am I supposed to comfort him or offer my own story? I don't know, but I can't let his honesty pass by silently.

"I have a brother, too," I say, the words rising unexpectedly. "I told you about him. Samir. Did you know he built his first robot when he was four? My parents still talk about it. Now he's on our school's robotics team. I…barely understand science *or* math. I put in so much effort to get good grades in those classes, but even then, I just barely scrape average. *He* has to help me sometimes."

Ace pulls out his phone. When he offers me an earphone, I take it without question. A soft instrumental song plays as the stars move around us.

He breaks the silence.

"I don't want to go to Yale," he says, voice hollow. "I want to go to NYU for piano performance."

I pause, my heart heavy. It's almost painful to keep my gaze focused on the ceiling when I want nothing more than to look at his face. "You've never said anything before."

Ace laughs but the sound is choked. "It just seems…so useless. I'll always be second to Xander. He'll take over dad's business with his Yale degree someday, and I'm going to be left in the dust. What's the point?"

I reach out, intertwining our fingers. "This is why you practice the piano three hours a day," I say, understanding dawning. "Why you take lessons. Why you miss school for competitions all over the world. Ace, it's obvious this means so much to you. Have you…" I pause, realizing the hypocrisy in my next words. *Have you considered telling the truth?* My shoulders suddenly feel as if they're carrying the weight of all the planets around us. "Does anyone know?"

He exhales quietly. "My dad might pay for the lessons, but I don't think he pays enough attention to realize it's more than a hobby for me. Ever since my mom left—" He cuts off, the words choked. I squeeze his hand again until he gains a hold of himself. "The piano is the one thing that still connects us. She's a world away, and I'm here, but our love for music—it's constant. It will never go away. It's how I keep her with me. She's the one who flies me out for international competitions, meeting me halfway. It's our *thing*. Whenever I play, it's like she's still with me." He shudders and I press my shoulder against his. "I can't imagine a future without the piano, but I don't know if my dad or Xander will ever understand that."

I wish you'd tell them the truth. I wish you'd do what makes you happy. I try to say the words, but I can't.

How can I, when I'm in the same situation? I can't tell him to apply to college any more than he can tell me to change my major.

"So what are you going to do?" I ask softly.

"I don't know," he says. In my peripheral vision, he ducks his head, staring at our joined hands. "All I know is that I don't want to do what they want me to."

The silence folds around us and my eyes grow wet with all that's left unsaid. "I don't want to do what my family wants, either. I want to go to Columbia for English." My voice cracks as I say, "I want *so much*, but I'm afraid I'll never have it."

Ace sighs and offers me his other hand. I take it, and we sit in silence for the next ten minutes, his fingers tracing the lines in my palm. In the quiet, I can hear our hearts breaking.

wishing wells are for those
with fortunes much larger than I

in my pocket, I hold a single gold coin
in your pocket, you hold my heart
I carry your dreams inside my ribs
you carry mine between your hands
we board a ship sailing for the stars
hoping to wish on them instead
but then the ocean demands a price
and slowly, carefully, hopelessly,
we sink alongside our anchor

It's only after those ten minutes that I remember it's Friday. I turn to him in alarm, wiping my cheeks hastily. "I thought you had a family dinner?"

"My dad's out of town," he says but gets to his feet, helping me up. His eyes gleam with unshed tears, and I pretend not to notice for both our sakes. "I should take you home, though. I'm sorry for bringing up...you know."

"Hey," I say, brushing my fingers against his jaw. The touch is gentle, given without any expectations. "No saying sorry."

He rests his forehead against mine. "No saying sorry."

And though neither of us can heal the rift between us and our parents, between us and our dreams, I wonder if we can't heal whatever is left. If we can't heal together, at each other's sides.

29

T-MINUS 16 DAYS

I hate coming to community parties.

They're worse with my parents around, but they're bad regardless. The problem isn't my cousins—or at least, the problem isn't a *majority* of my cousins—but rather the adults.

There are dozens of brown aunties and uncles hovering over our heads, picking us apart with their eyes and turning us to dust with their words.

The only solace is the relatives I actually like. My favorite cousin, Fatima, is sitting next to me tonight. We're at some fancy restaurant in Queens that looks out on a glistening bay, which I'm pretty sure leads into the East River. The restaurant hosts over a hundred attendees, and waiters dressed in blue walk around offering refreshments.

Fatima is a junior in college. Despite the four-year gap between us, we've always banded together in favor of the horde of elementary kids running around. The only rough spot in our relationship is how uneasy I become when we talk about her academic interests. She's majoring in biology, and I'm almost positive it wasn't her choice.

For a moment I consider asking her how it all went down, but I'd hate to recount any fight with my own parents, so I refrain.

"So what'd you get Sana?" I ask instead, nudging a piece of butter chicken with my fork.

Fatima sighs, resting her head on her hand. She seems uncomfortable tonight, continuously tugging on her heavy earrings. "What is there to get her? She already has everything she wants."

I grimace. She's not wrong.

Sana is every stereotypical brown parent's dream come true. Since she was little, she's always excitedly gone on and on about how she wants to be a doctor.

Now, a freshman in college, she's actually on that path.

Admittedly, it doesn't hurt that she's fair-skinned, beautiful, and an only child. She plays by all her parents' rules without complaint, and in return they dote on her endlessly.

I can't imagine a life abiding by my parents' standards, but Sana is obviously more than happy to do it. I guess it helps that most of her goals and views align with theirs, unlike the rest of us.

Out of respect and slight fear for myself, I avoid her outside of niceties. A lot of our relatives have suffered the consequences of befriending her; notably, my cousin Nabila, who confided in Sana that she was bisexual.

Sana went to Nabila's parents and outed her. To this day, I'm still horrified Sana valued her parents' rules over her cousin's safety.

Nabila's parents threw her out of the house—it's rare for queer people in our community to be accepted with open arms, since it's still illegal in Bangladesh—and none of us have heard from her since.

Or if we have, we don't talk about it. It's almost taboo to bring up her name.

It's frustrating not being able to do more for Nabila. I've seen support groups for Bangladeshi queer youth on social media before, so it's comforting to know that there *is* a safe space within our community, but it sucks that we can't always count on our parents to be a part of it.

I just wish we could all live our lives in peace, without these expectations that seem to dictate our every breath.

When everything went down with Nabila, I reached out over Instagram almost immediately afterward. She told me not to worry and that she'd moved in with her best friend. From her posts on her private social media accounts, she seems almost happier nowadays. But I don't know if I can rely on social media for the whole truth. She's definitely safer, but I can only *hope* she's happier.

I don't know if I would be.

The thought leaves a bitter taste in my mouth.

I wish everything didn't have to be so... I wish a lot of things. I know my parents aren't bad people, and I know they want the best for me, but I'm almost certain their definition of *best* isn't the same as mine.

My dad leans too much into my mother. I think it's easier for him that way. But it certainly isn't easy for me—I have to bear the consequences of having two parents who look down on me whenever I take one wrong step.

It's hard, because I *know* they love me somewhere deep down. I know they're not acting maliciously. And yet it doesn't change the fact that their beliefs don't always align with my own. It doesn't change the fact that I have to often sit here and pretend to be someone I'm not. I wish they were more like Dadu or my other relatives, who accept and support their kids no matter what. I know it doesn't have to be like this, so why is it?

I glance across the restaurant to where Sana is sitting on a fake throne, smiling brightly as an auntie talks to her. I wonder if she regrets what she did to Nabila. I can't imagine living with that weight.

Maybe it's not even a weight to her. Maybe she genuinely thinks she did the right thing.

That's somehow even more horrifying.

"We got her a gift card in the end. What did *you* get Sana?" Fatima asks, poking my arm, bringing me back to the conversation.

I shrug, trying to push away any remaining dark thoughts. "Dadu and I picked out some perfume. I couldn't think of anything else."

"That's a safe present," Fatima says. "Where is Dadu anyway?"

I glance around and catch Samir's gaze briefly as he goofs around with some of our cousins. He wiggles his brows, and I roll my eyes, ignoring him in favor of seeking out a white saree. I finally spot Dadu near the drinks. "Over there," I say, inclining my head with a fond smile.

Dadu has been making her rounds, and my youngest cousins follow her around like little ducklings. Any time she sits down, people trip over themselves to grab the seat next to her.

"Oh." Fatima's shoulders slump. "I needed to talk to her about…never mind."

My brows knit. Fatima is usually my polar opposite—outspoken and confident. Seeing her despondent feels *wrong*.

"Can I help?" I ask.

Fatima's mouth quirks. "I don't think so, Myra. But thank you."

"Let me know, though," I say, playing with the gold churi

on my wrists. "Even if it's just to talk about whatever's bothering you, I'm here."

"I know," Fatima says, smiling before her expression shifts.
"Actually, there is something I wanted to talk to you about."

"Oh God, that's not a good sign," I say, grimacing. "All
right, hit me with it. What did I do wrong?"

Fatima shakes her head and bumps shoulders with mine.
"You didn't do anything *wrong*. Relax. I was just curious—
there was a boy on your Instagram the other day...are you finally breaking away from your goody-two-shoes reputation?"

"I don't have a goody-two-shoes reputation," I say calmly,
even as my heart starts racing.

Some of my most-trusted cousins follow me on social
media, only because I know none of them would ever do
anything like what Sana did. Still, I didn't expect Fatima to
bring it *up*.

We all have things that go unspoken. Half my cousins post
pictures in which they're wearing shorts and crop tops, flaunt-
ing hidden tattoos and piercings, and even drinking or smok-
ing—all things that are strictly forbidden by our parents—and
I always silently like their posts and move on.

No one ever brings attention to the things we do behind
our parents' backs. And yet, here we are, talking about Ace
anyway.

Fatima rolls her eyes. "Yeah, Myra, you do. You're obviously not Sana over there, and thank Allah for that, but you
definitely play by your parents' rules a lot more than some
of us."

A lot of my cousins are more vocal about their displea-
sure when it comes to some of our restrictions. Samina, who
wants to go to college in California and is being manipulated
into staying in New York. Naureen, whose brother told their
parents about her Filipino boyfriend—taking away all her

freedom. Arun, who acts too feminine for his family's taste and had all of his clothes and makeup thrown away without warning.

But it's not always like that. There are so many wonderful Bangladeshi parents out there.

For example, Maheer, whose mother is probably my coolest aunt. She supports his dream of becoming an actor, even if it means spending all her time working in order to afford his private acting lessons. Or Liana, whose family promised her she could go to college wherever she wanted, and they'd move with her whenever she made her decision. Their parents are willing to hear them out and understand their side and support their hopes and dreams.

Then there's me.

My case isn't quite as extreme as some of the others, so Fatima's comment makes sense. I've never spoken out against my parents and, at this rate, I don't know if I ever will. It doesn't mean I *agree* with the way they act, but I'm not exactly actively fighting it.

I know a lot of my cousins hate their parents, but I don't hate mine. I *love* them and, in some ways, that's worse. If my parents ever kicked me out, I think I'd still miss them.

Because of that, I've always kept under the radar. Since no one knows my English aspirations, this thing with Ace is my first visible act of going against my family's rules.

"He's just a friend," I say eventually for lack of anything better.

Fatima snorts. "I saw your friends' comments on the post. Cora and Nandini, right? They have a ship name for you two."

"They're just being silly," I say, looking at my plate.

"Is that right?" Fatima says, her voice teasing, but then there's a visible shift in the air. "Listen… I want you to be happy, but I know your parents. If you're going to rebel, maybe start smaller. I don't think dating some random white guy will go over well."

I know, I almost say.

Ten, nine, eight, seven, six, five, four, three, two, one.

Ten, nine, eight, seven, six, five, four, three, two, one.

Every time someone reminds me how out of place my relationship with Ace is, my heart sinks lower and lower.

I am taking a *huge* risk with Ace. I know my parents, too, and I know Fatima is right. If they ever find out, they will in all likelihood murder me and bury my body in our backyard.

I lock those thoughts up tight in the back of my head. That's the *least* of my problems right now. If I'm going to fight my parents over something, it's going to be my English degree.

"Don't worry." The words burn as they leave my throat. "I know better."

30

T-MINUS 15 DAYS

My brother and I are sitting in the living room, basking in the midafternoon light, when the doorbell rings. I glance up from my book.

Samir is on the floor in front of me with a biology textbook cracked open and his phone in his hand, his fingers moving rapidly. It must be his friends.

"Are you going to get that?" I ask.

Samir groans dramatically. "Okay, you don't have to whine."

I roll my eyes and turn a page.

"It's for you," Samir says as he comes back, a set of matching footsteps following him. "That dude you tutor is here."

I look up and freeze at the sight of Ace standing in my house, holding a bouquet of flowers. His leather jacket is missing, replaced by a fancy mustard coat overlaying a cashmere navy sweater. Even his hair is combed through, although a few dark waves slip free, falling into his sea-colored eyes.

"Oh my God," I say under my breath. Is he out of his mind?

Showing up at my house with *flowers*? I'm going to die. My family is going to legitimately strangle me. I should've taken Fatima's warning more seriously. "What are you *doing* here?"

"Is your Dadu home?" he asks instead of answering. I contemplate walking over and shaking him, but that would make the entire situation worse.

This is my fault. I should've said something last time he showed up unannounced, but I didn't think there would be a repeat occurrence.

At the sound of her name, Dadu appears in the kitchen doorway. She looks at Ace and then at me, eyebrows raised.

For a moment, sheer panic overcomes me. Only Allah knows what kind of assumptions Dadu is going to draw from this.

Ten, nine, eight, seven, six, five, four, three, two, one.

Ten, nine, eight, seven, six, five, four, three, two, one.

Dadu is still staring at me, so I shrug helplessly. I have no idea why he's here.

Ace holds the flowers toward Dadu. "I brought these to say thank you for hosting me the other day."

I've never seen Dadu shocked before, but I'm pretty sure I'm seeing it now, her eyes wide and lips parted. I don't think she understands what he said or why he's offering her flowers. To be fair, *I* barely understand. I glance at Samir, but he doesn't seem to find any of this strange, which is the only source of relief among all the screaming white noise in my head.

"Myra, what's going on?" Dadu asks me.

I hold my hands out defensively. "He wants to thank you for feeding him."

"Oh." My grandma softens and takes the flowers. "You're welcome."

Ace looks over at me and my brother hopefully. "I was wondering if you both would like to join my sister and me. We're going bowling, and we'd love some company."

"Both?" Samir and I say at the same time. His tone excited, mine horrified. Of all things, why did it have to be bowling?

"Yeah," Ace says, nodding. "My sister is waiting in the car, if you want to join." He glances at my grandma. "If it's okay with you, Mrs. Ahmed."

There's a moment of stark silence after I nervously translate. Ace probably doesn't notice, but I'm hyperaware of it. There's no way Dadu will say yes, which is definitely for the best. I don't want my brother and Ace anywhere near each other, because it'll inevitably get back to my parents.

But missing out will still suck.

I hold my breath, waiting and waiting and *waiting* for the blow.

Finally, Dadu looks away from Ace and glances at me. "Okay. If Myra says yes."

Wait, what?

"Really?" I say in disbelief. Dadu has always had my back, but this isn't something I thought she'd budge on.

Dadu considers me for another moment before nodding. "Yeah, Myra. He brought me flowers. You can go bowling with him." She pauses. "Your Dada would always bring me flowers, too."

Oh my God, only Ace would unwittingly charm my grandmother.

Samir looks at me hopefully. He might love bowling, but the risk of going with him *and* Ace...

My brother keeps pouting at me and my resolve finally breaks. "Fine. I'll get dressed." Still, I have to figure out a way to make sure Samir doesn't slip up and tell our parents something he's not supposed to. I can't risk it. I *won't* risk it.

Both Ace and Samir cheer obnoxiously. I open my mouth

to tell my brother to come upstairs with me but, before I can, Samir rushes toward the foyer and puts on his shoes. "Wait, before you leave—" I say, but he waves me off.

"Tell me in the car," he says, far too eager, and slips through the door.

I stare after him woefully. Mia and Ace will be in the car. I definitely can't talk to him with them around.

I sigh and head upstairs, hoping I'll have a moment alone with Samir once we're at the bowling alley.

In my room, I stare at my wardrobe in distress before plucking something from the back, where the clothes I hide from my mother reside. I slip on a tank top and skinny jeans with holes in the knees. The jeans aren't that bad, but wearing something without sleeves feels too bold. I'm already testing my luck by agreeing to this outing. After a moment's hesitation, I throw on a cardigan, covering my bare arms.

I hurry down the steps and nearly run straight into Ace, who's standing in the doorway. "Hi, Karina."

A swarm of butterflies rushes through me. "Hi," I say back, and force myself to turn around and shout, "Bye, Dadu!"

"Bye, Myra. Have fun!" Dadu says, which is strange to hear.

I turn to Ace, trying to get rid of the nervous jitters. God, I wish I could light a candle. "So...bowling?"

"Yeah," he says, smiling at me. Something loosens in my chest. "I'm letting Mia practice driving."

"So you're looping me into dying with you."

"That's one way to look at it," he says, laughing and offering me his hand. "Come on."

I almost slip my fingers through his but falter, staring past him.

Samir is already in the car, peering over Mia's shoulder. The windows are down, so I can hear when he says, "How far is it?"

"Like ten minutes, Rafiq. Relax," she says, rolling her eyes.

"Not now," I say to Ace, my throat tight. Samir isn't looking at us, but if he does, I'll be caught out before I can explain. "I can't—my family…"

Ace gives me a curious look, but doesn't press, lowering his hand. "Let's go, then."

I give him a small smile. "Okay."

Daniela is sitting in the front beside Mia, so Ace and I slide in the back beside Samir. His eyes are bright, his body vibrating with excitement.

My brother hasn't had the chance to go bowling in a few weeks. My dad usually takes Samir every weekend, some kind of father-son bonding thing I'm not privy to. All my mom and I ever do is listen to dreamy Bengali folk music together. She knits and I make origami—more for my anxiety than anything else—and after a few albums, we go our separate ways.

Samir looks *forward* to his outings with Baba, though, so it's no surprise he's eager now.

Mia turns the radio to a pop station and starts singing outrageously along as she shifts the car into Drive.

"Pay attention to the road," Ace says, exasperated. "I invited Santos *specifically* so you wouldn't attempt to murder us."

"Daniela and I will happily die together," Mia says without missing a beat. "Isn't that right, babe?"

Daniela's expression is uneasy, her fingers gripping the upholstery tightly. "I would die for you but maybe…maybe we could postpone the dying part until we're like twenty-two and drowning in debt."

Mia looks thoughtful. "Fair enough."

Samir looks between them, eyebrows lifted. "I didn't know you guys were dating."

"Is that a problem?" Mia asks, glancing at him in the rearview mirror.

Samir smirks and opens his mouth to say something unde-niably *obnoxious*, so I elbow him roughly. I know he doesn't have a problem with it—he was also one of the first people to reach out to Nabila—but he's still a teenage boy with the proclivity to joke around in favor of being serious.

Samir grunts and gives me a betrayed look. I narrow my eyes in warning, and he huffs, rubbing his side. "Not for me," he says after a moment. "But one of my friends has a crush on Daniela. At least now I can tell him it's a lost cause."

Mia sits up straighter. "Which friend?" she asks almost too pleasantly.

"Don't tell her," Ace says from my side, a faint grin tug-ging at his mouth. "She's not above homicide."

Samir turns to Ace, and a far worse smile spreads across his face. "Speaking of dating—" he starts to say, and I pinch his wrist, my heart already racing. He yelps in surprise, clutch-ing his arm. "Jesus Christ. Never mind. My sister is a tyrant."

"I'll make Mia turn this car around right now," I warn him.

Samir sighs, leaning his head against the back of Mia's seat. "All right, Darth Vader."

"Darth Vader isn't that bad," Ace says, nudging my shoul-der, a comforting warmth at my side. Some of my nerves set-tle. "But your sister is Rey Skywalker."

Samir's eyes light up, and he launches into a Star Wars rant about Rey's lineage. I shake my head, leaning back in my seat as Ace indulges him.

Thankfully, the rest of the ride is uneventful, and we don't die miserably in a car crash.

When we arrive, Ace gestures for Mia to get out. "I'm not letting you parallel park my car."

Mia scowls. "I can do it."

Ace snorts and looks at Daniela.

Daniela's eyes widen and she hastily exits the car. "Don't bring me into this."

Mia gapes after her girlfriend. "The betrayal," she says, clutching her chest. "You win this time, *Alistair.*"

"Thanks, *Cosmia*," Ace says, rolling his eyes as his sister leaves. "Karina, Rafiq? Do you want to go with them?"

Samir pushes open the door. "I can't sit in the same car as an Anakin Skywalker apologist."

"I'm not an *apologist*. I just think that the Jedi Council alienated Anakin—"

"I don't want to hear it!" Samir says, hopping out, but there's laughter in his voice. Ace looks similarly amused. The interaction makes my stomach twist with sudden awareness.

Not for the first time, it hits me.

Even knowing I shouldn't, I have feelings for Ace. Feelings that are nearly brimming over the edges.

"Karina, if you want to go with them you can," Ace says, holding open the door for me.

I shake my head. "I'll come with you."

The smile I receive in return causes my heartbeat to stutter.

Ace parks the car a few blocks away. Before we walk back, he takes off his coat and tosses it in the back seat. For the first time, I see the dark shape on his wrist clearly.

"Is that a tattoo?" I ask, reaching for him without thinking.

Ace nods, presenting his arm. The solar system is tattooed neatly across his inner wrist, the planets in shades of black and white. It's a simple design, not meant to be flashy. It fits him perfectly.

"I got it on my sixteenth birthday. I had to forge a note from my dad and drive to New Jersey, but it was worth it."

My jaw drops. "You did *what*? How are you still alive?"

"He doesn't know yet," Ace says, a mischievous glint in his eye. "I usually wear a watch over it."

"You're ridiculous." I shake my head. "I hope for your sake that he never finds out."

"What's the worst that can happen if he does?" Ace asks, shrugging. "I'll be fine. It's not like I got a tramp stamp."

Right. Our situations are different. Even as I learn more about him, Ace remains an oddity to me, someone bold and defiant. Things that I can't help but be drawn to, even as they leave me reeling.

I have a better understanding of him than I did before, but there are still some things I can't put my finger on. Mysteries yet to be unraveled. I still don't even know why he *asked* to be tutored, much less why he orchestrated the fake dating situation. I understand parts of it, but the rest is muddled.

After watching him in the car with Samir, a firm resolve has taken place. A conversation sits on the tip of my tongue, and with two blocks between us and the bowling alley, I'm tempted to give in.

In light of my discussion with Fatima, it'll be good to know all the facts. If this is something I'm going to take a chance on, if this is something I have to put *everything* at risk for at some point in the future, I need to know it's worth it. I need to know with absolute certainty that this isn't just a passing amusement for Ace. Not when it's growing to mean so much to me. "Why did you arrange this?"

Unsurprisingly, Ace isn't following my random train of thought. "Huh?"

"The tutoring thing," I say, biting my lip. "And the whole fake relationship thing."

"What do you mean?"

I shrug, even as my brain buzzes, my leg bounces, my fingers tremble. "Everyone knows your reputation. I've seen it myself. You don't care about school, and you definitely don't care about your classmates. Why bother studying for English?

And why bring me home, where you'd have to explain the situation to your dad? I just don't get it, I guess."

Ace falters, running a hand through his hair. The world moves in slow motion as he turns toward me. "I brought you home because I felt bad about missing our first session and I wanted to make up for lost time. But after Xander came into my room while we were studying, I knew he'd catch on inevitably. The only explanation I could think of for us spending so much time together was dating. And I *wanted* to keep spending time with you. I still do." He swallows, his throat shifting. "In retrospect, I should have warned you before making that announcement during dinner. It was wrong of me. I'm sorry."

I blink, attempting to process that. "Okay, but...the rumors..."

"There are a lot of rumors about me." There's a short pause. "But I'm here with you right now, aren't I?"

"Yeah," I say, my throat impossibly dry. "But why? And why me? Miss Cannon told me she tried tutoring you first. What happened?"

Ace looks at me, pressing his lips together. "I couldn't focus," he admits. "She wasn't holding my attention, and I wasn't learning anything. But with you, it's different. I... I see parts of myself in you, Karina. I know you can see parts of yourself in me, too. I think your heart runs as wild as mine and that's why this works. It's why you keep trying, even when anyone else would have already given up. You *see* me."

"Do I?" I peer up at him through my eyelashes.

Ace takes a step forward and I take an uncertain step back, causing him to smile faintly. "You do. Maybe that means you're foolish and reckless, but that's what I like about you. The spark you keep inside here." He taps once above my heart before his hand drifts up, his palm resting against my neck. "In your heart."

"How do I keep from going up in flames?" I ask, the words hoarse. My own hand drifts up to graze his, my fingers brushing against the back of his knuckles. He's so close. Too close. We're in broad daylight, and Ace is only inches away, his skin touching mine. None of this feels real.

"You don't," he says, his thumb skimming along my jaw. "Become a blaze."

I take another step back and inhale sharply when my back hits a brick wall. "Next you're going to call me an inferno. I'm a fool for indulging you, aren't I?"

He shakes his head and leans closer, our noses brushing. "You're a lot of things, but not a fool."

I laugh, nervous, breathless, afraid, hopeful. "Then what am I?"

He smiles. "You're a lionheart."

I let out a shaky breath. "Maybe I'm a foolish lionheart then."

Ace's gaze drops to my lips and my heart thuds painfully in my chest, too hard and too fast. "Yeah. My foolish lionheart."

"There you guys are!" Samir's voice calls, startling both of us. My head knocks against the wall and I wince, both at the sudden ache and the fact that I got so caught up in the moment I lost all sense of my surroundings. Ace's hand immediately comes up to caress the back of my scalp, his fingers cool against the sore spot, but I gently push him away. "Mia sent me to make sure you didn't get lost."

Ace takes a step back, his fingers running through my hair. Samir is standing at the end of the street, his eyes flickering between us.

"We're not lost," I say swiftly, gathering my wits and walking forward. Somehow, my heart is beating even faster. Samir is staring at me, a question in his eyes, and I quicken my pace, reaching out to grab his wrist with shaking fingers. "Please don't say anything. *Please*."

Ten, nine, eight, seven, six, five, four, three, two, one.

Samir blinks at me, his gaze darting over to Ace before returning to me. His lips curve, a smug expression overtaking his features. "I was right. You do have a crush."

"Samir," I say, my voice cracking. "You *promised*. Please."

Ace catches up, and I let go of Samir's wrist but keep staring at my brother desperately.

"Are you all right?" Ace asks me, eyebrows furrowed.

"Yes." I swallow. "Right, Samir?"

My brother nods after an achingly slow moment. "Yeah."

Ace frowns but after observing my expression, he doesn't push. "I guess we'd better head inside before Mia has a conniption then."

"Yeah, let's go," I say and squeeze Samir's shoulder, the material of his shirt clenched between my fingers. "We'll talk more about this later, okay?"

My brother nods again, expression pensive, but my worry doesn't dissipate. Ace tugs gently on a strand of my hair, and I jolt, realizing I haven't moved.

"Right, let's go," I say, walking ahead of both of them.

Ten, nine, eight, seven, six, five, four, three, two, one.

31

T-MINUS 15 DAYS

The inside of the bowling alley is a shock of loud voices matched with loud music, and it takes a few blinks for me to take in my surroundings. Little kids are running back and forth, parents are laughing together in the common area, and teenagers are shrieking in protest while bright strobe lights flicker overhead. It's utter chaos and distracts me from the disquiet tearing up my chest.

Ace laughs at the expression on my face and leads me to the counter, where Mia hands us two pairs of shoes. In response to the confusion on my face, she nods toward Samir. "He told us your shoe size."

I look at my brother, but he's already moving toward the bowling lane, grinning. My shoe size isn't the kind of thing I ever expected him to know. Maybe…maybe everything will be okay. I just have to pull him aside and explain everything as soon as I have the chance. My brother is a lot of things, but malicious isn't one of them.

Some of my anxiety eases, and I take a deep breath, counting down over and over until my pulse returns to normal.

Mia and Daniela head to get some snacks and I sit down and slip on my bowling shoes. When Samir goes for a bathroom break, I almost follow him so we can talk, but he disappears too quickly.

I groan and resign myself to doing it later. Hopefully our promise will keep him from doing anything stupid before then.

A few minutes later, Samir runs up to us holding a sparkly pink bowling ball. "I found the perfect ball! Let's do this!"

I squint at him. He seems unbothered by our earlier conversation, more focused on the game than anything else. I wish I could let things roll off me that easily.

I turn my attention back to Ace, who's fiddling with the touch screen in the front of the table. When Mia and Daniela return, I realize I shouldn't have left Ace in charge, since he put me in as the first player.

With a sigh, I walk over to the lane, testing the weight of a ball in my hands. "For the record, I suck at this."

Ace does nothing but chuckle in response.

"I'm serious," I say, but now he's grinning. His smile is like a punch to the heart, and my ribs are becoming steadily bruised.

"Give it a try," he says. "I promise I won't laugh."

I roll my eyes but look back at the lane. There's a smile on my own lips, slipping free without my permission. Still, I know it'll be a miracle if I knock down even one pin. Giving me a ten-pound piece of plastic that I have to throw down a lane is like asking me to do rocket science.

I take a deep breath and swing my arm back and forth before letting go. My eyes track the ball's trajectory nervously. As anyone could have predicted, it makes to hit one of the pins but skids to the side at the last second, falling straight into the gutter.

I sigh, shaking my head. "Why does this always happen to me?"

"It's not that bad," Ace says. His hand is covering his mouth, and I don't have to see behind his fingers to know he's smirking.

I glare halfheartedly and retrieve my ball from where the machine spit it back out.

When my ball goes into the gutter a second time, I plop down in the seat next to Samir and mutter, "This game is stupid."

"Sore loser," my brother says, grinning at me. I huff and stomp on his foot, but I doubt he can feel it through the bowling shoe.

Ace laughs and stands up, cracking his back and knuckles. He holds out a fist toward my brother and they fist bump.

"Gross," I say, more for the sake of saying it than anything else.

Ace sticks his tongue out at me like a *child* before strolling over to the lane, grabbing a red ball on the way. He studies the pins before swinging his arm back, and the bowling ball rolls steadily down the lane. My jaw drops as it hits dead center, knocking down all the pins in one easy motion.

Of course. He's gorgeous, sweet, and he can hit a strike on his first try.

Ace winks at me, holding his arms out. "It's just simple physics, sweetie."

"*Simple phy*—" I cut myself off and take a deep breath when I notice Mia and Daniela are giggling.

"You two are so silly," Mia says fondly. "We're here to have fun. It's just a game."

"That's because you're going to lose," Samir says without

missing a beat. He's almost bursting with hyperactive energy. "Guys are just better at bowling."

I flick Samir's ear. "Stop being misogynistic."

"I'm not!" Samir protests. "Is it my fault you and Ma suck at bowling?"

I give him an unimpressed look. "Don't make me call you an Uber."

Samir immediately mimes zipping his lips.

Mia just looks amused. "We'll see how much better you really are. Want to bet ten dollars?"

After they shake on it, Mia lines up for her shot. When she hits a strike, I cheer loudly, pumping my fist.

"It's a fluke," Samir says dismissively.

I glance at Ace and he shakes his head. "Your poor brother," he whispers. "I'd never bet against Mia."

Daniela takes her shot next and hits eight of the pins in one go. She hits the remaining two in her second shot.

Samir only manages to hit nine pins during his turn. A look of horror is spreading across his face.

I'm feeling a similar sense of dread. I'm definitely the weakest player here, which means I'm going to bring down the girls' side.

I'm lining up to swing when fingers brush my arm, stopping me. I freeze before I realize it's Ace, whose hands are reaching down to press against mine.

I glance at Samir, but he's arguing with Mia again, showing her something on his phone.

"You're holding it wrong," Ace says, lips brushing my ear. I try not to shiver at the touch, my attention falling back to him.

When Ace uses his body to maneuver my own, I move easily, even though I think my hands might be shaking. I'm pliant as he turns me the way he pleases and then pulls my hand back.

"Now let go," he says, giving my hand a gentle push. I do

as instructed. I'm so busy keeping myself from freaking out that when the ball hits the pins, I jump at the sound.

I focus in time to see all the pins fall over and I stare with wide eyes. "No. Way."

Ace laughs in my ear and pulls away. Almost instantly, I miss the feeling of his lean body against mine before realizing what a stupid thought that is.

"Ace! What the hell, dude? Whose team are you on?" Samir asks in disbelief. I look back at my brother, searching his expression nervously, but apparently he's more concerned with the competition than...whatever Ace and I were doing. "It's guys versus girls!"

"Nah, dude," Ace says. "It's you versus Mia and Dani. Your sister and I are on our own team. Right, Karina?"

I tug at my collar, trying not to blush. I hope my brother doesn't read into that, either. "Right."

"You guys suck," Samir says and thankfully turns all his attention toward Mia. "Their scores don't count then."

"Fine by me," Mia says, grinning a toothy smile. "You're going down, Rafiq."

The next hour is more fun than I expect. Ace's laughter is like music in my ears, and his smile greets me at every turn. I'm starting to worry I might be more besotted than I'm supposed to be for the two weeks we've known each other. If this were a movie, there would probably be literal hearts shooting out of my eyes every time I looked at him.

I think there might be hearts shooting out of his eyes too, though.

At the end of the game, Mia and Daniela average their scores and beat Samir, to no one's surprise except my brother's.

"Girls rule, boys drool," I say jokingly.

"Ace *does* drool every time he looks at you," Mia says. "But you're pretty, so I guess it makes sense. What do you think, Dani?"

"She's gorgeous," Daniela agrees before turning to Mia, playing with one of her curls. "I can't wait for us to be sisters-in-law. We're all going to have such cute little babies."

I nearly choke on air, and Ace has to pat me on the back. I glance at Samir to make sure he didn't hear that, but he's too busy frowning at the scoreboard, which is a huge relief.

Except then he turns to us, his brows climbing into his hairline. Oh no.

Ten, nine, eight, seven—

"I think we can all agree I'll be having the cutest babies of us all. Look at this face." Samir gestures. "Unparalleled beauty."

I stare at him, eyes wide. Is that it? That's his only comment?

"Let's move on," Ace says, offering me a bottle of water. I take a sip, but I can't stop looking at Samir. He meets my eyes and offers me an awful wink that does nothing to settle the nerves playing ping-pong in my stomach.

I promised, he mouths.

I stare at him for one more beat, trying to comprehend what that means. Is...is this okay? Is he going to keep all of this to himself? Am I safe?

"I'll return our bowling shoes," Samir says, looking away from me and hooking his fingers into his pair. "Be right back."

I watch him go, breathing a little easier. Maybe this really is okay. I've been so paranoid, so certain Samir would slip up, but maybe I underestimated him.

Next to me, Ace asks, "Santos, I heard you hit ten thousand followers on Instagram?"

I tune back in to their conversation and see Daniela smile

bashfully. "I did. It's so weird that people like my photography that much."

"You should take our prom photos," Ace says, gesturing to me. I flush, unable to meet anyone's eyes. "Can I get a brother-in-law discount?"

"No, but Karina can get a sister-in-law discount," Mia says, slinging an arm around Daniela's shoulders and smiling broadly at her. "You know, I should get some credit for your new wave of followers. I'm pretty sure half of them are there to see the pictures you take of me. You're so lucky to have such an inspiring muse."

Even though Mia is clearly joking, Daniela's expression softens. "Yeah, I am."

My heart melts in my chest when Mia leans forward to peck Daniela on the lips before pulling back quickly, her cheeks tinted red.

"You two are so cute," I say.

Mia shoots me an abashed smile. "Thanks, Karina."

Ace throws his own arm around my shoulders and, instead of shying away, I lean in. Samir promised. It's okay.

"We're cuter than them," Ace says. "Hashtag Karstair, right?"

"Oh my *God*," I say in sudden mortification. "Have you been speaking to Cora?"

Ace kisses my nose instead of answering, and I think I pass away. I'm ninety-nine percent certain my soul just exited my body.

"See?" Ace says, looking back at his sister and her girlfriend. "I told you we're cuter."

"What do you guys want for dinner? It's my and Ace's treat," Mia says as we all pile in the car.

"Mexican food," Samir says. "I know a great halal place."

I try not to sigh. Mexican food is my least favorite. I'm utterly incapable of eating a taco or burrito without spilling out all the contents.

Before I can protest, Mia nods. "I'd be down."

"I'm always here for Mexican food," Daniela agrees.

Ace shrugs. "It's fine with me. I don't really care."

Well. If everyone is okay with it, I'm not going to be the one to disrupt the peace.

"Cool," I say, my shoulders slumping.

Ace frowns at me, but I turn my gaze away. It's nothing for me to be upset over. I'll just have a salad or something.

When we get there, we order inside and take it to go. I step up to the counter and ask for a salad, but they look at me blankly and say they don't have a salad option. Of course they don't.

"It's fine," I say tiredly. "I'll just have a water bottle."

I move out of the way so Daniela can order, heading for the back to wait for everyone. Mia and Ace are speaking to each other quietly, but Ace falters when he sees me, his eyes searching my face.

I frown. "Is something wrong?"

He stares at me for half a beat before swiping a knuckle gently across my cheekbone. "You had an eyelash on your cheek."

"Oh," I say. "Should I make a wish?"

Ace shrugs and holds out his hand, the dark eyelash stark against his pale skin. "Go ahead."

What do I want to wish for? There are so many things I want, but using a wish on something that has such a small possibility of happening seems like a waste.

Then again, it's not like any wish I make is going to come true because I blew on an eyelash, anyway.

I wish for happiness, I think wistfully, *in whatever form it might be.*

I blow, and my eyelash disappears, lost to the wind.

"What did you wish for?" Ace asks, head tilted.

I smile faintly. "I'll tell you if it comes true."

Ten minutes later, we pull up in front of Ace's house instead of mine.

"Why are we here?" I ask, puzzled. This must be what Ace and Mia were whispering about. Samir is too busy staring at the Clyde residence in disbelief to pose a similar question.

"Mia and Daniela are getting out because I have to go somewhere after dropping you off," Ace says, flicking a finger at his sister. "Let me drive."

Mia unbuckles her seatbelt. "I still don't understand why you won't tell me where 'somewhere' is," she grumbles.

"Don't worry about it," Ace says, booping her nose as they switch places.

Mia blows a raspberry at him before coming around the back. I'm surprised when she hugs me tightly. "Come by again soon. Ace is so much more fun when you're around. It's nice."

Something warm passes through me. "You're so sweet, Mia. Thank you for inviting us to come out with you."

"Any time," Mia says, finally pulling away. "Bye Rafiq! Try not to bruise your ego any further!"

Samir rolls his eyes, but there's a hint of a smile in the corner of his mouth. I think he enjoyed himself today despite losing miserably to Mia and Daniela. "I'll do my best."

Daniela murmurs a soft goodbye, reaching over to pat my hand, before exiting the car and joining her girlfriend. Ace backs out of the driveway, leaving them behind holding hands.

It's another ten minutes before we arrive at my house. I reach for the handle as he shifts the car into Park, but Ace says, "Wait."

I pause and Ace turns to Samir, holding out his fist again. "Thanks for coming out with us today. It was really cool to meet you, bro."

Bro. Sometimes I seriously wonder if Ace has multiple stunt doubles he switches out based on his mood.

Samir fist bumps him back. "Yeah, bro, you too."

Before Samir can open the door on his side, Ace pulls out his wallet and removes a crisp ten-dollar bill. "Don't tell Mia."

Samir looks between the bill and Ace in disbelief before breaking into a grin. "I knew you were on my team, dude. Bros before hoes."

"No," Ace and I say at once.

I give Ace a surprised look but he's still looking at Samir. "Dude, respect women as much as you respect everyone else."

"And stop calling them hoes," I add darkly.

Samir rolls his eyes, but there's an embarrassed flush to his cheeks. "Yeah, okay."

I arch an eyebrow. "So you'll stop being misogynistic when a *man* tells you to?"

My brother groans, the tips of his ears turning red. "Don't start. It's not that deep."

Before I can say how deep it really is, Ace touches my wrist, staying me.

"Just do me a favor and respect your own sister, if no one else." He waves the ten-dollar bill toward Samir again. "Anyway, do you mind if I speak to Karina privately for a minute?"

Samir grins suddenly. "Sure, dude. Whatever." He takes the money, salutes Ace, winks at me again, and exits the car.

I sigh after him. "I hope he's not such a dumbass in a few years. I feel bad for his future girlfriends."

Ace laughs quietly. "I want to talk to you." He gestures to the passenger seat. "Before you argue, I'm going to use the magic word. *Please* come up front?"

I close my mouth silently, wondering when Ace came to know me well enough to predict my actions. I grudgingly climb into the passenger seat and turn to look at him. "What's so important it couldn't wait until later?"

"Put on your seatbelt."

"What? Your car is in Park."

"Still," Ace says. "Come on, Karina. It'll take a second."

"Who knew Ace Clyde was a safety nut," I say under my breath. "For all intents and purposes, you should be riding a motorcycle."

Ace gives me an amused look. "Why's that?"

"Your whole thing you've got going on," I say, gesturing vaguely. It's kind of hard to make a point when he's wearing a peacoat instead of his leather jacket. "With your…other jacket. And stuff."

"You and my leather jacket," he says in exasperation. "I'm not even wearing it."

"Still!"

"Hm. Seatbelt?"

I sigh and buckle myself in. "Happy?"

"Elated," he says and shifts the gear, pulling out of his parking spot with absolutely no warning whatsoever.

"Where are we *going*?" I ask, staring at him with wide eyes. "Is this the part where you finally murder me?"

"Yes," Ace deadpans.

I continue staring at him with wide eyes. I don't actually think he's going to murder me, but Allah knows what he has in mind. I might die *anyway*. If I die because of a white boy, my parents are going to bring me back to life just to kill me again. I'm almost certain I should be making better life choices, but it's hard when Ace is so… Ace.

"You don't have to look at me like that," Ace says, alarmed. "I can turn the car around. I was only joking."

"Right," I say and lean back in my seat, sending a silent prayer to Allah that tonight doesn't seal my fate.

"I was, I swear. I'm not kidnapping you or anything. I'm just taking you out to eat. Where do you want to go?"

That shocks me out of my reverie. "What? What do you mean?"

"Where do you want to go?" Ace repeats, stopping at a red light. "Do you have any preference? Or should we just hit up a Burger King or something?"

"We just ate," I say. "Not even half an hour ago. You had a chicken burrito, remember?"

"And what did you have?"

I fall silent.

"Yeah, I thought so. There's a diner up ahead. Do you like fries and milkshakes, or should I keep driving? The milkshakes aren't as good as the ones at Pietra's, but they're still decent."

"Fries and milkshakes are fine," I say, mystified. No one has ever paid this close attention to me before.

"Are you just saying that?" he asks, giving me a quick look as he turns into the parking lot. "Because there's a pizza place down the road and a Chinese restaurant the next street over. It doesn't matter to me where we go. I just want you to be happy."

My pulse quickens and I fight to keep my voice steady. "I love fries and milkshakes, Ace. It's perfect. Thank you."

"Always, Karina."

Always. It's such a big word, with promises of so much more.

I don't know about *always*, but I know about right now.

And right now, I know there's nowhere else I'd rather be than at this boy's side.

32

T-MINUS 15 DAYS

Ace drops me off thirty minutes later, after we finish eating french fries in his car. I take half my milkshake home and smile as I walk to my front door, the moonlight shining faintly overhead.

When I come inside, Dadu is sitting on the couch with a distressed look on her face.

I immediately rush to sit beside her. "What's wrong? Are you okay?"

Dadu looks at me, startled. "Myra. You're back." Her face crumples, and it sends a horrible sense of foreboding through me. It's the same look Dadu had when we were informed my cousin Nabila got kicked out of her house. "Your parents said to call them. They want to talk to you."

My skin prickles uncomfortably. "About what?"

"Samir...told them about how you went outside today with that Alistair boy."

Oh no.

Oh no.

I left him alone for *half an hour* and he went and blew my cover. I shouldn't have put any faith in him. How could I be so *stupid*?

"What did he say?" I ask, my heart racing. *Ten, nine, eight—*

She shakes her head. "I don't know, Myra."

I nod, my leg jiggling up and down. "Okay. Okay. I'm gonna go talk to him."

"I love you," Dadu says as I stand, squeezing my hand. "I gave you permission to go outside with him. Okay? Tell them that."

Ten, nine, eight, seven—"I love you, too."

I take the steps two at a time, hurrying to Samir's room. I knock once before letting myself in without waiting for his response.

"What did you tell Ma and Baba?"

He looks up from his laptop, bemused. "About what?"

"About going outside with Ace and his sister, Samir. Don't play dumb," I say, my jaw so tense I'm afraid it's going to break. I can't believe he told them. I can't believe that, after he promised me, after I asked him not to, *he told them.* "What did you tell Ma and Baba? *You promised me.*"

"Nothing," he says, giving me a strange look. "They asked me what I did today, so I told them we hung out with the dude you were tutoring. I didn't mention anything about the crush. I wouldn't break a promise. What's the big deal?"

The big deal is that Ace is a boy and they're going to kill me. The big deal is that Ace isn't Bangladeshi or Muslim and they're going to kill me. The big deal is that I trusted you to understand when you never will and they're going to kill me. The big deal is that you don't think before you speak and now they're. going. to. kill. me.

"How could you do that, Samir? God, you're the *worst*," I say as my throat tightens painfully, and I turn, ignoring the way his face falls as I leave his room.

In the privacy of my own walls, I brace myself for the conversation I'm about to have.

I light three different candles and take a deep breath.

Ten, nine, eight, seven, six, five, four, three, two, one.

One, two, three, four, five, six, seven, eight, nine, ten.

In and out. Inhale and exhale.

I press call.

"Myra," my dad says. Already, there's heavy disappointment in his voice. I wish for once, for *once*, he would take my side when it matters. I know it's too much to ask of my mother, but he was raised by Dadu. Just once, can't he let me have this? "Samir said you were outside with a boy today."

I swallow past the lump in my throat. There's only one card that's going to let me go unscathed: the reminder this is all for school. "Yes. I'm tutoring him because my teacher asked me to."

"On a *Saturday*?" my mom asks. Even through a phone screen, she's intimidating. "You should have told your teacher it's against your religion to be alone with a boy."

Stop blaming your rules on our religion. I don't say that. It won't matter to them.

"We're never alone," I lie. "We always study in the library, so there are lots of people around."

"What are you tutoring him in?" my dad asks, eyes narrowed.

This isn't going to go over well. I inhale deeply and murmur, "English."

A silence follows before my dad shakes his head at me. "That's a waste of your time. Assisting your teacher is one thing, but tutoring this random boy one-on-one is another. If we'd known Miss Cannon was going to leave you on your own, we wouldn't have agreed to let you help her. You should be focusing on science anyway. Samir said you do this *every* day."

I want to strangle my brother for his obliviousness. Why would he ever tell my parents that? It wasn't enough to say I was tutoring a boy, he had to go into *depth* about it? I never took him to be that clueless.

"It counts as a grade," I say, biting the inside of my cheek. The copper taste of blood floods my mouth. "Miss Cannon is substituting it for one of my projects."

My mom scowls. "So? Tell your teacher you can't do it anymore. She can't force you to tutor this boy if you don't want to."

But I do want to. Maybe it was a forced situation in the beginning, but it's far from that now.

"Private tutoring will look good on college applications," I say instead, lowering my gaze.

"Yeah, and will bowling with him look good on college applications, too?" Ma asks. "What were you thinking, Myra? How could you be so irresponsible?"

"I didn't do anything wrong," I say, but I know it's a futile attempt.

"Oh, is that so? You don't think you did anything wrong?" My mom looks at my dad, clear disappointment written in her gaze, causing my blood to curdle. In response, my dad's own expression darkens. It's always like this. As soon as she's upset, he follows suit. I hate it so much. "This is the daughter we've raised. Imagine what people will say once they find out. Astaghfirullah."

Why does anyone care? I want to scream. Why do people care how I spend my time? Why do my parents care what those people think? What does it matter?

"It was just one time," I say, and my voice cracks, making me wince. They'll see it as another sign of weakness. "It's not a big deal, Ma."

"You have no respect," my mom says, pinching the bridge

of her nose. "No respect for Allah or for us. That's why you're acting like this. No one else's daughter behaves the way you do. I thought we raised you better."

Ten, nine, eight, seven, six—

"Say *something*, Myra," Ma says. "Don't just sit there silently. Why would you go bowling with this boy? And why would you take Samir with you? You know he should be focusing on his robotic competition next week, but you're distracting him. You can't even focus on your own grades, and now you're dragging your brother down with you? Aren't you ashamed of yourself?"

"Sorry," I croak. I don't know how to make this better. I don't know what to say. I hate disappointing them. "I'm sorry."

"Sorry isn't good enough, Myra," Baba says, his gaze heavy. "This boy is a bad influence on you. Staying out late…dragging your brother into your foolish acts…prioritizing English over your more important subjects. It's a shame."

"I'm sorry," I say again, not knowing how else to fix this. My mind blanks out as they continue to berate me, berate my actions, berate all I've done in the past. I keep repeating a different variation of my apology, but it doesn't seem to do the trick.

Twenty minutes later, my dad puts an end to the conversation. "We will discuss this further upon our return, Myra. You will stop tutoring this boy at once. If there's a problem, we will speak to your teacher ourselves."

"And I better not hear anything else about you hanging out with him, much less dragging Samir with you," my mom says. "Now go to sleep. You'll have to get up early to make up for the studying time you lost today."

"Of course," I say quietly. "Good night, Ma. Good night, Baba."

"Good night, Myra. Remember what we told you."

Like I could forget.

They hang up, and I set my phone down. It takes two seconds for tears to slip free from my eyes, and I start sobbing, burying my face in my hands.

Nothing I ever do is enough.

My door cracks open and Dadu comes inside, sitting on my bed and wrapping her arms around me. "I'm sorry, my dear," she whispers, holding me tightly. "I wish they weren't so hard on you."

I can't manage a reply, my cries muffled against her shoulder.

"It's not your fault, Myra," she says, stroking my hair. "I'll talk to your dad when they get back. I know you're just trying to help Alistair. If I thought he was a bad influence, I wouldn't have let you go with him today, but he's very sweet and he's a good friend to you."

"Dadu, I—I don't know what to do," I say, nearly choking on the words. "I don't know how to do this anymore. I can't—I'm not the daughter they want. I'm never going to be."

"Oh, my darling," Dadu murmurs, holding me even closer. There's a pained expression on her face. "Don't ever think that. You're perfect as you are."

"Not to them," I say and burst into another round of tears. Dadu murmurs comforting words against my hair and keeps holding me until my sobs subside.

"Myra," Dadu says, using her saree to wipe the remaining tears off my face. "No matter what, I want you to know I'm proud of you. You are enough. You are more than enough."

However, she looks even more pained than before and it makes my own chest hurt. "Are you upset with me, too?"

"No," Dadu says quickly, her expression fierce, but it subsides into something more melancholy. "I just wish I wasn't failing you. Failing our family."

"*What?* You could never," I say, roughly scrubbing my face. "This isn't your fault."

Dadu's mouth twists and she looks away. "Your Dada would be so sad to see this current state of affairs. All of you are going through so much, and there's nothing I can do."

"Dadu, it's not your fault," I say more firmly. She's been my rock through this whole thing. I throw my arms around her and hug her tightly to get my point further across. My heart still throbs like an aching bruise, but this is more important. "I love you. Thank you."

She kisses the side of my head, but her voice is somber when she says, "I love you, too."

33

T-MINUS 14 DAYS

When I wake up at noon, I have multiple texts from Ace. Instead of reading them, I get out of bed, make Wudu, and complete the Dhuhr prayer. Once I'm finished, I start a group FaceTime with Nandini and Cora.

Neither hesitates to pick up, even though Nandini has to slip into the bathroom of her cousin's home and Cora has to duck into an alcove of the mall in order to hear me.

Cora takes one look at my face and says, "We're coming over tomorrow."

I laugh weakly, throwing my head back against my pillow. "Please do."

"Are you okay?" Nandini asks, voice low with concern.

I shake my head and swipe hastily at my eyes when tears begin to spill. I tell them everything my parents said the night before, and by the time I'm done, I feel lighter. Like a weight has lifted off my chest.

I'm so grateful to my friends for listening.

"I can't stand your parents," Cora says, her teeth grinding

together. "Why do they always prioritize their own wants and needs before yours?"

"They're not bad people." I sink deeper in my blankets. "They just grew up differently, so they have different expectations for me. I don't like letting them down."

"I know. I get it. We're second-generation Americans, and they want us to succeed in the ways that they couldn't," Nandini says. "I get it, Karina. I really do. My parents are the same. But that doesn't mean I have to live my life *for* them. You can respect your parents' wishes without becoming a puppet."

"They're projecting onto you, and it isn't fair," Cora adds. "They've restricted every part of your life. They don't give you any freedom. It's not *right*. Ace is just one of a million things they won't let you have. What about wanting to be an English major? You should be allowed to study what you want. It's your life. Not theirs!"

"This isn't a fairy tale," I say. I wish it was. I wish with all my heart this was a fairy tale with a guaranteed happy ending. "I can't miraculously claim back my freedom and then ride off into the sunset with the prince charming of my choice. You know it's not that easy."

"You've never even tried!" Cora says, throwing her hands up, her shopping bags rustling on her arms. "Karina, you can't let them make all your choices for you."

"Cora, calm down," Nandini says, shaking her head. "Yelling at Karina isn't going to help." She looks back at me. "I know it's hard, babe. You love your parents. But sometimes, it's okay to put yourself first."

"You know I can't," I say, my throat tight. "They'll never talk to me again. They'll take away all my freedom. I'll never see you guys outside school, I'll never be able to call or text you, I'll never be able to do anything I want. The little independence I have will be taken from me, and they'll never trust me again. They'll be so disappointed, and I—" This conversation is making me nauseated. "Can we talk about literally anything else?"

"You can't always just change the subject whenever—"

"*Cora,*" Nandini says pointedly. There are some things that Cora pushes that we wouldn't. Things she does that we couldn't. Nandini's brown parents are more lenient than mine, but Cora's father is a white guy from France. He met her mother, who's Chinese, when she was studying abroad, and they fell in love. Both of her parents are super modern and liberal and support her in almost all her decisions.

She still has it hard in other ways, especially with her sexuality, but for the most part, her parents have never restrained her the way mine have. It makes conversations like this difficult, because even though Cora tries to understand and be empathetic, there's only so much that fits with her own experiences.

I don't blame her for it. I know she wants the best for me and that she loves me. It's just hard to take her advice when our parents would react wildly different to us doing the exact same thing.

Cora looks between us and sighs. "Yes, we can change the subject. So what *exactly* did you and Ace do yesterday on your double date?"

I offer a small smile in thanks for not pursuing the subject, even though I can see she wants to. "It wasn't a double date."

"It was definitely a double date," Nandini says. "This, I'll let Cora grill you about all she wants. He invited you to go bowling with his sister and her girlfriend, Karina. That's a double date."

"Samir was there!"

"Yeah, and he was the strange fifth wheel."

"Oh my God, you two are horrible," I say, but the urge to hug them is stronger than ever.

At the top of my screen, another notification flashes. Another text from Ace.

I swipe up without looking and continue talking to Nandini and Cora late into the night. Before we hang up, we make solid plans for them to come over the next day since Ma has yet to revoke permission.

When I finally end the call, I have five missed texts from Ace.

I bite my lip, debating whether to click into them, before admitting defeat.

Alistair Clyde:
watching the great gatsby (aren't u proud) and maybe I am rich...

Alistair Clyde:
also what are ur plans for today?

Alistair Clyde:
karina are u feeling ok?

Alistair Clyde:
did I do smth wrong?

Alistair Clyde:
hey. sorry if I did anything to make you upset or uncomfortable. pls at least let me know ur alright when u can

I groan loudly and shove my face into my pillow.

Dadu happens to walk by my door then, cracked open from when she brought me dinner. She stops and looks at me with raised eyebrows.

I shake my head, not having an answer to explain my predicament.

"Do you want to watch *Beauty and the Beast*?" she asks. She knows it's my favorite childhood movie. "You don't have school tomorrow since it's spring break, right? So it's okay to stay up late?"

Maybe my parents are making my life a psychological horror film, but at least my grandma is here.

"Yeah, Dadu, I'd love that," I say, throwing my blanket off.

She smiles. "I just have to make one call and I'll join you."

I nod my agreement and head toward the living room to put on the movie. I make the active choice to leave my phone behind.

As I'm walking down the stairs, Samir climbs up them, and I avert my gaze. In the corner of my eye, I see a bewildered expression on his face, but I keep going without a word.

I've been avoiding Samir since yesterday. I don't know what to say to him, how to explain this rising resentment. At the end of the day, I know most of the blame lies on my parents, but he still *told* them. I don't know how to get past it.

When Dadu comes back, her expression is exhausted.

I falter. "Who were you talking to?"

She sighs. "Nabila. She's having a rough time."

Of course. I'm not even remotely surprised Dadu still reaches out to my estranged cousin, even though the whole family was supposed to cut her off.

I never doubted Dadu for a moment, but *knowing* she's willing to put aside traditional beliefs in order to support Nabila is a huge relief. I'm glad Nabila has that.

Selfishly, I'm also glad to know all of us, no matter what happens, will always have Dadu in our corner.

Dadu and I curl up together on the couch, and she counts

off beads on her misbaha as she hums along to some of the songs.

Halfway through the film, when Belle and Beast are in the library, Dadu glances at me. "You know, back in Bangladesh, I used to have shelves overflowing with books, too."

"Really? I had no idea."

"Yes," Dadu says. "I remember wishing I could read forever. Your Dada and I would read to your dad and your uncles when they were younger. It was the only way we could get them to fall asleep. They'd always ask for more. Stories are such beautiful things."

"They are," I say in agreement, leaning my head against her bony shoulder. "I love them. Sometimes I wish I could read Bengali so I could read your books, too."

Dadu squeezes my hand. "You remind me so much of myself when I was younger."

"No way," I say, shaking my head. "You're way too cool."

Dadu laughs but it's a dismal sound. She must still feel bad from yesterday. I wish she wouldn't. "You're cool, Myra. And you're so smart. You have so many books, I'm worried you'll need a second room just to store them all."

I nod seriously. "Let's kick Samir out. His room can become a library."

"*Myra,*" she says, exasperated. "We're not kicking Samir out. I just wanted you to know I'm so proud of you. You're becoming such an amazing woman."

"Dadu, stop," I say, cheeks warming. "You're too nice."

"I'm being serious. Every day, I grow more proud of you. You work so hard."

It's near midnight, but hearing her praise makes me feel like I'm basking in sunlight. "I don't know about all that."

"I do," Dadu says. "You're like Belle. Brave, beautiful, and smart. I'm lucky to have you as my granddaughter."

"You have to say that," I say, ducking my head. "You're my grandma."

"I'd be proud of you even if I wasn't your grandma. I hope you know I'll always support you no matter what."

I look at her and think about the conversation we had last night. I think about the conversation we had just a little earlier, about Nabila. I think about all the conversations I've been having with my friends. I think about all the conversations I've had with Ace. About my past and my future.

Maybe…maybe if Dadu supports me, there's hope. Maybe she can talk to my dad and he can talk to my mom, maybe, maybe, maybe. Just maybe.

"Dadu," I say slowly, focusing on her lap, rather than her face. "What if I don't want to be a doctor?"

She stops counting her beads. "You don't want to be a doctor?"

"I don't know," I say. "I'm not good at science."

"But do you like it? You don't have to be good at it. Practice makes perfect."

I shake my head. "I don't."

There's a beat of silence and I tense, waiting for her to tell me I'm being immature and ridiculous. Except, all she says is, "What do you want to do then, Myra?"

"I don't know," I say again. "I really love English. Maybe I could be a teacher or something."

"Oh. English. That makes sense," Dadu says, her tone thoughtful. I chance a glance at her and find her staring at me in consideration. "Have you talked to your parents?"

I grimace. "I brought it up briefly, months ago. It didn't go well."

"Are you set on your decision?" Dadu pauses the movie to give me her full attention.

Set on my decision? I haven't *made* a decision. "I don't

know," I say, once again. I sound like an indecisive airhead, but thankfully Dadu is still looking at me seriously. "I...don't want to be a doctor."

Dadu looks at me for a long time before taking a deep breath, as if she's bracing herself. "Okay. Do you want to tell your parents? We can figure it out together."

The painful relief that hits me is the best punch to the stomach I've ever felt. I would happily let someone hit me over and over if it felt like this. "You're not mad?"

"I could never be mad at you, Myra," Dadu says, patting my cheek. "If you killed someone, I would help you bury the body. If this is what you want, then I'll help you. Life is so short... You shouldn't have to spend it being unhappy. None of us should."

"I know but I thought—they... I don't know," I finish weakly.

"The older I am, the more I realize it's not worth it to prioritize things that make you miserable," Dadu says. "I don't want that for you. We're going to figure this out, okay? One day at a time."

I turn my face into her hand, nodding. This is the most comforted I've felt about this subject in a long time. Maybe ever. I don't know if I'm going to tell my parents, if I can ever be that selfish, but it's good to know that if I do, Dadu will help me. "One day at a time."

PART 3

inferno

34

T-MINUS 13 DAYS

"Wait, but do you really think it'd work?" Cora asks, her mouth stuffed with popcorn.

"You're the one who came up with the idea," Nandini says, raising a pointed eyebrow.

Cora shrugs. "Yeah, but I don't even know my own name half the time."

I laugh, nudging her foot with mine. It's the first day of our break and we're sitting together in my living room, Netflix on the television and snacks littered on the floor.

We had plans to see the new Marvel movie later in the evening, but we decided to forego the theater to stay in and spend time together. Mostly because Nandini's manager has gotten worse, and she can barely stand being under the same roof as her.

Cora and I are nothing if not supportive.

"I just don't know if the luggage approach is viable," I say. "I feel like you'll need something bigger if you're going to illegally sneak me into junior prom."

"What if we just stuff you in a car trunk?" Cora says with a grin and offers me the bowl of popcorn. I take a handful and pass it back.

"I sincerely hope the FBI doesn't actually monitor our phones," Nandini says, shaking her head. "Otherwise all three of us are about to go to jail for attempted kidnapping."

"Is it really kidnapping if I consent to being taken?" I ask, stroking an imaginary beard.

We're all still laughing when Dadu wanders through the living room on her way to the kitchen, her expression somber, still carrying the weight of yesterday on her shoulders. When she sees us, she pastes on a smile. "Do you need anything?"

"No," I say, offering a dismal smile back. "But thank you."

"Of course. If any of you beautiful girls need anything, I'm just upstairs. Let me know."

Then Dadu looks at Nandini and says something in Hindi, which she's fluent in. Nandini grins and says something in return.

When Dadu leaves, Nandini says, "Your grandma is honestly the best."

"I agree," Cora says. "But what did she say?"

"She just told me she liked my hair." Nandini pets her short curls. "I love her."

I smile faintly. "Me too."

"She really is the best." Cora reclines against the couch. "Anyway, where were we? Oh, yeah. So, I kind of want to ask Holly Harrison to junior prom. It's three months away, so there's still time. I know we said it was going to be a solo affair, but since Ace took the plunge, I thought maybe..."

"Don't mention Ace," I say halfheartedly.

Cora offers me an apologetic grin, tapping my knee. "Sorry, K."

"Holly is the cute girl from our chemistry class last year

who shaved her head, right?" Nandini asks, moving the conversation along. "Is she into girls?"

"I have no idea," Cora says, her lips pursed. "I want to say yes. My gaydar is going off."

"I think I've seen her on the GSA Instagram," I say, reaching for my phone to verify it. "That's not a guarantee, but it definitely raises the possibility."

"She's so pretty," Cora says, flopping into my lap. I smile down at her as I continue to scroll through our school's GSA Instagram page. "I just want to kiss her face."

Nandini snorts. "You're so weird."

"I embrace that," Cora says, and sticks out her tongue.

I hold out my phone, presenting the picture of Holly and a few other members of the club. "See?"

"Should I ask her then?" Cora says, looking between Nandini and me. "I won't mention you-know-who, but I'm assuming you two are still going together...?"

"Bold of you to assume I'm going at all," I say under my breath before nudging Nandini. "If my parents miraculously give me permission, you can be my date instead."

Nandini bites her lip. "Someone might have already asked me."

"*What?*" Cora and I say at once. Cora nearly knocks her head into my jaw in a rush to sit up and stare at Nandini.

"Since when?" I ask.

"And *who?*" Cora adds.

Nandini shrugs, looking self-conscious for once. "Timothy Chen. He came to the movies last week and we got to talking and...yeah."

"What? He's so cute!" Cora pinches Nandini's leg. I have the urge to repeat the motion, because Cora's right. "Why didn't you say something?"

"Because I didn't know if we were still going as a trio!"

Nandini glances at me. "Karina's you-know-who kind of threw a wrench in the mix. Since I wasn't sure, I told Timothy no."

"Oh my God, if you don't message him *right now*..." Cora lets the threat hang in the air, her finger pointed at Nandini. "Say yes!"

I nod eagerly. "Say yes."

"But if I say yes and Cora asks out Holly, then what will you do?" Nandini asks in protest. "You refuse to even mention his name."

Before any of us can contemplate that, the doorbell rings.

I have a feeling I know exactly who it is, and just the thought makes me feel like I'm about to break into hives. I got two more texts from Ace this morning, checking in on me, and I didn't reply to either of them. Maybe that wasn't the best decision.

"You summoned him," Cora jokes before she catches the look on my face. "That's not actually him, is it?"

"Uh." I'm at a loss. "It could be."

Nandini makes a shooing gesture at me. "Answer it!"

Before I can, Samir comes down the stairs, heading for the door.

Not Ace, then.

"It's for you, Myra Apu," Samir says seconds later, and I immediately clamber to my feet. Did I speak too soon?

When I come into the foyer, it's clear the world is colluding against me. Ace is standing there, hands tucked into his pockets. My heart swoops toward my stomach and erupts into a fresh scatter of butterflies that seem hell-bent on destroying me from the inside out.

"Karina," he says, eyes darting across my figure. "Are you okay?"

I rub my arms, a chill passing through me. "I'm fine."

"You weren't answering my texts, so I—"

"Oh my God, it *is* Ace!" Cora shouts from inside, making me wince.

Ace's expression shifts to surprise. "Do you have guests over?"

"Yeah, Nandini and Cora are here." I scratch my head, unsure how to proceed. "I'm sorry, but now isn't a good time."

"Oh. Okay," Ace says, his face falling. When his shoulders slump, I notice the bag strapped to his back and feel even *worse*. I honestly think about inviting him inside before I remember my parents' words and push that urge away.

"Okay." An awkward silence follows. "I'll see you at school next week."

"Next *week*?" Ace repeats, his voice quiet. "Karina, did I do something wrong?"

Samir is still standing there, looking between us with a forlorn expression on his face. My blood feels like it's boiling, blistering my skin.

I clench my hands into fists. "Samir, can you leave? This conversation doesn't concern you."

"Myra Apu, I—" Samir says, but I give him a sharp look, and he closes his mouth. "Yeah. Sorry. I'm going."

I look back at Ace, but I don't have an answer to his question. I don't know how to explain my parents. I don't think I have it in me. "I'm sorry. I can't talk about this now. You shouldn't have shown up at my house."

Ace falters. "I just thought..."

I press my lips together and some of my lingering bitterness sprouts to the surface. "I don't think you did think, Ace. You can't just show up at my house because I'm not answering your texts. And honestly, you probably shouldn't come here at all in the future, especially without a warning. My family isn't like yours. I could get in serious trouble if you keep doing this." I take a deep breath and lower my voice, my shoulders hunching. "I should have told you sooner, but I didn't think you'd keep showing up. I'm telling you now, though, and I need you to respect my boundaries. Can you do that? Please?"

He blinks at me in shock, but I don't take back the words. He can't keep doing this. I can't *let* him. I'm lucky Dadu is willing to look past Ace's behavior, but if he ever tries this when my parents are back…it's better I tell him now than face the consequences later. I know what being caught hanging around Ace entails. I only agreed to three weeks for a reason.

"My lines are not your lines," I say, when he keeps staring at me silently. "Please be careful about crossing them."

"Okay," he says again, looking down. "Of course. I'm sorry. I crossed a line. I won't cross it again."

I nod slowly. "Thank you."

Ace bites his lip. "This last weekend, when you weren't replying to my texts… I don't know what I did but I'm sorry for that, too. I didn't mean to do it."

It's not your fault, I want to say but I can't force the words past my lips. If I do, I'll have to explain everything. I can't do that on my doorstep, with Cora and Nandini one room over, and my grandma and Samir upstairs. There's too much to unpack.

It turns out I don't have to say anything because Ace swings his bag around front and pulls out a small gift bag. "I, uh, bought you some candles. I Googled anxiety a few days ago and saw that aromatherapy can help. When I was here the other day, I noticed you were using some, so I thought maybe… I got lavender-scented ones, because they're supposed to relax the body and mind."

My lips part but nothing comes out. He looked up anxiety? He bought me *candles*?

Ace doesn't seem to mind my lack of response, focused on pulling out an envelope from the gift bag. "It's a CD mixtape," he says at my incredulous expression. "I wrote down the Spotify link, too, in case you wanted to listen on your phone. It's songs that remind me of you. I just thought you should have it. Maybe it'll help relax you, too."

"Thank you," I say, looking down at it, utterly mystified. No one has ever bought me candles before, much less made me a *playlist*.

He stares at me, expression wistful, before he looks away. "Okay. I'll see you next week. Bye, Karina."

"Bye," I whisper, holding on to the gift bag with tight fingers as he walks away.

I close the door behind him and stare down at the bag, my breath caught in my throat.

Ace Clyde is an anomaly, and I have no idea what to do with him.

A Karina Ahmed Mixtape
"Light"—Sleeping At Last
"Bones"—Lewis Watson
"Almost (Sweet Music)"—Hozier
"Call Me Out"—Sarah Close
"Come Into The Water"—Mitski
"Hypnotised"—Years and Years
"Fuck Em Only We Know"—Banks
"Trust"—Alina Baraz
"Get You The Moon (feat. Snøw)"—Kina
"Your Hand In Mine"—Explosions In The Sky
★★Bonus: because I know how much you love pop music.
"Adore You"—Harry Styles
"Levitating"—Dua Lipa
"Treacherous"—Taylor Swift
"Euphoria"—BTS
"We Made It"—Louis Tomlinson

"Oh my God," Cora says in disbelief, looking at the hand-written letter Ace put inside the CD case, with each song title accompanied by underlined lyrics. "Karina, oh my God, he's literally in love with you."

"He's not in love with me," I say, but my voice is weak. "It's been like half a month."

"So?" Cora says, waving the letter in my face before gesturing to the expensive candles laid out in front of us. "Do you see this shit? Do you need glasses?"

Nandini finishes pulling the Spotify playlist up on my smart TV and we all silently stare at the title. *Lionheart.*

"What does that mean?" Nandini asks, poking me sharply.

I gape, unsure how to provide a proper definition right now. Ace made me a playlist titled *Lionheart* filled with *love* songs?

Cora starts typing rapidly into her phone before she looks at Nandini with wide eyes. "A person of exceptional courage and bravery."

"Karina."

"I don't know what to tell you!"

"Maybe tell me why this dumbass made you a *mixtape.*"

"I don't have the answer!"

We all stare at each other, at an impasse.

Cora looks away from me to grab the remote. "Let me hear this. I can't even grasp what's happening right now."

Listening to the playlist makes everything so much *worse.* The thought of Ace listening to songs this gentle and writing down lyrics in correlation to me...

"I think I'm dying," I say, knees weakening as I collapse against the couch. "This is the way the world ends. Not with a bang, but with a whimper."

"This is *not* the time to quote some dead old white man," Cora grumbles.

"There's never a time for quoting dead old white men," Nandini adds, but her gaze is more tempered. "Karina, you heard those songs. You must've had *some* sort of realization."

I throw myself face-first into the cushions and groan. I can't handle the thought of Ace liking me back, not when I know nothing can come of it.

"Karina," Cora whines, poking my rib cage. "This is *Ace Clyde*. He probably hates dogs, but he still likes you."

"He does not *hate* dogs." I look at her, disbelief momentarily staying my misery. "His dog is named Spade, and he's very sweet."

"I thought you were afraid of dogs," Nandini says with a raised eyebrow. "How did you come to learn Spade is 'very sweet'?"

"That is not the point!" I say, turning back toward the cushion. A barrage of memories burst like painful fireworks in my chest. The bakery, the bookstore, his honesty, my vulnerability, our secrets…

"I think that's exactly the point, Karina." Nandini joins Cora in her incessant poking. "You're different with him. Bolder. Braver. Stronger."

"You're just saying random words right now," I say. But I know they're not wrong. The fire inside me that Ace loves to write soliloquies about is burning brighter than ever.

"You look so much *happier*," Nandini says, reaching for my shoulder and forcibly turning me around. "You like him, don't you?"

"I can't."

"But you do," Cora says. "Admit it, Karina. You have a crush on Alistair Clyde. Maybe even more than that."

I press my lips together, refusing to say anything. I haven't said it out loud. Even with Samir, I denied it to the very end until everything blew up in my face.

If I say it to someone else, this becomes too real. The weight of my parents' disappointment becomes soul crushing.

"He likes *you*," Nandini says softly in response to whatever she sees on my face. "He likes you so much. Look at these candles. Look at this playlist. You couldn't pay my ex-boyfriend to do that."

"He could've bought the candles at any Duane Reade he passed by. And Ace *likes* music." I swallow painfully. "He probably didn't have to put that much effort into it."

Cora gives me an incredulous look. "He burned songs on a CD for you. Do you know what year it is? No one casually does that. He definitely put a lot of effort into this."

I've been thinking about that, too. I keep picturing Ace walking past a convenience store, catching sight of an assortment of candles and deciding to buy them for me. Or worse, in his room, waiting for me to text back only to receive radio silence, and then deciding to make a playlist for me to pass the time. They're such painfully sweet gestures that it seems like I must have made them up.

"We're just fake dating," I say. I'll live in denial about this for the rest of my life if I have to. "He has an image to keep up."

"In front of *who*?" Cora asks. "The only people here are me, you, and Nandini. He didn't even know we were going to be here. He came by specifically to give you this playlist and these candles and apologize to you for something he didn't even *do*. What part of that seems fake?"

"Don't do this," I bemoan, covering my face with my hands. Being reminded of how miserable Ace looked on my doorstep makes me want to die. I force myself to remember that he was in the wrong to show up at my house just because I didn't text back. I have to hold on to that, or else I'm going to give in to their pestering. "I'm not in an emotional state to argue with you."

"Because you know I'm right," Cora says. "Nandini, tell her."

Nandini sighs, patting my head. "Karina, sweetie, I love you, but this is too much. We're your best friends. If you can't admit to us you like him, who *can* you admit it to?"

"Oh, come *on*, don't play the best friend card."

"She has a point," Cora says. "I thought we were your best friends, Karina?"

"You both suck," I say fervently. They know I'm not going to dismiss our friendship. "Fine. Fine. I like him. Are you happy now?"

"I told you so!" Cora jumps up in excitement, nearly sending me toppling off the couch. "I fucking told you so."

Nandini snorts and helps me keep from falling with one hand stretched out. "We did tell you so. Now what are you going to do about it?"

"Absolutely *nothing*."

"My parents never found out about my ex-boyfriend," Nandini points out, nudging me. "You could keep it secret. We only have one more year until college and then we'll be in dorms, and none of this will matter. Your parents don't have to know."

She's right. I know she's right, but after my last conversation with my parents, I don't know if I have the strength to see this through, even in secret.

And I don't know if I can ask that of Ace, either.

"I'm doing nothing," I say again, staring up at the ceiling.

Cora does some kind of weird full body wiggle, poking my nose. "We'll see about that. I don't know a lot about

Ace, but I think it's pretty clear—he's used to getting what he wants."

I huff. "Well, not this time."

"Famous last words," Cora croons, not for the first time. I have a disturbing feeling she's right.

35

T-MINUS 12 DAYS

The next day, my relatives unexpectedly stop by. I'm in the shower when Samir knocks on the door and says, "Fatima and Labani are here with their parents."

Hearing Samir's voice is jarring in and of itself. We haven't spoken since yesterday afternoon, when he opened the door for Ace. But then the words register, and I'm even more confused. "Huh?" Since Fatima's family lives in New Jersey, they rarely visit us. Parties are one thing, but Long Island is a lengthy venture for a casual visit. "Why?"

"To see Dadu, so hurry up!"

I groan and start rinsing my hair.

After slipping into my room undetected, I change into a salwar kameez and dry my hair as fast as possible. By the time I come out, my relatives have settled in and are eating samosas and fuchkas.

"As-salaam alaikum," I say, bowing my head.

"Wa-alaikum salaam," they say back. My aunt and uncle are busy fussing over Dadu. They treat her like she's a fragile old lady ready to break her hip, and it's all too reminiscent of the conversation I had with Dadu about her brothers treating her like a precious jewel. I have difficulty hiding my grimace.

I wish I could help her, but I doubt anything I say will convince my aunt and uncle to stop hovering.

I sit down beside Fatima with a half smile. Labani is only ten years old, so we don't really talk to each other much. Samir is keeping her occupied, showing her his collection of robotic toys. I barely hold back a snide comment about him showing off in front of our uncle and aunt.

What would I ever show them? My poetry? Yeah, right.

"Are you feeling better?" I ask Fatima, trying to veer off that bitter road. It doesn't lead anywhere good.

"I'm okay." Fatima offers me a thin smile. That's hardly a good sign.

Now that I'm paying attention, there's a clear tension in the air.

"I like your salwar kameez," I say instead of prying. Whatever's bothering her is probably better discussed out of earshot of her parents.

"Thanks," she says, glancing down at the material. It's a pretty orange color, a fading sunset, with exquisite purple designs woven in. I wonder if I can find something similar in Ma's closet. "I like yours, too."

Ya Allah, this is awkward. She keeps eyeing her parents in a way that's making me increasingly uncomfortable.

"Do you want to watch something?" I ask. I'd suggest abandoning the room altogether, but I probably shouldn't leave before I have a chance to properly talk to her parents.

"Sure," Fatima says, and I click on the newest Netflix original movie.

Ten minutes into watching it, I understand Fatima's uneasiness.

"Fatima decided to double major in biology and psychology," Pooja Auntie says to Dadu, mouth curled in an unattractive sneer.

Oh jeez. Psychology isn't scientific enough for a lot of brown parents. I know this because I've asked my parents about it halfheartedly in the past, and they looked at me like I'd asked for a million dollars.

This explains what Fatima wanted to talk to Dadu about. I sigh internally, knowing even Dadu can't ward off the contempt radiating from Fatima's parents.

"Now she has to stay in her undergrad for another year," Mustafa Uncle says, rubbing his temples. "It's horrible."

"I *chose* to stay in my undergrad for another year," Fatima says, her voice sullen.

A small part of me is jealous of Fatima for pursuing what she wants, which is probably a bad thing. No, it's *definitely* a bad thing, because her parents look like they're one word away from dragging her outside and screaming at her.

"It's embarrassing, Fatima," Mustafa Uncle says, shaking his head. "You should have finished your biology degree. Now med school is going to be postponed."

If I tell my parents I want to pursue English, they're going to look at me the way Fatima's parents are looking at her right now. They'll never be able to forgive me, much less speak to me again. My heart constricts at the thought.

Ten, nine, eight, seven, six, five, four, three, two, one.

As discreetly as possible, I reach toward the center table and open one of the drawers, pulling out a candle and lighter. Within seconds, the scent of lavender fills the room, and my muscles relax infinitesimally.

"This isn't the place for this, Mustafa," Dadu says, giving her eldest son a hard look before turning a warmer gaze toward Fatima. "I'm very excited for you, dear. You're going to do amazing. Mashallah."

Fatima's expression lightens, and I'm glad to see it. As always, Dadu is ready to stand between us and the world. "Thank you, Dadu."

I can't help but wonder why *her* parents are like this. I wish I knew how all five of Dadu's sons ended up being so harsh and strict when she's always been anything but. At least in my case, I *know* it's because of my maternal side, but everyone else is a mystery. I wonder if this is why Dadu feels like she's failing us. Because somehow, despite her best efforts, her sons turned out into exactly what she tried to avoid.

It's easier for men, I guess. Traditional ways cater to them. But I would think—I would hope—being around Dadu would set them off those ways.

And yet here sits my cousin, as miserable as me. And here sit her parents, as hell-bent on shaping her into something she's not as my own.

My phone buzzes in my pocket, and I glance at it quickly. thinking of u. text me if u feel up to it.

Ace's words cause my heart to skip a beat. *Lionheart*, I think to myself, recalling the playlist that's been on a loop in my head since yesterday.

A burst of adrenaline rushes through me and I say, "I think it's really cool, what you're doing."

Fatima looks at me, eyes wide. I don't think she expected me to say something. *I* wasn't even expecting it. "Thank you, Myra."

I nod and try to ignore the way her parents are staring at me. Fatima looks relieved. Even if my words result in blow-back, it's okay if I helped her feel better.

"And what have you been doing in school, Myra?" my aunt

asks sharply. "Samir told us all about his robotics club. Are you in something similar?"

I should have expected that. "I'm in Pre-Med Society," I say, the words heavy on my tongue.

"I see," my aunt says before turning her gaze toward my brother. "Samir, won't you tell us about your last competition? Your mom said you guys came in first."

"Of course, Pooja Auntie," Samir says with a grin. "I actually have a competition tomorrow, too, but I'm not as worried as last time. I really thought we'd lose."

I roll my eyes. I remember his last competition. He didn't look distressed. In fact, he looked as confident as ever.

"Oh, don't be silly, Samir," Mustafa Uncle says, clapping him on the back. "You're on the track to MIT at this rate. Making the whole family proud."

"I was actually thinking of CalTech," my brother says, sudden affliction passing across his face. He chews on his bottom lip and asks, "Do you think Ma and Baba will let me go?"

"I don't see why not," Pooja Auntie says, smiling widely. "You're such a bright young boy. It's nice to see *someone* in this family take initiative."

When she glances our way, I know she's looking at Fatima, but I can't help but feel like her dark gaze is aimed at me.

"I'm proud of you," I whisper to Fatima when her mother finally looks away.

Fatima gives me a hug so tight that it's almost difficult to breathe. "Thank you," she murmurs.

I squeeze back. "You're so inspiring," I say, low enough that it doesn't reach past her ears. "Thank *you*."

Little things are starting to add up. Nandini and Cora's encouragement. Ace's kinship. Dadu's support. Fatima's bravery. I'm not alone.

Hours later, after Fatima and her family leave, Dadu and I

are cleaning up the dining room and she says, "What you said today was very kind."

I glance at her as I wipe down the glass table. "What did I say?"

"To Fatima," Dadu says, analyzing me. Her expression is more withdrawn than usual. "That you're proud of her."

I bite my bottom lip. "She has so much courage."

Dadu sighs, looking down. "So do you, Myra," she says. "I wish I could do more to help you kids. All of you have such big hopes and dreams and I want you to accomplish all of them. I'm starting to realize it's not as easy as I thought."

I blink in surprise. "What do you mean, Dadu?"

Dadu shakes her head gravely. "Our family. There's so much wrong here. I wish I knew what to do."

For the first time, I'm at a loss when it comes to my grandmother. All my life, she's been this confident, strong figure I've looked up to. I've never seen her this dejected before.

I don't know how to help.

"You're everything right with our family," I say. I've never been more certain of anything in my life.

"No, Myra." Dadu smiles weakly. "You are. I can't wait for the day you realize it, too."

36

T-MINUS 11 DAYS

Midland High has a different energy when school is out. It's calmer, somehow. I didn't expect to find myself here on the Wednesday of spring break, but when Samir knocked on my door this morning, asking if I was still coming to his robotics competition, I couldn't bring myself to say no.

Maybe it was because of the way he was fidgeting awkwardly in my doorway, or maybe it's because I've never missed one of his competitions before. Even now, sitting in the bleachers, the thought of missing one leaves a bad taste in my mouth.

The competitions are year-round, and this is the fourth one. Our school is hosting, and twelve different high schools have crammed into our gym. The judges are near the bleachers, handing out points for visuals, presentation, functionality, team spirit, and whatever else.

My brother's team is gunning for first place, trying to snag as many points as possible.

In a minor act of defiance, I keep my earphones in and listen to Ace's playlist on repeat instead of paying attention to the student commentator's play-by-play of the competition on the overhead speakers. Dadu and I are squeezed between two families who are far too enthusiastic.

I cringe away from the cheering mother on my left and hunch toward my grandma as she fiddles with her misbaha. The bleachers are far from comfortable, but Dadu isn't complaining, so I won't either. I distract myself by texting Nandini and Cora until Samir's group comes forward.

My brother is in his element, our school's colors painted across his cheeks. He spends a third of his time controlling the robot, another third cheering on his teammates, and the last third discreetly looking at the bleachers. His gaze is focused far above me and Dadu, where a lone girl is sitting with a book in her lap, toying with a cross necklace.

I squint, trying to figure out why she looks familiar before it clicks. She's one of the students that I used to tutor in English after school. What was her name...?

Leah.

I look back at my brother, but he's paying attention to the competition again. I barely understand what he's doing, but there's a huge smile on his face.

Something painful twists inside me. I wish I was that comfortable with my own passions.

After a while it becomes hard to look at Samir's beaming face, so I direct my attention back to my phone. As the minutes pass, I resist the urge to text Ace. It's hard. Harder than it's ever been to ignore someone's texts.

I miss him. A lot.

Sitting in the bleachers gives me a lot of time to think. About who I am, who I want to be, and who I can be. The choices I want to make. The sacrifices those choices will require.

My friends are right. I like Ace. Being around him makes me happy in ways I didn't know I could be. I want more than three weeks, and I don't want our relationship to be a pretense we put on for other people. I want it to be real.

But no matter what, it's something I'll have to hide from my parents. They'll never approve of him, no matter what I say, no matter what I do. It's not a fight worth attempting, not because I don't want to fight for Ace, but because it'll be pointless. They'll force me to stop seeing him, and I'll lose their trust forever.

But I want to be with him.

I want to go prom with him, like any other teenage girl. I want to look across a dance floor and see him walking toward me, holding twin cups of punch. I want to slow dance with him under flickering lights, the sound of our heartbeats echoing in our ears. I want it all.

I'm willing to lie to my parents and hide our relationship from them if that's what it takes. I was afraid at first, but the longer I go without speaking to Ace, the more certain I am that this is something I don't want to lose.

Studying English is something I can't do without confronting my parents, without fighting them over my future, but this thing with Ace doesn't have to be.

This can be mine and mine alone.

when prometheus promised us fire
did he know it would live inside your eyes?
did he know I would turn to ashes
to keep that flame alive?
I will kindle all that remains
even if my skin becomes a torch
even if my mouth tastes like a dying sun
I will burn for you
I will burn for you
I will burn for you

If he's okay with limitations on our relationship, if he's okay with understanding that, until we get to college, this is something we'll have to be careful with, then there's no reason for me to sit by and let these feelings pass without acting on them.

I didn't think I had it in me to be this brave. But after everything, I know I don't have any other choice.

I *have* to be brave.

For my own happiness.

The competition ends too quickly. I look up and realize Samir's team won.

I guess it's not that surprising, because he *is* smart, but I can't help but wonder what it'd be like if he lost. I wonder if my parents would care. Maybe they'd yell at him instead of me for once.

When we get home, I head to my room, but Samir stops me. His expression makes me uneasy. "What, Samir?"

"I'm sorry, Myra Apu," he says, scratching the back of his neck. "I didn't think you'd get in trouble because of what I said. I should've realized they'd be upset because Ace is a dude, but I figured it wasn't that deep. I thought as long as I kept the crush thing to myself, it'd be fine. That was my bad. I'm sorry. Really."

My resentment falters. I wasn't expecting an apology, but I realize a small part of me hoped for one. I'm both surprised and relieved.

"Thank you for apologizing," I say quietly.

"If you ever want to..." He doesn't finish the sentence. "I won't ever mention Ace to them again without talking to you about it first. I promise. For real this time. Sorry again."

I swallow past the sudden lump in my throat. "Thank you."

He stands there awkwardly for another moment before he nods and turns away, heading to his room as I head for mine.

Samir's apology stirs something in me, and I'm struck with

the urge to act now. I need to make an apology of my own. I need to make a *confession* of my own.

I can do this.

I light a cinnamon-scented candle and take a deep breath. Before I can overthink the situation, I grab my phone and text Ace, I'm sorry.

What I don't expect is for my phone to start vibrating. Alistair Clyde would like to FaceTime...

I waver, looking at myself in the screen. I look like I've been lying in bed all day, my hair ratty and piled in a high bun and my eyes droopy with dark circles underneath. I didn't put any effort into looking good for Samir's competition. I regret it now.

But I'm not ignoring Ace anymore. I don't want him to think I am.

With trembling fingers, I accept the call.

"Karina?" Ace says, his voice hesitant.

I lick my lips. "I'm sorry I took so long. Things have just been...a lot."

"No apologies, remember?" Ace smiles but it fades quickly. "You picked up."

"I did," I say quietly. He's leaning against his bed frame, in a sweater that looks fuzzy and warm. I want nothing more than to wrap my arms around his neck and breathe him in. But there are more important things. If I don't say this now, I'm never going to. "I want to do this."

"Do what?" Ace asks, blinking at me.

I take a deep breath. *Ten, nine, eight, seven, six, five, four, three, two, one.* "This thing you and I have. I want it to be real. I don't want to pretend anymore."

It takes a moment but then Ace's lips part. He's staring at me like I'm going to disappear right before his eyes. "You want to—really?"

I nod, worrying my bottom lip between my teeth. "It's not going to be easy." My phone is shaking in my hands. "It's going to be so far from easy."

Ace's gaze is so intense that I feel pinned to the spot. "I don't care what's easy, Karina. You're worth it."

I laugh, half-hysterical. "You would say that."

"I'm serious," he says, conviction heavy in his voice.

I smile faintly. "You should back out while you still can. Doing this…this thing with me is a lot to handle. I have a lot of lines. I'll understand if you want to call it quits. You don't owe me anything."

Ace starts shaking his head before I even finish speaking. "I'll take my chances," he says. He scans my expression before he asks, "What made you change your mind?"

"It wasn't a what," I say. These words are too honest, too truthful. But they're the right words. "It was a who. Someone who said they saw a spark in me. They helped me realize that I could be brave. A lionheart, even."

Ace laughs breathlessly. "They sound wise."

"They are," I say, my smile shaky. "But they're also beautiful and thoughtful and patient and so very lovely."

"Yeah?" Ace says, a smile pulling at his own lips. "You shouldn't say things like that. They might get the wrong idea and think you like them."

"It's a good thing I do, then," I say, the words unfamiliar and terrifying. *Ten, nine, eight, seven, six, five, four, three, two, one.* "I like them so much, it's kind of crazy."

Ace's smile stretches even wider, familiar dimples popping into view. "Say it again."

"I like you, Alistair Clyde." There's something bright and colorful and warm blooming inside me, growing flowers in the gaps between my ribs and alongside the edges of my heart. "I like you so, so much."

Ace's eyes shine brighter than they ever have before. The midnight sky doesn't begin to compare. "I like you beyond explanation, Karina Ahmed. You drive me insane and I wouldn't trade that for the world."

"I drive *you* insane?" I say, raising my eyebrows. My lips are stretching so wide that my cheekbones hurt. "You're the one that won't study no matter how much I beg you."

"Actually…" He disappears from the screen and comes back holding a copy of *The Merchant of Venice* with colored tabs marking the pages. "I finished this."

My eyes widen. "Are you serious?"

"Is Portia a cross-dressing fake lawyer?" Ace throws back.

There are explosions in my chest, little fireworks of glee injecting themselves into my bloodstream. "You really read it."

Ace's face softens. "I did."

"I'm proud of you," I say, my heart swelling with affection. "Maybe you'll pass the Regents, after all."

He laughs, throwing his head back. "Yeah, maybe."

There's a moment of warm, comfortable silence before Ace breaks it. "I want to ask you something." For the first time since I've met him, he looks bashful. As if he's somehow *nervous* to ask me whatever it is.

"Okay," I say. My pulse is loud in my ears, because Ace is watching me like I'm holding the universe in my hands.

Ace looks down, his cheeks a lovely pink color I've only read about in books. "What do you think about dinner and a movie tomorrow?"

I knew it was coming, and yet my breath still hitches. "Are you asking me out?"

Ace's smile doesn't waver as he tilts his head at me. "Yes, I am."

I think I'm choking on my lungs. Ace wants to go on a date. With me. A *date*.

"Okay," I say, my voice high-pitched.

"Okay?" Ace repeats. There's the beginning of what looks like it could be a full-blown grin hinting at the corner of his mouth.

Before I can second-guess myself, I nod. "All right."

"All right," Ace says, as if it's that simple. The grin comes to life. It looks like the sun is shining from Ace's eyes—the sun, the stars, and the moon, all together. "It's a date."

I'm helpless to do anything but grin back, butterflies fluttering in my stomach. "It's a date."

37

T-MINUS 10 DAYS

I'm the stupidest person alive. Why would I *ever* agree to a date with Ace Clyde?

"I am *freaking* out," I say to my laptop, where Nandini and Cora are on FaceTime. "Why would you ever let me do this? What kind of friends are you guys?"

"Don't start," Nandini says. I don't have to look away from the mountain of clothes piled on top of my bed to know she's rolling her eyes.

She's in the middle of assembling a puzzle with her brother, and Cora is in the bath, bubbles hiding half her face. They've been trying to calm me down for the last twenty minutes.

Four candles are burning in my room right now, and frankly, I'm worried I'm one candle away from starting a house fire. "I've never been on a date! How does this even work?" I start pacing back and forth, my fingers buried in my hair.

I told my grandma I was going out with a friend today, and she didn't ask me who—I have a feeling she knows—but anxiety still tugs on my heartstrings.

"You're being ridiculous, Karina," Cora says, her voice shockingly gentle as she blows a bubble at me. "Relax. Don't put out on the first date. Or do. Just enjoy yourself."

"I haven't even *kissed* a boy and you think I'm going to *put out* on a first date?" I ask, eyes wide. "Do you think Ace thinks that, too? I'm meeting him at his house."

"I was joking," Cora says, eyebrows raised as she lifts a bottle of face wash. "Does Ace seem like the type to pressure you into anything?"

"Yes," I say, thinking of him urging me to live my life to the fullest. Nandini drops a handful of puzzle pieces and Cora squirts out a ridiculous amount of face wash. I look up to see the alarmed expressions on both their faces and hurry to add, "No. No, sorry, I—no. He wouldn't pressure me to do anything."

Even the times when Ace has crossed my personal boundaries, he's always been willing to listen and apologize. He learns from his mistakes and doesn't make them again. I can't put into words how important that is to me.

"Then just relax," Nandini says, her voice soothing as she gathers puzzle pieces again. It helps my nerves only slightly. "So what are you going to wear?"

"Oh God, don't remind me." I fall backward onto my bed. *Ten, nine, eight, seven, six, five, four, three, two, one.* The fear of getting caught and the fear of messing up are terrifying, and both have made a home inside of me. "I want to die. I'm going to jump off my balcony. This is the end."

"Karina," Cora says softly on the other end. For a moment, I feel pathetic at how worked up I must sound just because I'm going on a date. It's not like Ace asked for my hand in marriage.

"Yeah, okay. Will you guys help me choose?"

Nandini smiles. "Always."

★ ★ ★

When I arrive at Ace's house, my jaw drops. He sent his driver—apparently he really *is* that rich—to pick me up and bring me to his house, and now I'm staring at a rose-petal path.

I text Ace in confusion, and his only reply is, follow the roses ♥

The heart results in a strange swoop in my stomach. I follow the petals along a stone path, leading to a greenhouse. Ace is waiting for me inside with a candlelit dinner and a stupid grin on his face that I feel the strange urge to kiss.

As I step closer, I realize they're lavender-scented candles. My lips turn up of their own accord.

"What's this?" I ask, wiping my sweaty palms against my skirt.

Nandini and Cora helped me pick out an outfit, a deep blue blouse interwoven with silver designs of flora and a high-waisted black skirt that I wore over black tights. More importantly, they helped me pick out jewelry which I borrowed from my mom's collection. Maybe wearing traditional Bangladeshi jewelry for a first date is a little over the top, but I think it's fitting.

Ace has abandoned his leather jacket for a white button-down shirt and black slacks paired with dark loafers. I try not to feel giddy at the thought of him dressing up for our date.

"Well, this is filet mignon in mushroom sauce with a side of parmesan risotto. It's halal, too." He looks down, fiddling with his rings. "I might have asked my mom for help over Skype."

I can't help but *awwww*. "Really?"

"Yeah," Ace says. There's a hint of pink to his cheeks that causes a pang in my chest. "She loves cooking, so she was happy to help."

He pulls out my chair and gestures for me to sit down. "Bone apple teeth, madame."

I burst into laughter. "Bone apple teeth? You're so weird."

Ace shrugs. "You like it."

"Strangely enough, I do," I say, lowering my gaze to my plate. The food smells delicious. It's fancier than anything I've ever eaten before. "Bone apple teeth, sir."

He asks about my ride here as we start our meal and I can't help poking fun at the fact his family has a driver. He takes it gracefully, which is more than I expected. I didn't think he'd throw a fit or anything, but seeing him laugh it off is a pleasant surprise.

As I'm spreading my napkin across my lap, Ace taps my wrist. I look up to see him watching me, eyes bright. "You're the loveliest flower in this entire garden."

Laughter spills from my lips. "Is that right? Aren't you just the smooth talker?"

Ace's eyes crinkle in amusement. "The smoothest."

Without thinking about it, I lean forward to brush a stray strand of hair out of his eyes. "You've wooed me," I tease.

He catches my wrist and holds me there, suspended. "*Wooed*? I've wooed you?"

I pout at him halfheartedly. "I was trying to be nice and this is what I get—"

"No, no, I like it," he says, playing with the cuff of my sleeve. "That's going to be my job from now on. To always woo you. Expect to be wooed frequently and as often as possible."

"You're ridiculous," I say affectionately, pulling back my wrist. "I think you overestimate your prowess."

"Don't use SAT words," Ace says, nudging me underneath the table with his foot.

I slant him a look. "*Prowess* isn't an SAT word."

"It is," he insists. "I saw it in a workbook the other day."

I falter. Last I heard, Ace wasn't taking the SATs. "Why were you practicing?"

Ace falls silent, and his jaw tenses. I reach over to gently touch his hand.

He looks down at our fingers and exhales. "I've been thinking a lot…and I don't want to throw away my future."

My eyes widen. "So, you're going to take the SATs? You're going to apply to NYU?"

"Yeah," he says, biting his bottom lip. "Yeah, I think I am. I was kind of…the thought was lingering in my head, you know? When I started failing English, I had a moment of panic where I realized there's no way I was going to get into college if I *failed* a class, especially not a school like NYU."

"That's why you decided to get a tutor," I say, the pieces clicking together.

"Yeah." Ace isn't meeting my eyes. "But I didn't want my dad or Xander to know. I already said I wasn't going to college. I already said I didn't care about school. My dad was so mad at me—he's still mad at me, honestly. But it's better than being invisible."

"How could you ever be invisible?" I ask, thrown by the concept. Even before I was tutoring Ace, I knew of him. Everyone in our grade knows of him. "You're so…bright."

A smile touches Ace's lips. "Yeah?"

"Yeah." My cheeks warm at the admission. "Back to what you were saying. Does your dad know you're going to apply?"

"No. I'm not going to mention it to my dad or Xander, but I'm going to do it. This isn't for them. It's for me." He glances at me and then looks away. "My family wants me to go to Yale, anyway. My grandfather went, my dad went, and now Xander's going, too." He shakes his head. "I'd rather go to NYU. If I can't do that, I want to study astronomy anywhere except Yale."

My heart feels like it's going to burst with pride. "What changed your mind?"

"You," Ace says simply.

I almost bite my tongue off in surprise. *"Me?"*

"Yes," he says. "I thought about what you said about how hypocritical I was being, and realized you were right. I was telling you to live your life for yourself when I wasn't living my own that way. And you were right about how that was a very privileged way to see things. We're from two different worlds...but that doesn't mean they can't overlap. Even if it's just one small, tiny inch. That's enough for me."

"How do you exist?" I ask, floored by the fact he's sitting here with me and having such an open conversation. "How can you be real?"

"I ask myself that about you every day," Ace says, reaching across the table to tuck a strand of hair behind my ear. His skin is warm where it grazes mine.

A question rises to the tip of my tongue and, in the gentle glow of the candlelight, I let myself ask, "Why didn't you show up that first day? To our tutoring session?"

Ace flushes, his cheek blooming with color, and looks away. "It's stupid. Xander was nagging at me for slacking off so much, for focusing on the piano instead of my grades. He didn't know about the tutoring thing, and I definitely wasn't going to tell him. But then he got our dad involved and things went downhill."

"What happened?" I ask.

"My dad grounded me and told me to come home immediately after school and study, and I—it was the first time in a while that he sounded concerned about me. Like he cared about me. I probably should have just told him the truth, but I couldn't." Ace grimaces. "So I went home instead of going to the library. I'm sorry. It was a jerk move."

Having an explanation for that first day is strange. It feels both like it was weeks ago and just yesterday he failed to show up. "And then the next day? My study guide?"

Ace grimaces, running his hands through his hair. "Xander and I had a fight that morning. Ever since our mom left, we've grown apart. Before they split up, I was Mom's favorite and he was Dad's, and it evened out. But after she left, it wasn't even anymore. He and Mom rarely talk anymore. I don't know why."

Briefly, I recall Xander checking out an Italian cookbook. I can't help but wonder now if it was an attempt to connect with his estranged mother, who apparently loves cooking. I keep the thought to myself, unwilling to speculate about Ace's family.

"Since she's gone, Xander acts like we're competing for our dad's love. As if it's something to *win*. I can't stand it. I was skipping class that day, but then he saw me in the hallway and the first thing he did was rat me out to Miss Cannon."

"So that's why he showed up during English class," I say, the memory flickering through my brain. "God. What's his problem?"

"When you find out, let me know," Ace says, a frown pulling at his mouth. "While we were talking, Miss Cannon said you left something on my desk, so I grabbed it."

I nod, remembering his entrance all too well.

"When I came back out with the study guide, Xander saw it. 'Ace, you're actually studying? I'm so proud. I never thought the day would come. Miss Cannon, it's a modern-day miracle!' I didn't have it in me to stand there and put up with his condescending bullshit, so I threw the study guide in the recycling bin, flipped him off, and walked away. I came back for it later, but I guess you must've gotten to it before I could." Ace looks up at me, a rueful expression on his face.

"You're lucky the recycling bin was empty," I say lightly, nudging his foot under the table.

"I'm surprised *you* didn't tell Miss Cannon what I did. You know, that's why I was intrigued by you at first. I'm so used to being in trouble because of Xander, and it was kind of nice to not have to worry about that." A sheepish smile flits across Ace's lips. "I might have a trust issue or two."

I consider his words, flipping them over and over in my head as I try to work through them. The first thing he ever asked me was why I didn't tell Miss Cannon about him skipping our meeting. It makes sense now.

What doesn't make sense is his relationship with his brother. As upset as I was with Samir this past week, I don't think the two of us have ever been that volatile.

"What…happened between you two?" I ask hesitantly. "There are rumors you sabotaged Xander's presidential campaign. Is that true?"

"Yes," Ace says, leaning his other elbow against the table and sighing. "That might be one of the few rumors about me that is actually true. Mom and Dad had been separated for a few years by then, but she didn't move to Italy until last year, around the same time Xander was running for student body president. Xander and I were always fighting, and he kept telling Dad about every single little thing I did. It was driving me up the wall."

"Who could blame you," I mutter.

"Xander could," he says, a muscle ticking in his jaw. "I asked Mom if I could go with her to Italy, because I couldn't take it anymore, but Xander overheard and told my dad. Dad thought it was because of him. He was heartbroken, and Xander was elated, and I was *furious*. The next day, I set out to ruin his campaign—not that it worked, since he's clearly student body president. Since then, he's been spreading rumors about me as payback."

I blink. "What the fuck," I say, unable to form anything more coherent. "Just...*what*?"

Ace exhales deeply. "I really don't know. I can't wait until he goes to Yale in August and all this ends. I'm exhausted."

I reach across the table and place my hand over his. "I'm sorry." I wait a moment before offering a timid smile. "At least there's Mia?"

"At least there's Mia," he agrees, lacing our fingers together. "After you and I talked, I told her the truth about everything. She demands *real* double dates in the future."

My smile widens. "I'm happy to oblige. I'm glad you have her."

Ace nods, locking gazes with me. "And now I have you, too."

Warmth spreads through me. I try to mask the butterflies raging beneath my skin by extending the conversation. "You know, for someone who *asked* for a tutor, you spent an awful lot of time in the beginning not studying."

"You're more interesting than English," he says, grinning.

I raise an eyebrow. "Sure."

He chuckles, squeezing my hand. "I told you before, Karina. I saw a spark in you."

"Every time you say that, you sound more ridiculous," I say, but I don't pull away.

"Good," he says before his eyes light up. "Hey, I just remembered I want to show you something. Are you done eating?"

I glance down at my plate, which is almost empty. I didn't realize how hungry I was. "Yeah."

Ace leans over, blows out the candle, and takes my hand. "Come on."

38

T-MINUS 10 DAYS

The piano. That's where Ace is leading us.

After he flicks on the lights in his room, he gestures for me to join him on the piano bench. "Sit with me."

I take a seat, eyeing the beautiful piano curiously. Is Ace going to play something? "What did you want to show me?"

Ace looks torn for a split second, but his expression eases at whatever he sees on my face. "It's hard to play in front of other people," he says, pressing his thumb against a key. "My friend Ben is a natural performer. He loves crowds. Me...not so much."

I give him a curious look. "You've mentioned Ben before. How'd you two meet?"

His mouth turns up in the corner. "It was during a competition in Brussels. He accidentally dropped coffee on my sheet music. Ben—he's a prodigy. Shines brightest on stage. I think it intimidates people, but I don't really care about all that, you know?"

I bump shoulders with him. "Yeah, I know. You can be pretty intimidating yourself."

Ace huffs a laugh. "So I've been told. But yeah, I think Ben expected me to freak out, except I just took it in stride. I know shit happens sometimes. From then on, we stuck together when we saw each other at competitions." He pauses. "He told me to say hi to you, by the way."

I grin. "Did he now?"

A flush spreads across Ace's cheekbones and he looks down at the piano. "Anyway, during competitions, I have to pretend no one else is around. I used to be able to play only in front of my mom. But she's in Italy now, and I'm here, so…"

"Why is she in Italy?" I ask. I've wondered for a while now, but it never seemed like a good time to ask.

He sighs, hands faltering. "She's a boutique fashion designer. She's been opening up branches across the world, and her flagship is in Italy. Even though we talk all the time, I don't get to see her much anymore, for obvious reasons."

I lean my head against Ace's shoulder. "I'm sorry. That sucks."

"It's not either of our faults," he says. "When I asked her to take me with her, I wasn't thinking straight. She travels too much for me to go with her while still attending school, and I wouldn't want her to sacrifice her dreams to stay with me."

A new fact about Ace. Instead of accusing his mother of abandoning him or whining about her being gone, he chooses to absolve her of blame. He chooses to be selfless.

I admire him more every day. "You're so different from what I thought you'd be."

"Not the bad boy you expected?" he teases.

"Not at all," I say, but can't help adding a quip. "Although, you should probably stop wearing a leather jacket."

He laughs and gently shoves me. I pretend to flail but he

wraps an arm around my waist before I can fall. "Sit still for a moment, okay? I really do have something to show you."

I make a show of rolling my eyes. *"O-kay."*

Ace ducks his head, but that doesn't stop me from seeing the dimples pressing into his cheeks. "You already know I play the piano but, uh, I like to compose songs, too. I haven't had a lot of inspiration lately, but…something changed these last few weeks." He takes my hand and presses his lips against the inside of my wrist. "This song is called 'Spark.'"

My breath catches. There's no way Ace wrote a song for me.

I don't know what to say. But maybe I don't have to say anything, since Ace's focus is on the piano now.

He starts with one hand, pressing down lightly on the keys. With each soft note, my heart begins to melt. As he repeats the keys over and over, he grows more confident and presses down with more enthusiasm. Soon after that, he adds his second hand.

The tempo strums on my heartstrings. I don't know what to look at.

I have the option of watching Ace's capable hands dance across the keys, his rings stark against the black and white. His wrists look incredibly delicate, and I'm all but held captive by the way his hands move.

But there's something about Ace that's even more arresting: his expression. A look of peace settles across the planes of his face, soft and open, as he presses key after key. He's losing himself in the familiar motions, and it's strange, because it looks so natural—like Ace was born to play the piano.

For the first time since I've met him, Ace looks naked with emotion. With each note, I feel more alive.

He's stunning like this. I wish I had a way to capture this moment, to put it on billboards and magazines. Everyone in the world deserves to know that Alistair Clyde is completely and utterly beautiful.

My eyes begin to water, because there's something familiar in this tune. I don't know how to place it, but there is. *It's me.* He's somehow turned me into a song, into a series of notes.

The song starts slow and quiet but there's a strength hidden, woven through as the song grows more and more intense. Something infinitely tender overlaps with something harsher.

In this song, I hear everything he thinks of me. I'm a dichotomy between quiet and bold, between soft and brave.

When Ace finishes playing, he's hesitant again, the last few notes soft. He presses one final key before he lets out a breath and sits back on the bench. The moment he turns toward me, a tentative expression on his face, everything collapses inside me.

I lean forward and kiss the corner of his mouth without thinking. It takes a moment for my own action to register, and I shift away, heat prickling the back of my neck. The song is pulling such a strong reaction from me, and I don't know what to do with it.

He blinks at me, lips parted. His shock lasts only a moment before a breathtaking smile breaks across his face. "Karina," he whispers, my name a gentle caress, before he leans in and presses his lips against mine.

He's kissing me.

Oh my God, he's *kissing* me.

I part my lips and Ace moves closer, kissing me deeper. His mouth is soft, but his teeth are sharp where they catch on my lips, and it's somehow perfect. One of his hands cups my face, his thumb gently brushing my cheek. My own hands find their way into the dark strands at the back of Ace's neck and I tenderly card my fingers through them, pressing closer.

I don't know how long we kiss, but suddenly Ace is laughing into my mouth and I can't help the giggle that bursts from my own lips.

We pull apart, but his forehead rests against mine and he's still smiling. "Hi," he says. "Did you like the song?"

I smile back, closing my eyes. There aren't enough words to answer his question. "Hi. I did. It was beautiful. You're beautiful."

Ace huffs another laugh. He's close enough that I feel his breath against my face.

I blink my eyes open. "God, you're ridiculous. Who writes an entire *song* for someone?"

"Who said the song was about you?" Ace says as he places a featherlight kiss between my eyebrows. I nearly go cross-eyed trying to watch him. "It could've been about Spade."

"Oh?" I raise my eyebrows at him. "Do you often write songs about your dog?"

"Perhaps," he says, his nose brushing against mine. "Spark. Spade. Only two letters off."

"Shut up." I shove him away, laughing. "I can't stand you."

Ace nudges me. "It's a good thing you're sitting down."

"You're *horrible*."

"It's all a part of my charm."

I consider him for a moment, from his bright eyes to the sweet dimples indenting his cheeks to his messy unruly hair that I just ran my fingers through. "Yeah," I say, more breath than words. "It is."

By the end of the night, I realize I've made the worst possible mistake ever, because I'm now terribly, terribly besotted with Ace Clyde. There's no way to come back from this.

It's not like I expected to like him this much—it's not like I *wanted* to. But Ace is a ridiculous boy with a warm smile, and he's so lovely sometimes that I don't know what to do with myself. He listens to me and respects my boundaries and *learns* from his mistakes. It's perplexing and addicting.

I lie in bed, staring at the poems on my ceiling. This is the happiest I've felt in a long time. And I can't help but feel stupid for it.

I want to be selfish for once. My parents accuse me of being selfish all the time, but this is the first time it's ever been true. I rarely do things for myself, but I don't want to give this up. If this is the only thing I can allow myself, if this is as brave as I can be, then I want this for as long as I can have it.

Ace is wonderful. Wonderful enough that I'm willing to ignore the possibility of doom in the future. When my parents come home, this beautiful, blossoming thing that we have might wither under the strain. It'll become lying, hiding, and sneaking around. We both deserve better than that, but it's all I can offer.

I'll deceive my parents if I have to. I'll find a way to be with Ace, even if it means doing something ridiculous, like sneaking into junior prom in a duffel bag. This isn't something I'm willing to half-ass.

If Ace leaves, I'll let him go. But it's not going to be me that steps away from this, not unless I have no other choice. I want this. I want him.

I want to be happy.

39

T-MINUS 9 DAYS

The next day, I look back at the poem Ace found a while back. "Unshakeable."

I never finished it. Writing about myself makes me uncomfortable in a way that's hard to explain.

It feels too honest, too vulnerable.

I remember writing it the day after my parents lectured me against pursuing anything that wasn't STEM. Sitting at my desk and not being able to push down the anxiety. Counting *ten, nine, eight, seven, six, five, four, three, two, one,* to no avail.

Then I sat down with my journal and the words poured out for the first time. I couldn't figure out what happens past *it's dark, it's light, a hand reaches out* then, but now I think about Ace's smile, Ace's patience, Ace's kindness. I think I finally have the answer.

> *somewhere there are birds that fly free*
> *here, I am caged and can barely breathe*
> *there is so much to say*

these thoughts never fall from my lips
I am scared of so goddamn much
afraid these flames will burn
my fingers, they hurt from clinging so hard

I'm lost, I'm bruised, I don't know what to do
I never thought I'd give up
but I'm starting to think I'm going to lose

it's dark, it's light, a hand reaches out
I hold, you pull
somehow I find the will to keep on
unshakeable, you whisper
I exhale my first clean breath
unshakeable, I whisper
freedom tastes sweeter than I'd expect
unshakeable, we whisper
you guide me through the fire
unshakeable, we whisper
you hold every key I thought I'd never find

some days, my hands, they tremble with doubt
you take them, you press them
against your chest where your heart beats steady
when I shiver, you sing to me
the sweetest of songs
the sun is brighter than it's ever been
and I think for you, I'd join the fight again

unshakeable, you whisper
unshakeable, I whisper
unshakeable, we whisper

"Unshakeable," I whisper to myself. I finished it. I opened myself to that vulnerability.

Unshakeable.

It's what I want to be. It's what I hope to be.

I close my journal and take a deep breath, letting that sink in. Unshakeable. If I was unshakeable, there are so many things I would do.

T-9 days.

Nine days until my parents are back and everything changes.

Nothing terrifies me more than my parents' disappointment. Of losing their respect and love. Those things feel flimsy most days as it is. To lose what little I have is the most horrifying thing I can think of.

I know I'm not the only one who struggles to find the balance between loving their parents and being who they want. A lot of other brown people I know have dealt with situations like this. My experience isn't singular.

But that doesn't make it any less scary. I might not be entirely alone in this experience, but I *am* alone.

Then I think of Dadu in the next room, and her unwavering support of me, and I adjust that thought. I'm not alone. I have her.

I have to believe that if she can support me, my parents can, too.

I hope.

I stumble into Dadu's room. She's sitting on a chair, praying. Her knees are too creaky for her to pray on the prayer mat, so an allowance is made for her to do her rackats from a chair. I blink in surprise, but then grab a janamaz, joining her for the Maghreb prayer.

When I finish, I look from side to side, murmur a few surahs, blow out a long breath into my palms—asking Allah for guidance in the next few days—and turn to look at Dadu.

"Are you okay, Myra?" she asks.

I nod. "Just thinking." Being around her is enough to make me breathe easier. Having someone in my corner—having *her* in my corner—is more than I could've ever hoped for.

Yet I still can't bring myself to make the definitive decision to tell my parents about wanting to study English.

Nine days to decide.

I technically have until college applications in the fall, but I know if I don't do it when my parents come back, I probably won't do it ever. Especially because Dadu will go home to New Jersey and I'd have to do it on my own.

And facing my parents alone about *this*? Just the thought makes me want to walk into traffic.

No, if I do this, it has to be the day they come back.

But I don't know if I have the strength. I don't know if I can throw all my parents' hard work back in their faces.

"Dadu, why is life so hard?" I ask, flopping onto her pillows.

She squeezes my ankle. "Your Dada used to ask me the same thing."

"Did you have an answer for him?"

My grandma laughs lightly and looks at her bedside table. A photo of her, Dada, and the rest of our family is framed there. "Of course not. I don't think he was ever genuinely asking. Life is hard because it is. There's no easy answer. It's just a matter of whether we're willing to face the hardships. Even when life was hard, your grandpa was always willing to face it with me."

"It makes sense," I say, smiling. "Everything is easier with your support."

"Easier," Dadu echoes, her gaze still focused on the photo. "But not easy."

I sigh wistfully. "Yeah. But not easy."

40

T-MINUS 8 DAYS

With only eight days left, Ace and I agree to make the most of our time.

For our second date, Ace doesn't tell me what we're doing. Instead, he blindfolds me before I can even walk out of my house, which is all kinds of ridiculous. It's clear how fond of him I am, because I mutter only one insult and indulge him otherwise, even though I'm *pretty sure* we're in a different car.

We drive for maybe twenty minutes before Ace stops the car. "We're here," he says, and I can *hear* the grin in his voice.

"What a lovely view," I say, still blindfolded.

Ace sighs in exasperation. "Hold on." His long fingers come around the back of my head, untying the cloth. His rings brush my ear, cold against my skin.

It was already late when Ace picked me up. The sun had set a few minutes prior to his arrival. Now, when I pull the blindfold away, the sky is completely dark.

I look around, trying to figure out what we're doing, but there's nothing around us for miles. We're in a clearing beside a cluster of trees, and Ace is smiling like we're at the top of the world.

That's when I realize what type of car we're in. It's some kind of pickup truck that looks like it belongs in a junkyard. I'm surprised we made it this far without the vehicle breaking down. "Who did you rob to get this death machine?"

He bumps his shoulder against mine. "No one. It belongs to my stepmother."

"Are you going to kill me or something?" I'm only half joking. "This truck will definitely lead to my death somehow."

Ace rolls his eyes and climbs out of the truck. I laugh and follow him.

When he pulls away the built-in tarp, I see how nicely decorated the truck's bed is. There are piles of soft blankets and fluffy pillows alongside a basket filled with junk food and soft drinks.

Ace watches me with a hopeful expression.

"What's this?" I ask softly.

He shrugs sheepishly and gestures toward the sky. "I thought maybe we could watch the stars? I come out here when I can. It's a little hard where we live because of light pollution from the city, but it's pretty clear over here. I thought you might like it."

"Are you kidding?" I ask, climbing into the back of the truck. I settle into the blankets and offer Ace a reassuring smile. "I love it. Thank you for putting it together."

He laughs and he looks *nervous*. My heart honestly hurts. "Really?"

"Yeah." I pat the spot next to me. "Let's look at some stars, Ace."

And so we do.

We watch the stars, and Ace points at the brightest one and mutters something outrageous about how it's not as bright as

I am. All the while I try not to break my face from smiling too big.

Ace is beautiful, the pale moonlight washing over him in ways that highlight the shadows on his face. When he speaks, he's focused solely on whatever he's talking about. He points out his favorite star constellations and tells me all their stories. He might just be the most captivating human being I've ever met. I'm still listening to him talk when he suddenly sits up and shrugs off his leather jacket.

I'm confused until Ace rolls his shirtsleeve up and points at his solar system tattoo. "Sometimes, I bring my telescope out here, and I can see some of the planets when I use the right settings. It's what inspired me to get this."

I smile, lying back on the blankets. "I hope you know your tattoo still contributes to your bad-boy reputation." I giggle when he hits me with a throw pillow. "What? Am I wrong? You're a sixteen-year-old with an illegal tattoo!"

"How can you lecture me about what's illegal when you're a thief?" he asks, raising his eyebrows. "You've stolen my heart, after all."

I attempt to scowl. I really, really do. It just doesn't work, not when I have all this bright lightning zinging through me. "That was terrible."

"I don't think you have much of a problem with it," he says, lips twisting into an impish grin. "You can't even frown at me."

I force my lips into the best frown I can manage, but he just keeps grinning. I hold it for maybe ten seconds before I huff a laugh and shove his chest. "Whatever."

"I win," he says and darts in to kiss my cheek before I can so much as blink. "Lie down with me, I'll tell you the story of Orion."

I start to nod when my phone rings, a picture of my dad

flashing across the screen. I sit up abruptly, my breath caught in my throat. "*Fuck.* Oh my God. Oh my *God*, what do I do?"

Ace is half tangled in the blankets as he tries to sit up, looking equally startled. "Uh. Do you want to get back in the car? Maybe you can pretend you're with your brother or something?"

I scramble up, almost falling off the truck bed in my haste. *Ten, nine, eight, seven, six, five, four, three, two, one.* "You got my brother's number the other night, right? Can you call him?"

Ace nods, climbing off the truck after me, typing rapidly into his phone. My heart is jackrabbiting, attempting to burst through my chest as I run around the side of the truck.

We slip into the front seats and my phone falls silent. I wince, knowing my parents are going to be upset I didn't pick up immediately.

Ace's dial tone starts ringing and we wait for Samir to pick up, sitting on the edge of our seats. There's a rustle on the other end of Ace's phone and then, "Ace? What's up, dude? Is my sister okay?"

I grab the phone from Ace. "Baba is FaceTiming me. I need you to pretend you're with me. I'm going to put you on speaker, okay?"

"Oh shit," Samir says in surprise. "Yeah, yeah. You got it, bro."

I call my dad back on FaceTime audio. I'm not even going to attempt video, knowing that'll end in my untimely death. I have no excuse for being in some random truck at 8:00 p.m.

"Myra?" my dad asks. He's alone for once, which is a minor relief. "Why didn't you answer before? And why audio?"

"Baba! Sorry about that. I don't have a lot of charge right now," I say, my eyes flicking to Ace. He's watching me quietly, teeth pressed against his bottom lip. "Video will drain the battery."

"Why don't you plug it in?" Baba asks. "Are you outside?"

I bite the inside of my cheek to keep from screaming. "Yes. Samir and I went to Duane Reade because we ran out of... tape."

"Yeah!" Samir chimes in. "Myra Apu and I checked the entire house, but we couldn't find any. We asked Dadu, but she doesn't know. We didn't want to bother you guys, so we just went to the store instead."

There's a moment of heavy silence. "Samir, why do you sound so strange?"

My eyes widen and I look at Ace hopelessly, but Samir immediately starts coughing over the phone. "I think I'm getting a little sick. Don't worry, I'll ask Dadu to make me some chai."

"Oh," my dad says and his tone relaxes. "I won't keep you long then. I just wanted to check in to see how things were."

"Things are fine," I say, forcing my voice to stay even. "I should go before my phone dies, though."

Baba hums in agreement. "Good night, Myra. Good night, Samir. I hope you find the tape soon."

"Good night," we both say at once, and I hang up.

We all sit there, breathing in tandem. I hold my head in my hands. The world is spinning out of control.

Holy shit. Holy *shit*.

"Oh my God," I say aloud. "Oh my *God*."

"Myra Apu? Are you okay?" Samir asks, a note of concern in his voice.

My vision blurs until Ace reaches out, his fingers wrapping tightly around my wrist. The motion grounds me enough to exhale harshly. I remind myself to breathe. *Ten, nine, eight, seven, six, five, four, three, two, one.*

I look up. Ace is staring at me with wide eyes, and I feel the strange urge to cry.

"We're good. Thank you, Samir," I say, my voice choked.

"Jesus Christ," my brother says on the other end, his exhaustion palpable. "I think I actually need some chai."

"I'll make you some when I get home," I promise, unable to look away from Ace. His grip loosens on my wrist and his fingers slip away, leaving my hand suspended between us. "Thank you again."

"It's what we do, right?" Samir says, and there's something regretful in his voice. A call to his last promise. "I've got your back."

Despite the tension still stringing my body, I manage a quiet laugh. "I've got your back, too."

Samir hangs up, leaving me and Ace alone. Only our quiet breathing exists in the silence.

"Sorry about that," I say, my cheeks burning with unspoken shame. I lower my hand slowly.

Ace swallows, throat shifting with the movement. "No saying sorry, remember?"

I look down, my limbs heavy with awareness. "I know this isn't what you signed up for."

He shakes his head and cups my cheek. "Yes, it is, Karina. I want you with all your lines."

A tremor runs through me. "All my lines?"

Ace nods, resting his forehead against mine. "All your lines."

"There are so many," I whisper and my voice cracks. "You should give up now."

He smiles faintly. "That doesn't change anything. I want you, Karina Ahmed. That means lines and all."

He leans in, and I meet him halfway, our lips brushing together in a soft kiss.

A tear slips down my face without permission and he pulls back, stroking a careful thumb against my cheek. "I'm not giving up on us unless you are."

I shake my head. "I don't want to give up on us. I choose this. I choose us. I choose *you*."

"Then I'm here to stay," he says, and he leans in again, pressing a gentle kiss below my eye. "Come out back with me?"

I nod and follow him to the truck bed again, my chest flooded with warm, dizzying emotions.

Ace whispers luminous stories to me for another hour before we finally call it a night and he drives me home.

The truck idles in front of my driveway, and I unbuckle my seatbelt. I turn to find Ace watching me. "Thank you. For the date and the ride. And everything else." My pulse is racing for no discernible reason. Or maybe it's because I can still feel the ghost of Ace's lips against my skin, still hear the echo of his words in my head.

"And you thought the truck would kill you," Ace says, eyes dancing in the pale moonlight spilling through the window.

"No," I say quietly. "I thought you would." *I still do.*

Ace blinks as if he didn't expect that answer. I offer him a small smile and climb out of the truck.

I shut the door behind me, then hesitate. I turn back around and knock on the window. Ace peers at me in confusion and I tap again insistently.

He leans over the seat and manually winds the window down. I give him a pointed look but refrain from making a comment about how old the truck is. "Did you forget something?"

I shake my head. "I want you with all your lines, too," I say and duck forward to press a quick kiss to Ace's cheek.

In front of me, Ace's mouth snaps shut. I can't help but smile at his gobsmacked expression before I turn around and walk to my front door.

His truck continues to idle until I unlock the door and slip inside. Outside, the engine rumbles, and I watch from the window as he disappears down the street.

"Myra," Dadu says, making me jump twenty feet in the air. I turn around with a hand clutching my heart.

"Dadu," I say. A small wave of panic pushes at my chest. Did she see me kiss Ace's cheek? She doesn't look mad, which is a good sign.

She observes me for a moment before smiling faintly. "Tell Alistair it is 10:02 p.m. He promised me 10:00 p.m. If he does this next time, I might have to make your curfew 9:58 p.m. instead."

I laugh hoarsely. "Okay, Dadu. I will."

41

T-MINUS 7 DAYS

A knock on my bedroom door startles me from my failed attempt at yoga, and I hit my arm against the side of my desk.

I've moved on to the next coping method. Candles have proven useful, but I want to have as many options as possible.

Hence why I'm trying yoga to help with my anxiety. Not that it's going well.

"Yo, Myra Apu?" Samir says, peeking his head in the door. "Can I talk to you for a minute?"

"Yeah, sure." I rub the side of my arm. "What's up?"

"I need your help," he says.

I falter and look at him. What could Samir possibly need my help with? "With...?"

Samir lets himself in and shuts the door behind him before sitting at my desk. He levels me with an extremely serious expression. "It's top secret. You can't tell anyone."

"Who am I going to tell?" I ask, exasperated. In the days since his apology, we've returned to normal in the way only siblings can after a huge fight. Last night, his help in hiding my date from our parents only proved it further.

"*No one* can know," Samir emphasizes.

I roll my eyes. My brother is the world's strangest specimen. "Just spit it out."

Samir lets out a deep sigh. "I need to know more about Leah."

"About *who?*"

"Leah Jimenez," Samir says, his tone despairing. In the back of my head, the girl from the bleachers appears. "She goes to Miss Cannon's after-school tutoring. She said you helped her with *Fahrenheit 451.*"

I blink at him several times. "Okay, and…?"

"What do you mean?" Samir runs a hand through his hair. "Bro, come on, just tell me what's up. What's she like? What's she into?"

"I'm not your bro," I say, raising my brows. "And I'm sorry, but I don't really know her. She was just a random freshman I helped."

Samir makes a horrible sound like he's dying. I'm starting to wonder if maybe he's secretly related to Cora. *"Myra."*

I narrow my eyes at him for withholding the honorific for older sister, *Apu.* "Don't call me Myra."

"Oh my God, I can't call you bro, I can't call you Myra. What do you want from me?"

I throw a wad of paper at him. "Get out of my room if you're going to be a clown."

"No, no, don't kick me out." He holds his hands out in a pleading gesture. "Please, come on. Just give me something to work with. I really like her."

"How can you like her if you don't know anything about her?" I ask, shaking my head.

"Well, I'm *trying!*"

I huff a laugh. Trust boys to do the bare minimum and chalk it up to effort. "Try a little harder. Maybe talk to her yourself?"

"If you asked me for help with Ace a few weeks ago—" Samir starts and I throw another piece of paper at him. "*What?* There's no one else here. Come on, I just covered for you yesterday! Are we going to pretend you're not attempting to date some random white guy?"

"Leah isn't Bangladeshi *or* Muslim," I say pointedly. "That's two facts right there. Did that help?"

Samir groans again. "I know *that* already. But if you can do it, maybe..."

The sentence stops me in my tracks, and I stare at my brother imploringly. *Lionheart,* whispers a treacherous voice in the back of my head.

"Come on, Myra Apu. Please?" Samir says.

I sigh. "If I tell you something about her, can we both return to peace and quiet?"

"Obviously. You think I *want* to be in your room? It smells disgusting in here."

I gape at him. "It smells like cinnamon."

Samir wrinkles his nose. "Yeah, and lavender and vanilla and peppermint. None of that shit goes well together. Stick to one." He waves a dismissive hand. "Just tell me the thing."

"You are the most annoying human ever," I say, but the words hold little heat. "All right, fine. Her favorite book is *Jane Eyre.*"

My brother squints. "Her favorite book? Really?"

I sigh and point at the door. "Out. Out, out, *out.*"

"No, wait," Samir says, raising his hands placatingly. "That's cool. Do you have a copy?"

I do, somewhere around here, but God knows what condition Samir will return it in. "Nope."

Samir worries his bottom lip between his teeth. "Where can I get one?"

I almost tell him to Google the closest bookstore, but then I take note of how earnest his expression is.

I *guess* it wouldn't hurt to go a little above and beyond to help him. Ace and I planned to meet at the aquarium today anyway, and it isn't that far off from where I have in mind. "I might know a place..."

Two Stories is as magical as last time. I catch sight of Genesis near the register, but she's with a customer this time.

"Knock yourself out," I say to Samir, my own eyes snagging on the young adult shelves.

"What? I don't know where anything is." Samir gives me an aghast look. "How am I supposed to find *Jane Eyre*?"

I shrug. "Beats me."

"What kind of sister *are* you?"

"The kind of sister who came to a bookstore with you when I could've easily sat at home and minded my business," I say, poking his shoulder.

Samir groans. "You're the worst," he says, before his eyes fall on Genesis. "She looks like she works here. Let's ask her."

"She's clearly busy," I say.

"I'm a paying customer, too. She can make herself available," Samir says and walks off before I can protest what an entitled mindset that is.

Ugh.

I linger behind him, regretting all the decisions in my life that led me here. When he reaches her, Samir says, "Hey, can you tell me where to find *Jane Eyre*? My sister won't help me."

I glare at him. Behind Genesis, the other customer wanders off, so at least there's one less witness for when I inevitably murder my brother.

Genesis turns and her expression brightens when she sees me. "Oh my God, hi, Karina! Is Ace with you?"

I shake my head. If only. "Not this time. I'm here to help my annoying little brother find a book."

"Forget about her," Samir says, waving me off. "I am literally *begging* for your help to find *Jane Eyre*. Dude, please."

Genesis raises her eyebrows. "Begging me? Well, I guess I'd better help then." She looks at me and adds, "Come by with Ace next time. I miss that little punk."

I don't have a chance to reply before she whisks Samir away, leaving me alone. It's not like I mind, anyway.

The young adult section is empty when I get there, so I have the freedom to pick through titles without worrying I'm taking up space. As I run my fingers along the bindings, my phone buzzes in my pocket.

I take it out to see a text from my cousin Fatima.

hey sis!! I saw your last post on IG and I just wanted to check in... still just friends??

My last post on Instagram was Ace and me holding hands on top of his piano. I don't see any way I can lie myself out of that.

With a sigh, I reply: a little more than friends...

Fatima's reply is immediate. not to sound pessimistic but is this rlly the move, myra???

I wince. it'll be okay but thank you for checking in!!! I hope things are going well w/ you! always rooting for you ♥

Fatima's response is slower this time, but when it comes, it settles in my chest heavily. I'm always rooting for you too!!! I just don't know how long you can make this work I'm sorryyyy.

I don't have anything to say to that. I have no idea how long I can make this work, either. I want it to last as long as possible, but I know as we keep moving forward, the riskier this becomes. If we're together years from now, I will have to decide whether Ace is worth risking my family's wrath. It's inevitable.

And even though I'm terrified of that day, it's not enough for me to give up on what we have together *now*.

For now, I'm willing to give this my all.

I want to believe I'm going to win in the end.

Samir and I part ways after he buys *Jane Eyre* and then chips in to buy me the young adult book I wanted, too. Maybe I can forgive him for being a nuisance.

I meet Ace at the aquarium and the entire time we're in line for tickets, he playfully grumbles about how the zoo would be a better date.

His silly complaints do make me feel oddly better. I try not to think too much on why that is.

"Zoos *smell*," I say, wrinkling my nose. "And these animals are in glass tanks so they can't try to kill us."

He sighs dramatically before resting his palm against my neck, a bright grin on his face. "I'll stop complaining for a kiss."

I shake my head at him. It feels like I'm in some ridiculous movie. Things like this don't happen to girls like me. "You're *terrible*," I say but stretch onto my tiptoes to kiss him anyway. He tastes like mint chocolate ice cream and peppermint ChapStick, both of which are quickly becoming some of my favorite flavors.

When I pull away, there's a warmth spreading through my chest, a small fire that roars with the heat of a million shooting stars. "Terrible," I repeat and run away from him, toward the dolphin exhibit.

He laughs behind me. "Terribly infatuated with you, yes."

We're wandering aimlessly when I hear a familiar voice. "Can you stop being an asshole for *two seconds*?"

I turn around, looking for Cora, and come to an abrupt stop when I see her next to someone equally familiar.

"Is that your brother?" I ask incredulously.

"What?" Ace turns around, following my gaze. *What?*

"You read too much into everything," Xander says to Cora dismissively. There's a horde of students behind them, some I know, some I don't. It must be the student council.

Now that I think back on it, Cora did send a Snapchat streak this morning that said: dealing with the white devil today,,, but I hadn't given it much thought. It makes sense now.

"It's classist to insist every member of student council has to pay an entry fee for a mandated trip during *spring break*," Cora says darkly. "I know you're a trust fund baby that's never worked a day in his life, but some people aren't that privileged."

I glance at Ace for his reaction, but in the face of Cora's bluntness about his socioeconomic status, he looks amazed. "I think Cora is my new best friend."

I snort. "Get in line, buddy."

Cora looks up at the sound of my voice and a smile breaks across her face, wiping away any lingering irritation. "Karina!"

She runs toward me and I open my arms, accepting her hug. She squeezes me tightly before pulling back, glancing at Ace. "Your brother is the worst."

"I know," Ace says, grinning.

Cora blinks in shock. "Are you…*smiling at me?*"

I steady her, trying not to laugh at her dismay. "It's a rare sight, I know."

Seconds later, Xander comes to stand beside Cora, his eyes flicking between me and his brother. Ace's smile has vanished, replaced by an indifferent expression.

"Karina," Xander says, nodding at me.

I wave awkwardly. "Xander."

To Ace, Xander says, "I thought you had a piano lesson today, Alistair."

"It was canceled," Ace says, his gaze cool.

Xander clicks his tongue. "I highly doubt that. Does Dad know you're at the aquarium instead of your lesson?"

Ace smiles thinly. "I'm sure he will soon."

"You're even a dickhead with your *family*," Cora says, startling both of them.

I giggle and attempt to cover it with a cough. Xander is too busy staring at Cora with an appalled expression to notice.

"I think Ace and I are going to take that as our cue to leave," I say, pushing Ace back with one hand and squeezing Cora's hand apologetically with the other. "It was nice seeing you...both."

Without another word, I slip my hand into Ace's and pull us toward the jellyfish exhibit, almost running in my haste to get away.

Behind me, Ace chuckles as he follows along. When we're safely away from them, he gives me a grateful look. "Thanks. He's just...aggravating. I wasn't even lying—my piano lesson really was canceled. My instructor has the flu. Not that he cares." Ace sighs, scratching the back of his head. "I'm sure he'll tell Dad either way."

"And he'll look stupid when he does," I say, squeezing Ace's hand. "Forget him."

He huffs a rueful laugh, pulling me closer and leaning his chin against the top of my head. "I wish."

I sigh, wrapping my arms around his waist. "Family, am I right?"

"Family," Ace agrees solemnly.

Later, we're holding hands and walking back to Ace's house when something splashes against the back of my neck. When

I turn to Ace, there's a drop of water sliding down the ridge of his nose.

A clap of thunder sounds, and I jump in surprise, clutching Ace's hand tightly enough to cut off circulation.

"Are you scared?" he asks, having the nerve to sound amused.

I scowl. "No. I just don't want to get a cold. Your house is a *long* walk from here."

Ace rolls his eyes but his lips curl up in one corner. "You'll be fine, Karina. Plus, haven't you always wanted to kiss in the rain? It happened in like half the Bollywood movies we watched."

"You've seen like *four*."

"It still happened."

"I resent that."

Not a moment later, the rain decides to pour down in buckets, drenching us both.

Ace laughs in delight, because I'm apparently dating a lunatic. His bad mood from before has all but evaporated, as if the rain is the equivalent of sunshine for him.

He slips his hand out of my grasp and extends his arms on either side. I watch as he tilts his face toward the sky and closes his eyes, a wide smile across his face.

"What's *wrong* with you?" I say, shouting to be heard over the pouring rain.

"Join me!" Ace says back, eyelashes fluttering open to reveal striking kaleidoscopic eyes. "Live a little."

I give him an unimpressed look as I push wet hair out of my face. "You can't keep saying that, you know. I live just fine, thank you."

Ace laughs again and shakes his head. "Baby, come on."

I jolt at the endearment and the way my pulse starts rocketing. It's nothing like his joking *sweetie* in front of his family, in front of my friends. This isn't for show.

This is me and him, alone in a storm, and he's giving me the most beautiful smile and calling me *baby*.

Despite the freezing rain, I feel impossibly warm.

A bolt of lightning flashes across the sky, capturing Ace's attention before he can press further. He looks up with wonder written across his face. "Isn't it amazing?" he asks before looking back down at me. "It reminds me of you."

Holy shit, he's going to kill me. "You're ridiculous," I murmur.

Ace somehow hears me through all the noise, and his cheeks dimple.

I cross the distance between us and press my lips against his before he can say anything else. Maybe it's to shut Ace up, or maybe it's to stop myself from saying something completely foolish. Either way, I'm kissing him in the rain, just like he wanted.

When we pull apart, I tilt my head and ask, "If I'm lightning, then what are you?"

Already, I can imagine Ace teasing me but instead, he smiles and says, "I'm thunder. I'll follow you wherever you go."

I don't have an answer for that. He doesn't look like he needs one.

"Karina," he says softly, his hand coming up to brush my cheek. "Will you go to prom with me?"

"I already said yes," I remind.

He shakes his head. "You said yes when we were pretending. Will you go to prom with me?"

I stare at him for a long beat of silence, warmed by the stars in his eyes. "Yes."

Ace laughs quietly and leans forward, kissing my temple and pulling me into his arms.

When Ace shifts again, it's to shrug off his leather jacket. "Here," he says, holding it out for me. "I don't actually want you to catch a cold."

"*Now* you're worried about my health," I say, but slip my arms into the sleeves, letting him situate it around me. The smell of cinnamon makes my heart sing. "You can explain this to Dadu."

A look of horror passes over his face and I laugh, tangling our fingers together as we start walking toward his house again.

That night, I lie awake and listen to the storm. Ace is on FaceTime but he's fast asleep. The sound of his breathing is soft compared to the harsh beat of the rain against the roof. Slowly, it lulls me to sleep.

rain, rain go away
come again another day...
that's what they always say
but what if you want rain to stay?
being addicted to the storm
wanting to see it transform
I'm lightning, he's thunder
my God, he's a wonder
I'm quick, I'm fast, I glow
and him?
he follows me wherever I go

42

T-MINUS 6 DAYS

"Be prepared."

Ace looks at me in alarm as we swipe our ID cards and walk into school. "For what?"

I shake my head. "You sweet, naive soul."

It takes approximately two seconds for Cora and Nandini to show up and approximately one second after that for Nandini to drag me away while Cora stares at Ace with her arms crossed and foot tapping.

"Karina?" Ace says, gaze darting between Cora, Nandini, and me. His expression is cooler than I'm used to. However, I've come to accept that Ace has trouble being his true self around people he's not fully comfortable with.

Hopefully he'll be comfortable with my friends one day soon. I don't doubt it will happen. I just don't know when.

"Alistair, sweetie, so nice to see you again." Cora smiles warmly at me before she looks back at Ace, her expression shifting to something cold and terrifying. "All right, let's talk business."

"Uh, okay?" he says.

"It has come to my attention that you and my wonderful, lovely, one-of-a-kind best friend Karina are doing whatever it is you two are doing. For some reason completely beyond me, she seems happy. However, if she's anything *less* than happy, *ever*—and I don't care if you did it or if someone else did it, because I'm going to assume it's still your fault—just know I've seen every *Mission Impossible* movie and I know how to kill someone with a pen."

Nandini lets go of me to join Cora, throwing an arm around her shoulder. "When you fall asleep tonight, keep your third eye open. We'll be watching."

I stifle a giggle. My friends are so ridiculous. Now that everything's out in the open, I honestly don't care if they threaten Ace twenty times a day so long as he isn't bothered by it either. I know my friends are dramatic, and that's part of why I adore them.

Ace blinks. "Noted."

Cora returns to normal in a second, grinning cheerfully as she claps him on the shoulder. "Great! Glad that's settled."

Without another word, she skips over to me and loops her arms with mine. When she starts pulling me away, I falter only to smile back at Ace. "I'll see you later."

His eyes are fond, even if the rest of his face is unmoved. "Yeah, you will."

I'm sitting in the library, outlining new study questions for Ace when someone loudly approaches our table.

I'm alone, because I forgot my copy of *The Scarlet Letter* and Ace went in search of another. I wish I'd gone instead when I see who's standing over me.

"Xander," I say slowly. I've never been alone with Ace's brother before, and I don't want to start now. "Hello."

Xander's expression is dark. "Where's Alistair?"

"He's…in the bathroom," I say, glancing down at the notes, books, and papers scattered across the table. Xander isn't supposed to know I'm tutoring Ace.

I need a quick lie. I don't want to mess this up.

Anxiety bubbles in my stomach. *Ten, nine, eight, seven, six, five, four, three, two, one…* "He likes to keep me company while I study."

Xander hums, eyes narrowed. "Is that right?"

My mouth dries. His tone makes it sound like he knows, but how he could *possibly* know? He saw me and Ace on a real date just yesterday.

"Yes." My hands are sweating. "Would you like me to pass on a message?"

"I'll wait," Xander says, taking the seat beside me. We're *way* too close. I can't help scooting away. My skin prickles from just being around him, but it's worse with him watching me like a hawk. "So, Karina. How exactly did you and my brother start dating? I'd love specific details. It's not every day Ace gets a girlfriend."

"Uh." I bite my lip, looking around for Ace. "He—um. Like we said, we sat next to each other in English."

"My brother isn't exactly the friendliest company," Xander says, which makes my blood boil. It fizzles away some of my anxiety, enough that I straighten and reach for my things, pushing them toward my side of the table. "What about him won you over?"

"I honestly don't see how that's any of your business," I say coldly.

Xander raises his eyebrows. "He's got you acting like a guard dog?"

I glare at him. "Are you comparing me to an animal? Is that the hill you want to die on?"

He lifts his hands in apology, but I don't buy it. I've always said Xander Clyde is on his way to being US president. I've never believed it more than when he offers me a charming smile after likening me to a dog. "I'm not trying to insult you. You know, you kind of remind me of Cora."

"Do I?" I ask, smiling sweetly. "Perhaps it's because neither of us enjoy speaking to you."

Something flashes across Xander's face too quickly for me to decipher. "Is that right?"

Thankfully, Ace comes back then, and I don't have to singlehandedly fend off his brother anymore. He stops short at the sight of me glowering at Xander, and his own gaze grows dark.

We're tucked into a back corner, and there's no one else in our vicinity, otherwise I'm sure this scene would draw far too many eyes. I'm itchy just thinking about it.

"Why are you here?" Ace asks, setting *The Scarlet Letter* down and sliding it toward me. I catch it before it can slip off the table, but my stomach twists at the sight of Xander's gaze following the book.

"Mia and I were speaking earlier, and she mentioned something very interesting," Xander says, raising his eyes to meet his brother's.

Ace grows very still. "Did she?"

Xander laughs. The sound grates on my nerves. "At first, it seemed ridiculous. I thought she was joking. But then she tried to cover it up so fast that I began to think, *Is it true?* Could Alistair really be stupid enough to *pretend* to date his tutor?"

"Hey," I cut in, gritting my teeth. "Don't call him stupid."

Ace shakes his head slowly. "This isn't your fight, Karina."

I bite my lip, wishing it was. I hate seeing Xander demean Ace like this.

"Oh, enough," Xander says, rolling his eyes. "You can stop the act. I know you're not dating."

"You're so fucking annoying," Ace says, pinching the bridge of his nose. "Go then. Run off and tell Dad how I'm a fraud. I'm sure he'll love that."

"Honestly, Alistair." Xander sighs deeply, leaning his elbow against the table. "Don't you get tired of disappointing Dad? He just wants you to succeed."

I have a strong urge to kick Xander down a flight of stairs. If Ace hadn't specifically told me to stay out of it, I think I would've told Xander to fuck off. It makes sense why Ace is reluctant to talk to our classmates if his own brother is such an ass.

"And what do you want, Alexander?" Ace smiles coldly. "To make me look bad so you can look good? Your superiority complex is pathetic."

A sense of pride fills me as I watch Ace casually take out a lollipop and unwrap it.

"I don't have a superiority complex," Xander says, raising one eyebrow. "I worry about you, Alistair. If Dad and I don't keep you in line, what's going to happen to you? Ever since Mom and Dad's divorce, you've had no drive, no motivation. I only want the best for you."

I gape at Xander. He speaks as if he hasn't sabotaged Ace repeatedly, as if he hasn't spread rumors about him, as if he hasn't consistently thrown Ace under the bus.

Ace has the most drive and motivation of anyone I've ever met. He spends hours practicing piano, sought a tutor when he was doing poorly, and is active in almost every aspect of his life. He knows what he wants and goes after it.

And yet his brother unabashedly calls him lazy and apathetic, without even making the effort to learn what kind of person Ace truly is.

Ace is silent as he pops the lollipop in his mouth. *Tell him,*

I want to urge, but I also know why he won't. Ace's choices have nothing to do with Xander or his father.

"Talk to me, Alistair." Xander reaches across the table, but Ace leans away. "You're being childish."

"And you're trying to gaslight me," Ace says evenly.

"Gaslight?" Xander snorts. "Where'd you learn that word? Was it from your little 'girlfriend' over here?" He gestures to me with a wave of his hand. "I guess the tutoring is paying off."

"Don't bring her into this," Ace says, his voice low, before he exhales and looks away. Under the table, I loop my ankle around his, hoping to comfort him in some way. A fleeting and barely there smile passes across his lips. He looks back up at his brother, expression weary. "I'm tired of this, Xander. You're Dad's favorite son. I know it. You know it. Can we please stop doing this?"

"I don't know what you're talking about," Xander says dismissively.

"Don't you?" Ace asks. "Ever since Mom and Dad got divorced, you've been taking it out on me. You turned Dad *against* me. It's not my fault Mom left. It's not my fault you and Mom barely talk. Stop blaming me for things that are out of my hands."

Xander's cool expression slips, his gaze suddenly heated. I shift farther away from him, waiting for the blow to follow.

"It is your fault," Xander hisses. "She talks to you all the time and never gives me the time of day. And when we do talk, she only ever goes on and on about *you*. It's always Ace this, Ace that. I told her I got into Yale, and immediately after congratulating me, she asked me what your plans for college were. It's *always* about you."

Ace stares at his brother like he's grown a second head. "And that's *my* fault? Why don't you talk to Mom about it instead of trying to *ruin my life*?"

His brother sniffs with an air of disdain, but there's a crack in his demeanor now, in the way he carries himself. "You always overexaggerate. I haven't ruined your life."

"You told Dad I wanted to go to Italy with Mom and acted like it was because of *him*. Dad hasn't looked at me the same since! You know the reason I wanted to leave was because of *you*, you fucking asshole. Back then, all you ever did was pick fights with me over nothing. But instead of factoring that in, you let Dad think I hated him. Your relationship with Mom isn't my fault, but my relationship with Dad *is* yours."

Xander's mouth thins into a straight line. "What does it matter to you? You have Mom. You don't need Dad, too."

My mouth falls open in disbelief. What kind of logic is that?

Ace seems similarly aghast. "What are you even talking about? He's my *dad*." He shakes his head. "You have no idea. Mom *misses* you. She tells me all the time she wishes you'd call more. But you'd rather spend your time ruining my relationship with Dad, I guess."

Xander falters. "Mom misses me?"

Ace looks up, taking in his brother's expression. His gaze slips briefly to mine, and I offer him a timid smile, hoping it reassures him.

In the face of it, Ace seems to deflate. He scrubs a hand over his face, a sigh escaping his lips. "All right." He pushes back his chair. "I guess we're doing this."

Xander narrows his eyes, looking between us. "Doing what?"

"Talking to Mom and Dad." Ace stands up, gathering his things before coming around the side of the table to crouch near me. "Hey."

I carefully brush a strand of dark hair from his eyes. I don't know what to do with the fight I just witnessed, but I know I want to be there for Ace. "Hey."

He catches my hand to press his lips against my wrist. "I have to go deal with this. Can we get a rain check?"

"It's not raining," I say, trying to lighten the mood.

It works because a real smile touches Ace's lips. "A sun check?"

I smile back, glad to see his face brighten. I still have the urge to stab Xander with a pencil, but that's neither here nor there. "Yeah. We can get a sun check. Call me tonight?"

"Of course," he says before hesitating. "I hope you know I wouldn't be brave enough to even consider doing this without you, lionheart. Wish me luck?"

Even now, in the middle of such a tense situation, he manages to make my stomach do cartwheels. "Always." I lean forward to kiss his cheek. "Good luck."

Ace's face flushes as he pulls away. To Xander, he nods shortly. "Let's go."

Xander's expression is a mix of distrust and bewilderment. When Ace walks away, he has no choice but to follow, leaving me alone.

Ace is going to face his family, and he says it's partly because of me. I don't know about that. Sometimes I wonder who the real lionheart is in this relationship. During moments like these, I'm almost certain it's him.

When Ace calls me, I fall off my bed in an attempt to answer and nearly knock over the candle on my dresser.

"Are you okay, Myra?" Dadu calls from the next room over.

"I'm great!" I say and slide my thumb across my screen. Ace shows up a moment later. There's a smile on his face that makes me want to smile, too. "Hi."

"Hey. Are you busy?"

"Not at all," I say, turning my phone so he can see the epi-sode of *Avatar: The Last Airbender* paused on my laptop. "So what happened?"

Ace chews on his bottom lip and I stay silent, not wanting to rush him. "I talked to my mom and dad. About everything."

"Everything…?" I wait for him to elaborate, settling more comfortably in my bed and holding him up on my pillow.

Ace nods and lies down on his own bed. Seeing him shirt-less on my screen doesn't cause me to fling my phone across the room, which is a definite improvement from last time.

I know odds are we'll never spend a night lying next to each other without pulling some kind of reckless stunt. This has to be enough. It *is* enough. I love seeing him like this, warm and natural and soft.

"I told my dad how I felt about the whole Xander situation. I don't think he realized it was that bad. He's not…happy with me about certain things, but I'm not happy with him either, you know? But at least now he knows I wasn't trying to leave home because of him. We both agreed to try going forward. I didn't tell him about the college thing yet, but I'll work up to it. I don't want this to be a thing I did *for* him. It's a me thing. I want it to stay a me thing as long as it can."

His smile makes sense now, and it makes *me* happy to know things are working out for him. "That's amazing, Ace! I'm so happy for you. I'm glad he was understanding about it. What about Xander?"

"Xander is… Xander. I think he also didn't realize how serious it was. For him, it's always been a competition. I don't think he ever realized I wasn't playing. He talked to Mom on his own, so I don't really know what went down there, but he seemed different afterward. Better."

"Will he relax then, do you think?"

Ace laughs. "We can *hope*. He's still Xander, though. I don't know if he can help himself."

"Brothers," I commiserate, but then I soften, seeing how bright his eyes are shining. "I really am so happy for you. This is everything you deserve."

Ace's smile stretches even wider. "God, you're so sweet. I wish you were here, baby."

My cheeks warm as I laugh. "I wish I was there, too."

He tilts his head, considering me before he presses two fingers to his lips and lifts them to the camera.

I lift my eyebrows. "Are you attempting to kiss me through the phone?"

Ace shakes his head, amused. "What else am I supposed to do? I can't exactly come over. Your grandma is great, but even she might protest me throwing rocks at your window at 11:00 p.m."

"Not might. She would *definitely* protest," I say before pressing two of my fingers against my own lips and holding them to my camera. "Happy?"

"Ecstatic," he says, and he looks like he means it.

I fall asleep to the sight of his smile, but despite the happiness I feel for him, my mind can't help straying to my parents.

Ace's family accepted everything he told them. They sat down and tried to understand his side of things. I don't know if that will ever be in the cards for me.

I want to be lionhearted, too. Not because of Ace, not because of my friends. I want to be a lionheart for me. I want to apply to Columbia for English and go on to have the future I've always wanted.

With six days left until my parents' return, desperation claws at my chest, begging me to save myself. But I still don't know if I have it in me to try.

43

T-MINUS 5 DAYS

Inspired by Ace, I decide to talk to Samir the next day. I don't know what I'm going to do about my parents yet, but maybe if my brother understands what I go through, things will be a little easier around here.

After I come home from school, Ace dropping me off with a kiss to the side of my head, I knock on Samir's door.

Wednesday is one of the rare days my brother doesn't have an after-school activity or work at the deli, so he opens the door a second later.

"Can I talk to you?" I say, trying to push down the nerves. I can be brave. I can do this. "It's kind of important."

Samir furrows his brows but opens his door wider for me to come inside.

I make a face at the dirty wrappers, empty bottles, and clothes tossed around. "Astaghfirullah." *I seek forgiveness in Allah.* Throwing the word around callously is probably bad, but I think only a prayer can help Samir fix this mess.

My brother rolls his eyes. "You're the one who came to my room."

"Right, right, sorry." I take a seat on the one clean part of his bed. *Jane Eyre* sits beside me, and I run my finger along the edge nervously. "I wanted to talk about what happened the other night. With Ma and Baba."

Samir looks at me with wide eyes. "I already said I was sorry. I helped you the other night. I thought we were good."

"We are," I say, licking my lips nervously. "I'm not mad at you. I just want to talk about it."

"What about it?" Samir asks, scratching his arm as he sits down at his desk.

"I...have you noticed how differently Ma and Baba treat us?"

He blinks at me. "Just because of one time?"

"It's not just one time." I don't know how he could have failed to notice it over the years. It feels so obvious to me. "It's all the time. Part of it is because you're a boy. They let you have all the unchecked freedom you want but don't—*won't* do the same for me. The other part is because you're...perfect. You love math and science. You want to be an electrical engineer and go into robotics. You're charismatic and good around others. They constantly brag about you. They always put you first. No matter what it is, they always take your side."

Samir looks shocked. "That's not true, Myra Apu."

"It is," I say, looking down and fiddling with a loose string from my pajama pants. "I'm the odd one out. I love books and reading. I care about things outside their realm of understanding. I'm shy and don't talk to anyone I don't already know. I constantly disappoint them. If they could have two of you, they would do it in a heartbeat. They're so hard on me because of that. Sometimes, I can't even breathe around them, because I'm worried they'll tell me I'm doing it wrong."

"Since when?" Samir asks, biting his lip. "How come I've never noticed?"

"Because you never had to," I say, trying not to let my bitterness taint the words. It's not his fault our parents treat us differently. "I know they're not doing it to be cruel. They just don't…understand me. You fit perfectly into all their boxes. I don't. I always have to watch myself for missteps, because everything I do wrong gets scrutinized. If you do something wrong, they'll move on within five minutes. It's just how it is."

Samir sits there for a long moment, grappling with the information. I wait it out even as my hands start shaking. I shove them underneath my thighs to keep Samir from seeing them.

"How can you live like that?" Samir finally asks. He makes a move as if to reach for me before seeming to think better of it. "Why don't you say something to them?"

"What good would it do? They're not going to change because of me. At this point, all I can do is try to meet their expectations. Maybe one day they'll be proud of me. I'll wait until then." Even as I'm saying the words, they sound desolate. *Ten, nine, eight, seven, six, five, four, three, two, one.*

My stomach is tied into painful knots, but Samir is reacting better than I hoped. I expected more denial. Maybe a little ignorance. But he's listening to me.

It's a relief, even if I'm nauseated enough that I feel like running to the bathroom.

Samir shakes his head, his expression growing tight. "But that's horrible. You're not a puppet. You shouldn't have to worry about every single thing you do. I'm sure Ma and Baba would understand if you told them the truth. I know they're proud of you. Remember when you cooked biryani for the first time? Ma bragged about it to *all* the aunties. And every time you get straight As, Baba prints out your report card and puts it on the fridge."

I smile weakly. "It's nothing compared to the way they treat you. You're blinded by their love for you."

"Myra Apu…" Samir frowns. "How long have you felt like this?"

I suck my bottom lip into my mouth, considering how honest to be. "My whole life, Samir," I say finally. This conversation isn't the place to lie. "It's nothing new. I'm sorry I never talked to you about it before. I wasn't… I wasn't brave enough." I swallow roughly. "But I'm trying now."

"That's ridiculous," Samir says sharply. I look up with wide eyes, worried I mistook his tone of voice earlier, but then he says, "Dude, you silently lived through that without ever complaining. That's mad brave. How could you ever think otherwise?"

My throat closes up. Those were the last words I expected from him. "I don't quite know about that."

"I do," he says, unfaltering. "I'm sorry if I helped contribute to…the situation. I'll be careful in the future, and if there's anything I can do to help, tell me. If you need me to cover for you again or make up an excuse to get us out of the house, or you just need to, I don't know, vent, I'll figure it out. I don't want you to go through this alone."

A tear slips down my cheek and I use my sleeve to wipe it away. "Thank you, Samir."

"Oh, don't cry," he says, looking disturbed. "It wasn't that deep."

I laugh hoarsely. There's the brother I know. "It was definitely that deep." I stand up and walk over to him, holding my arms out. He sighs but doesn't move away, which I take as invitation to wrap my arms around him from behind.

"It's no big deal." Samir looks up at me and winces slightly. "Hey listen, I've got your back and all that, but uh…is this thing with Ace really worth it?"

I freeze. "What do you mean?"

He sighs, shifting his gaze to the ground. "You know Ma and Baba are never going to approve. Is this worth it? Have you really thought about it then?"

Ya Allah, if *Samir* is concerned about this, there's no way I'm going to get out of this situation unscathed. I swallow down the fear coating my throat. I can't afford to be worried about this right now. There's nothing I can *do*. This is a problem for future Karina. "It is what it is," I say. "He makes me happy. I don't want to throw that away."

Samir nods as if he expected that answer. "Okay. I just want to make sure you know what you're getting into."

I offer him a strained smile. "Trust me. I understand. I'll worry about it when I'm in college."

There's a moment of layered silence, a million things left unsaid. "I'm sorry," Samir finally says. "I'm sorry you understand."

"It's not your fault," I say, and I mean it. "Thank you for looking out for me, though. You have no idea how much it's going to help, having you in my corner."

He squeezes my arm. "Sorry I wasn't there before."

I close my eyes and hold on to him tighter. "You're here now. That's what matters."

Samir nods before giving me a curious look. "Does this mean you'll help me with Leah now, too? Tit for tat or whatever?"

"Oh my God, you ruined it." I drop my arms, but there's a genuine smile threatening to split my lips. "You're so annoying."

"I'm just *saying*."

"Don't say anything. Ever," I suggest and leave his room. The smile finally breaks free. My brother is an absolute mess, but when it matters, he listens.

★ ★ ★

My parents call that night, and I grimace at my phone. I'm on FaceTime with Ace, who's curating his end-of-month playlist while I finish reading a new book I got from Two Stories.

"Can I call you back?" I ask, drawing his attention away from his laptop. "My parents are calling."

Ace frowns. "Of course. Are you going to be okay?"

I huff fondly. "I'm good. Thank you for checking."

"I only wish I could do more," he says under his breath but raises two fingers to the camera again, his sign of a kiss.

I raise two back and answer my parents' call. For once, my mom is *smiling* at *me*. "Myra!"

"As-salaam alaikum?" I say and it comes out like a question. "What's going on?"

"Nothing." Ma gives me a strange look, like I'm weird for questioning her optimistic mood. "Your dad and I just got home from a going away party. We had to leave because he wasn't feeling well."

"Don't blame me," Baba says from off the screen. "You're the one who threw up."

My mom glares at him but turns back to me with a smile. Now that I'm paying attention, she definitely looks ill. "We leave so soon, it's strange. It feels like it went by so fast."

You have no idea, I want to say. "I know. I can't believe you come back on Sunday. What time does your flight get in?"

"We come at night." Her face is warm and welcoming, even though it's slightly ashen and there are dark circles under her eyes. "I can't wait to see you and Samir again."

My dad comes into the shot, loosening his tie, and a smile takes over his face, too. *Both* of them? Maybe they're drunk. We're not supposed to drink alcohol because it's haram and we're Muslim, but I can't think of another explanation. "Myra!"

"As-salaam alaikum," I repeat, scratching my head. "Did you have a good time tonight?"

"It was okay," he says, sitting next to my mom and squishing his face into the frame. Oh, he looks sick as well. I should probably be less surprised, since I also fell ill last time I went to Bangladesh. Even though visiting is always lovely, the air pollution is difficult to handle. The food also sometimes affects our stomachs, which *sucks* because my relatives always put so much effort into making extravagant meals that look and taste fantastic. With that in mind, I discard my drunk theory. They're definitely being nice because they're sick.

"I can't wait to get home," my mom says, rubbing her eyes. "And hug you and Samir."

"It's miserable here," my dad adds, even though my mom swats him on the arm. "I've never missed home so much."

I smile, but I'm worried they're a ticking bomb. *Tick, tock, tick, tock.*

God, I need to calm down.

Ten, nine, eight, seven, six, five, four, three, two, one. Okay. *Okay.* If they're in a good mood right now, I might as well enjoy it while it lasts. Looking a gift horse in the mouth is bad practice, after all. "I'm excited to see you both again, too."

"Mashallah, our beautiful girl," Ma says, holding a hand to her heart. "How have you been doing? Are you eating enough? Sleeping enough? Doing all your homework?"

"Yes," I say, trying not to fidget. "How about you guys?"

"Don't worry about us," Baba says. There's a faint look of nausea on his face, but he's clearly fighting past it. "You guys are what's important. Is there anything specific you want from Bangladesh? Gifts or anything? Your mom already bought you a lot of clothes, but is there anything else?"

"Uh. A pillow?" I say. I definitely prefer the pillows from Bangladesh to the ones from America. They're much more sturdy, yet still comfortable. I didn't think I was going to be able to ask for one with the mood they were in last time we formally spoke. "If that's okay?"

"Of course," my mom says, laughing. "We'll make sure to leave room in our luggage."

My smile is painful to hold, and I keep counting backward in my head. "Thank you."

My dad nods. "And how's your Dadu? Samir?"

"Good and good," I say. *Tick, tock.* I really don't want to be here when they lay down the law again. "Do you want to talk to Dadu? I'll put her on."

Without waiting for a reply, I slip off my bed and take the phone to my grandma's room. She raises her eyebrows at me when I hand off my phone, but she doesn't question it.

I go back to my room and pull out my janamaz for the Isha prayer, before I falter. I sit down, staring at the patterns woven into the prayer mat, my brain whirring. I always tell everyone my parents aren't bad people, but sometimes I forget it, too. I'm always on edge around them, trying to please them and do what will make them proud, and sometimes I forget they're my parents and they're supposed to look out for *me*. I forget they might not love me as much as Samir, but that doesn't mean they don't care about me at all. They wouldn't be so invested in my success if they didn't want me to do well.

Maybe I can try telling them again. Maybe they won't react badly this time.

But then again, maybe they will.

44

T-MINUS 4 DAYS

Ace and I are in line at Pietra's Sweet Tooth when Pietra squints at us from behind the counter and says, "There's something different about you two."

A flush starts to creep through my body. I didn't realize Ace and I were so bad at fake dating that someone could tell the difference when we started really dating. "Maybe it's Ace's lack of jacket," I say, gesturing to where it's settled on my own shoulders.

Now that I've started to associate the scent of cinnamon with relaxation, it's almost calming to wear Ace's jacket. I think he knows, which is why he lends it to me whenever I start looking even slightly anxious.

Pietra tilts her head, looking between us. "That's part of it, but there's something else. I'll figure it out eventually."

"Karina just likes me more than she did before." Ace pointedly pulls a lock of my hair between his fingers. "Which I'm very happy about."

"You know what? That might actually be it," Pietra says,

tapping the side of her chin before beaming. "You two are so cute."

My cheeks burn. "Thank you."

"You're making her blush," Ace says, grinning at me. I swat his hand away when he tries to cup my cheeks.

"So cute," Pietra emphasizes. "What'll it be?"

"Cheesecake and coffee for me," I say.

"Milk with three spoons of sugar," Ace adds offhandedly, his gaze on the desserts display. "Can I get a vanilla milkshake and a cup of cherries?"

I try to contain my smile but it's hard. I know how thoughtful Ace is, but experiencing it in the moment is different. It sets me on fire from the inside out to know he remembers the little things about me.

We go to our usual table, and Ace gestures for me to sit next to him instead of across from him. "I want to show you a playlist," he says, holding up his earphones.

I shrug and sit by him, taking one of the earphones. "I'm Yours" by Jason Mraz is playing and I shake my head at him fondly. "Wooed."

"That's the goal," Ace says, winking at me before offering me some of his milkshake. There are two straws, so I'm not surprised when he leans in the same moment that I do.

I flick his nose, and he grins at me. "We're supposed to be studying."

"Then let's study," he says. "I'm not the one holding us up."

I grumble but take out our notes. As I pull out a few discussion questions, Ace's hand brushes against my wrist and I look up.

"I wanted to talk to you about something." He's biting his bottom lip and he looks almost...nervous?

"Okay," I say, turning toward him fully. "What's up?"

"Remember how I said I was going to apply to NYU but if I didn't get in, I'd pursue astronomy elsewhere?"

"Yeah," I say, my brows drawing together. "Did you change your plan?"

"No." He looses an uneven breath. "I've just been looking around a lot, and if I get a high enough score on my SAT, Columbia…"

My eyes widen. I don't know where he's going with this, but my heart is already racing. "Columbia…?"

He looks down. "Columbia has a really good astronomy program."

"And you're thinking of…applying?"

"Yeah." His fingers tap against the table, the metal of his rings clinking and echoing through the shop. "If I get an A in all my classes this year, my GPA should be high enough, especially with my music extracurriculars. English is my weak point, but I think it'll be okay." He glances up briefly, offering me a mild smile, and my heart stutters. "It's one option of many. NYU is still my top choice, but it's only half an hour away from Columbia and…" He cuts himself off. "I don't know."

I can hardly breathe. "Only half an hour?"

He nods and finally meets my gaze. "Fifteen minutes if we meet in the middle. I know there's no guarantee you'll still want to be together by then. But I thought, maybe…yeah."

He's thinking about our future together. He *wants* a future together, after all these studying sessions, after junior year, after prom, after college applications, and even after that.

He wants this. He wants us.

Something settles in my heart. If I do somehow miraculously win in the end, it won't be alone. We're partners in this.

I peer through wet lashes to see Ace gazing at me hopefully. "What do you think?"

"I think that's wonderful," I murmur. The smile spreading across my face is too wide but I'm helpless to stop it. "I think it's really, really wonderful."

Ace's responding smile is like gazing directly into the sun. "Yeah?"

"Yeah," I say, unable to contain a soft laugh. "You know, I was thinking of applying to NYU, too. Either way, fifteen minutes doesn't seem like that bad of a trek."

"Not that bad at all." Ace's eyes are bright as he holds out a pinky. "Fifteen minutes in either direction?"

"Fifteen minutes in either direction," I promise, linking our pinkies together.

Ace kisses my palm softly. "We have so much future in front of us."

"I know," I say, squeezing his fingers. "It's a little terrifying."

"It used to be," he says, his lips skimming along the underside of my hand. "But it's starting to look a lot brighter."

45

T-MINUS 3 DAYS

English class is different now. Fewer people stare at Ace and me, which is always a good thing. Even better is that Nandini and Cora sit in front of us and don't gape or watch us discreetly from the corners of their eyes the entire time. Instead, everything is as ordinary as any other day, except for the fact that Ace is sitting next to me. We're creating the new normal. I love it.

Nandini gives Ace a dark look when she sees me nudge him to pay attention, but otherwise, everything is fine.

"I like your friends," Ace says in a whisper, lips brushing my hair. "They look out for you, even if that means glaring at me."

"Yeah," I say, glancing at them. I don't see much other than the back of their heads—Cora's platinum blond hair is plaited into a french braid, and Nandini's short black curls are held back with a speckled headband. "They do."

"Stop whispering," Nandini hisses, startling us.

"Or at least whisper louder," Cora grumbles.

"I take it back," Ace says. "I don't like them."

I snort and shove his shoulder halfheartedly. "Don't start."

Class passes in a breeze, and Nandini and Cora leave for lunch first, but not without promising to save us seats. I'm still packing my stuff away when Miss Cannon approaches. "Karina, Alistair."

"Miss Cannon." I wave with my free hand. "What's up?"

"I wanted to check in and see how the tutoring is going," she says, sitting on the edge of a desk. "Good, I hope?"

Ace offers me a mischievous grin. "You could say that."

"Shut up," I say, swatting him. Honestly, he has no shame.

Miss Cannon raises her eyebrows, looking between us. "I see you two have grown a lot closer. That explains all the whispering I hear back here."

My cheeks grow impossibly warm, anxiety rushing through me like a waterfall. "I'm so sorry. I didn't mean to disrespect—"

"It's because she's explaining things to me that I don't understand," Ace cuts me off, resting his hand on top of mine. The motion is grounding. "It's my fault."

Ten, nine, eight, seven, six, five, four, three, two, one. I take an uneven breath before nodding. "Yeah."

Miss Cannon's gaze drops to our hands. "I see… I'm glad to hear you're learning a lot, Alistair."

"It's all because of Karina," he says. "She's an amazing tutor. She's so passionate about English that it's hard not to care about it after listening to her."

"Ace."

"What? It's the truth." He shrugs, unbothered, but his hand squeezes mine. "Thank you, Miss Cannon. I'm sure I'll pass the English Regents with flying colors."

Miss Cannon beams. "I'm happy to hear that. Have you guys started the poetry project yet?"

"I thought I was excused," I say, biting my bottom lip. Now

that I know she's not mad at me, the anxiety is easing. It helps to have Ace and the scent of cinnamon near.

"You are," she says. "I meant have you two started working on Alistair's together?"

"Oh. Yes," I say, glancing at Ace. He hasn't let me see any of his poems, but we've gone over the parameters several times. "He's been doing really well."

"That's lovely," Miss Cannon says, clapping her hands. The sound batters around in my skull, echoing. "I was thinking you could present first, Alistair? For extra credit? It would help boost your grade. I think we can get you to an A by the end of the year."

"I guess I'll really have to bring my A game then," Ace says and nudges me. Slowly, I nudge back. "But it should be easy since my name is Ace."

"Shut up," I say, a laugh slipping from my lips involuntarily. "What's wrong with you?"

"It's not my fault you can't appreciate the fact I'm a true comedian," he says. "It was funny, wasn't it, Miss Cannon?"

Miss Cannon is looking between us, a look of understanding dawning on her face. I think her smile might even be wider than before. "Hilarious, Alistair."

Ace winks at me. "See?"

"Yeah, I see," I say, rolling my eyes.

Before we leave, Miss Cannon rests a hand on my shoulder. "Could I speak to you briefly, Karina?"

I nod, gesturing for Ace to go ahead. He lingers in the doorway for a moment but when I wave insistently, he disappears, the door closing behind him. "What's up, Miss Cannon?"

She presses her lips together, considering me. "I received an email from your parents over the break."

My heart plummets. "You did?" I say, voice shaky. "What did it say?"

Ten, nine, eight, seven, six, five, four, three, two, one.

She leans against the whiteboard. "They said you wanted to stop tutoring Ace. Is that true?"

"No," I say immediately, my fingers clenching into fists. "No, it's not. They're just—it was a misunderstanding."

Miss Cannon looks me over in concern. "Are you sure? This is a safe place for you to speak your mind."

"I'm sure." My nails dig into my palms almost painfully. "I want to tutor Ace. Really. Please disregard their email."

"That's not what I was referring to," Miss Cannon says quietly.

I falter, unsure what to say. The same way Ace can't save me from my parents, neither can Miss Cannon. She already does enough by providing me a safe haven at school.

"I'm sure," I say again, looking away from her earnest expression. "Thank you, Miss Cannon."

She sighs softly. "If you need anything, I'm here, Karina."

I nod and leave her classroom. Ace is waiting outside and at the sight of my expression, he silently offers me his jacket.

I smile faintly as I accept it, but my mind is whirring. None of this is going to be easy. My parents are going against me at every step, knowingly or not.

For as long as I live under their roof, this will be my life. Refusing to live by their rules is the start of a war I don't know how to fight.

you look at me across a bloody battlefield
and I swing until my knuckles are bruised
I will run until my lungs collapse
for you
I will kiss death and smile
for you
even in hades, I will fight
for you

46

T-MINUS 2 DAYS

Ace is trying to ruin my life.

"I'm not *dressed*," I say. "I can't meet your dad in a hoodie."

"You've already met my dad," Ace says, shaking his head at me. He looks amused, as if this is funny and he's not trying to drag me to his house against my will.

Drag might be an exaggeration, but still. He didn't tell me where we were going until we arrived, and now it's a match of wills.

"Yeah, but I didn't *care* then! Now we're like…dating. And he's your *dad*."

Ace huffs fondly. "Karina, my dad already likes you. I told him everything, and he thinks you're a good influence. It's just dinner."

"No offense, Ace, but that sounds really fake," I say, planting my feet solidly on the ground and refusing to budge. "Your dad probably hates me. I *lied* to him the first time I met him. Ya Allah, he definitely hates me."

"He doesn't hate you," Ace says, squeezing my shoulders.

"Ace, I look *disgusting*," I say, crossing my arms. I falter for a moment but then push forward, because I need to assert my boundaries. "You should have told me we were going to do this. We're supposed to be in this together. You can't just make decisions for the both of us. It's just—I'd appreciate if you told me next time."

Ace's expression falls. "I just thought that—no, never mind. You're right. I'm sorry. It was wrong. There's no excuse, but I promise it won't be a repeat occurrence. I'm still learning your lines, but one day I'll know all of them and I'll never cross them again."

I examine his expression, trying to see if he really understands. It's more obvious in some moments than others that we come from two different worlds, and this is sadly one of them. But he looks genuinely contrite, so I nod. "Okay. Thank you."

He offers me another apologetic smile. "Always."

There's a moment of silence Ace breaks by clearing his throat. Tension slips from both of us as we settle back into our usual routine. I'm glad I told him my feelings, though. That's the only way this relationship is ever going to work. And I *want* this to work, despite the odds stacked against us.

"If it helps, I think you look great," Ace says, brushing a strand of hair from my eyes. He hesitates and reaches for my braid, untying it. He runs his fingers through the strands until they come loose. "There. I don't know how anyone could look at you and not see the most beautiful person in the world."

Blood flows to my cheeks fast enough to give me a head rush. Or maybe that's just Ace. "You need glasses."

He shakes his head, smiling. "I've got twenty-twenty."

"I doubt that," I say but shake my hair out, arranging it around my face. My hair tie is missing, and I find it on his wrist. "Are you going to give that back?"

"Nah," he says, lacing our fingers and pulling me toward his house. "I'll hold on to it for you."

The whole family is at the table again, but this time I sit beside Ace. Still, I expect dinner to be awkward.

It's surprisingly not. The weird tension that was there last time seems to be mostly—if not completely—gone. I keep glancing between Xander and Ace, expecting a fight to break out, but neither of them seem inclined to pay attention to each other.

"Ace tells me you've been tutoring him in English," Albert Clyde says, gazing at me thoughtfully. *Ace?* I wonder. *Not Alistair?* "How's he doing?"

"He's actually doing really great, Mr. Clyde. Today he corrected *me* about something. I've never been prouder." I grin at Ace. "He's improved so much already."

"I'm glad to hear that," Albert says. There's a small smile on his lips, which is shocking. I was expecting change, but not this much. Ace looks similarly amazed by it. "So you two are really dating now?"

I wince. "Yes. I'm sorry about lying to you before. I hope you don't think less of me for it."

"I would never blame you for going along with my son's... wild inclinations." Albert looks almost fond as he stares at Ace. It's surprising, but it makes my heart warm all the same. "He explained the situation to me. I understand you're part of why he felt comfortable enough to talk to me in the first place."

"I didn't do much," I say, cheeks burning. "Your son is a lot braver than he gives himself credit for."

"Yes," Albert says, eyes crinkling. "He is."

"Yuck," Mia says jokingly, but she's also smiling brightly. "Too many feelings."

"I agree," Xander says.

I turn to glare at him, but his expression is solemn—mildly curious, even—as he looks between his dad and brother.

"You two get enough love," his stepmother, Tina, says with a laugh. "Let Ace have his moment."

They're trying. The realization hits me like a brick. Ace told them the truth, and they're *trying*. Xander is keeping his comments to himself, and Albert is making the effort to reach out to his son.

"To Ace," I say, holding out my glass of water. He deserves a toast after all this.

"You're embarrassing me," Ace says with a smirk, but holds up his glass.

I raise an eyebrow. "You don't look embarrassed."

"I'm not," he admits. "Too happy for that."

We all clink our glasses, and continue eating. Halfway through our meal, something nudges my foot and I nearly jump out of my skin. I look down and see Spade pressed against the side of my leg.

Uh.

I glance at Ace, but he's in the middle of talking to his father. I press my lips together and force myself to take a deep breath.

It's just Spade.

I reach down and gently scratch behind his ears. Spade barks excitedly and presses closer. I can't help but laugh and scratch again.

When I look up, Ace is watching me with a crooked grin. I return it.

I continue eating my food. Occasionally I see Xander looking at Ace as if he's seeing his brother for the first time. It might be because Ace keeps poking and prodding at me with his fork, but I think it's because of the bright smile on Ace's face. It's nothing new to me, but it seems like it's new to Xander—and new to Ace's father, too.

They're truly trying, and it fills me with a strange sense of hope.

We end up in Ace's room, and I toy with one of the stars hanging from his ceiling, lost in thought. Seeing Ace with his family was unexpectedly heartwarming, but it also stirred something uncomfortable in me, especially after my conversation with Miss Cannon. Could I ever have something like that?

I just don't know.

"Karina."

I look away from the star to see Ace sitting on his bed. "Yeah?"

"Sit with me for a second." He pats the spot next to him. "I want to talk to you."

My brows pull together. His tone is serious. "Okay." I sit down facing him and cross my legs pretzel style.

"Your parents come back this weekend, right?" Ace asks, rubbing the back of his neck. "What's going to happen then?"

I tense, not having expected that. I should have. I just met his parents. It's natural he would ask about mine.

"With us?" I say, biting my lip. This is a hard question, because I don't know how he's going to take my answer. "I want to stay together. That's not even a question at this point. But it's not going to be...easy. For either of us."

A wrinkle forms between Ace's brows. "What does that mean? You said it before, too. You know I'm not going anywhere, right?"

I sigh. I was hoping to avoid this conversation for as long as possible, but now that it's here, I can't give him false promises. The only way for this—for us—to work is to keep it a secret as long as possible. He deserves to know that, too.

"My family isn't like other families. I need you to know that. You saw as much during our date...but this isn't a temporary thing. This is the way it's always going to be. We can never tell them we're together. If we do, they'll fight us at every step. They'll see you as a distraction from school, and it doesn't help that you're white. They're never going to accept you." I fiddle with my sleeve, unable to meet his gaze. "I don't want them to take drastic measures."

"Drastic measures?" he repeats quietly.

My bottom lip quivers. "Yeah. I'm sorry. I never want you to think I'm embarrassed of you or ashamed to be with you or anything like that, but I can't ever tell them. You're never going to be able to have the experience that I'm having right now, where you get to sit and eat with them. They'll never make us pose for prom pictures. They'll never clap you on the back or joke around with you. Just...all of it. They'll never approve, and they'll never allow it."

Ace's frown becomes deeper. "They'd be that upset you're dating me?"

"Yeah. That's just how they are." In an attempt to lighten the mood, I add, "Knowing them, they'll probably start looking for potential husbands when I graduate from college. Maybe we can drop the bomb on them then and run off into the sunset."

Ace tilts my chin up. "Like an arranged marriage? They'd force you to do that?"

I shrug, even though my skin is crawling from just discussing this topic. "Not exactly. They wouldn't force me. But deeply encourage me? Probably."

His eyes are sad. "Is that—is that what you want?"

"What?" I ask, lips parting. "No, of course not."

"How can you talk about this so lightly then?" Ace asks, letting go of me to run his hand through his hair in a quick, agitated movement. He's clearly frustrated, and I don't know how to make it better. "I don't understand, Karina. You don't have to tell your parents about us if you don't want to, but is it your choice? Is any of it? First your major, now your relationships? What's next? When does it end? Maybe it's not my place to ask, and I'm sorry if I'm overstepping, but I just... I want you to be happy."

I understand where he's coming from, but it doesn't make it any easier to have this conversation. "They're not choosing for me. They're just worried about my future," I say, but the words are empty. "And I—I can't disappoint them."

"Why not?" His gaze is beseeching.

I blink. How do I answer that? "They're my parents, Ace."

He sighs. "I know, Karina. But that doesn't answer my question."

"They're my *parents,*" I repeat, not knowing what else to say. "I can't let them down."

"What's going to happen if you do? Would they stop caring about you? Stop loving you?"

"Maybe!" I bite my tongue. I didn't mean to say that.

Ace looks at me in surprise. "Is that true? Would they stop loving you because you're not who they want you to be?"

"I—I don't know," I say, my breaths coming faster. *Ten, nine, eight, seven, six, five, four, three, two, one...*

He scrubs a hand over his face. "Listen, I don't care about telling your parents about us. I don't care if they never know. As long as you want to be together, that's enough for me. We respect each other's lines, right? But what about you? You have to hide *so* much of yourself from your parents. Do they even know who you are?"

"They know enough," I say, swallowing painfully.

"Do they?" he asks lightly. "I'm asking genuinely. It's your life, not mine. I'll never ask you to do something you don't want to do. That's not my place. But is this enough for you? Is it enough to have their love, even if it means hiding who you really are? You're their daughter, Karina. You shouldn't have to change yourself to make them happy. If their love comes with terms and conditions, what's the point?"

"They're my parents." My voice cracks miserably. "I can't— I can't…"

Ace reaches for me, but I move back unthinkingly.

"Karina," he says, his own voice pained. "I want you to be happy. I want *you* to want yourself to be happy."

"I am happy." I blink back tears. "But I'd be happier if I made them proud."

"You make me proud," he says softly. "You make Nandini and Cora proud. You make Miss Cannon proud. You make your Dadu proud. Can't that be enough?"

I heave on a sob. It's not enough. It's not enough, and I wish so badly that it was.

Ace reaches for me again but falters halfway. "Can I please touch you?"

Another sob tears its way out of my throat, and I nod. I need something to ground me.

He wraps his arms around me, and I bury my head in his chest, crying. I wish it didn't have to be like this. I wish it was enough to have other people look at me with pride. I wish I didn't feel like I owe this gigantic debt to my parents and the only way to ever pay it back is to succeed in their eyes.

"I hate seeing you so miserable," Ace murmurs into my hair. "I'm sorry for bringing it up. I know there are no easy answers, but I'm worried about you. I don't know how much longer you can do this before you burn out, Karina."

I wish I had the breath to reply that I've already burned out. The fire he sees inside me is actually just the ember that remains from a once-roaring inferno.

Ace holds me closer, stroking my hair with one hand and wrapping the other around the back of my neck, squeezing gently. "Breathe with me. Come on."

His chest moves under my head as he takes deep breaths in and out, and I try to copy him until my own breathing evens out. Tears still spill down my cheeks, saltwater stinging my tongue.

"Hey," Ace says, leaning back so he can cup my face. His thumbs brush across my cheeks, wiping the tear tracks. "You deserve to be happy, Karina Ahmed. Your life shouldn't be about making other people happy at your expense. Please believe that."

"I wish I could," I say, sniffling. I still feel the urge to rip out my heart and throw it somewhere far, far away, where it can't bother me anymore, but I'm calmer. Ace is right in that I have to make a decision about my future career in two days. The question of which one to choose haunts my every waking moment. "But it's easier said than done."

Ace's eyes are sad. "I know. This entire situation is the worst. But if anyone can find a way to come out of it on the other side, it's you. My lionheart. It's always going to be your decision, but I hope you know I believe in you more than anything."

I close my eyes and lean into his touch, trying to soak in his warmth. "I wish I was as brave as you think I am."

I am not a spark. I am not a blaze. I am not an inferno.

"You are," Ace says, pressing a soft kiss to my forehead. "You are."

47

T-MINUS 1 DAY

One day.

T-1.

My parents come back tomorrow. Everything is going to change. It's back to constant supervision and intense lectures and watchful gazes I can never fully shake, even when I'm out of their sight.

It means goodbye to my dates with Ace, goodbye to having Dadu around, goodbye to my newfound happiness.

Goodbye to the indecision that plagues me constantly.

My motions are slow today. I wake up and brush my teeth. I eat breakfast and watch Dadu read the newspaper. I kneel on a janamaz and pray to Allah to help me find an answer. I lie down with a book in the living room but end up watching Samir play video games. I sit outside on the porch and attempt to do homework, all to no avail.

Ace texts me, more than once, telling me he misses me. My eyes burn when I read the messages, but my mind is somewhere else, fixated on a singular, terrifying thought. Should I defy my parents? Should I tell them I want to study English?

The idea has infested my mind like a disease. This past month has changed me. I can feel it in the marrow of my bones, something deeper than words can explain.

I'm different.

But I don't know if I'm braver.

I don't know if I can do this.

"Dadu," I say. I'm sitting in her room as she packs for her departure tomorrow. Just thinking about it fills me with dread. "Do you think I'm a coward if I don't tell my parents the truth?"

She stops folding a saree midway and her fingers clench around the material. "Of course not. Did someone tell you that?"

In that moment, I'm certain if someone *had* called me a coward—an auntie or a cousin or a random person on the street—Dadu would hunt them to the ends of the earth.

I wish that helped. I wish there was someone to blame.

"No," I say, swallowing the lump in my throat. "But I feel like I'll be one. It shouldn't be this hard to tell them I want to be an English major."

"No one has lived your life, Myra," Dadu says. She loosens her grip and touches my hand. "So no one can pass judgment on you for your decisions."

"*I've* lived my life and I can pass judgment on myself. I—I want to tell them so badly, but I'm afraid of disappointing them. I'm afraid they'll say no. Then what will I have?"

Even the thought of them saying no feels like it's going to kill me.

"You will have your heart," she says fervently. "Don't let the fear of disappointing them stop you from living your fullest life."

"It's terrifying," I whisper.

Dadu sighs and sets her saree down to sit next to me. "I know. And you don't *have* to do it. If you do, do it because you want to. Not because other people are telling you to. Not because you want to make someone else happy. Whatever you decide, make sure it's your choice."

"What if my choice is wrong?" I ask. My voice is small.

"It won't be," Dadu says, wrapping her arms around my shoulder. "No matter what choice you make, it will be right because it's yours. And if, down the line, you change your mind, that's okay, too. No matter what, I will be proud of you and I will support you, Myra."

I stare at her face, earnest and warm, and look away in shame. In the end, even Dadu's support isn't enough. I love her so much, but I don't see how she can stand against my parents. I don't see how anyone can.

I know my choice. It's not one I'm proud of.

In the end, I will always care more about making my parents proud than my own happiness, no matter how much I wish I didn't.

If they want me to be a doctor, I will be. Their expectations have shaped me too much for me to disappoint them in this. I can't do it. I don't have the strength.

48

T-PLUS 0 DAYS

My mom hugs me when she arrives. It's nice but so unbelievably strange.

She still smells like roses and citrus shampoo but also like jasmine. In Bangladesh, there's a garden in my grandparents' backyard with jasmine shrubs. It seems she brought the scent with her. I'm wistful for half a moment, wishing I'd gone to Bangladesh with them.

"We missed you so much," Ma says, squeezing me in her arms and peppering me with kisses. I grimace at the amount of lipstick she probably just smeared across my face. Then her words register and my mouth falls slack. They *missed* me?

"It's great to see you again, Myra," Baba says, patting me on the shoulder. "How was the ride here?"

"The Uber driver had nice music," I say, unsure how else to answer. Having my parents greet me warmly has thrown me into a state of confusion. Samir is smiling as if this unprecedented change makes sense when it doesn't. "How was Bangladesh?"

"Good," my dad says, and then begins speaking to my grandma in quiet murmurs. Dadu isn't coming home with us. Uncle Mustafa is already here to pick her up and take her back to New Jersey. My stomach twists at the thought of not seeing her for weeks when I've become used to seeing her every day.

"We went to a mela almost every week, and we got to see a lot of our relatives. So many of them sent back gifts for you and Samir," my mom says, gesturing to their luggage before coughing into her sleeve, clearly still sick. "We also went for fancy dinners and visited carnivals. Also your little cousins said hello. I have videos of them to show you."

"Your mom did *lots* of shopping," my dad adds, rolling his eyes. He's not much better off than my mom, judging from his pallor. He's more pale than when he left, which is the opposite of what should happen when going to Bangladesh. "Half our luggage weight is just the things she bought."

"It's less expensive over there," Ma says, sniffing. She takes a tissue from her bag and wipes her nose. "Both of them needed new clothes anyway."

"I'm just glad to be home," Baba says, wrapping an arm around Samir's shoulders. "No more shopping for your mother, and finally some rest for me."

"But we're going bowling this weekend, right?" Samir asks, nudging my dad.

Baba makes a face. "Maybe next weekend. I don't think I'm quite up to it yet."

"I, for one, can't wait to go home and *sleep*," my mom says, fanning herself. "And have some decent medicine."

Samir laughs. "You just need a good dose of NyQuil, Ma."

She nods in agreement. "That's exactly what I need. That and my two kids."

Without warning, she pulls us both into another hug. I

blink at Dadu over my mom's shoulder, and she only shakes her head, looking equally mystified.

My parents are being *too* nice. It's uncomfortable. There's a weird tension in my gut, my muscles strung tight.

"What's wrong with them?" I whisper to my grandma as we head for the parking lot, where my uncle is waiting to pick her up.

She nudges me. "Maybe they had a change of heart. Being sick on vacation is never fun. Perhaps it made them grateful for the finer things in life. Life lessons come when you least expect them, trust me. Dada and I learned many in surprising places."

"I can only hope," I say, watching my parents poke at Samir's ribs, complaining he's barely eaten since they left.

As we enter the lot, a wave of sadness strikes me. It's time to say goodbye.

Dadu says farewell to Samir first, hugging him and ruffling his hair, telling him to take care of himself.

Then it's my turn.

"Myra," Dadu says, gently cupping my face. "I'm so proud of you. In this last month alone, I've watched you grow incredible amounts. I'm going to miss you so much. Please be kind to yourself when I'm gone, and call me if you need anything. I'm always here for you."

"Get a cell phone so I can text you," I joke, even though my heart is heavy. I don't want her to go.

She nods seriously. "I'll look into that with your uncle. Until then, you can always call my home phone. Okay?"

"Okay." I hug her tightly. "Thank you for everything, Dadu. I'll miss you."

Please don't go, I want to say. *Please stay forever.*

But there's no stopping this. It's inevitable, like most things in my life.

Before I know it, Dadu is gone, waving from a window as my uncle's car drives away.

I miss her already.

"Oh, don't look so sad, Myra." Baba squeezes my shoulder. "We'll visit her again soon and now you have us back."

"Yeah," I say. *But how long will this last? How long until I become the daughter that constantly disappoints you again?*

By the time we get home, I'm feeling despondent. I want to lie in bed and sleep forever.

I head for my room to do just that when my mom calls me back. "Let me show you the gifts we brought."

"I thought you were feeling sick?" I say but pause at the base of the stairs.

"Yes, but I missed you more. Come here," she says, waving me over.

I hesitate, worrying my bottom lip between my teeth before I nod. Maybe Dadu was right. Maybe they thought about things and changed their minds.

I want to believe it's true.

I sit down next to her. My dad is busy looking over his plants to make sure they're still alive, inspecting their leaves with a careful eye, and Samir is watching videos of my baby cousins on my dad's discarded phone. "What'd you bring?"

My mom takes out gorgeous lehengas and sarees and salwars and rolls and rolls of beautiful fabric. "Nanu insisted on these so you could pick and choose your own outfit design."

"They're so pretty," I say, running my hand along a roll of pale blue chiffon with golden designs woven in.

"And I brought you some jewelry, too," Ma says, pulling out velvet boxes and unlatching them. "Some tikkas and anklets and bangles. Oh, and some nose rings. I think I have some regular rings, too."

My mom presents a row of shiny golden rings to me, and my first thought is of Ace. He'd love one of these.

I quickly discard that thought. My parents and Ace do not fit in the same sentence, even in the safety of my head.

"I love them, Ma," I say, slipping one on. I study the sapphire stone, glinting in the light before looking back at my mom.

She's smiling warmly. The look on her face makes my stomach clench uncertainly. "It looks good on you."

I nod, turning back to the accessories. I can't second-guess myself now. Dadu isn't here to support me. If I tell them the truth, it'll be by myself, and what if they don't approve?

I don't know if I could cope. I'm not as brave as everyone keeps saying I am.

By the end of the night, they've run out of things to show me. I retreat to my bedroom to light a candle and text Ace, still feeling out of sorts, when there's a knock on my door.

"Come in," I say, setting my phone down.

It's my dad, and he's holding a giant package. I furrow my brows. "What's that?"

"Your pillow," he says, shaking it around. His eyes are crinkled with amusement. "It saved me a fortune since your mom had to stop shopping. It was so big she couldn't find any room to fit in more clothes."

I laugh, reaching for the pillow. "Glad I could be of service."

Baba sits on my bed, patting the spot next to him. "I wanted to talk to you about our phone call last week."

My blood curdles. The ball is about to drop. I've been expecting it all night.

"I think we were a little harsh on you," he says, scratching the side of his head. *Wait, what?* "Your Dadu told me how upset you were. Ma and I wanted to say sorry. We know you're doing your best in school."

Ma pops her head in. "Did you call me?"

"I was just telling Myra we're sorry about how we spoke to her on the phone last week," my dad says.

My mom looks a little hesitant, but then she sighs and comes inside, taking the seat on the other side of me. "Yeah, we're sorry."

I blink. They're *sorry*? They know how hard I've been working? They recognize their faults?

Did I somehow die and go to heaven?

"It's okay," I say, my head spinning. I can't believe Dadu convinced my dad to *apologize*. I can't believe my mom somehow agreed to this. I can't believe any of it.

"We're proud of you for giving school your best effort," Baba says. "We're not happy you're tutoring a boy, but it shows you have a good heart."

"And you said it will look good on college applications, right?" Ma asks.

The mention of college applications causes my heart to race. I look between my parents, both watching me with earnest expressions. They're *apologizing*.

My heart flutters nervously. Can I do it? Can I tell them the truth?

"Yeah, it'll look good on college applications," I say.

"That's good, then. Before you know it, every college will be accepting you into their premed program," my dad says, smiling.

Do it, do it, do it, a part of me whispers fervently, despite my sweaty palms, my prickling skin, my racing heart.

If I don't do it now, I never will.

Being brave in this one moment might be enough to serve me a lifetime.

It's time I take control of my own life and ensure my own happiness.

Ten, nine, eight, seven, six, five, four, three, two, one.

Okay. Time to be a lionheart.

I brace myself.

"Actually," I say, biting my bottom lip. "I've been thinking, and I don't want to study medicine. I don't want to be a doctor. I really love English, and I want to study that instead."

I did it. I told them the truth.

Silence follows my proclamation, broken only by the sound of my mother's laughter. "That's funny, Myra. But be serious."

Oh.

Oh no.

No, no, *no*.

"I wasn't joking," I say weakly. I fucked up. I've made a horrible, horrible mistake.

I shouldn't have said anything.

My dad stares at me. "What do you mean you want to study English? Your whole life, you've wanted to be a doctor. Why would you change your mind now to study a useless degree?"

It feels like there's a dagger twisting into my heart. "I never wanted to be a doctor. You wanted me to be a doctor."

"What are you talking about? Are you saying we *forced* you to become a doctor?" Ma asks sharply.

I shake my head. I want to disappear, I want to run away, I want to be anywhere but here, in this situation. "No, but I don't—"

"How can you be so selfish?" my mom asks, shaking her head. "You only think of yourself and what you want. Your dad and I have worked tirelessly so you could have a better future and you want to throw it away for an English degree?"

Ten, nine, eight, seven—

"I'm not throwing away my future," I say quietly. Tears press against my eyes but I won't let them spill. Not here, not in front of them.

"No, you're being lazy. You want to study English because

it's *easy*. Because math and science are hard. What kind of daughter did we raise, Hussain?"

Six, five, four, three—

My dad's expression is grim. He exchanges a look with my mom, and I see the moment all sympathy swings away from me. The moment he fully takes her side. "You will get nowhere in life with an English degree, Myra. You have to know that. I'm so disappointed in you for even thinking of doing something like this. How can you be so ungrateful for all we've done for you?"

Two, one.

Zero.

"I'm not—I'm not *ungrateful*," I say, because that's so far from the truth. I know everything they've sacrificed for me to have a better future. But it's *my* future. "I just thought—"

"That's the problem with young girls lately," Ma says, cutting me off. "You think too much, and yet too little. Back in my day, we would never say something so stupid. Don't be silly, Myra. You will be a doctor. That is final."

No.

Please don't do this to me, I want to say, but I can't speak. My throat has closed up.

"And get those foolish ideas out of your head," Baba says, standing up. "This is what happens when we leave you unsupervised…" His eyes meet my mother's, and he mutters, "Disgraceful."

He walks out without another word and I stare at his retreating back, breathing harshly.

"You should be ashamed of yourself, Myra," my mom says, shaking her head as she also gets to her feet. "One day, you will learn. Until then, we are here to guide you. In the future, think before you speak."

She leaves, closing the door behind her, and my heart finally collapses in my chest.

★ ★ ★

I wait until I hear their voices disappear down the hallway to let the tears flow, unrelenting as they are.

I don't know why I expected anything else. I don't know why I got my hopes up. I don't know why, I don't know why, I don't know why.

I don't know why they can't let me have this.

I'm not asking a lot. I'm not asking *them* to do anything. I want this for me, for myself. For my future.

Because it's mine, isn't it?

At least, it should be.

I bury my face in my pillows and take ragged breaths as sobs rack my frame. Someone knocks on my door and Samir's voice calls, "Myra Apu? Can I come in?"

I don't answer, instead muffling the sound of my cries as best as I can. If Samir can hear, my parents can, too. I don't want them to think any less of me than they already do.

Samir knocks again. "Myra Apu, let me in."

"Go away," I say, my voice cracking. "*Please.* Just go."

The knocks subside. My phone lights up with a text from Samir, but I can't make myself read it.

It feels like something is ripping me apart from the inside out. Some kind of monster that's slipped inside my chest and decided to ravage my insides. No matter how many painful breaths I take, I can't get enough air inside my lungs. I've never felt this much heartbreak.

Everything I've ever known feels like it's turning on its head. Ace's words echo in my head: *If their love comes with terms and conditions, what's the point?*

I don't have the answer. I don't know what the point *is*. All this time I thought it was my own fault, that I wasn't doing enough as their daughter—but what *haven't* I done?

Don't I deserve to be happy, too? Don't I deserve a family willing to try?

I've never felt the sting of their disapproval like this. Not only does it burn, it's blistering over. All I feel is constant, aching, writhing sadness.

Sad isn't the right word. *Sad* doesn't even begin to cover it. *Devastated* is better, but still falls short.

Destroyed.

I'm destroyed.

I wish for nothing more than my grandma's arms around me, comforting me, but she's miles and miles away.

I've never felt more alone.

Why can't I have this? Why can't I choose the path of my own future?

What am I supposed to do now? Paste on a smile and pretend I'm happy with the decision they've made *for* me?

Pretend that the world hasn't stopped turning?

But the truth is that everyone else is living their life as they always have. It's me who's stuck in slow motion.

The thought of having to face anyone ever again makes me nauseated. I'll have to explain that my parents don't love me unconditionally—that their love comes with a million hidden clauses—and that I have no choice but to do exactly what they want. Even now, bile burns in the back of my throat. I'm choking on my own anguish.

I don't know how much longer I can do this.

I don't know.

I don't.

I.

Is this what it's like to have your parents disappoint you? This paralyzing devastation?

I don't know what to do. I don't know if there's anything I can do.

I'm sixteen, and my future is out of my hands.

My head starts pounding so hard I have to sit up and tuck

my head between my knees to keep from blacking out. Every breath I take is ragged and painful.

My hands are shaking. My entire body is shaking. My soul is about to vibrate out from underneath me, disappearing into the wind. Not my countdown, not my candles, not my prayers, not a single thing can help me now.

Unshakeable, I think bitterly.

I've never been unshakeable. I only fooled myself into thinking I was.

I don't even try to count backward in my head. I don't see how that can help me anymore.

I clench my eyes shut, as if that'll stop the tears from burning the backs of my eyelids. The future that lies in front of me is bleak.

This is the end, I realize. *This is the end of my life and the beginning of the life my parents want for me.*

But maybe I never had my own life in the first place.

49

T-PLUS 1 DAY

Forcing myself to get up for school the next morning is the most miserable experience of my sixteen years.

There's a strange numbness that's slipped under my skin. It creeps closer to my heart with each passing moment. It's as if there are shards of glass twisting inside me, tearing into my flesh and forcing me to become hollow.

I'm empty. I'm broken.

I'm alone.

Despite texts from my brother, from Nandini, Cora, and Ace, I feel completely and utterly alone.

None of them have ever been in this situation. None of them will ever be.

I wouldn't *want* them to be. It's the last thing I would wish on anyone, but it doesn't help the fact that I have no one to turn to now who really understands how I feel. Maybe my cousins, but I can't handle the thought of them knowing, looking at me in pity whenever we cross paths.

This pain is my burden alone.

Even the thought of trying to explain it to my friends feels impossible. How can I explain this bruising ache spreading through my entire body? How can I explain the crushing pressure on my heart, weighing me down to the bottom of the ocean?

How can I explain that I'm no longer the same Karina Ahmed I was just a few days ago? That I'm just a shell of her? Of her bravery, of her boldness?

I don't know how to do it. I don't know if I'll *ever* know how.

And I don't know how to be the person they're expecting me to be.

Walking into school takes more energy than I have, but staying home would be worse. Not that my parents would let me in the first place.

"Karina!" Cora says as soon as I swipe my ID card. I look at her, with her sunny smile, adorable blond space buns, and bright yellow overalls, and my face crumples.

I can't do this.

"Karina?" Cora repeats, her own face falling as she sees mine. She looks at Nandini in confusion, but I know Nandini doesn't have an answer either. I haven't been answering anyone's messages.

"Sorry," I mouth and duck my head, slipping into the crowd of students exiting the cafeteria, hoping to elude my friends if they follow me.

I spend my free period in silence, tucked away behind a row of lockers in the history hall. My mind is buzzing loudly with white noise and my eyes are glazed over. I don't know how many students pass by or who any of them are. Time moves both too fast and too slow.

When the bell rings, I bang my head into the wall by accident, jarred. I rub the back of my skull with a sigh and head to my second period class.

Halfway through AP Physics, my nausea becomes too much to handle. I quietly raise my hand, ask my teacher if I can go to the nurse and slip away with a signed pass.

That's how I spend the next two periods. Sitting in the nurse's office trying to stave off an anxiety attack while she asks if she should call my parents.

It means I miss English class. My phone is buzzing in my pocket, but I ignore it. I don't have an answer for anyone right now.

I leave the nurse's office during lunch, mostly because if I stay any longer, I'm afraid the nurse really will call home, and that's the last thing I want.

For lunch, I sit on my own again, finding an abandoned stairway. I stare out a window and wait.

I wait for something to spark to life in my mind—some solution that can fix all this and get rid of the horrible pain infecting my heart.

Nothing comes.

Instead, after ten minutes of simply sitting there, I reach into my backpack and grab my journal, flipping through the pages for something to grasp on to.

if a whisper is all I have left of you
then I will never make a noise
I will live in silence
if it means your voice will sing in my ears

I turn the page.

never did I know a heart can ache
for a soul it cannot see

yet when an arrow slices me open
blood pours from my veins in the form of you

I turn the page.

the world swore to me
you would always return
this is the promise that echoes
in the abyss of my head
when I cannot find relief

It's funny in retrospect. All these poems are a product of watching too many TV shows and reading too many books, sympathizing with characters to the point that they inspired words from me. Only recently was I able to put my own story on the page. But none of those poems fit right now.

I reach for a pen and force myself to think past the ringing in my ears, the heartbeat thudding too hard in my chest. My hands shake as I write in messy loops of cursive.

I'm drowning out of water, I'm burning out of fire
I was young and I was bold, I am different, I am cold
my heart no longer beats in tune to the universe
kept under lock and key, every step is a luxury
the ghost of my future haunts me at every turn
I miss the stars that used to live in my eyes
no longer do I dance under the moon
my knuckles are bruised and bloody from fighting
from surviving a battle I was destined to lose
a knife dangles over my head, on the precipice
I am h u n g r y
but I am scared of wanting ever again

                           —*death is desire, k.m.a.*

Desire certainly feels like death. Why would anyone want anything if it means risking this feeling when it doesn't work out?

I don't have the answer.

When the bell rings again, I contemplate just sitting here and letting what happens happen. But again, the fear of my parents being called spurs me into action, and I head for APUSH with my shoulders slumped.

I'm almost there when I see a familiar figure across the hallway. My eyes lock with Ace's, and his expression breaks with relief. "Karina, there you are. I've been looking for—"

No, no, *no.*

I can't do this.

I can't look Ace in the eye and tell him I tried and it wasn't enough. I can't do it.

I can't relive that moment again.

"I'm sorry." I look away, hurrying inside my classroom, where he can't follow.

"Karina!" Ace calls after me. I can't see his face, but he sounds distraught.

I swallow roughly but don't look back. I don't have the strength to face him. I don't have the strength to face anyone.

Even after everything, I still want to be with Ace. That's the one thing I'm certain of. But I can't right now. I need time to sew up the gaping wound in my chest, to find a way to grapple with the future I've lost.

By the time Italian rolls around, I have no choice but to see Cora and Nandini.

They're waiting for me outside the classroom. As soon as I see them, my hearts starts racing impossibly fast. I don't want to explain. I don't want to do *anything.*

"Karina," Nandini says, reaching for me and pulling me

into her arms. I comply, mostly because I don't want to make an even bigger scene. "What's going on?"

I shake my head and take a shaky breath, my nose buried in her neck. *Ten, nine, eight, seven, six, five, four, three, two, one.* "Please don't make me talk about it."

"Was it—was it Ace?" Cora asks in concern, wrapping her arms around both of us, maneuvering us into a three-way hug. "Do I have to kill him? He seemed worried but that doesn't mean anything. I can sharpen my knives within the hour."

I wish I could smile. I wish I had the energy.

"It was my parents," I say, and that's as much of an explanation as I'm willing to offer. "I don't want to talk about it. Please."

"Oh, sweetie," Cora says and hugs me even tighter.

The bell rings and we huddle through the door, pulling apart. They're both watching me in worry, and I love them for it, even if I'm not in the headspace to react properly.

"If you need anything, we're here," Nandini says in a hushed voice, squeezing my hand. "Anything at all. We love you."

"Anything," Cora agrees, squeezing my other hand.

I nod and look away. "Thank you."

Class passes by in a blur. Nandini and Cora keep shooting me looks—I can feel them—but I don't look back. I can't.

When ninth period comes, I head for Miss Cannon's classroom. There's still one thing left to do.

50

T-PLUS 1 DAY

When I get home, I have multiple texts from Ace. I don't want to look at them but he deserves better than that. I have to say *something,* if not everything.

He deserves that much.

I light a candle and brace myself to look through the messages.

Ace Clyde ♥:
are you okay?

Ace Clyde ♥:
what's wrong? pls talk to me?

Ace Clyde ♥:
miss C said you canceled our tutoring sessions for
good.

Ace Clyde ♥:
pls just text me back

Ace Clyde ♥:
karina please

Me:
I talked to my parents and they said I can't be an
english major. I don't want to talk about it. please
leave me alone for now

Ace Clyde ♥:
that's bullshit wtf i'm so sorry

Ace Clyde ♥:
is there anything i can do?

Ace Clyde ♥:
pls talk to someone if not me

Ace Clyde ♥:
what does ur dadu think?

Ace Clyde ♥:
karina...

Me:
ace please drop it I can't do this rn

Me:
can we pause for a few days? just until I get my
head on straight. I need some time

Me:
this is a line for me please please please don't
cross it

Ace Clyde ♥:
okay i won't

Ace Clyde ♥:
even if we're on pause i'm always here if you need anything

Ace Clyde ♥:
just lmk

I throw my phone away and bury my face in my pillows. The future looks bleak.

I hate it but I'm helpless to it.

T-PLUS 5 DAYS

The week passes in a haze. Oscar Wilde once said, "To live is the rarest thing in the world. Most people exist, that is all." I've never more thoroughly understood the sentiment than right now.

I'm just existing. My body goes through the motions, but my brain barely processes them.

Everyone around me is worried. I know it as well as I know the back of my hand.

Samir checks in on me every night and finds an excuse to do his homework in my room. He tries to broach the subject of our parents, but after I shut him down for the third time, he settles for providing silent comfort. It's nice to know he's stayed true to being in my corner, but it doesn't make the situation better.

Cora and Nandini follow me around protectively even when I'm despondent and unresponsive. Ace watches me constantly and texts me near as often. He doesn't ask about my parents, but he does ask about me. Every day, I get a variation of *How are you doing?* interspersed with random updates about his day, even though I rarely reply.

Miss Cannon looks at me with a crease in her brow every time I walk into English. Ever since I told her I had to quit tutoring Ace because of a family issue, she's been concerned. She offered to talk to my parents, but my vehement refusal stopped her. However, with each passing day she looks like she regrets that decision more and more.

I even go to Pre-Med Society once. I end up leaving half-way through, unable to stomach that this is my future now, that this is really happening.

With each passing day, my heart cracks a little more.

Ironically enough, even my parents have noticed. Every-thing they ask me to do, I do, but in complete and utter si-lence. Every time I look in the mirror, my eyes are dead, and I have to assume they're even more dead when I'm around them.

Once or twice, Ma gives me a sharp look and asks what's wrong. I shake my head and continue on my way. Baba only frowns at me. When they think I'm not looking, they ex-change inscrutable looks.

The one person I refuse to let worry is Dadu. I don't tell her about anything that's going on. I don't know *how* to tell her. I'm afraid that, if she finds out what my parents said, it'll set something bigger and scarier into motion.

Back when I thought there was a chance of my parents agreeing, it was okay to involve my grandma. Now, know-ing they're against it, I wouldn't dare bring her into it. I don't want to imagine my parents' anger if they thought I turned her against them.

Even worse, Dadu might feel guilty for my misery, and I can't stand that idea. She has enough weight on her shoulders from all the loss in her life, without me piling onto it. It's not her fault our family's a disaster.

Every day is as monotonous as the last. Nothing in the present matters anymore now that my future is written.

It's Friday when things are uprooted from the ordinary.

I'm gathering my things from my locker during my lunch period when someone's shadow looms over me.

I tiredly turn to face them, and I'm taken aback at the sight of Xander Clyde.

"What?" I ask. My voice sounds dead even to my own ears. If I had the energy, I'd wince.

But I'm not going to fake a happy expression for Xander, of all people. He's low on the list of people whose opinions I care about.

"I wanted to talk to you," he says, glancing around half-heartedly before looking back at me. There's no one in the hallway, since it's already fifteen minutes into lunch and most people are inside the cafeteria or outside enjoying the burgeoning spring weather. "Is now a good time?"

I turn back to my locker. "No."

"You don't look busy."

"Can't you take no for an answer?"

"You're being difficult," Xander says, closing my locker. "No wonder you and Cora are best friends."

I give him a flat look, but there isn't much heat behind it. He's an irritating fly buzzing near my ear when I'm in the middle of facing off with a pack of wolves.

"Fine. What is it?"

"I…wanted to make sure I didn't do anything to drive you away from Ace." Xander looks contrite for the first time since I've met him. "I haven't seen you two together for a while, and I realize I might've been a little rude when we last spoke to each other."

I stare at him in disbelief. He came to me in concern over *Ace*?

"No, you didn't do anything," I say. "Now can I please open my locker?"

"If I didn't do anything, why are you avoiding him?" Xander says as he furrows his eyebrows. My heart thuds miserably. He and Ace have the same thick brows that seem to commandeer their face.

"Did Ace send you?" I ask quietly. "Because I really don't want to talk about this right now."

"No, I'm just worried about him," Xander says, tucking his hands into the pockets of his khaki pants. "He's always been somewhat of a broody asshole, but he's been extra broody lately. I assume it has to do with you."

This is so uncomfortable. Xander Clyde isn't winning Brother of the Year anytime soon, but apparently he's trying anyway. I'm glad for Ace that his brother isn't as much of an asshole as we thought, but I also don't want to deal with this at *all* right now. Especially not when there are tears pricking the back of my eyes.

I turn away from him, blinking away stray moisture. "And what? You came here to convince me to run back into his arms?"

"I mean…would you?"

I can't believe this guy. "I'm sorry, but no. I'm glad you're trying to be a decent brother to Ace, but please just—just leave me alone."

Xander sighs. "I tried." He starts to turn away but falters and looks back at me. "He really misses you, you know. I'm not just saying that. He's been playing that song he wrote for you a lot. Drives Mia and me up the wall to hear him go on and on all night, but Dad's being soft on him now, so he doesn't make Ace stop."

There's a lump in my throat that's painful to swallow past. "Xander, please go."

"I'm going," he says, shaking his head. "All I'm saying is that he cares about you a lot."

Before I can reply, he turns around and walks away, whistling merrily as if he didn't just take a dump on my entire day.

My heart hurts thinking about Ace missing me. My heart hurts thinking about all of the missed opportunities ahead of us.

I laugh bitterly to myself when I remember prom. It's out of the question now. I don't know why I ever got my hopes up.

No matter how much I wish things were different, they're not.

Not that any of it matters anyway. I'm not in the mental headspace to hold a conversation with someone, much less be part of a relationship.

But I miss him, too, and this is hard.

For now, this is the way it has to be. I hope I can take us off pause soon, but that future seems impossibly far away and I don't know when I'll reach it.

I can only hope he's still there when I do.

51

T-PLUS 12 DAYS

Another week passes. It's no surprise that I forget our poetry projects are due in English the upcoming Friday. I realize only after I walk into English—heading for the front of the room, alone, rather than the back where Nandini, Cora, and Ace are—and take a seat.

I did my project. After I quit tutoring Ace, I didn't want anything tying me back to the sessions, so I finished the project in its entirety. I refuse to present it, though. If I'm called up, I'll take the grade reduction in favor of skipping the presentation.

"Alistair Clyde," Miss Cannon says, drawing my attention. "You're first to present."

Oh. Right. I forgot I was there during that conversation.

For the first time in two weeks, a quiet part of me stirs. I never read anything he wrote. I don't know if he even finished his project.

Ace stands and makes his way to the front of the classroom. He's as beautiful as the first day we met, and it *hurts*.

He hands Miss Cannon a stapled set of papers but takes out a folded sheet of loose-leaf from his pocket to read from. It's slightly crumpled, and Ace smoothes the edges.

Then he turns to look at me.

"This is my free verse poem. It's called 'Lionheart,'" Ace says, his intense gaze meeting mine. "I wrote it for someone special to me."

My breath catches. He wrote a poem for me? He's going to *present* a poem he wrote for me?

"Here goes nothing," Ace says under his breath. I'm lost to his next words.

promises are meant to be broken, that's what people always say
but what if I want to keep mine?
to this day, I'd sooner break my bones
than go back on any of the words I said
so dearly to you
we're so young, God, we're so young
only sixteen with a pocketful of big dreams

the world is in our hands, that's what people always say
but what if I'm afraid to carry it?
what if I don't want to be Atlas?
you, my dear, are unshakeable
you hold your cards close to your chest
courage finds a home in the space between your ribs

I'm too young to understand, that's what people always say
but I am old enough to see
there's a forest fire in your eyes that sets me alight
a bravery in your heart that beats in tune to mine
my darling, you're something out of a story
poetry doesn't begin to do your soul justice

change is inevitable, that's what people always say
but what if that change is good?
there's a lightness to my steps there wasn't before
there's a brightness in my heart there wasn't before
if you held me up to a candle,
my silhouette would be covered in your name

before you, I used to care what people always say
your lovely heart led me astray in unexpected ways
sometimes I think I'm going to burst into flames
from the spark you struck inside my chest
I wonder, how do you keep from setting yourself afire?
but then comes the startling yet undeniable understanding
you are fireproof, lionheart
and now I am, too

Silence follows the last line. My pulse is rocketing under my skin, pressing against my neck as if it's trying to escape. I'm barely breathing.

Tears threaten to spill from my eyes and I can't do this, I can't *do this.*

I get to my feet and run out of the classroom, despite the protest I hear from Miss Cannon.

I run into the staircase and heave a deep breath, my tears flowing freely. *You are fireproof, lionheart.* Then why do I feel like I'm burning alive?

Ten, nine, eight, seven, six, five, four, three, two, one.

Despite pressing the heels of my palms forcefully into my eyes, the tears won't stop. I just want them to stop.

I just want everything to stop.

"Karina."

"No," I say, voice cracking. I can't face Ace right now.

"Please just look at me," he says softly. His hands are gentle when they touch my wrists, tugging on them until I finally drop my hands from my face.

"What?" I wish he wasn't staring at me. I don't have to look in a mirror to know I look as horrible as I feel.

Ace frowns, his thumbs swiping across my cheeks carefully. "What's going on?"

I laugh hoarsely. "I wish I knew."

He keeps staring at me with his wide, concerned stormy eyes, and I don't know how to explain, how to say what's happening, how to say his poem hit somewhere deep inside of me that's still trying to heal.

Tears pool in my eyes again and Ace shakes his head, murmuring, "Please don't cry."

"I'm so lost," I say through harsh breaths. "I don't know what to do."

"It's okay," he says, pulling me toward his chest. He rests his chin against the crown of my head and strokes a hand down my back. "It's okay. You don't have to."

"It's not okay," I say, my voice muffled. It's so hard to breathe. "It's *not okay*."

"Shhh," Ace murmurs, his lips pressed against my hair. "You'll figure it out, whatever it is. I know that. I know you."

"I don't even know me," I say, wishing it wasn't the truth. I'm a stranger in my own skin. I'm a puppet on strings, playing out my parents' dreams.

"Of course you do," Ace says before squeezing my shoulders. "Please breathe. Follow me, come on."

I exhale deeply and try to breathe with the movements of his chest. It clears my head enough to say, "Nothing about me is even real. I'm just the person my parents want me to be."

"No," Ace says, his voice fierce enough to jar me. I'm suddenly hyperaware of my surroundings, of his wool sweater pressed against my cheek, the faint scent of cinnamon in the air, the thump of his heartbeat beneath my ear. "That's not true. How can you not be real? You're the realest thing I've ever known."

"Maybe you need to broaden your horizons," I say weakly. I forgot how easy it is to talk to Ace. It's the most natural thing in the world, somehow, to joke with him even when I feel five seconds away from a mental breakdown. Maybe six seconds away now. With every passing moment, it seems like a further-off possibility.

"Why? You already light up my world unlike anybody else," Ace says, pulling back to brush my hair out of my eyes.

"Are you quoting One Direction?" I ask. Again, for the first time in weeks, I feel the urge to smile even though I can't quite bring myself to actually do it.

"Yes," he says, pressing a kiss to my forehead. "I absolutely am. It's not my fault they wrote a song about you."

"Hm." I close my eyes and rest my head against his chest again. In turn, he wraps his arms around me.

Maybe for five minutes, I don't have to think about my future.

Maybe for five minutes, I can have this.

A long moment passes in silence before Ace tenderly strokes my cheek with his thumb, making me open my eyes. "What happened back there?"

Well. That was a nice five minutes while it lasted.

"I'm just really overwhelmed right now." I look down to avoid his earnest gaze. "Your poem was…a lot."

"I meant it," Ace says, tilting my chin up. His rings are cold against my heated skin. "You're so brave. Even if things didn't work out the way you wanted, you *tried*. You conquered your fear and put your heart on the line, even though you knew it might get broken. That's the bravest thing someone can do."

"I'm still so afraid," I whisper. It's the first time I've admitted it out loud. It feels like a fresh breath of air, even if it makes me slightly queasy. "I don't want to disappoint them."

"Worry about them less." His hands slide down my throat to cup my neck, his thumbs still tilting my face toward him. "Can I offer you some honest advice? You don't have to take it, but I just can't—I can't watch you struggle like this."

"I don't know if it'll help," I say but I nod, wiping at my own face to get rid of the tear tracks. "Okay. I'm listening."

"Stay as strong as you can," Ace says fervently, his eyes dark. "I know that it's rough and unfair right now, but you're not always going to be living with your parents. There's a future past all of this where you have your own life and your own rules. Their expectations won't be there anymore, and you can decide who you want to be. We just have to get through the present. All you can do right now is take care of yourself. No matter what happens, you're going to come out of this even stronger. The fact you've been doing this for so long shows how strong you already are. Just don't give up on your happiness. That's all I'm asking."

The words strike something inside me, a part of me I thought was sealed away for good. A light has switched on in the darkest recesses of my heart.

I always thought if I had this conversation with Ace, he'd try to foolishly step in. Or worse, he'd tell me to fight against my parents or run away from them. Things I could never do. But he's not doing any of those things.

He's telling me to stay strong. To not give up. To keep hope. He's telling me exactly what I need to hear.

I don't understand, I remember him saying. But it seems like he does now, or at least he's *trying*. That's more than enough.

"This is temporary," Ace says, pulling me from my thoughts. He's biting his lip, like he thinks I'm taking this conversation poorly. As if it's not the opposite. "We're only sixteen, Karina. There's still so much future ahead of us. It'll be better. You just have to hold on to the strength and bravery I know you already have."

I lean forward on my tiptoes and pull him into a hug, wrapping my arms around his neck. "Thank you."

He returns my hug, pulling me closer and squeezing me so tight I feel it down to my bones. "I missed you so much, baby," he murmurs into my neck.

My heart skips a beat. God, he's still so *much*.

I close my eyes, breathing in the familiar scent of cinnamon. "I missed you, too."

Ace brushes a light kiss against my neck before sighing against my skin. "Do you think Miss Cannon will take points off my project for running out?"

"You're unbelievable," I say, and Ace pulls away almost immediately, only to greet me with a wide, dimpled smile.

"There's my girl," he says, tucking a strand of hair behind my ear. His expression shifts minutely, and he looks almost bashful, his cheeks dusting pink. "What'd you think of the poem?"

"I think you're ridiculous," I say lightly. "But it was gorgeous. I didn't know you could write like that."

Ace's teeth flash behind his beautiful smile. "I had a good tutor and an even better muse."

"Yeah, you did," I say, reaching up to squeeze one of his hands. I shift my gaze for my next words. "But I still... I just need a little more time. I'm still struggling with... I'm sorry."

"No," Ace says, his thumb stroking the back of my neck. "There are no apologies between you and me. If you need me to wait, I'll wait. However long you need. If it's until next week, okay. If it's until next month, okay. If it's until next year, okay. If it's until college, *okay*. There's no deadline on this. On us. I promise."

I can't believe Ace is real. I can't believe I somehow got this lucky.

Right now, none of my other worries exist.

This is one thing I will never let my parents touch.

"I don't deserve you," I say.

"You're right," Ace says, his face softening. "You deserve better. You deserve the world. My foolish, beautiful, fire-proof lionheart."

I shake my head, warmth rising through me. "Only one part of that is right. The part where I'm yours."

"And I'm yours," he says solemnly. "I'll wait for you."

There's hope in my future. It's small, but it's there, and it's growing with each passing moment. *Stay as strong as you can* echoes in my head.

I'm going to try. That's all I can do.

52

T-PLUS 13 DAYS

I'm eating breakfast Saturday morning when my mom tosses a salwar kameez on the table. "Get ready."

I look between the beautiful red garment and my mom. "Where are we going?"

"To visit your Dadu," Ma says, before taking away my half-eaten roti. "I'll wrap this. Get dressed."

I want to protest and say I was in the middle of eating when her words register. We're going to visit Dadu.

I still haven't told my grandma what happened, but now I don't think I'll have much of a choice. I almost contemplate faking an illness to avoid this situation, but then I get a hold of myself. It's Dadu. She's not going to *try* to make my life any more miserable than it already is.

And I miss her. Maybe more than anything else.

This visit was going to come inevitably. The whole family goes to see Dadu every few weeks, to make sure she doesn't get too lonely out there. The anniversary of her daughter's death is approaching, and we tend to visit more frequently around then. It completely slipped my mind, and I feel horrible about it. I'm not the only person going through things.

For Dadu, I'll brave my relatives.

I silently get dressed and pile into the car with the rest of my family. Samir gives me a concerned look, but I ignore it. Still, he sits a little closer than usual, and his warmth is a comforting weight.

My dad keeps up a steady stream of conversation the entire ride there, mostly with Samir, but I keep my earphones in. My skin is already crawling and my knee is jiggling up and down.

Ten, nine, eight, seven, six, five, four, three, two, one.

It'll be fine. It'll be okay.

I run Ace's playlist on a loop through my earphones.

Halfway through the drive, Samir starts texting me ridiculous memes. I snort at one despite myself, and he flashes me a thumbs-up. I smile at him briefly for attempting to cheer me up, but the texts are only a momentary distraction from my anxiety.

By the time we get to my grandma's house, I'm concerned my heart might beat out of my chest. There's a bead of sweat sliding down my temple. My palms are so sticky that wiping my forehead will barely help.

I greet my grandma with salaam, and there's enough of us at first that she doesn't seem to notice how down I am. My cousins are already there, which at least means I can go unnoticed.

Fatima catches my eye and waves me over, but I shake my head. I don't have the energy. She frowns but lets me go with an understanding nod.

I'm slinking away to find an abandoned room when Dadu grabs my wrist, turning me toward her. "Make sure to come by my room after I'm done praying, okay, Myra? I want to know what's new in your life."

My smile is strained. "Okay."

I manage to escape for an hour, sitting in a corner on my phone, but eventually one of my little cousins comes up to me, tugging on my pigtail. "Dadu wants to see you."

With a sigh, I get to my feet and make my way to her room. Dadu prefers the comfort of her room to the large living spaces, and I can hardly blame her. My uncles are so *loud*, arguing over some cricket match, and my youngest cousins are running around in a frenzy. I pass my parents, who barely notice me, engrossed in conversation with one of my aunts about the upcoming election.

When I get to Dadu's room, she's sitting at the small table tucked beside her wardrobe, sipping a cup of chai. I sit down across from her, where there's another cup prepared just the way I like it.

"So what's wrong?" she asks.

We're getting straight to the point then. I didn't even realize she noticed I was off.

I slump in my seat. "I talked to my parents about college."

Dadu's face falls. "What? When? Why didn't you tell me?"

"The night after you left." I sip my chai to avoid answering the rest.

"And then…?"

I grimace, knowing I've backed myself into this corner. "I told them the truth."

My grandma's grip tightens on her mug. "Why don't you start from the beginning? I thought you weren't going to talk to them."

"I wasn't," I say, keeping my gaze on my mug instead of my grandma. If I keep looking at her face, I'm going to start crying, and I've cried enough this week. "But they were in a good mood. I thought maybe…maybe they'd be accepting. Maybe they'd approve. I was being stupid."

Dadu's face hardens and she reaches across the table to squeeze my hand. "You're not stupid, Myra. What did they say?"

I close my eyes and shake my head. "I can't—" I cut myself off, forcing myself to breathe in and out. *Ten, nine, eight, seven, six, five, four, three, two, one.* "They said I was being selfish and lazy. That I was only thinking of myself and that I would get nowhere in life."

"Myra, sweetheart," Dadu says hesitantly, but I shake my head. I need to get this all out in one go.

"They said they were extremely disappointed in me, and that I was ungrateful for everything they've given me—which isn't *true.* I am grateful for everything they've done and sacrificed, but—I wanted this one thing. That's all." My throat closes and I can't say any more.

When I open my eyes, the look on Dadu's face is pained. "They said that to you?"

I nod, swallowing against the bile rising in the back of my throat. "I'm so scared," I whisper quietly. "I don't know what to do, Dadu."

"The light in your eyes has died out." Dadu gently touches my cheek. "Myra, darling, please don't let your parents stop you. If you want to study English, do it. Be happy."

"It's not that easy," I say and dig the heels of my palms into my eyes before the tears can flow. "They'll hate me, Dadu. They'll never forgive me."

"To hell with your parents," she says, and it would be funny if I wasn't on the brink of a mental breakdown. "I can't believe after everything, your dad would—no. I guess I can. Ever since he married…" She takes a deep breath. "Regardless. Listen to me, you can't let them make your decisions for you. It's your life, not theirs. I believe in your future. Do you?"

I'm silent. I don't know what to say in response.

"Myra? Is this really what you want?" she asks quietly.

I exhale shakily and lower my hands. "More than anything. Does it matter?"

Dadu makes a decision then. I see it in the set of her jaw and the fierce glint in her eyes. "Of course it does. Myra, if you want this, you have to fight for it. But that doesn't mean you have to fight alone."

I stare at her, trying to make sense of those words. "You think I should try again? But what if—what if I make things worse?"

"How can it get worse?" Dadu asks gently. "I know you're scared, but you've always been so strong, and I know you can do anything you set your mind to." Her eyes are filled with an understanding that I almost wish wasn't there. It strikes a flame of hope in my heart that would be better left unlit.

Again, a voice in my head chants, *Do it, do it, do it.*

Dadu is right. How can it get worse? What more do my parents have to take from me?

I take a deep breath and nod. This is my last chance to be brave. I want to be a lionheart. "Okay. One more time. I want to try."

"Then we'll try," Dadu says, squeezing my hand before leaving the room.

When she comes back, it's with both my parents. She locks the door and gestures for them to sit on her bed.

"Go ahead, Myra," she says, squeezing my shoulder in encouragement.

I clear my throat and meet my parents' eyes. "I want to be an English major. I know we already talked about it before, but I—"

"This *again*?" Ma narrows her eyes. "Myra, we already told you no. How dare you bring this up again? And in front of your Dadu? Do you have no shame?"

Ten, nine, eight, seven, six, five, four, three, two, one.

I am a spark. I am a blaze. I am an inferno.

I force myself to speak again. "Ma, I don't want to be a doctor. Please, just listen—"

My mom looks at my dad, shaking her head. "I can't believe how disrespectful—"

"*Farah,*" Dadu snaps.

The room goes silent, all of us staring at my grandma with wide eyes. I start counting down from ten right as Dadu unleashes *hell*.

"What is wrong with you two? Your daughter is so smart and so talented, and you turn her away when she's honest with you? You *shame* her? Are you absolutely *insane*?"

Baba blinks in surprise, looking between his own mother and me. "Ammu, I don't know what Myra told you—"

"Oh, don't even start, Hussain," she says, waving a finger in warning. "I'm so disappointed in you. You wanted Myra to be a doctor. She told you she doesn't want to do it and that she wants to study English instead. Then you yelled at her for being a shame on our family. Is that right or wrong? Don't even answer that. I already know the answer. I almost watched a repeat performance mere *seconds* ago."

I wince at her brutal recap and the way my mom starts giving me the evil eye.

Still, I don't cower away. I *want* this. I have to stand on my own two feet.

"Eyes over here, Farah," Dadu says, noticing my mother's gaze. "Your daughter is so respectful of both of you. You treat her as less than she is, and she never says a word. The one time she wants something, you kill her dreams? How dare you? Where is *your* shame? What would Allah say about this? You are supposed to love your children unconditionally. Your Abbu and I never treated you this way, Hussain, so why are you doing it to Myra? She's done nothing to deserve the way both of you dismiss her passion and skills. If she wants to study English, what's the problem? Is she killing someone? Is she robbing someone? Is she breaking a law? Where in the Quran does it say she has to be a doctor, that you two are so adamant about it?"

"Ammu, we're only looking out for her," Baba says, scratching the top of his head. He's beginning to look contrite. My stomach starts doing cartwheels. Could this actually work?

"How is this looking out for her? She's *miserable*. All this will do is make her resent you in the future, when she's on a career path she doesn't want. Then it won't matter how much you shame her, because she'll remember *this*. This moment when you ruined her life and didn't care about her feelings. This is your daughter, Hussain. Not some kind of servant to do your bidding. She's a real human being and she's trying *so* hard to always do right by you. When will you do right by her?"

"English, though?" Ma's expression is doubtful. "What kind of success will she have with that?"

"Stop thinking about her future success and start thinking about her future happiness," Dadu says darkly. "And do not doubt your daughter. She is an incredibly hard worker. She will be amazing at whatever it is she chooses to do. But it's *her* choice. You don't get to make that decision for her, do you understand?"

"Ammu…"

"Don't 'Ammu' me," she says to Baba. "Tell me you understand. If for some reason you don't understand, I'll pack my bags and come home with you and Farah so you can *also* live with a parent that shames you for your choices. Is that what you want? I can start packing now."

"Ya Allah, Ammu," my dad says, scrubbing a hand over his face. "No, you don't have to do that."

Dadu shakes her head. "Then ask Myra what she wants. Ask her and *listen* to her."

My mom frowns deeply but doesn't raise another argument. My dad looks exhausted. I know how much he values Dadu's opinion. Maybe even more than he values my mother's. It's clear this denouncement is weighing on him. "What do you want, Myra?"

Stay as strong as you can. Ace's words echo in my head.

I swallow the fear coating my throat. I can do this. I have to do this. My future is at stake. "I want to study English. I love reading about new worlds, and I love writing about them even more. It's all I've ever dreamed about. English is *everything* to me." I suck in a deep breath. "And I want to go to Columbia. Their program is incredible, and it's an Ivy League school, and I know I would do amazing there. It's the right choice for me and I can prove it. I have graphs, analyses, whatever you want. Just give me a chance."

My parents are quiet as they stare at us and Dadu squeezes my shoulder again. My stomach swoops uncertainly as the silence stretches.

Ten. Nine. Eight. Seven. Six. Five. Four. Three. Two. One.

"Please let me have this," I say, my voice breaking. *Please.* "I promise you won't regret it."

"Okay." The word comes out painstakingly from my dad's lips. "You can study English."

Okay.

Okay.

Okayokayokay.

My mouth falls open and no words come out. Dadu steps in for me. "And you will cast *no* judgment on her for this decision. If I hear or see you doing something of that manner, you're going to wish it was me who died instead of your Abbu. Not that he would approve of any of this, either."

"Ammu," Baba says, aghast. "Don't talk like that."

"I'm being serious," she says, sitting down across from me and sipping her chai. "It's settled then. In the fall, Myra will apply to Columbia to study English and you will support her wholeheartedly."

My heart is racing. Is this real? Can this be real? Did we do it? Did *I* do it?

All the heaviness weighing on my heart is slowly lifting like a strange fog. The world looks clearer, sharper.

Both my parents seem resigned. "Okay."

As one, they rise and leave the room, shutting the door behind them. I blink after them in disbelief. "Am I dreaming?"

"No, Myra," Dadu says, reaching over to squeeze my hand. I turn my attention back to her. My eyes feel like they're about to bulge out of my head. "This is real life. You did it and I'm so proud of you for being brave. Please tell me if there are any issues. I'll handle them, okay? I won't let this family fall apart. You will have your happiness."

"Dadu," I say, my voice choked. I don't bother to stop the tears this time. "Thank you. Thank you, thank you, thank you."

I lunge across the table and wrap my arms around her bony shoulders, squeezing as tightly as I can.

"Oh, Myra," she says softly, hugging me back. "Don't thank me. You did this. I simply helped."

When I pull back, tears still streaming down my face, she gestures to my eyes with a small smile on her face. "The light is returning. Mashallah, Myra. Your Dada would be so proud, too. Maybe there's hope for our family, after all."

I exhale in such painful relief, it hurts. "I think you're right, Dadu."

53

T-PLUS 14 DAYS

My house is silent.

There's an awkwardness in the air. I don't think either of my parents are mad at me. They're definitely irritated, but it seems directed more toward my grandma than me.

Samir comes to my room and gives me a quick hug, mumbling how happy he is for me. "I never did that," he says a second later and walks out, which I should have expected.

Yet I can't stop smiling afterward.

Sunday night, I slip a packet of research I did on Columbia's English program under their door. Later, I hear my parents arguing with Dadu on the phone. I have to light two candles to stay calm enough to listen. The conversation starts loud but ends quietly. When my dad comes out of their room, he looks even more resigned than before.

"We'll start looking at the best colleges for English in the summer. We saw your research, and the English program at Columbia looks decent, but you need to have backup options if it doesn't work out," Baba says on his way to the bathroom, and I gape at him. He doesn't notice, already closing the door, but I can't even process the words.

I did it. Things worked out somehow, and I can—I can have the future I want.

And I can have my parents, too.

That's all I ever wanted.

One day, I know we're going to fight over my general lack of freedom, and we're definitely going to fight about Ace. But I have to believe those fights will be worth it.

I'll be stronger. Braver. Bolder. I will win in the end. And Dadu will always support me.

Now that everything is resolved, now that my future is in my own hands, I can recognize Ace was right.

My true bravery was always there, hidden within my strength.

I text Nandini and Cora immediately with the good news, and they FaceTime me in tears. Cora is at the hairdresser and Nandini is at the movie theater, but neither hesitated to call. Of course they didn't.

"We were so worried about you." Cora sniffles. "I didn't know what to do and Nandini said there wasn't anything we could do, but I just love you so much and want you to be happy."

"I was right," Nandini says, but she's rubbing at her red-rimmed eyes, too. "It wasn't anything we did. You saved yourself, Karina. I'm so proud of you. We both are."

"You guys did *so* much, though," I say, refusing to let them gloss over their support. "You were there for me. You gave me the space I needed. You supported me from the beginning. I don't know what I'd do without you."

Cora starts crying again, which sets off my own tears. Nandini tries to maintain a cool image, but her eyes are glassy, too.

"We're so happy for you." Cora wipes her nose hastily. "I'm going to give you the biggest fucking hug when I see you."

"This is everything you deserve." Nandini's expression is so earnest I have to look away and take a deep breath to keep another round of tears from slipping free.

"Thank you." I wave a hand in front of my eyes like the cool air will keep them from watering. "I missed you both impossibly. Thank you for putting up with me these past two weeks."

"You're stuck with us for life," Nandini says.

I smile shakily. "Pinky promise?" I raise my pinky toward the camera.

"Pinky promise," Nandini says, holding her pinky up.

Cora nods eagerly, holding up her pinky. "Pinky promise. NCK forever."

All three of us start laughing and it feels right. I've missed this. I've missed them.

But there's still one more person I need to talk to.

T-PLUS 15 DAYS

Monday morning, I wait in front of Ace's locker. It means not seeing Nandini and Cora until English, but this is something I have to do in person.

My heart is racing in my chest but, for once, it's for a good reason. I'm nervous but I'm also excited to tell him everything.

Earlier, Ace said I was the reason he found the bravery to talk to his family. As it turns out, he's also the reason I found the bravery to talk to mine.

Maybe we bring out the best in each other. That's not something I'm willing to lose.

I'm staring out the window at the end of the hallway when someone walks up behind me.

"Karina?" Ace says incredulously, and when I turn, he's stopped in his tracks, staring at me with wide eyes.

I smile. "Are you still waiting?"

Ace looks gobsmacked, his lips parted with no words coming out. He finally shakes his head, as if he's trying to gather himself. "Yes. Of course, yes."

I take a small step closer. It's dizzying to have Ace so close but so far. "You can stop."

"Stop…waiting?" Ace asks. He looks even more dazed than I feel.

My smile widens. "Yeah. I'm here. To stay."

Ace's eyes glitter. "Yeah? What happened?"

One more step closer.

"I talked to my parents again, but with Dadu's help this time. I convinced them to let me study English." It's so hard to contain the hope rising inside me, trying to burst through the surface. It doesn't help that Ace is looking at me like I'm the only person in the world. "I'm applying to Columbia in the fall. I was thinking we could work on our college essays together, if you want. Maybe after prom?"

Ace laughs breathlessly. "My English tutor might get jealous."

Another step. The butterflies in my stomach are growing jittery, fluttering around in a frenzy. "That's too bad. I think your girlfriend takes priority over your English tutor, though."

He raises his eyebrows, a beautiful and familiar grin tugging at his lips. "My girlfriend?"

I nod, cheeks warming. "If that's okay with you."

Ace makes an incoherent noise in reply and crosses the distance between us, pulling me into a kiss.

I laugh against his lips. It's easy to kiss him back. More

natural than anything. I melt into the kiss, curving in toward him. My heart is beating like a sledgehammer in my chest, as if it's moments away from giving out.

If I die in Ace Clyde's arms, I'll die happy.

Ace is the one to pull away, resting his forehead against mine. His eyes are somehow impossibly brighter, shining with the brilliance of a thousand lightning bolts. "Karina Ahmed, I'm so crazy about you. I always knew you were the bravest person I've ever met."

A giggle slips past my lips. "Ace Clyde, I'm completely mad about you, too. Thank you for believing in me."

We stand there in the middle of the hallway, just breathing in each other's presence. Ace's fingers are tracing the slope of my nose, as if he's trying to memorize me, when I'm reminded of something incredibly important.

"You wrote a *poem* about me."

He smiles, dimples popping into existence. "I remember."

"I'm so proud of you," I say, pinching one of his cheeks. He grabs my hand and keeps it pressed against his face. "It was really good."

Ace chuckles. "I guess that means I'm going to *ace* the English Regents after all."

"I'm going to break up with you," I say.

He shakes his head, kissing my nose. "No, you're not."

I smile. He knows me well. "No, I'm not."

Ace leans forward and kisses me again. I laugh, foolishly happy.

He was right about me.

I am a lionheart.

54

T-PLUS 69 DAYS

"Karina, I think we're good—"

"Just stay still," I say, cutting Ace off and adjusting his tie. My boyfriend apparently can't make a knot to save his life. "You keep fidgeting, and it's messing me up."

"It's not a big deal, it's just—"

"Alistair Clyde, if you say it, I'm going to gag you with this tie."

Ace rolls his eyes, but there's a hint of a grin in the corner of his mouth.

We have five minutes before Cora and Nandini come inside and bodily drag us out of his room for taking so long. Ace kindly offered his family's estate for junior prom photos, trying to win points with my best friends, but he looks like he regrets it now. I don't blame him.

Fixing Ace's outfit is helping me calm down. I think he can tell, because aside from his minor protests, he doesn't try to stop me.

He's in a perfectly fitted navy blue suit with a lavender

pocket square that matches my dress. His hair is combed back for once, and he looks so well put-together it's hard to believe I ever thought he was some kind of delinquent.

I'm wearing a traditionally South Asian outfit, more beautiful than any prom dress could ever hope to be. It's a floor length cream-colored anarkali suit with beautiful floral patterns in the navy blue of Ace's suit. It swishes with every step I take and flows when I spin. My dupatta keeps falling off my shoulders, but Ace catches it before it slips every time.

It was hard to convince my parents to actually let me go to junior prom with Nandini and Cora, but they relented after Cora's parents promised to pick us up and drop us off. I neglected to mention the brief visit to Ace's house to pick up our dates, but that's neither here nor there.

I still can't believe we're going together. I still can't believe I somehow *survived* the last two months. It's the second week of June and Regents are next week, but I have no doubt Ace is going to kill it. I have more faith in him than I have in almost anything else.

My fingers keep fluttering around Ace's neck. I can't help bouncing on my toes and making circles around him to ensure nothing is out of place.

Junior prom is something I thought I'd never have, so just being here in and of itself feels like a victory. But I'm also afraid someone is going to pull the rug out from underneath me any second.

Ace takes my hands in his, rooting me in place. "Hey. We don't have to go if you don't want to. I can go outside and tell Nandini and Cora to fuck off. I don't mind being the bad guy."

I smile at him, a fraction of my nerves easing. "You could never be the bad guy."

He snorts and laces our fingers together. "I'm serious. If you want, we can stay in and watch Netflix."

"No," I say, shaking my head. I won't admit defeat *that* easily. "I want to go. I'm just…nervous. I don't know why. I can't explain it."

My anxiety has been better in the last few months as I've learned better coping mechanisms. I still rely on the countdown the most—I think I always will—but I'm growing and learning and doing better every day.

It's just…this is junior prom. I'm *here*. I'm going.

And I'm nervous.

"Don't be," he says, squeezing my hands. "I won't leave your side all night. No matter what happens, I'll be here with you."

My smile widens. I already knew that but it's nice to hear it again. "I know. I guess we should go then, shouldn't we?"

Ace lets go of my hands to wrap his arms around me. "Nah. They can wait one more minute."

I laugh and slip my arms around his waist, leaning against his chest. "Just one. Otherwise Cora will come in here, guns blazing."

"I don't doubt that."

I close my eyes and let myself have this impossible moment. He's humming in my ear, a tune I recognize from the countless times he's played it for me on piano.

There's something so warm and comforting about being in Ace's arms. A feeling more familiar than home.

He's safe. He's mine.

"Oh, enough!" someone shouts from outside. It's the unmistakable voice of my dramatic best friend. "It doesn't take that long to put on a corsage and boutonnière."

I pull back hastily, eyes wide. "We didn't even do that yet. She's gonna kill us."

Ace laughs and pulls out a small plastic box from his pocket. "Here."

I offer him my hand, and he slips the navy blue rose corsage onto my wrist with gentle fingers.

When he's finished, I pin the lavender-themed boutonnière to the lapels of his suit jacket, next to his pocket square.

"Perfect," he says as Cora knocks furiously on his door again. He sighs. "She's definitely gonna kill us."

"At least we'll die together?"

Ace shakes his head but holds out his arm to me. There's a crooked grin on his face that makes my knees weak. "Shall we?"

I place my hand on his elbow. "Onward."

"And you say I'm strange," he says, pressing a kiss to my set curls before walking us to the door.

"There you two losers are," Nandini says in exasperation. She's sitting with her date, Timothy Chen, on a chaise in the hallway.

Cora is pacing while her own date, Holly Harrison, watches fondly. Cora stops when she sees us. "*Finally.* Come on, let's take our junior prom pictures! NCK first. Come here, Karina."

I reluctantly let go of Ace and make my way to my best friends. "Ridiculous," Cora mutters to Nandini. "She gets a boyfriend and becomes too uppity to take pictures with us."

"*Hey,*" I say but Nandini is laughing as she wraps an arm around my shoulder.

"Leave her alone," Nandini says, nudging Cora with her other arm.

Cora grumbles but there's an unmistakable grin on her face. "I *guess* I can forgive you, but only if you let me take at least ten pictures."

I sigh and nod. It's all for show, because I'm beyond elated and grateful to be here with them. I wouldn't trade this for the world. "If that's the price I have to pay."

She laughs and leans over to hug me. "I told you we'd all go to junior prom together."

It feels like she said that a lifetime ago. Before I met Ace, before I told my parents the truth, before I made my future happen for myself. It was so long ago, and yet barely any time ago at all.

"You did," I say, leaning my head against her shoulder. God, I'm so happy. "It's no surprise you're always right."

Nandini snorts. "I don't know about *always*."

Cora flips her off before pulling away. "Come on! Pictures!"

I get looped into a half an hour of taking photographs on Ace's lawn while Mia and her mother coo from the front porch. Ace FaceTimes his own mother for a few minutes amidst the chaos and I try not to blush too much when he shows me off, waving grandly in my direction.

"You're too much," I whisper, nudging him lightly.

Ace offers me an impish grin. "It's not my fault you look like the sun brought to life."

His mother's warm laughter rings in the background.

After Ace hangs up, his father stops by to clap him on the shoulder and whisper something in his ear that I can't hear. Even Xander comes by to adjust Ace's tie, which is unnecessary since I spent a ridiculous amount of time perfecting it, but he's *trying*, and it makes Ace smile, so I don't say anything.

There's even a moment where Xander says something to Cora and a wisp of a smile appears on her face before she abruptly stomps on his foot and walks away with her date.

Nandini meets my eyes over Ace's shoulder and shakes her head as Cora mutters insults under her breath.

I laugh in response.

At one point, I slip my phone into the mix and manage to get a picture of Ace and me in our complementary outfits, which I text to Dadu with a heart emoji.

Daduuuu ♥:
Mashallah u look beautiful

Daduuuu ♥:
Love u

Daduuuu ♥:
So proud

I smile at the texts and put my phone away.

Despite all the hardships, things worked out for the better. I have a long path ahead of me, but each step I take brings me closer to my goals. For now, this is enough. I'm happy and my future is my own.

By the time we get to the venue, my nerves are hitting again. I lead Ace to the double doors marking the entrance and falter. *Ten, nine, eight, seven, six, five, four, three, two, one.* I take a deep breath, and Ace squeezes my wrist lightly, a reminder that he's here.

He's always here.

"Ready?" he asks.

Ready for this? Ready for us? Ready for the future?

I exhale and straighten my shoulders. "Ready."

Ten: Thunder shakes the world around us. I tremble, you glow. All I see is you.

Nine: I am not a princess. My hair grazes my waist. You scale an ivory tower.

Eight: Constellations tear through the sky. I am never lost. You are my true north.

Seven: The earth is cruel. It takes relentlessly. When I am unsteady, you ground me.

Six: Not every lock has a key. I am shackled. You learn to break chains.

Five: Bridges are meant to burn. You strike the match. I am a spark, a blaze, an inferno.

Four: My wings are crippled. Your touch is featherlight. I remember how to fly.

Three: I am buried in the dark. A lone candle flickers. Iridescent stars live in your eyes.

Two: My mind is elastic. It snaps. You mend the edges.

One: You love me. That will always be enough.

—counting down with you, k.m.a.

★ ★ ★ ★ ★

ACKNOWLEDGMENTS

Taps mic Testing, testing… Not to be crass, but to be a little crass: *holy shit, bro.* I never thought I'd be sitting here writing the acknowledgments for a real book. I always hoped, but it never seemed possible. Isn't it wild when dreams come true?

I'd like to start by thanking you, the reader. Thank you for coming with me on Karina's journey. We are both infinitely grateful for your time and support.

Going forward, I'd like to thank my agent, JL Stermer, for believing in this book and believing in me. Thank you for *seeing* Karina, and understanding why I wanted to tell this story. The world worked miracles to bring us together, and I'm grateful for it every day. You get my New Yorker heart more than anybody else! Here's to more books (and pretzels!) in the future. And thank you to the rest of the team at New Leaf Literary—especially Suzie Townsend, who introduced me to JL.

Thank you to my former editor, Natashya Wilson, for taking a chance on Ace and Karina. Being with you on this journey has taught me so much, and I'm a better writer for it. You saw the heart of this book, and helped make it shine even brighter. Thank you to my current editor, Rebecca Kuss, for being so supportive of this book and loving it like it was your own acquisition. Your enthusiasm is appreciated beyond words, and I'm glad to have you along for the ride. Thank you to the rest of the Inkyard team, including Bess Braswell, Brittany Mitchell, Laura Gianino, and Linette Kim for cheering this book on and helping to bring it into the world with a bang! Thank you to Gigi Lau for designing the cover, and Samya Arif for the cover art. I'm absolutely in love with it!

And now, to get a little weepy, thank you to my family for all your love and support through the years—most importantly, to my own wonderful Dadu. And thank you to my favorite Bangladeshi teenagers: Zareen Khan, Fabia Mahmud, and Shannon Ali. I write for you, and I write for us.

Thank you to ones who are far away, but close to my heart. To Fari Cannon, for sharing the same ten brain cells with me, and being my found family. To Kris Urbanova, for claiming my children as your own, and indulging "Tashie After Dark" too many nights in a row. To Genesis Mendoza, for teaching me to be a better person, and looking out for me like a mother. To Holly Hughes, for being the other half of the dream team, and opening every single can of worms with me. To Z. Ahmadi, for having my back since spring break in Tokyo, and always picking up my phone calls. To Chloe Gong, for letting me scream about [redacted], and always experiencing the exact same brain waves as me. To Hannah Vitton, for allowing me to pull you into the book world, and crying over Instagram edits with me. To Alyssa Cavallaro, for reading the first words of this book in Penn Station, and always sending hugs when I'm in peril. And to Nina Petropoulos, for being the Stumbleina to my Twinkle Toes, and sticking with me through thick and thin.

Thank you to the ones that are even farther than far. To Lorena Valenzuela, for being the sweetie to my honey, and shedding tears over my characters. To Sofia Tulachan, for reading every single word I write, and inspiring me to be more hardworking. To LinLi Wan, for having the biggest galaxy brain, and trying to send me ice cream from another continent. And to Kaity Findley, for loving Stiles as much as I do, and getting up way too early just to spend time with me.

Thank you to the ones who are close by, and close to my heart. To Pietra Ibrisimovic, for believing in me from the moment we met, and being my book bum soulmate. To Akvinder Kaur, for being the other side of the same coin, and being my #2 for life. To Rachel Koltsov, for letting me talk your ear off for hours, and always dropping everything you're doing to join me on an adventure. To Juliana Ogarrio, for loving Rockefeller Center as much as I do, and offering me a place to stay the first night we met. To Kadeen Griffiths, for showering me with constant affection, and always fine dining with me. To MSRB—to Zuzu Bicane, Sophia Monsalve, Sydney Martinez, Kayla Ryan, and Stella Gomes, for being my favorite bookish babes. To Raisa Bhuiyan, Helen Urena, Sadia Alam, and Unwana Abasiurua, for reading my words in their early stages, and loving them anyway. And to Emily Tom, Bailey Disler, and Dhervi Kapoor, for supporting me wholeheartedly without having read a single line.

Thank you to the angels that make publishing so much easier. To Leah Jordain, critique partner (and friend) of the century—this book would not be what it is without your guidance, and I am so grateful for you. Thank you for offering to cut words a lifetime ago, and never leaving my side since then. To Christine Calella, for being the best mentor in the world, and the first person to believe in me. To the Gen Z author squad, Christina Li, Zoe Hana Mikuta, and Racquel Marie (and Chloe again), for always indulging in my chaos. To Crystal Seitz, Nora Sakavic, J. Elle, Vanessa Len, Shelley Parker-Chan, Mae Coyiuto, Nora Elghazzawi, Anne Zoelle, Naureen Nashid, Adiba Jaigirdar, and Nina Varela for being a part of my publishing journey, whether through reading this book or supporting me. To Avi Lewis, Emily Miner, Page Powars, and Kalie Holford, for being the most wonderful beta readers. And to AMM R6 Write Club—Brighton Rose, Meryn Lobb, Shana Targosz, Cristin Williams, Carrie Gao, Janice Davis, Natalie VanderHeydt, Zoulfa Katouh, Nicole Chartrand, Kiara Medina, Christie Megill, Gwen Flaskamp, Kimmy Wisnewski, Finn Longman, Lindsey Hewett, Savannah Wright, Laila Sabreen, Tamar Aleksandr, and Russell Armstrong, for being the best greasy foxes around.

And thank you to all the people on social media that support my random snippets, my ten million aesthetics, and my general chaos, including Lilian Hillary, Humnah Memon, Jo-elle Wellington, Aishwarya Tandon, and Amy Holford.

Of course, a huge thank you to the authors who read an early copy of this and blurbed it: Mark Oshiro, Emma Lord, Sabina Khan, Rachel Lynn Solomon, and Jenn Bennett. I'm honored to have your names on my book jacket!

Thank you to my day one supporters. To Marisa Lysachok, Andie Gomes, Anam Sattar, Valerie L., Michelle Bader, Lavender Ruffman, and Claire Malchow, for your unending support of Karina and Ace. And to Madison Taylor Bast, Katie Foster, Ira Petrova, Grace P., Rachel Leach, Vanessa Fuentes, Lina El Gharbi, Ellen Leung, Lois Salvacion, Taina Malavazzi, and Rachael Rodriguez, for following me on this journey since the beginning.

And, of course, thank you to S and T. I couldn't do it without you.

Glances off camera Did I get everyone? No? Oops. Well, thank you to anyone I might have missed. Sending you all the love!

Turn the page for a sneak peek at
Tashie Bhuiyan's next big-hearted novel,
A Show for Two!

There are three things that people applying for the Golden Ivy student film competition should know.

One: film transitions can make or break you.

Two: casting yourself in the film is as good as accepting defeat.

Three: having a celebrity make some kind of ridiculous guest appearance *always* wins points with the judges.

While our short films always have great transitions, and Rosie and I live strictly behind the camera, we've never had a celebrity make an appearance, ridiculous or not, in one of our films.

"Every single time," Rosie says, running her hands through her auburn hair, nearly wrenching out the curls. The rest of the seniors aren't much better, alternating between various stages of distress.

I frown, leaning an elbow against the desk. It's our first film club meeting after winter break. More importantly, it's our first film club meeting where we're actively working on our short film after the literal hell of submitting college applications.

The projector is broadcasting last year's winner on the classroom's whiteboard, one of the many short films we're watching for research purposes.

The freshmen sitting on the floor look bemused at our coinciding irritation. One of them, Brighton, looks imploringly at Rosie and hesitantly speaks up. "Every single time…what?"

Rosie is too busy pulling her fingers down her face in frustration to answer, so I point at the whiteboard. All of the freshmen follow the movement with wide eyes.

On the screen, some random popstar is smiling at the camera, as if mocking us for our inadequacy.

"Almost every year without fail, the winner of the competition snags a celebrity endorsement," I say. "And as all of you know, we have yet to manage such a feat."

Brighton blinks before turning her head toward the back of the room, where Grant is sitting. "What about Grant?"

I snort, and Grant sticks out his tongue at me. "Grant doesn't count. Being the son of someone famous isn't the same as being famous."

"Still more famous than you," he points out, but there's no heat behind his words.

Rosie leans against my leg, seated down below with the freshmen. I pat my best friend's head in a weak attempt at reassurance.

"Our film concept is strong," I say quietly, in part for myself. "There's still a chance we could win."

We have to is what I don't say.

She groans, burying her face in the rough material of my jeans. "This is our *fourth* year trying to win."

"Yeah, but this is our first time in charge," I say, flicking her hoop earring.

Astoria Academy of the Arts and Sciences has been applying to the student film competition at the Golden Ivy Film Festival for many years now, long before either of us enrolled.

When Rosie and I joined AAAS's film club as freshmen, we sat here just like this, watching the previous winners' films. Since we're co-presidents this year, I'm responsible for writing the screenplay while she's responsible for directing.

Planning the film wasn't that hard. Accepting our inevitable defeat to some random school in Los Angeles with connections to half a dozen celebrities is proving to be a lot more difficult.

It's been my dream—and Rosie's dream—for four years now. Winning means everything, starting with a scholarship and ending with visibility in the film community.

But as important as all of that is, I need to win for an entirely different reason. If we win, I'll finally have proof that choosing to double major isn't a mistake. My parents will be forced to accept that I'm capable of standing on my own two feet and making a path for myself.

And more importantly, they'll honor the agreement we made months ago and pay for me to attend USC in the fall.

If I get accepted.

"Next one," Rosie says, waving a hand in Grant's direction. "If I have to watch one more second of this, I'm going to *scream*. I still don't understand how we lost last year. This film isn't even that good."

I shush her. "You're going to set a bad example for the freshmen," I say, before offering the rest of the room a reassuring smile. "This just means we have to work that much harder when we're putting together the film. We still have two months left. Everyone has March twenty-nine marked in their calendars, right?"

The thirty-five people in the room nod. I pretend not to notice as half the freshmen discreetly take out their planners and mark the date.

Our supervising teacher, Ms. Somal, has long since checked out of the meeting, sitting beside Grant with her earphones in, flipping idly through a graphic novel. She looks up once in a while to make sure we haven't set the classroom on fire, but aside from that she seems more than content letting us do what we want.

Grant clicks into the winning film from two years ago, and we all fall silent as the opening credits begin rolling. I try not to grimace, in full agreement with Rosie. Our film was better than the winning films the last three years, but we've still never gotten past semifinals.

We watch around three more short films before the bell rings at five, signifying the end of after-school activities. I stand up, stretching my sleeping limbs. My entire body feels jittery with the anticipation of finally starting this project after months of prepping and planning.

One of the freshmen walks over to Rosie, shyly asking her a question. I leave her to it, gathering my things instead. My earphones are loosely splayed across the desk beside a scattering of different colored pens, three different journals labeled by project, and a planner filled to the brim with Post-its. My phone buzzes, and I glance at it briefly.

Anam Rahman: hurry homeeeee I don't wanna deal ma and baba by myself anymore

I type out a quick response. sooooon!

As I'm setting my phone down, Rosie wraps her arms around my neck, pale white skin contrasting against light brown. "Mina. I'm going to die."

"Hm?" I ask, glancing at her over my shoulder, meeting her blue eyes. "Why?"

"The Nutritional Science lab," she says, dropping her arms so she can lean against the desk. "Do you think you could help me? My dad will be here soon, but he can wait—"

I shake my head, eyes flicking toward my phone again. "Anam needs my help fending off the parental figures, so we might need to take a rain check. Maybe we can FaceTime later?"

Rosie grimaces and tugs on my dark braid. "I have a thing tonight with my dad's girlfriend. Maybe tomorrow? It's due Monday, right?"

I shake my head. "I have a community party on Saturday," I say, but I'm already rearranging my schedule to make room for a call. With only a few days until casting begins, I've been making final tweaks to the script in my free time. "How about Sunday afternoon?"

Rosie smacks a kiss against my cheek. "Perfect."

I wrinkle my nose, wiping away the leftover strawberry lip gloss residue on my skin.

She rolls her eyes and blows me another mocking kiss as she packs up her own things.

Rosie and I have been best friends for four years now, bonding over a shared love for Studio Ghibli films during freshman year. We've been attached at the hip ever since. Last year, instead of running for president of the film club individually, we both agreed to run as co-presidents, even though it wasn't *technically* allowed. But we made it happen, because we refused to do it without each other.

As we both leave the classroom, waving to Ms. Somal, Grant catches up to us, running a hand over his buzzed head. "Yo, so I was thinking—"

I slant him a look. "What?"

Grant pouts at me, and Rosie giggles. "Why are you like that? You're always so quick to jump the gun for no reason. Rosie never does that."

"You never hit on Rosie," I say offhandedly.

"I'm *not* hitting on you," Grant says, but he has the good sense to look slightly ashamed.

At the same time, Rosie says, "Because I'm gay, dumbass."

I shake my head at both of them. "What do you want, Grant?"

"Ignore her," Rosie says, nudging me out of the way. "What's up?"

Grant smiles at her, white teeth flashing bright against his dark skin. "About the famous celebrity, my dad—"

"I know your dad's famous, but he's not a celebrity," I cut in before he can finish. During freshman year, Grant attempted to impress me by bringing up his father every five seconds. The man's Wikipedia page is practically seared into my brain. Speaking from past experience, it's best to cut this topic off at the root. "Producing the next big blockbuster film is cool and all, but I don't think it's going to win us brownie points."

Grant grunts. "That's not what I was going to—"

I sigh, my shoulders slumping with exhaustion. This isn't worth bickering over. Not when I've had my fair share of arguments this morning. "Fine. What is it?"

He stares at me for a long moment before he shrugs. "You know what? It wasn't that important anyway."

"Hey," Rosie says, tugging Grant's sleeve. "Ignore Mina. You know how she is."

I give her an affronted look in response but don't argue. Between the two of us, I'm admittedly the more standoffish one, but I wasn't trying to be rude. I just—I'm *tired* and I don't want to deal with this right now. Is that a crime?

"No, it's fine," Grant says, shrugging her off. "Never mind. I'll see you guys in class on Monday."

He walks away, slipping on his hood, and I can't help but feel distinctly unsettled. I didn't mean to upset him.

Rosie turns a look on me. "Seriously? What if he was trying to tell us something important?"

I try not to squirm under her gaze. "Like what? Was he going to offer to produce a celebrity out of thin air?"

Her lips thin. "You're always doing this, Mina. You know this competition is just as important to me as it is to you, but it's not the only thing that matters. There are other things in life that are also important."

I look away, tugging the collar of my turtleneck. "That's not—we have to win this competition, Rosie."

"I know," she says softly, laying a hand on my arm. "But we have to accept that there's every chance we might lose."

My throat is suddenly tight. Rosie needs to win as much as I do. Without the scholarship, it's going to be a lot harder for her family to pay the tuition for NYU.

But at least her family supports her dream of becoming a film director. At least her family believes in her.

I cough and paste a smile on my lips, turning back to my best friend. "Yeah, definitely."

Rosie scans my expression and huffs a quiet breath. "You're a terrible liar, Mina." She saves me from responding by grabbing my arm, pulling me in the direction of her locker. "Come on, before your parents kill me for making you late."

I follow her, all the while trying to push her words to the back of my head.

We have to win the competition. We *have* to.

If I have to spend another year at home, if I have to spend another year with this awful weight on my shoulders—with this tiny, familiar voice in the back of my head taunting me relentlessly—I'm going to lose my shit.

You're never going to win. You're never going to be good enough.

Sometimes I can't tell whose voice it is.

And sometimes…it sounds like my own.

Loved Ace Clyde?
Now meet Emmitt Ramos.

"You'll fall head-over-heels in love with these characters while they fall in love with each other."
—**Chloe Gong**, *New York Times* bestselling author of *These Violent Delights*